SWIFT RETRIBUTION

BRIAN SWIFT & KAYLEN ROBERTS
MYSTERY / SUSPENSE SERIES, BOOK 3

HEATHER AMES

WELL OF IDEAS PRESS

CHAPTER ONE

BRIAN SWIFT SPOTTED a small crowd milling around in front of Roselia's coffee shop as he drove into the parking lot to pick up his to-go order. The coffee shop, which opened routinely at 6:00 A.M., appeared to be closed.

Instantly, Brian's mood flipped from anticipation for the meeting with his Cold Case staff at Miami-Dade Police Department into a state of high alert. A tingle he hadn't felt since his days as a homicide detective inched its way up his spine and flowed down both arms into his wrists. His grip tightened on the Camaro's steering-wheel.

He eased up on the gas, cruised over the cut curb and coasted to a stop in the side lot. Roselia's had become his favorite place to pick up breakfast for himself and his team on the way to work. An hour ago, Antonio, the owner had assured Brian his order would be ready at eight o'clock sharp. Brian's 8:30 A.M. meeting with his staff preceded a briefing for Chief Hal Shaw and Homicide supervisor, Lieutenant Darrell Trehorn, on the squad's unexpected progress in solving Lila Kowalski's murder, which had long gone cold for lack of new leads.

Twelve years had passed before Lila's neighbor decided his business had outgrown his shed and her bones had been discovered beneath the concrete floor the work-crew had begun to break up. Yet another case of a dysfunctional family taking care of business in a sloppy way, Brian thought. His team had linked the chain of evidence to Lila's brother and sister-in-law, and were ready to file charges.

Brian knew once he laid everything out, he'd get those two suspects to confess. All he needed to complete his morning was to pick up hot coffee, bagels and cream cheese. Instead, he'd arrived to find what might be a potential robbery in progress.

He kept the engine running and remained behind the wheel, but rolled down his window while he swore under his breath and scanned his surroundings. He wondered if the three-alarm fire bells ringing in his head and the sensations pulsing through his body were really warranted or whether he was over-reacting. But if he *was* making something out of nothing, then why wasn't the crowd forming a line? Why wasn't anyone going in or out of the front door? And why in hell was the coffee shop staff ignoring the accelerating level of noise?

Brian checked for signs of a power outage. Although surrounding businesses in the warehouse district didn't need signage in broad daylight, a well-lit open loading dock on the opposite side of the street told him any outage at the shop had to be localized.

He watched a thick-framed, middle-aged white man in heavily splattered painter's overalls pound his fist against the front window as a thirty-something Hispanic man in a suit repeatedly jerked the door handle unsuccessfully. The front door was obviously locked. Brian's adrenaline crept up another notch.

Antonio's van sat under the shade of a tree growing out of the easement between the coffee shop's paved lot and the industrial park behind it, where so many of the shop's customers spent their working hours. Brian put the Camaro into first gear and took his foot off the brake. He slowly turned the wheels to maintain a low profile as his vehicle glided along the side of the building. He stopped the car's momentum several feet from the side door, which stood slightly ajar.

Brian rolled down the passenger's side window and listened intently. An 18-wheeler pulled up opposite and began backing into the loading dock. The shrill beeping that accompanied the truck's movement brought a couple of uniformed workers out of the office. They walked toward the dock at a leisurely pace. Brian heard shouts from customers in front of the coffee shop. A couple of car doors slammed.

He shut off the Camaro's engine and warily stepped out, taking another look around before quietly closing his own car door. A warm breeze stirred leaves on the palm trees edging the sidewalk, lifted a white paper from the easement and carried it scraping across the blacktop on a puff of brown dust.

Brian welcomed the heightening of all his senses. He'd worried frequently whether, after almost two years, he'd lost the steady calm that usually poured through him when he approached a dangerous situation. Relief joined the disconnected remoteness that always removed fear. The elimination of doubt was the best feeling he'd had in far too long. His training as a homicide detective had kicked back into high gear without missing a beat.

Strident voices filtered from the front lot, blending together in discord. One voice jumped out from the rest: "Where the hell *are* these people?"

That had to be the painter. The guy seemed to feel his role was to ignite a mob mentality. Brian decided the first thing he'd do after securing the scene would be to take care of that man and his mouth in whatever way was needed.

Bringing his focus back to his assessment, he scanned the immediate area again. Nothing remarkable jumped out at him except the partially-open side door, which was enough of an anomaly in itself. Antonio never left that door unlocked. Too much of a risk, he had told Brian. He didn't care if it got hot in the kitchen. He wasn't going to give bums the opportunity to steal or invite a stick-up.

The breeze sighed away around the back of the building as Brian pushed his jacket behind the belt holster housing his Glock, the movement as automatic as it had been before the arm injury that had almost cost him his career and relegated him to his current position as Cold Case's supervisor.

He needed to check out the scene and report his findings if this was, indeed, more than a power outage. But the last thing he wanted to do was summon assistance to a scene that didn't need it and become the butt of jokes at the precinct. He'd finally restored faith in his integrity after bribery accusations were proved to be unfounded. He had to determine whether his alarm signals were warranted or his senses were totally fucked.

Moving closer to the side entrance, he spotted a brick wedged between the door and its frame. Definitely something out of place. Brian ran over details he knew about Antonio's business...three employees, none of whom would be outside smoking during the morning rush. Two large dumpsters at the back of the lot were both tightly closed, so no one was in the middle of a trash run.

Flanking both sides of the company van stood two old clunkers Brian recognized. One, a battered red 1994 Toyota extended-cab pickup was owned by Aurelio, the baker. The other, a 2012 white Chevy Caprice with a dented rear fender, belonged to Antonio's right hand, Rigo, whose cheerful "Buen dia; good morning; and what can we do for you today?" greeted every customer as he or she walked in the door. To anyone who asked, Rigo would proudly say his greeting reflected his Argentinian roots.

All of them would have been at the shop by 4:00 AM at the latest to make donuts and bagels, brew coffee and ready the shop for their opening. Aurelio's nephew, Moises, had been added to the employee roster six months ago. He cleaned, polished, swept up and took out the trash. He had also graduated recently to assisting with bagging orders if the line of customers stretched out the front door, as it had on an increasingly frequent basis during the past few months.

Antonio had fired his previous donut-maker and hired Aurelio, who had a knack for creating light and crispy donuts and a mouth-watering, seemingly endless variety of bagels that changed day to day. Morning meetings in Cold Case had become enjoyable events, leading Brian to break his own rule of never taking a predictable route to or from work.

An old bicycle Moises used for transportation leaned against a pole topped by a rusted-out sign for the taco stand that had once occupied the building. Parked at the curb directly across from the open door, and partially obstructing a clear view of the warehouse dock across the street, sat a nondescript beige van. Behind it, two other dented and dirty cars completed the available space between the back entry into the parking lot and a designated 'no parking' area that allowed trucks from the frozen food plant across the street unobstructed access to or from the dock. Brian looked for a paint truck and saw one parked in a secluded and shady space between the dumpsters and the alley access to another set of dumpsters at the back of the burger shack next door.

He stayed close to the wall as he approached the coffee shop. No cooking odors wafted out. No smell of coffee. None of the usual sounds of voices and equipment in use. The back of the store was in darkness. He weighed going inside alone against calling for back-up and waiting for the results. If he entered and disturbed a robbery in progress, the outcome could turn bad really fast, despite the element of surprise. If he waited for a cruiser and more than one perp attempted to exit the store, that outcome might not be much better. He had no cover beyond his Camaro, which couldn't be moved closer without announcing its presence.

He also needed to avoid inciting the crowd at the front of the store into taking a closer look if any of them spotted him. He could either gain a small group of vigilantes or run the risk of being shot by someone seeing his gun but not the badge clipped to his belt.

How well he reacted to this situation would be reviewed not only by his superiors but by all of Miami-Dade's staff, he thought, retreating to call for back-up. Some still doubted he'd been ready to return to active duty. Others remained convinced he should have been placed on permanent disability. And more than a few probably thought he was unfit for other reasons. He pushed those thoughts aside as he radioed in, requesting one cruiser. No lights, no siren, he instructed the dispatcher.

While he waited impatiently, he used his phone to make a quick check for power outages, found none and brought his flashlight from the car. The crowd in front of the store continued to swell and became increasingly vocal. Their leader, waving his arms and glancing frequently at Brian, was the man wearing painter's overalls. In a booming voice, he demanded the store open. He asked the crowd why they couldn't get what they wanted. He encouraged them to knock on the windows and beat on the door.

Other would-be customers arrived and left, their cars cruising in and out of the lot, some quietly, others leaving with a strident screech of tires and the smell of burning rubber. The overall mood pitched increasingly toward hostility, and Brian hoped the cruiser's arrival would lower the volume to a dull roar before he was forced to intervene. Crowd control was definitely not one of his specialties. He had no patience or sympathy for dealing with people who had already lost theirs. He'd contribute to the melee, without a doubt.

Three very long minutes passed before a cruiser rolled through the lot's rear entrance. Brian showed his badge to the two officers. He knew the driver, Officer Santiago Milagros.

"What's up?" Milagros asked in an undertone, nodding toward the crowd, which had continued to swell now rush hour was in full swing. "Looks like a riot in the making."

"Shop's locked at the front. Possible robbery in progress. But no one's exited the building since I arrived close to seven minutes ago," Brian said. "Glad to you guys were close."

Milagros nodded. "Hope you're still gonna say that when I tell you Rojas is a rookie." He jerked his head toward his fellow-officer, hovering several paces behind them, his attention focused on the unruly mob. "They dispatched us only because of our proximity. They're sending another unit, but that one's wrapping up a citizen complaint. I figured, once I heard it was you needing assistance, we'd do okay until the other cruiser rolls in." He grinned at Brian. "So, you wanna go in that open door now, Sergeant?" Officer Milagros put his hand on the butt of his gun.

Brian nodded. "That's the plan. You and I'll go in. Rojas can do crowd control until the others arrive. Tell him to keep the mob away from the front door. If he's got some balls on him, he can try getting them to break it up. Tell 'em there's a salmonella outbreak or something. Place is quarantined. That should get rid of a few."

"Okay." Milagros nodded. "I'll have him radio for additional support first. That crowd's turning ugly."

"Yeah. Tell him the guy in the painter's overalls is the instigator. If Rojas can cut him from the pack, maybe the others'll calm down."

"It'll be a good learning experience for him." Milagros walked back to talk with his rookie partner.

6

While receiving his instructions, Rojas shot a quick glance at Brian, guarding the door. Brow furrowed, he returned to the cruiser. Both Brian and Milagros took out their firearms and turned on their flashlights. At Brian's nod, Milagros pulled the door fully open and blocked it with the brick. Nothing stirred inside. Brian's adrenaline, already pumping hard, shot into high gear. He stepped inside, Milagros at his back. Both flashlights pierced the darkness as they did a sweep.

A walk-in freezer filled the right side of the narrow passageway. Straight ahead, silhouetted against light streaming in through the front window, shapes of kitchen appliances became dimly visible. Brian motioned Milagros to check the freezer. The officer cautiously took a look through a pane of glass at face level before opening the door. He shook his head and closed it back up.

Failing to locate a light panel, they advanced slowly toward the vat where the donuts were fried. Overwhelming aromas of grease and powdered sugar, a telltale metallic odor blanketed the space in front of Brian. On the floor beside the vat, a white uniform contrasted with the darkness. Brian motioned to Milagros, who moved forward, squatted, checked for a pulse on the motionless figure and silently shook his head.

Damn.

Brian's eyes had adjusted sufficiently to recognize Aurelio, blood haloing his head and splattering his uniform. Milagros stood back up and carefully stepped across the body. They were now walking through a crime scene and contaminating evidence, but Brian judged it more important they secure the scene than wait for reinforcements. Unless someone was crouching between the counter and the supplies stacked along the passageway, the robbery was no longer in progress. Although Brian doubted they were going to find anyone else alive, they needed to make sure.

Trying to keep their tampering to a minimum, the two men stepped cautiously through the kitchen, finding another body face down, balding head pointed toward the front of the store. Rigo. Multiple gunshot wounds to his back and head.

Bastards.

Brian's anger seethed. Those men had been shot from behind. Unable to defend themselves, they had fallen where they worked.

His feet crunched on something and he stopped. He realized he was treading on coffee grounds. A lot of them. They littered the counter, the floor and even the back of the body right in front of him. A large canister had to have been knocked over, and it had been done after the shooting. He again motioned for Milagros to check for signs of life as he skirted the body, which he felt was far beyond help. Blood covered the floor and trailed toward the counter.

The till stood open. Brian stopped again. He'd heard a sound, definitely coming from within the confines of the counter area. Faint, but definite movement. He put up his hand. Milagros stopped behind him, the officer's uniform rustling faintly. Brian strained his ears against the roaring silence inside the shop and the muted disruption outside. He swore he'd heard something or someone moving ahead of him only a moment before. He continued to listen, senses quivering.

There it was again.

Indistinct but definite movement.

Where?

Behind the counter. To the right. Where Rigo always stood as the unofficial greeter with his cheerful baritone and big smile.

Brian felt an acute pang of loss. He pushed the unwanted emotion aside. This was no time for anything but a keen sense of observation. He might no longer be an active member of the Homicide squad, but he needed to record everything while continuing to secure the scene before they arrived. The first order of business was to not only find out if anyone was alive, but whether a robber was crouching in the darkness, more than ready to blow their heads off. Brian was still wondering whether their failure to locate that light panel was going to work in their favor or against them.

The flashlight's beam crept forward until it illuminated Antonio slumped over in a seated position, his back to the wall. Blood flowed through his fingers as he clutched his neck. Swinging the beam around, Brian saw no one else. He moved to the end of the counter, lifted the heavy flap and took a fast look. No one hiding on the other side. The robbery part of this crime was apparently over.

The crowd spotted him. Renewed pounding on the window caused Brian to lock gazes with the painter. What the hell were all those people still doing at the front of the store? The mob had actually doubled in size. Rojas should have had them corralled at a safer location. It looked like the rookie's career choice had been a poor one if he couldn't even command enough respect to control a group of disgruntled, hungry and caffeine-starved people.

Brian made the necessary calls to get paramedics, homicide detectives, the medical examiner and CSI unit moving. He requested further back-up for crowd control as Milagros used a wadded-up towel to staunch the blood flowing from Antonio's wound. Soon an army would arrive to take over what was now a multiple homicide investigation.

Brian squatted down beside Milagros and Antonio. "What happened?" he asked the coffee shop's owner.

Antonio opened his mouth, but nothing came out except a whisper of air.

"He needs help fast," Milagros said.

Brian placed a reassuring hand on Antonio's shoulder. He looked unwaveringly at the frightened man, whose eyes reflected pain and dread. "You're gonna make it," he said. "Paramedics are only moments away."

Antonio's bloodied hand crept up from his lap to grasp Brian's shirt. Brian placed his own hand over the store-owner's. "I swear to you, we'll find whoever did this," he assured the wounded man. "Save your strength. I'll talk to you at the hospital." He looked at Milagros. "One employee's missing. I'm going outside. Maybe he's at the back of the store."

"Find out what Rojas is doing," Milagros said as Brian got up. "Why the hell are people still yelling and beating on the door?"

"I'm gonna put a stop to that right after I make sure Moises isn't lying outside somewhere."

Walking briskly back through the store, Brian finally found the light panel hidden under a rack holding jackets and a couple of aprons. He flipped all the switches. Fluorescents flickered before humming to life. A muted cheer broke out on the other side of the front window. Customers renewed their efforts to get inside. Brian felt more than a stir of annoyance at Rojas. Just how green *was* that goddamned rookie?

Partially blinded by a combination of stark fluorescents and bright sunlight pouring in through the open door, he blinked before crossing the threshold. His eyes adjusted to find a fresh trail of blood crossing the floor to disappear beneath the freezer door. With a sinking feeling, he opened it.

Rookie Officer Rojas lay sprawled on his back, eyes staring blankly at the ceiling, his throat slit from ear to ear.

CHAPTER TWO

"LET ME GET THIS STRAIGHT, SWIFT," Lieutenant Darrell Trehorn said. "You came to pick up an order. You found the owner badly wounded, two of his staff dead from gunshot wounds, and the third missing." He leaned forward, bouncing on his toes. "And while you and Officer Mila-gros were investigating, the rookie officer, Rojas, got his throat slit and was dumped in the cooler his first morning on the job."

"That pretty much sums it up." Brian had learned to offer little in way of explanations or any other comments to Trehorn. It avoided thinly-disguised pissing matches and allowed Trehorn to draw his own conclusions.

"You saw no one and heard nothing." Trehorn shoved his hands into his pants pockets and snorted his disgust.

"I didn't say that." Brian felt even testier with Trehorn than usual. To save time at home he'd skipped brewing his own coffee, leaving him with a mild headache. Then he'd walked into the scene of what appeared to be a store robbery gone really bad and completely missed the murder occurring right behind his back. Not his finest moment, but did Trehorn really need to point that out?

"But you didn't see who murdered Rojas," the lieutenant continued, as though Brian hadn't responded. "And by the time you got to the back of the store, the perp was long gone." Trehorn's raised eyebrows as well as his tone registered complete distain for Brian's observational skills.

Brian felt his jaw tightening. "That part's right. But there had to have been more than one perp to do that much damage without Rigo or Antonio responding. Rigo has a shotgun behind the counter at all times. It hadn't been moved, let alone fired. And there has to be a motive for Rojas's murder. He was told to talk to Dispatch and then do crowd control while Milagros and I went inside. But it looks like he never even got to the front of the building. I checked with Dispatch…he didn't radio in that request for more assistance. While Officer Milagros and I were securing the scene and giving aid to the survivor, Officer Rojas must have tried to intercept a possible suspect and gotten himself murdered. Why whoever it was took the time to drag Rojas's body into the freezer, not to mention the risk, I can't tell you. If the goal was to conceal his body, then why leave a blood trail?"

He glanced over Trehorn's left shoulder to see how few members of that large crowd had stayed on-scene after the barrage of first responders arrived. Where was the painter who'd been pounding the window or the young guy in the suit who'd been pulling on the door handle? Brian had also noticed a woman in a yellow and white checked dress who'd been carrying a grocery bag in one hand and a large red purse in the other. She was gone, too. So were two young guys in uniforms of blue and white striped shirts over black pants.

Evidently, a lot of onlookers had scrambled back into their vehicles or taken off running when they heard the sirens. Since there was a bus stop on the corner, Brian wondered whether some of them had managed to leave on public transportation. As if losing possible witnesses wasn't enough of a problem, he noticed two news vans, their crews quickly readying themselves for broadcasting. He became very aware that his suit and shirt were heavily stained with blood.

Striding briskly toward them across the parking lot was the detective who had been placed in charge of the case…an early-forties African-American detective named Trent Buxford, who had been personally recruited by Trehorn into MDPD's Homicide division from Atlanta.

Detective Alex Ramirez stood interviewing a young girl who was crying and shaking her head. Brian remembered Ramirez had been one of the department representatives at Tim's funeral. The loss of his brother still weighed heavily on Brian, especially in stressful moments. He pushed that unwanted emotion aside.

He didn't know much about Buxford, who had come to the department while Brian was out on disability, but he knew Ramirez was a good investigator, clear-headed and able to communicate effectively with shaken-up witnesses. One positive in a sea of negatives.

Trehorn took a call and moved away after shouting "Don't go anywhere," over his shoulder.

So much for all that progress on the Kowalski murder, Brian thought. He knew his own investigation would have to take a back seat to an active multiple homicide. He also knew Trehorn was poised to trounce all over him, yet again. This time with what might be some merit, Brian admitted, watching the medical examiner supervising the removal of Rojas's body.

"I put out a BOLO for the missing employee, Moises Delgado," he told Buxford, who had managed to detour around the news crews and an impatiently-pacing Trehorn. "The owner was able to give me the kid's last name before he got loaded into the ambulance. We'll have access to an address in Delgado's personnel file as long as Antonio keeps good records. The kid's bike is still leaning against the post opposite that loading dock on the other side of the street. I got CSI to process it without removing it. Whether Moises left under his own power or was abducted is still up in the air because Antonio doesn't have a good surveillance system."

"You're Cold Case, Swift, so there's no 'we' to this investigation," Trehorn said from behind Buxford, who jumped and then grimaced at his own reaction. Trehorn had managed to approach and eavesdrop with admirable stealth. "You're a witness," he told Brian. "Limit yourself to facts. No speculation or trying to manage the scene. Your clothing's gotta be processed, and we'll take the rest of your statement back at the precinct."

"Noted." Brian gave Trehorn a curt nod. "I'll head back, then, since you don't want me to complete my report here." He tried not show irritation at Trehorn's reprimand. "I keep a spare set of clothes in my locker.

After CSI gets done with me, I'll shower and change before I give my formal statement."

Trehorn looked like he wanted to argue about Brian not wearing a jumpsuit to leave the scene, but cast a sidelong glance at Buxford, who shrugged and jerked his head toward the news vans. Two reporters were looking right at the three detectives clumped near the coffee shop's side door. Brian knew they would focus on him as soon as they realized who he was; not only was he the one covered in blood, but the notoriety surrounding Tim's death continued to single him out of any group. Suddenly, he shared Trehorn's wish to get him the hell out of there as fast as possible.

Buxford cleared his throat. "Swift hadn't finished giving me all the details I need," he told Trehorn.

"Then get the rest of it faster," Trehorn said from between clenched teeth.

Brian gave a quick glance toward the news crews, already recording footage as they advanced toward the crime scene tape, flapping within ten feet of where he stood with Buxford and Trehorn. "So where do you want me to hang out while I finish up with Buxford?" he asked the lieu-tenant. "Those reporters already have a bead on us."

"Damn it." The lieutenant waved at two patrol officers standing close to the tape's perimeter. "Get over here."

Both men obediently jogged up to him, their faces expectant. Brian wondered whether they thought Trehorn was going to tell them to take Cold Case's supervisor to their cruiser and put him in the back.

"Keep the scene secure," Trehorn instructed them. "No reporters or camera people back here. And take that tape out to the edge of the lot, dammit."

One of the officers started widening the taped-off area. The other headed over to the news crews and made them move their vans. Neither crew looked happy when they were forced to find street parking. One of the reporters had managed to get inside the taped-off area. She trotted toward them, microphone poised.

"No!" Trehorn held up his hand like a traffic cop. "Get back behind the tape!"

The young woman, wearing a tight black leather skirt and flower-print blouse, her credentials fluttering in a plastic holder at the end of a long lanyard around her neck, faltered. Brian noticed she was wearing green high-heeled shoes. Not the usual garb for a streetwise reporter, he thought. The other one, who had retreated immediately when told to do so, remained on the outside of the tape. She wore flat beige sandals, beige pants and a white t-shirt under a navy jacket. Brian recognized her…Mireille Shagassi, a seasoned investigative reporter. She looked ready to chase any story in a professional manner. Brian noted she was already back to broadcasting the scene, her cameraman having driven the van across the sidewalk to its current position at the curb before following her every move as she slowly walked toward the store's front parking area.

"The press has rights," shouted the reporter in the tight skirt, waving her microphone. "Our viewers want information. Have you made any arrests?"

"You'll get an interview when I'm ready," Trehorn called in response. "No comment right now."

"Is that man injured?" The reporter pointed a shaky finger toward Brian. The rogue reporter's camerawoman had also come inside the taped perimeter. She started shooting footage of the detectives.

"Stop that!" Trehorn's roar would have intimidated a pride of lions.

The camerawoman lowered her equipment. The reporter stopped walking and stood uncertainly tottering on heels that wouldn't stay upright on the cracked blacktop beneath her feet. Brian made out her name on the fluttering credentials: Cassandra Bunting.

"You." Trehorn glared at Brian. "Get in your vehicle and stay there."

"Fine with me." Brian turned toward his Camaro, which placed him directly in front of the startled reporter. She stared at him with widened brown eyes, her long black hair streaming behind her as the wind gusted. "I'm okay," he told her.

"Don't give her any details," Trehorn warned.

"I'm not." Brian didn't feel the need to qualify anything else either for the reporter's benefit or Trehorn's. "You give me the word, I'll go back to the precinct," he told Trehorn. "Whoever's going to process my clothes can meet me in the locker room. I'm not stripping in the garage."

When he got into the Camaro, the interior could have cooked eggs. He left the windows down but blasted the a/c to clear the air.

"How about a few comments?" asked Mireille Shagassi as she leaned through the passenger's side window, her microphone unwavering as it pointed in his direction. "You must have had to render first aid when you first arrived on-scene. There's a lot of blood on you, but you don't seem to be injured. How does it feel to be back at an active homicide scene after all these months, Sergeant Swift? Excited? Ready for action? Any lingering signs of post-traumatic stress?"

CHAPTER THREE

KAYLEN ROBERTS OPENED one eye in response to the buzzing phone on her nightstand. She looked at the caller-ID: Angela Crossfield. She put the cell on her pillow and punched the speaker. "Hello?"

"Turn on the news," Angela said. "Turn it on quick. I'm watching NBC."

Kaylen patted around the nightstand, located the remote and tuned it to WTVJ. A local news report appeared, giving a panoramic view of a parking lot crowded with emergency vehicles.

"Brian's there," Angela said. "He looks fine, but there's blood on him."

"What?" Kaylen's lethargy fled as she bolted into a seated position. She brushed unruly curls away from her face and stared at the screen, her heart thumping. She saw a jumble of unfamiliar faces with a building in the background. "Where is he? I don't see him."

"They just panned across the lot," Angela said. "It's a coffee shop. Something really bad must have gone on in there. I heard three people died, one of them a police officer, and the owner was wounded. I don't think Brian could have been injured. See, he's getting into his car."

Kaylen *did* see him. Her heartrate slowed from a full gallop to a heavy trot. "Thanks, Angela. I'll call him right now. I'll get back to you as soon as I find out something." She cut Angela off without saying goodbye, but she figured she could apologize later. As she waited for the call to go through, she watched a reporter lean into Brian's passenger's side window, a cameraman behind her.

"Can't talk now," Brian told Kaylen when he picked up. "I'm okay; not my blood."

"Thank God." She told him she loved him, but wasn't sure he heard her, as she found herself talking to an empty phone line.

She looked back at the TV screen and turned up the volume. The footage had abruptly cut to images of a chaotic scene with multiple victims being transported out of a coffee shop Kaylen knew was on Brian's regular route to his Thursday morning meetings with his Cold Case staff. A voiceover cut into the ambient sound, ghosting across stark noises of shouting, sirens and screaming, lowering them to a background clamor. A calm, female voice reassured viewers the police had the situation in hand. Mireille Shagassi's name flashed across the lower-third of the screen. Kaylen remembered Shagassi as a respected local investigative reporter whose broadcasted reports gave substantive details versus lingering on sensational revelations.

She pulled two more pillows behind her head as she continued to watch and listen to more details. Miami-Dade police department had sent a supervisor, who had refused to give an update. The fire department's coordinator had been more cooperative with the news teams, reporting one victim en route to the hospital. It was believed the other workers at the popular neighborhood coffee shop were deceased. No wonder Brian had blood on him, Kaylen thought with a frisson of fear.

What if he'd arrived there earlier? Or had he, and been involved in a shoot-out?

She gave herself a mental shake and told herself not to jump immediately to that scenario. But Brian was Brian. If he had witnessed any altercation, he would have waded right into the middle of it.

Estimates were as many as three or four people had been found dead inside the building, Mireille told viewers, her tone exhibiting concern. More cutaways to hysterical customers in the parking lot revealed stories of gunshots, gunfights, masked robbers fleeing the scene and a poor police response.

Kaylen flipped to another station, where a man in heavily paint-splattered overalls declared to a reporter in a flowered V-necked blouse and black leather skirt that this was a gang-related shooting in pay-back for some altercation that had taken place the week before, and that the detective who was involved in the entire situation was well-known to everyone. He had recognized Detective Sergeant Brian Swift, who, the painter said, had a reputation for shooting first and asking questions later. Facing the camera head-on, that reporter, whose name was revealed to be Cassandra Bunting, gave a shaky recap of her initial arrival at the scene and the chaos she had observed around Brian Swift, who had run out of the building covered with blood and waving a gun around.

Kaylen bristled. Brian would never run from anything, including a multiple homicide, much less wave his Glock around in front of a crowd of bystanders. She called Angela back and told her not to believe anything she heard until a report came in from Homicide supervisor Darryl Trehorn or Chief Hal Shaw, then went into the kitchen where she started a pot of coffee by spilling grounds and water all over the counter.

After cleaning up the mess and starting the brewing cycle, she took a shower in an attempt to rid herself of lingering effects from too little sleep and a case of the jitters. Her new nightclub, Treasure, was scheduled to open in two weeks to great fanfare and the highest hopes for success from all her backers. She hadn't seen her bed until close to dawn, and now here she was, on four hours sleep, trying to function when it looked like Brian was about to get into more hot water with the public and Miami-Dade Police Department.

Between towel-drying her hair and trying to run a pick through the tangles, Kaylen scrolled down multiple emails. Four were from Rob, her manager at Bannisters. Five were about problems with and at Treasure. She decided to deal with all of them after she made sure Brian was okay, at least for the immediate future.

Thankfully, there were two new text messages from him. One told her he hadn't been injured but he'd witnessed the aftermath of a crime. He'd have to give a statement and get debriefed, so she wouldn't hear from him for a while. The other text, much shorter, and evidently sent as a very welcome afterthought, told her he loved her. Kaylen felt a lot calmer, drank two cups of coffee, and called Angela to give an update.

"I'm coming over," Angela said. "You need company, or you'll sit and worry. I'll bring lunch. Once Brian contacts you again, or you get too busy with work, I'll leave. I've got some really good news to share, so don't tell me 'no.'"

"Okay. You like to railroad me into things, but this time I'll let you. You do sound excited."

"I am. Salad from Chebaks with their fantastic tuna, or a strawberry muffin from Mizell's?"

"Better make it Mizell's. It's a lot faster, and not out of your way. She's got omelets now, too. I'll call and place the order. What do you want with that strawberry muffin? Ham and cheese?"

"An omelet sounds good, but mushrooms and spinach with cheese for me. Thanks. I'm dressed and on my way. Say thirty minutes for the pick-up?"

"Okay. You'll catch me looking pretty much *au natural,* but I showered, so at least I'm clean."

Angela laughed and hung up.

Kaylen placed the order and dressed in a pair of gray capris with a white t-shirt under a gray and black abstract-print blouse. She didn't know where she was going to end up that afternoon, and she wanted to be ready for anything.

She worked on the emails and a couple of voicemails while she waited, surprising Rob with a much earlier than usual call and catching her new manager for Treasure, Paul Centis, right after he had gotten out of the shower. He promised to call her back in ten, so she went on to the next message, a response to her request for a plumber to resolve a repeatedly-blocking drain in Bannisters' kitchen. She arranged for Rob to meet the plumber in an hour and managed to extract a verbal promise from the company to finally fix the issue before Emrico, her theatrical but highly-talented head chef made good on his promise to walk out in protest during the dinner rush the next time he found himself in danger of standing in dirty water.

Paul returned her call, and they were able to finish running through the list of problems at Treasure before Kaylen punched in the code to get Angela and their meal into the building.

"So, what's your big news?" Kaylen asked as soon as Angela had set the take-out bags on the kitchen counter.

Angela's beaming smile went along with a glowing complexion that had very little to do with makeup. "I'm pregnant," she said. "Two months."

"Oh, Angela, that's wonderful! I'm so glad for you and Jonathan."

Kaylen managed to hug her friend before her landline started ringing. She glanced at the caller ID: Brian.

CHAPTER FOUR

"I RAN into trouble on the way to work," Brian told her. "I know it's all over the news, hon, but why aren't you sleeping? I could have filled you in later without the dramatic crap I know you've been watching." He sounded irritated.

Kaylen felt a little defensive. "Angela called and woke me up." She heard the sharpness in her voice, but if he could be irritated, so could she.

"I should have guessed," he said.

Also not a good remark, Kaylen thought. She needed to tamp down the bristling response she wanted to give him. He was probably shaken up and trying to hide it.

"She picked up breakfast for us and came over," Kaylen told him with a quick smile to Angela, who no longer looked elated but worried. "I'm so relieved to hear your voice and know you're okay," she added. "You are, aren't you? You're not lying to me while you're getting stitched up at the ER, are you?"

"Of course not." His voice sharpened even more. "I promised I'd never lie to you again, remember?"

Definitely tense, Kaylen thought. He had every reason to be, and she shouldn't add to that. She needed to sound supportive…grateful he'd taken time out of his stressful day to call her. Keep her comments short and to the point.

She remembered how he'd reacted to his brother's disappearance and murder. Like a powder keg with a tight but cracking lid. The coffee shop's staff had become closer to friends than acquaintances, from what he'd told her. Working exclusively with cold cases since his return to active duty, he couldn't possibly have been prepared for what he had witnessed that morning.

"I do remember," she said, unable to think of anything more profound at that moment. "Of course I do."

Silence.

It lengthened.

Kaylen couldn't even hear Brian breathing, but she was sure he was still there.

She decided she should ask him something about the crime. That, he'd expect. She needed to act interested, but without wanting explicit details.

"Can...er...can you tell me anything about the murders?" *That sounded lame.* "Or maybe I should wait for the press conference?" She hoped that sounded like a response from any cop's girlfriend.

"I can give you a *few* details." He didn't sound so irritated. "Some I'd rather you heard from me than the news crews."

"Thank you," she said, thinking of Cassandra Bunting's hysterical reporting.

"I arrived after a robbery went down." He paused. "The scene's complicated," he said slowly, as though trying to figure out what to tell her. "You'll hear whatever else the department's willing to release if you tune in to the chief's news conference at two o'clock. The blood you saw on me, or maybe Angela told you about, was all from the victims. I've showered and changed into clean clothes already, so nothing to see here."

Kaylen felt a lump form in her throat and swallowed with difficulty. When he'd taken the Cold Case supervisory position, she'd felt over-whelming relief. She'd told herself that he'd be protected from the most dangerous elements of his former career as a homicide detective. The murderers he now dealt with day to day had to be less of a threat to his well-being. They'd be older, slower and less apt to shoot Brian immediately he arrived on their doorsteps. Kaylen had even managed to assure herself he'd stop wanting to return to Homicide. Now her little insulated bubble had been popped. If there was trouble, Brian would always wade right into the thick of it.

She hoped he couldn't hear the anxiety in her voice as she mumbled: "I'm really glad you stayed safe."

She bit her lip and fought symptoms of PTSD. The smell of fresh blood threatened to fill her nostrils. She grabbed a napkin and wiped her nose, breathing in the reassuring odor of paper. What she really wanted to tell Brian was how horrified she'd been when she'd seen him on TV that morning, but she wouldn't do that to him. What else could she say? She hadn't practiced giving platitudes after a shooting because she'd thought she'd never need them.

Brian would share anything he thought she needed to know when and if he could, Kaylen assured herself. Or if he decided she really *did* need to know.

The *Need to Know*...that boat of his was very aptly named, she thought, wallowing in the irony of Brian's stonewalling reticence over so many aspects of his life. After all the time she had been with him, the only thing she knew about his childhood and the abuse he'd suffered was that the profound scarring on his body had resulted from his stepfather throwing scalding liquid on him and beating him with not only a belt, but the buckle.

The day after she had brought a container of Emrico's excellent tomato bisque home and served it with a sandwich for their lunch, Brian had told her the scalding liquid that had burned him was tomato soup, and he'd never liked it much after that. How he'd managed to eat half the bowlful she'd set in front of him, she still couldn't imagine. She didn't think she could have done it.

Brian had finally and reluctantly confided details about his childhood to his psychologist after being told that was the only way he would get cleared to return to active duty. But no one else knew anything. Not even his best friend and neighbor, Jim Paxton.

Jim had assured her of that, but now he was preparing to leave for

Baton Rouge to research Brian's background, he'd probably end up learning a lot more about how Brian had developed such a strong and forceful personality. Brian had told her there were so many questions about his past, and especially about what had happened to his father, that he didn't feel he could move forward with their relationship until he knew more. Perhaps when Jim returned, Brian would finally open up to her. Or perhaps not.

"Yeah, I'm fine," Brian said in her ear. "Another day at the office, or should I say on the way to the office." He sounded like he was trying to make light of the situation.

Realizing he was waiting for her to comment, and knowing his penchant for gallows-humor, she decided to try for cheerful and off-topic herself, instead of what she knew could turn into a one-sided conversation about whether he'd been in as much danger as she was imagining.

"Are you going to be able to come to the club tonight, as we planned?" she asked.

It took him a couple of beats to answer. "Probably not," he said slowly, as though still considering his response. "I don't want you or your clubs mixed up in anything. A couple of news crews were conducting impromptu interviews, one of which involved some guy yelling slurs about me. The other reporter tried to interview me while I was waiting to finish giving my report to the lead detective, and I...well, you know me with reporters...I didn't respond well."

Kaylen could well imagine Brian in a state of "not responding well." He'd probably broken his promise not to swear...multiple times.

"I guess you missed that part," Brian said. "Or you'd be telling me I came off sounding like a jackass." He sighed. "And you'd be correct. Jack and Gabe were monitoring, and they told me a lack of tact was probably the nicest way to put what I said to her. They also heard the accusations being thrown around by some guy in painter's overalls. Apparently, he sang another verse of the same song about me being dirty and involved in all of Tim's shady deals, then finished up by saying I was responsible for Tim's death. Good thing I didn't hear any of that. I'd probably have assaulted him, maybe on live TV."

Kaylen's heart contracted painfully. Needing privacy, she mouthed

"Brian's okay,' to Angela, practically ran into the bedroom and closed the door. "Oh, Brian," she began.

He cut her off. "I'm giving you advance notice, hon. I don't want to hear anything else about all that today. I've already heard more than enough from Hal."

Kaylen skimmed quickly over the top of Brian's disagreements with the media, Hal, Trehorn, Internal Affairs, and the rest of MDPD's staff. "Not again with the accusations," she said, her mood shifting from wary relief to indignation and anger. "What is *wrong* with these people? Can't they ever let you alone? You nearly died trying to protect me and make those responsible pay for Tim's murder. You were investigated and cleared from taking kickbacks. There was the commendation ceremony…"

"All of that means nothing, except the bribery charges. Everyone always remembers the bad shit. It sticks to me like crap on a cracker."

Kaylen winced. He was swearing again, which either meant he'd gotten back into the swing of investigating alongside his coworkers in Homicide or he was really upset.

"I thought everything had been a little too quiet since Tim's funeral and the cartel members' roundup," Brian said. "Someone's stirrin' the pot again. Unfinished business. You watch yourself, hon. Let me know if anything's not looking or sounding right in your life."

Our life, Kaylen wanted to say, but she kept silent. Brian always distanced himself when he thought she might get sucked into the fringes of his professional life and those bribery allegations. He was right…the lingering dirt from Tim's cartel-related activities continued to dog him. Kaylen wished Brian's mother had never re-married and given birth to Tim, but then, she reminded herself, she would never have met Brian, and regardless of all the complications that had brought, she remained very glad she had him in her life…*their* life.

"Hang on a second," Brian said.

She heard murmuring male voices in the background.

While she waited, her already-jumbled thoughts sailed off to a contemplation of the roses Sam Wilson had sent her months ago. A dozen red, and a half-dozen white. Symbolic of both his relationship with her and hers with Tim's. She'd thrown those roses into a dumpster and hoped against hope that was the last reminder she'd have of the man she had once called her mentor and most-trusted friend.

Had it really been that long since she met Brian? *Yes.* In three months, they would have their second anniversary of that fateful morning.

After nothing more transpired, and no further sightings of Sam had occurred, she'd really begun to believe the past was mostly behind them, even if Brian still carried tarnish he couldn't seem to shake. Now, she wasn't so sure, and she knew he wasn't, either.

Unease prodded at her. Why hadn't Sam Wilson resurfaced? Where had he been hiding out all those months? Had he renewed his relationship with the cartel while it patched itself back together? Were the new versions of both Sam Wilson and the cartel about to ruin Brian's rebuilt career? Kaylen felt nauseated and wished she'd skipped that second cup of coffee.

Brian was back. "I don't mean for you to go looking for things," he said. "I'm sensing you're beginning to stress, and it won't do any good. I got involved in an active murder case instead of a cold one. I gave a statement, and apart from the mess I made of things by letting my temper loose on those reporters, my connection will probably remain low-key. Trehorn would like to keep it that way, and for once, I'm in agreement with him. No smoke, no fire where the media's concerned."

"I'll try to keep away from reporters the next few days myself," she said. "But as you know, they tend to stalk me on a regular basis, and with Treasure's opening only a couple of weeks away, interest is booming. I need publicity, but not the negative kind." She shuddered at the thought of going out the door to find reporters shoving microphones in her face, too. "I'd better stay home from the club this evening. I don't want to risk being blindsided by someone asking questions I can't answer or don't want to."

His sigh sounded both deep and profound. "I'm sorry, hon. I know you need exposure for the new club, but maybe not tonight. You don't want my name linked with yours right now."

"It's a little late for that, Brian. Tim's murder shone a spotlight on us both. When the public first became aware we were dating, there were plenty of nasty comments posted everywhere on social media. The haters are always ready to jump on anything positive."

"Let's not get into dragging up not-so-ancient history." His voice had sharpened again. "You know how I feel about that. What went on between you and Tim...I told you...it's in the past. I don't want any blow-by-blow descriptions."

She rushed to reassure him. "Don't worry, you won't ever hear them from me. But I have to think about my reputation as well as yours. There's still that sex tape floating around somewhere."

"You always bring up that tape."

He sounded angry, and he had every right. Kaylen could have kicked herself. This call was supposed to be about reassuring each other everything was okay. She asked herself why she had even broached the subject of that tape, while knowing the answer...she dreaded it surfacing at the worst possible moment. So many of her backers were conservative, older friends and business associates of her deceased husband, George. Those people would never understand the perils of modern life, when your most intimate moments could become fodder for everyone and anyone who happened to look at social media.

"Look," Brian said, "nothing's been seen or heard of that tape since Sam sent you a clip from it last year, and nothing's been seen or heard of him, either. Maybe he's dead. I hope he is. As far as I'm concerned, he can rot in hell."

"If he's going to resurface, you know he'll choose to do it at the worst time, and it sounds like this could very well *be* that time. My club opening, and now suddenly you arrive at a murder scene, where accusations start flying around about your involvement in Tim's businesses? His murder?"

"That's enough, goddammit!"

"Wow," she said, taken aback. "You haven't shouted at me like that since we were on the run together. And swearing at me? I don't like it. You know that. Don't do it."

She waited, listening to nothing but dead air. Just when she thought he may have hung up on her, he spoke again.

"You mustn't jump to conclusions." His voice was calm. Deadly calm. "That's my area of expertise, and then it's called calculation. You need to confine yourself to getting the bugs ironed out of your club opening. I know you've got more than enough there to keep you away from idle speculation on subjects you know nothing about."

His voice was so cold, goose bumps formed on her arms. He'd completely dialed down his emotions and detached himself. Kaylen wasn't sure if she felt relieved or angry he could throw that switch so quickly.

"You sound preachy," she said, hurt and disappointment vying for the top spot in her own emotional response. "I don't like it when you take that tone with me." She sounded petulant, even to herself, but why was it okay for him to tell her what he thought while she was supposed to keep quiet?

He didn't answer immediately, even though she expected him to deliver some sort of zinger. Maybe he was biting his tongue to keep from snapping at her. Kaylen found herself as eager as she imagined Brian was to get off the phone...before either of them said something that would bring a lot of regret later.

"Oh, hon, let's not get into an argument," he said, his tone not only flat but lifeless. "I feel it brewin.' You need more sleep, an' I've gotta get back to work. The wrap-up on one of my cases is now on a back burner due to this morning's events, but I've got plenty of other old murders to work on."

She felt for his frustration and reluctantly pushed hers aside. *For the common good,* she told herself.

"That painter didn't mention you or your own relationship with my brother," Brian said. "There's some good news for *you,* at least."

Kaylen definitely felt the irony in that statement. He was telling her she was a lot luckier than he was, and she begged to differ. Their relationship was well-known throughout Miami. Her reputation was now dependent, to a certain degree, upon his.

She heard voices in the background again. Whatever quiet corner Brian had found wasn't quiet any more. She told him she loved him, because despite their tense conversation, she most definitely did, and heard him say he felt the same way about her. He hung up before she did.

She sat on the end of her unmade bed with the phone in her hand and listened through the closed door to the TV in the living room. Angela had turned up the volume, probably to give her friend some additional privacy. Kaylen imagined Angela was probably still camped out on the couch with her feet up on two pillows.

Kaylen needed a few minutes to herself. She made her bed and tidied her bedroom and bathroom before opening the door and going back into the living-room. Angela was indeed still on the couch, feet up, fast asleep. On the coffee table, a full mug of coffee sat with a thin layer of cream congealing on top. Angela had only picked at her omelet, but she'd eaten most of the strawberry muffin and finished half her milk. Kaylen didn't want to disturb her friend, but she needed to watch the upcoming press conference. She took her laptop into the bedroom, plugged in earbuds and sat on the bed to watch, the laptop balanced on her knees.

Hal Shaw made a good chief, she thought as she watched him detailing what they knew of the coffee shop murders. He'd always had the ability to command, a talent of which she was acutely aware from the times she'd met with him in an official capacity. He made eye contact with reporters. He gave succinct details that didn't reveal more than she thought was probably the bare minimum of known facts. He named the two murdered employees and reported the surviving owner was out of surgery, but said the hospital would issue any reports on Antonio Camardi's condition. He stated one employee, Moises Delgado, was still missing.

He then spoke about the department's own personal loss in Officer Luis Rojas, a newly-minted graduate of the academy with a bright future; a future that had been ended by his senseless slaughter while assigned only to keep citizens at a safe distance from the crime scene. Kaylen felt Shaw's empathy as he publicly delivered his condolences to the officer's family before concluding his report.

"Kaylen, are you okay?" Angela knocked loudly on the bedroom door. "Kaylen, please answer me!"

Kaylen jumped and hated her startled response. She couldn't always control her over-reaction to any sudden movement or sound. She took out her earbuds. "I'm fine," she called. "I'm watching Chief Shaw's news conference about the murders. Come in."

Angela joined her on the bed, curled up and rested her head on

Kaylen's shoulder to better share the small screen as Shaw fielded questions from the media.

"Did he mention Brian?" Angela asked while a reporter requested Shaw speculate on the whereabouts of the missing coffee shop employee, which the chief refused to do.

"Not by name." *Thankfully,* Kaylen added silently.

They watched as the chief wrapped things up. He told the restless and increasingly-vocal media that he couldn't comment any further, but would issue a new statement as soon as he had more details. One reporter tried to ask about the off-duty officer who had arrived after the murders, calling out to Shaw as he left the podium. He didn't respond.

Kaylen noted the woman was the same reporter who had stood obediently by while that painter spewed outrageous lies about Brian. She was wearing the same outfit, which looked more appropriate for a social event than a somber police department press conference. Kaylen thought maybe she was being too critical and didn't say anything to Angela. After all, Cassandra Bunting might have been too busy in the middle of a work day to stop by her home to change, or perhaps she didn't ever need to wear anything but fun clothing for her normal beat.

"That's a relief for Brian, and for you, too," Angela said, moving away from Kaylen's shoulder to stretch and yawn. "I doubt you'll have to worry about reporters trying to sneak into Bannisters tonight."

Kaylen shut down the laptop. "Hopefully not, but I'm staying here this evening. I'm not sure if Brian's going to be able to come over or not." The patio door to her balcony was open, and she drank in the fresh air, laced with a hint of the ocean.

"I should go and let you sleep," Angela said. "I'm sorry I woke you. You look really tired."

"I'm fine." Kaylen patted Angela's hand lightly. "Let's change the subject and talk about something way more fun. Come on, spill the beans about your pregnancy." She genuinely wanted to hear more of Angela's wonderful news. She knew the odds had been stacked against her friend conceiving. "I'm so excited for you, and I'm so, so sorry your news had to be delivered to me in the middle of such a horrible event. I want you to know if this was a normal day, it would have taken precedence over anything else."

Angela smiled. "I know. Don't worry about hurting my feelings." She grabbed Kaylen's right hand and squeezed. "It was so unexpected. I had a small period last month. My GYN assured me that sometimes happens, and it won't harm the baby. It also means I'm further along than I thought. I've been bursting to tell everyone, but was afraid I'd miscarry. No prior experience with that, but I was so worried our happiness would be short-lived. Jonathan's over the moon about us becoming expectant parents."

Kaylen managed to put the laptop aside without it sliding to the floor. She turned to face Angela head-on and placed her other hand on top of her friend's. "Did you have an ultrasound? How long before you know the sex?"

As Angela chattered excitedly, they moved from the bedroom back to the living room. Kaylen drank another cup of coffee, ate a blueberry scone and wished Brian would come home early, but to her condo, not the *Need to Know,* anchored at the Coconut Grove Marina. She needed to hold him tight and know he was fine, instead of him merely telling her.

He'd had a lot of blood on him, she thought, a shadow passing through her soul, as it always did when symptoms of her PTSD nagged. She'd seen Brian covered in blood one other time, when she'd nearly lost him. Memories of that night came surging into her mind. The deafening noise she now knew was a gunshot. Flying glass. The blood running down his face; his arm. All that blood…

Although she was using every technique she'd been given to stave off the horrors of her memories, her breakfast began to give her heartburn, and when Angela insisted on leaving, Kaylen didn't object. She needed to process all the information she'd received and convince herself everything was going to be okay.

She knew it would be a tough sell while her adrenaline kept surging. She asked herself why any reporter would want to dredge up that horrible business with Tim and cast doubt on Brian's integrity yet again. Would it never stop, regardless of how much time had elapsed? How long would the sensational aspects of Tim's murder keep circulating on what seemed a regular basis with the local news organizations? As long as Brian was still alive and fodder for the tabloid community? The online haters? The bottom-feeders eager to destroy anyone they could?

Maybe she was being too paranoid, Kaylen thought as she stepped onto her balcony and watched palm fronds swaying gently in the breeze as she leaned against the rail and raised her face to the sun. Maybe after the second anniversary of Tim's death had passed, their ordeal would fade into the background, its place taken by even more sensational crimes.

Then again, maybe not.

CHAPTER FIVE

BRIAN WATCHED a rerun of Cassandra Bunting's interviews with bystanders and potential witnesses outside the coffee shop. He wondered if her news van had been diverted from its intended destination. He paid particular attention to her interaction with the scowling man in painter's overalls. The more the guy gestured, the more uncomfortable Cassandra became. When he pointed at the camera and shouted Brian's name, she became visibly distressed, grabbing her blouse and twisting the neckline into a knot as she took a couple of steps back.

"Brian Swift's responsible for this!" the painter yelled. "He's a dirty cop. He caused these murders!"

"How…how do you know that?" Bunting stammered.

"He's in bed with a drug cartel," the man told her. He grabbed the microphone and pulled it toward him, dragging her hand along with it.

Her extended arm shook badly. Brian reckoned at that point, she was on the verge of bolting.

"Brian Swift murdered Tim Madison for his brother's share of the drug money," the guy shouted, his face contorted and reddened. "The crime was covered up by other dirty cops."

Despite the many barbs that had been thrown at him in the past, Brian found himself reacting. "Fucker," he said to the screen. "Lyin' sack of shit. Who the hell *is* this guy?"

He replayed that portion of the footage, thinking he'd missed the guy's name, but he hadn't, and the second time around, Brian became even angrier. Once he had an ID, he'd confront the son-of-a-bitch and make him take back those baseless accusations.

"Coffee," Gabe said from the doorway. He walked in and placed a mug on the desk. "Here. Pause that garbage for a few minutes and drink. I've got much better news for you."

Brian wanted to throw the coffee, but knew Gabe would only bring him more. After they wrapped up the case in Tampa, Gabe had lost his fear of Brian's legendary temper and became his right hand in the office. Out in the field, Jack Mills had that sometimes dubious honor. Between them, they had kept their new supervisor on a straight course through a difficult period. Brian highly appreciated both his coworkers in Cold Case.

He muted the footage, picked up the mug and drank. Gabe's coffee always tasted better than anything else, including his own home-brew. If he'd asked Gabe to go in early and make coffee instead of taking that ill-fated breakfast run himself that morning, Brian knew he wouldn't have walked into that crime scene and certainly wouldn't be listening to the crap that painter was spewing. But what was done, was done.

"So, what's good about this morning?" he asked Gabe.

"I put out feelers for more information on the Hester Bowman case and got a bite. A neighbor who had moved away. Her sister still lives in the area and contacted the woman after my call. She's willing to talk with one stipulation…she wants me to go with you, and she'll only meet us in a public place." He cleared his throat and made a big production of straightening two papers on the edge of the desk. "She saw the news footage from the coffee shop this morning."

Brian's anger at the painter found a new outlet. He slammed the empty mug down on the table. "For Christ's sake, Gabe…what's she think I'm gonna do…beat her up? Shoot her fingers off one by one?"

Gabe looked like he might want to squirm. "Maybe," he muttered without making eye contact. "She might have mentioned something like 'putting the screws to me.' Anyway, she gave me a location and time.

You want me to call her back and confirm? I can tell her you're bringing Detective Mills instead of me."

Never shoot the messenger, Brian reminded himself. Gabe was definitely the good news genie that day.

He rubbed a hand over his face. "Days like this, I want to take a job on the west coast, where I might stand a chance of remaining anonymous. Any time my face gets on the news here in Miami, half the population recognizes me. Sometimes that's because I'm seen with Kaylen, but other times, I know people remember Tim's murder and his cartel connections."

"Boss, this wasn't your fault," Gabe protested. "You can't take responsibility for whatever happened at that coffee shop before you got there."

"I'm not so sure I agree." Brian pointed to the screen, where an image of the coffee shop surrounded by emergency vehicles was overshadowed by him mouthing something at Cassandra Bunting that he knew was crass and unwarranted. "I managed to make things even worse for myself this morning. I've brought down more crap on my head, and probable fall-out for Kaylen, too."

He'd thought he was done with the media after Mireille Shagassi cornered him with that microphone through the window before opening the Camaro's passenger door and dropping into the seat. But only moments after she left, Cassandra Bunting was trying to jab her own microphone into his face through the driver's side. She'd had the gall to open his door. He'd given her a few uncensored comments about what he thought of her and her TV station before wrestling back control of his door, slamming it and escaping, gravel from the Camaro's back wheels flying in his wake. Bunting's camera-operator had captured every little detail in hi-def.

"It'll stop eventually," Gabe said, breaking into Brian's churning thoughts. "The chief doesn't react. He's steered his course, and he always supports you."

"A lot more than Trehorn." Brian leaned back in his chair. His left shoulder was aching, and he needed to relax his muscles before they started cramping. It had been a while since he'd felt so tense.

"Anyone is more supportive than that guy." Gabe grinned. "He's even less touchy-feely than you are, and that's saying a lot."

"Oh, for God's sake get back to work, will you?" Brian had to smile, however reluctantly. "You can go on the field trip with me this afternoon. Call that woman back to confirm. Two o'clock?"

"She said two-thirty. But don't you need to reschedule that meeting you missed this morning?"

Brian thought about the limited amount of available time that afternoon. "The meeting over the Kowalski case may have to be postponed. Hal's got bigger fish to fry with this multiple homicide. Call his admin assistant. Let her know about the possible conflict. Give the chief and Trehorn some choices. Jack Mills can present the evidence at two-thirty. I can do it after we get back, say four-thirty. Or let them pick another day that'll work better for all of us."

"Gotcha." Gabe nodded. "Boss, you want lunch? I can order in."

"No. My appetite went south this morning. I'll wait for dinner with Kaylen."

Gabe didn't look like he thought skipping two meals was a good idea, but he left, closing the door quietly behind him as Brian resumed watching the remaining news footage with the volume turned back up.

He reviewed the interview with Mireille Shagassi again. It started off with a different, more reasonable perspective despite her invasive entrance into his car. But after he told her he couldn't comment on the case except to confirm the blood all over him wasn't from some wound he'd gotten by confronting the perpetrators, the tone had deteriorated on both sides. He'd told her he wasn't giving her anything else, and if she didn't get out of his car, he was going to arrest her for disturbing his peace.

He noted that goddamned painter had turned up again while he was preoccupied with Cassandra Bunting's shenanigans. The guy had presented himself to Shagassi, and her report had given him another opportunity to put in his two cents and over-extend his 15 minutes of fame by a wide margin.

"Brian Swift of Miami Dade Police Department is a dirty cop," the painter shouted, his refrain already familiar and repetitive.

Brian bristled and pounded his fist against the table. His notebook fell into the trash can, and the coffee mug almost hit the floor.

"Are you okay, Boss?" Gabe called.

"Fuck no, but yeah. Sorry." Brian got up and closed the door.

"You need to act like the investigative reporter you're always telling Miami you are," Brian heard the painter spouting at Shagassi.

He turned around and watched the man leaning over the reporter, his fists clenched.

"Get him to tell the truth about what he did to his brother. Why he took bribes," the painter told her.

Brian wished he'd clipped the guy with his car on the way out of the parking lot.

To her credit, Mireille Shagassi looked completely unphased, like this was a normal day for her, which it probably was, given the number of volatile assignments Brian had seen her cover. He watched her interrupt the tirade to ask the painter's name. When he refused, she calmly told him she had to have it before she'd air his complaints. She asked him why he felt so strongly that Brian Swift's motives needed further investigation, and why did he want to revisit those questions when the detective's arrival may have saved the life of the coffee shop's owner?

The painter lunged for her microphone in the same manner he'd gone for Bunting's. But he'd reckoned without Shagassi's street smarts. She sidestepped, pulled the microphone to her chest and made a slashing motion across her throat for her cameraman to cut the feed. Looking completely unflustered, she beckoned the closest patrolman as the Camaro flashed past behind them.

Brian remembered missing the cut curb in his haste to place as much distance between himself and the news crews as possible. The Camaro slammed down into the gutter, ramming his left arm against the door and sending pain shooting through his shoulder. He broke his promise not to swear by reciting a litany of highly-satisfying curses that ate up several miles on the way to the precinct.

He still felt the effects of that morning in his shoulder. He took a break to replenish his coffee before reviewing the remaining footage. Afterward, he felt too angry and tanked up on caffeine to work on anything until the time came to leave for the Hester Bowmen case's interview.

"I'm going for a drive," he told Gabe as he strode through the outer office. "I'll be back to pick you up at one forty-five."

Gabe, talking on the phone, gave him a thumbs-up and returned to jotting notes on a pad and peering at his computer screen while continuing to give information that sounded like it was to obtain coroners' reports.

Brian drove out of the dim garage into bright sunlight. He worked on dropping his level of anger and struggling to regain his objectivity even while the news-feed continued to replay in his head.

Overall, the painter's demeanor seemed fueled by righteous anger, Brian decided. But how could his arrival at the scene be anything but contrived? Brian remembered seeing the guy pounding on the coffee shop's front door when he arrived.

He knew he'd made no moves that would have attracted any attention from the crowd in front of the coffee shop until he was seen checking behind and in front of the counter. He should not have been recognized.

He called Gabe. "I need you to find out everything you possibly can about that painter on the news footage. I want to know where he lives, works, shops, eats and shits," he told the clerk.

Still mulling over the morning's events, he realized he'd unconsciously driven into all-too-familiar territory...the immediate area around Woodland Park Cemetery. He pulled through the gates and parked. Whenever he felt stressed, sooner or later he'd end up where Tim was buried. Another somewhat predictable trait, he thought, disquieted. *Like the coffee shop.* He'd have to change his ways or he could be tracked by any fool with a grudge.

He'd keep that in mind for the future, but at that moment, he refused to miss out on an opportunity to decompress. Brian knew he'd never given Tim any credit for insightfulness while his brother was alive. Brian's opinion had been that Tim's attributes only included extreme bull-headedness, a stubborn streak even larger than his own, and a perverse delight in self-centered behavior. Brian had thought his brother's intention when insisting he be buried at Woodland Park had been to make sure no one ever forgot him, and for Brian's guilt to be sufficient enough to ensure regular graveside visits.

But as the months stretched out to a year and beyond, Brian realized Tim really *did* understand how dangerous his lifestyle was, and must have considered he might die younger than his robust health indicated. Not only had Tim purchased a cemetery plot and headstone, he'd made sure the plot was situated where Brian would have a place to go that pretty much guaranteed uninterrupted peace and solitude.

Tim had succeeded one thousand percent on the serenity aspect, Brian thought, feeling the load slide from his shoulders and the darkness surrounding his soul begin to lighten. He walked on paths between neat rows of headstones to sit on his favorite bench under the shade of a spreading oak tree. Ten minutes into the breathing and meditation exercises he'd been so resistant to practice when he first started sessions with his shrink, Dr. Fleming, he felt calmed and cleansed enough to Google both reporters.

What he learned confirmed his deductions about Cassandra Bunting. She usually handled the social beat. Many of her interviews dealt with restaurant openings, craft fairs and on what might be a brave day for her, musicians. Although he already knew the other reporter, Mireille Shagassi regularly covered breaking news, Brian still learned a few additional details he might find useful in the future.

Shagassi had a knack for convincing people to disclose details they probably wouldn't have revealed to others. She had a reputation for doing her research before conducting in-depth interviews. She always seemed to have a firm handle on the type of personality she'd be dealing with, and was ready for a head-on confrontation with any member of the local political scene, government office or law-enforcement bureaucracy. She could think on her feet, and she usually concentrated on facts while throwing out conjecture.

Brian ran through a mental checklist of interviews she had conducted at the crime scene. She'd spoken with the young Hispanic in the suit, two other bystanders Brian had noticed hanging at the back of the crowd, and a guy with a bicycle. Brian snapped out of mental viewing mode and scrolled back through his memories to the beginning of Shagassi's last interview. The bicycle...was it the one that had belonged to Moises? The one he'd had CSI process and leave chained to the post?

He pulled out his cell. "Call Moises' family," he instructed Gabe. "Get every detail about his bicycle, then have CSI send you pics and a description from their processing. I want info on paint, scrapes, nicks, everything. If the family has any photos of it, get 'em picked up. Then see about enhancing the last interview subject on the tape from Mireille Shagassi's footage. Get it from the TV station if they'll give you a copy. Otherwise..."

Gabe interrupted. "I know, boss. I'll get you the best footage ASAP and all the info."

Brian felt more than marginally better. As a warm breeze stirred the leaves above his head, he debated whether to call Buxford or Ramirez to give them an update or whether he should stay the hell out of the morning's homicide case unless asked to investigate further. But if he didn't at least notify one of the other detectives after he'd contacted Moises' family and CSI about the bicycle, then what did that say about him?

He leaned back and watched the branches above his head swaying in the breeze, dark green oak leaves rustling gently. If he said nothing, he could be accused of hiding important information that might help locate a witness, identify Moises as an accomplice, or even reveal him to be a hostage.

Brian felt a headache coming on, and he'd sworn off taking any kind of pain relievers. Time for coffee. He checked his watch. Maybe the headache was more from a lack of food than anything else. He had just enough time to cruise into a fast-food drive-through before picking up Gabe.

He'd promised Kaylen he'd try to limit his intake of food on the run to a couple of times a week. He'd already passed that goal. He shrugged and stood up. No one was perfect, even Kaylen, and she'd want him to eat.

He knew of a burger joint right on his route back to the precinct. But first, he'd take a moment to stop by Tim's grave, say hello and throw out the dead roses in the urn. Kaylen went on Thursdays to replenish the flowers, and it would save her a trip to the dumpster.

He saw the white roses when he was still two rows away, and his stomach churned in a way that had nothing to do with hunger. He quickened his pace, even though he knew Kaylen wasn't going to suddenly appear and get a nasty surprise. Those roses had to be from Sam Wilson. Although he found no card tucked into the flowers when he searched, Brian's belief wasn't shaken…Tim's signature weekly bouquet for Kaylen had been a dozen red roses. Sam Wilson's was always a half-dozen white.

As he tossed both the withered red roses that Kaylen had left the previous week and the half-dozen fresh white ones into the dumpster on his way back to his car, Brian felt relieved he had spontaneously driven to the cemetery that day. Otherwise, Kaylen would have been the first one to get the message that her former mentor had surely returned to Miami. The question was, Brian thought, stifling the anger he felt at Wilson's audacity in defiling Tim's grave, whether Sam Wilson was merely paying a short visit and taking the time to taunt Kaylen, or whether he was potentially going to develop into a much bigger problem by staying around long-term.

Whatever, he thought as he cruised out of the parking lot. He'd deal with good ole Sam as soon as he got his hands on the guy. *Both hands.* He flexed the fingers of his left hand. Sam's cartel buddies had almost ended not only his career but his life. If Sam thought he was going to face a weakened foe, he was in for a real shock. Brian thought with relish about sinking the fingers of his left hand into Sam's neck. It'd be worth going to prison for the satisfaction of ridding Miami and Kaylen's life of one useless piece of shit.

But then he'd never get to hold Kaylen and be with her again, except through a thick piece of glass, Brian reminded himself. He swore under his breath, felt bad about adding that infraction to his weekly tab of backsliding but still ordered a cheeseburger and fries from Holland's Burgers and Shakes. His order came with a large soda. He drank and munched while he drove back to the precinct.

He'd have to tell Kaylen about Sam's reappearance. The unease they had both felt over the last few months about when and how Sam Wilson was going to mess with Kaylen's life and her business would turn the imaginary caution light Kaylen had said she felt was hanging over her head from yellow to red.

But she wasn't alone this time. She wasn't as vulnerable and as unprepared for trouble as she had been when she first opened Bannisters. She had a homicide detective as a boyfriend, loyal and protective employees at her supper club that included manager, Rob Diaz, and friends like Jim and the Crossfields. Between all of them, they would make sure she stayed safe.

He'd break the news to her as soon as he finished his interview, Brian decided as he drew into the parking garage and saw Gabe waiting outside the elevator. In person, not over the phone. There would be time. He doubted Wilson was ready for a face-to-face confrontation yet, or he wouldn't have had the roses delivered to Tim's gravesite, the bastard.

CHAPTER SIX

TREHORN CALLED while Brian and Gabe were on their way to meet their new witness in the Hester Bowman case. Brian considered letting Trehorn chat with his voicemail, but if the lieutenant needed more information on the triple homicide, a delay wouldn't only jeopardize solving the case, but cause unnecessary friction between the cold case squad and the hard-working detectives at the homicide bureau.

In Brian's opinion, one tyrannical lieutenant had been replaced by another. The deceased William Hastings, late supervising lieutenant of the Vice squad, had met his match with the new troublemaker brought into MDPD by Hal Shaw. Different position, but similar result. Excluding the randomness of a coin toss, Brian thought Hastings still kept the prize for being top asshole, but since Trehorn had been in his position for 18 months, he still had ample time to cruise into 1st position.

Brian took the call. "What can I do for you, Lieutenant?" he asked, striving for an uninterested and slightly bored tone that didn't quite stoop to condescension. He noticed Gabe grabbed both his seat belt and the dashboard as they cruised off the ramp from the expressway at 30 mph over the posted limit.

"Get back to your office and make yourself available," Trehorn barked. "Buxford told me your squad room's completely empty. Where the hell is your clerk? No one's picking up the phone. You don't even have a way to leave a message. Is that the norm for your outfit? I'm writing you up and submitting a formal complaint to the chief."

"I don't have to answer to you or be available to you or any of your staff whenever you happen to drop by the basement," Brian snapped, tossing away any attempt to control his insolence. "You called, I picked up. Gabe Weston's with me at the request of a potential witness, who feels she's got rapport with him. Jack Mills is working the Kowalski case. You decided to postpone this afternoon's meeting because of the coffee shop homicides, so there's no need for any of us to be working from the precinct." He ignored a snort from Trehorn that probably superseded an interruption. "If Buxford or Ramirez need me to come back for another interview, then I can make myself available after I've finished my own. Now, what do you need that can't wait until I get back?"

"Buxford needs to go over the timeline with you again. He wants you to look at mug shots." Trehorn sounded slightly less confrontational. "And the chief is going to want to discuss the accusations flying around on TV about your hand in your brother's murder."

"Yeah. I heard that garbage on TV. Hal would never go anywhere near that route over Tim's murder. I had nothing to do with it. You can ask anyone at the precinct. No one believes that crap. And the evidence ruled me out. I loved my brother. I'm still dealing with his death. Tell Buxford to call me." Brian hung up.

Gabe cleared his throat. "That was completely unprofessional and uncalled for."

"Don't you turn on me, too." Brian jammed his foot down hard on the brake as they almost ran into the back of a pink Cadillac that had abruptly stopped when the light ahead flipped from green to yellow.

Gabe had braced for an impact that didn't come. He took his hands off the dash and settled back into the seat. "I didn't mean *you.*" He turned to look at Brian with eyes still wide from shock. "I wouldn't be working for you if I had any doubts about your involvement in Mr. Madison's case. If you want to file a formal complaint about the lieutenant's behavior, I'll back you up."

Brian felt tension ease from his back and left shoulder. "Thanks, Gabe."

The Cadillac turned right on a green arrow, and Brian began working through Fleming's methods for tamping down his anger. *Deep cleansing breaths. Visualize the words flowing off like rain water or a cleansing shower.* While he practiced the calming techniques, he slowed the Camaro to the posted limit and lowered his window to circulate fresh air through the car.

"Sorry to doubt you," he told Gabe.

Gabe let out a long breath before responding. "I don't want you to be sorry, Boss," he said, keeping his gaze fixed on the road ahead. "I want you to fight back. You've got good cause. I don't know why the chief doesn't see what Trehorn's doing."

"Yeah, sometimes I wonder why I'm on the short leash and Trehorn's allowed to range all over my territory as well as his own, but I've gotta figure the chief's testing me. Tryin' to make sure I've really changed; that I don't blow up at any provocation, however personal. Maybe, deep down, he still has doubts about whether I'm completely innocent of any involvement in Tim's prior activities with the cartel, too."

"Boss, if the chief had any doubts, you wouldn't be in charge of Cold Case."

"Where I can do the least damage?" Brian raised an eyebrow at his clerk.

Gabe shook his head. "The doubts are all on your side, not Chief Shaw's. But you're letting Trehorn yank your chain, and I've never seen you do that before."

Brian had to disagree. Hastings had done plenty of chain-yanking before his own son shot him to death. And even after the length of time that had passed since his return to work, he frequently felt he was still skating on very thin ice where belief in his innocence was concerned.

"If the lieutenant's questions about my involvement in Tim's death gain any footing, there's gonna be a lotta shit flyin' around again," he told Gabe. "Watch you don't get hit."

"I can take care of myself." Gabe's mouth formed a grim line as the Camaro weaved its way through traffic. "Don't you worry about me, Boss." He clutched the seatbelt again as they cleared a clump of cars crawling along behind a semi. "But if we could stop doing close to fifty in a thirty zone, and you do more of those relaxation exercises you've told me your shrink gave you, then I think we might be able to avoid you picking up a speeding ticket before scaring our witness into running away."

Brian checked the speedometer and found Gabe wasn't exaggerating. He eased off the accelerator and watched the needle sink to the posted limit before lowering his window all the way to take deep breaths of air heavily-laced with diesel fumes while he tried to rid himself of the burning sensation tightening his chest. "Thanks, Gabe. I can always count on you when I need a little perspective."

"Glad to provide it," Gabe said. "Maybe we should stop at that fast-food restaurant I see up ahead? I could do with a soda, and I bet you could, too."

"Okay." As Brian maneuvered his way over to the drive-through's entrance, his phone rang again. Buxford, that time. "Damn," he said under his breath.

"Why don't you park, and I'll go inside to pick up those drinks while you're taking this call?" Gabe suggested.

Brian nodded and eased into the first space. Gabe jumped out as Buxford's expressionless monotone asked Brian where the hell he was.

"On the way to interview a witness on a cold case," Brian said. "I heard you want me to go over mug shots. I can do that after I get back to the precinct. What else d'you need? You already have my statement."

"There are a few holes in it," Buxford said slowly, as though he was reading the statement while they talked. "I can't understand how neither you nor Officer Milagros heard the rookie getting his throat slit. The attack on him had to have happened inside the store, otherwise there would have been witnesses in the parking lot. Did he really give himself up without a fight?"

"I didn't think there was enough blood either inside the store or outside of it for Rojas to have been killed in either location," Brian said. "My theory, if you want to hear it, is he was murdered elsewhere, and then dumped in the cooler."

"Why would anyone take the risk of getting seen or heard dragging a body into the back of the store? That makes no sense."

Brian made no attempt to hide the impatience he felt. "Not all murder scenes make sense on the first pass. You and I both know that."

"We're going to find more than one victim's blood on your clothing, I suppose?" Buxford said.

"You'd suppose right. The owner grabbed me, and then I checked Rojas for a pulse after I found him." Brian saw Gabe sauntering toward him with two large sodas. "I've gotta go," he told Buxford. "I can call you back later or talk with you in the squad room after Gabe and I get back from this interview."

"Come over and talk to me in Homicide," Buxford said. "What time?"

Brian saw any plans he'd had for the rest of the afternoon fly out his lowered window. "How about four-forty-five?" he suggested, rolling the window up. He turned on the a/c to counteract the smell of fast food grease and exhaust fumes.

"I'll be waiting," Buxford said before hanging up.

"I'm sure you will," Brian muttered as he watched Gabe stop to take a drink from one of the sodas and pass the time of day with an elderly man who had just left his vintage red Pontiac Firebird in a handicapped space.

Brian scrolled through his text messages and found one from Kaylen. She was going to Bannisters for a couple of hours. Rob had too much on his plate. Brian swore under his breath. That meant he'd have to go to the club, regardless of the risk. News crews might be hanging around Bannisters, but if he didn't talk to Kaylen about those roses, he was taking a chance Sam Wilson might try to contact her, and she wouldn't be expecting it.

Gabe climbed into the Camaro and handed Brian his drink. He drank half of it while finishing the drive to Shore Acres Park. The cold soda felt good going down but didn't ease the churning inside Brian's gut. Anger, frustration and worry for Kaylen all circulated like they hadn't for months.

He pushed hard against his surging emotions, once so easily controlled. Opening up to Dr. Fleming and allowing himself to love Kaylen had done serious damage to his protective armor. Monthly sessions with the shrink had given him what he now knew was a false sense of security. Suspending those sessions three months ago had been a mistake. Between the crime scene that morning and the prospect of having to deal with Sam Wilson's bullshit again, he realized he wasn't as ready for the delivery of a full load of crap as he'd believed.

Definitely time for a tune-up from Fleming, Brian told himself. He felt fragmented. Scattered. Speeding and snapping at Buxford were symptoms he recognized. Before meeting with the homicide detective later that afternoon, he'd call Fleming's office. Even making that decision seemed to alleviate some of the stress.

Let it flow away, like a cleansing shower.

Brian silently intoned that mantra for the last few minutes of the drive. Gabe drank his soda and chilled until their arrival at the park, where Brian found a space for the Camaro adjacent to a playground.

A number of children swarmed over the equipment. They shouted from a jungle gym, screamed on swings and milled around like a stampede of miniature wild horses. Brian and Gabe strode past a barrage of strollers, tiny bicycles, tricycles and adults seated on benches and retaining walls. The one thing Brian dreaded was Kaylen suddenly deciding that at the age of thirty-four, she needed to become a mother. With bestie Angela pregnant, he feared his chances of that happening had probably doubled.

"She said she'd be on the fourth bench on the right side after the fountain," Gabe said as they walked briskly along a serpentine pathway beneath tall palms. He sounded slightly breathless.

They were power walking without reason. Brian slowed to a more moderate pace. No need to draw attention to themselves. His jacket flapped open on that thought, and he saw a young woman pushing twins in a double-wide stroller glance at his waistband, where his badge was prominently displayed as well as his firearm. Her brows drew toward each other. He buttoned his jacket and tried giving her what he hoped was a reassuring smile. Apparently, he succeeded. She returned the smile as their paths crossed.

He started counting benches after they passed the fountain and continued walking a path that curved first toward the water, then back toward the parking lot.

"That must be her." Brian nodded toward a figure in a pink and turquoise print pantsuit. A large floppy hat covered her head, which seemed to be resting on her chest. "I wonder how long she's been sitting there? She must have dozed off."

Gabe checked his watch. "We're on time."

A woman with a dog passed close to the bench. The dog stopped to sniff the woman, who didn't move. The owner shouted "Sorry" and pulled on the leash. Dog and owner moved away, but Mrs. Dewett didn't even stir.

"I've got a bad feeling about this," Brian said as he broke into a jog. Gabe kept pace.

"Mrs. Dewett," Brian said loudly when they were both standing over her.

No response.

Christ, was she dead?

"Mrs. Dewett." He squatted in front of her and tried to peer beneath her hat.

"I'm not dead," a voice said from behind him. "She's not, either, although she sleeps like she is."

Brian turned to see a tall, thin woman scowling down at him. Dressed in purple capris and a beige long-sleeved shirt, her sunhat was only marginally smaller than that worn by the sleeper, but sat at a jaunty angle. A sunflower tucked into the hat's pink headband flapped rhythmically in the breeze.

"That's Gertrude Pensky." Mrs. Dewett pointed a long, bony finger in the direction of the sleeper, who was now snoring. "We live in the same rest home. She always wants to walk with me after lunch, but then she tires, and I have to leave her behind." Mrs. Dewett squared her shoulders. "I walk two miles every day. She only manages the two blocks from the rest home and crossing the street to the park before she wants to sit." Mrs. Dewett formed a pair of air-quotes. "Her 'I only need five minutes' always turns into an hour-long nap."

"Oh, dear," Gabe said when Mrs. Dewett glared at Mrs. Pensky, whose snoring had increased in volume.

Passers-by stared. Brian quickly stood back up. "Let's walk to the next bench. It's in the shade, and we can talk without disturbing her."

"All right." Mrs. Dewett nodded, her scowl easing. "Let's get this over with, so I can wake up Gertie and get us back before we miss our afternoon snack, such as it is. Lord forbid we're late; they'll send out a search party." She rolled her eyes. "You like stale crackers and sickly-sweet lemonade with powdered mix floating around in it, Sergeant?"

Brian smothered a smile. He was beginning to like Mrs. Dewett's dour spirit. He thought she might be an excellent witness. "I don't," he told her. "I think we could get you a much better snack than that, don't you, Gabe?" He winked at his coworker. "After we finish talking, we'll get both of you ice cream and whatever else you'd like from one of those cafés across the street."

Mrs. Dewett's scowl eased. She stood ramrod-straight as she eyed Brian from head to foot. "You're not as scary in person as you looked on TV," she said. "You're not as tall as I expected, either," she added, looking from Brian to Gabe, who was slightly taller than his supervisor.

Brian shot a warning look at Gabe, who was one of his staunchest defenders, before the clerk tried to correct her regarding Brian's ability to terrify anyone he chose, and point out that she was lucky she wasn't one of those people. Brian could definitely live with Mrs. Dewett mistaking him for a mild-mannered domesticated house cat. He sensed she'd be more apt to open up. Having spent her working life teaching middle school, he figured he'd get more out of her with sweetness than vinegar.

"Let's chat about the years you lived next to the Bowmans," he suggested as they strode toward the bench, Gabe following. He wondered what this spry woman was doing in a rest home.

"Very well." Mrs. Dewett sat on the right side of the bench and patted the seat beside her. "What do you want to know about Hester?" She eyed a cart filled with assorted cans and bottles on the other side of the park. "It would really make things go a lot smoother if your assistant would kindly get me something to drink. I'm quite parched, and very partial to orange soda."

Gabe nodded. "I'll be right back." He took off at a brisk pace.

"No hurry," Mrs. Dewett called.

Gabe slowed down. Mrs. Dewett settled back.

"You lived next door to the Bowmans for how long?" Brian asked.

"Close to ten years. Hester worked in the same school for eight of those, although we had very little contact during that time. Mrs. Dewett tugged down first one cuff of her blouse, then the other. "She was a cafeteria worker, not a cook," she clarified. "She served meals and cleaned up."

Brian's mother had served meals in a school cafeteria for a while. He didn't like Mrs. Dewett's condescending tone. "What about the husband?"

"He was a public works supervisor. They were ill-suited, if you want my frank opinion. At home, the arguing would start around nine o'clock most evenings and continue until eleven, when I suppose they both went to bed."

"Why didn't you tell the detectives about that when you gave your original statement?" Brian asked.

"I didn't like their attitude." Mrs. Dewett gently tossed her head. The sunflower waved at Brian. "They acted like they were in too much of a hurry to really listen to what I had to say. You let me set the time and place for this interview, and you're treating me with respect."

"I'm glad we understand each other," Brian said.

"You're not really a nice man, are you?" She looked steadily at him.

"No," he said. "I'm not."

"I like that about you." She smiled. "No bullshit. Let's get down to business. You want to record this or what?"

CHAPTER SEVEN

"How were the Bowmans with their neighbors?" Brian asked.

He waited impatiently for an answer while Mrs. Dewett guzzled orange soda, then bit into the chocolate chip cookie Gabe had brought from a café across the street.

Mrs. Dewett directed a sharp look toward Brian's lightly tapping foot. "Cordial," she said around a mouthful of cookie. "They usually turned up last minute at barbeques and pool parties, and if they brought anything to contribute to the party, it was always cheap beer or pretzels." She looked disapprovingly at the empty soda bottle before propping it beside her on the bench. "He was always dressed in one of those tiny little bathing trunk things for the pool parties..." She stopped, apparently searching for the right word.

"A Speedo?" Gabe suggested from his lounging position against a nearby palm tree.

Mrs. Dewett shook the remains of the cookie at him. "That's right; a Speedo. He looked awful, and he'd leer at all the teenage girls and puff out his chest while strutting around the pool like he owned the place."

"How about Hester?" Brian prompted when Dewett paused, apparently lost in thoughts of Bowman and his party attire.

Mrs. Dewett shrugged. "Oh, Hester was all right." She popped the last piece of cookie into her mouth and brushed crumbs from her pants. "Better than him by a mile. I wondered why she'd married that crass creature, but she didn't have a lot of education, so perhaps she'd felt her prospects were severely limited and said yes to the first man who asked. She was very plain. Wore her graying hair pulled back in a bun and no makeup. I've never liked makeup, myself. Makes you look cheap." She shot a look at Brian. "Your girlfriend wears a lot of it, but somehow it doesn't look cheap on her. I suppose she can afford the expensive stuff. Maybe that's what makes the difference."

Brian wasn't there to discuss Kaylen or her makeup with Mrs. Dewett. "Let's keep talking about the Bowmans," he redirected. "They had one child..."

"Wallace." Mrs. Dewett scowled, either at the thought of Wallace or because Brian hadn't taken the bait she'd thrown out. "Good for nothing. Always out of a job and going back for a hand-out. Hester complained to me one time, when she must have been even more upset with him than usual. She had told Wallace he couldn't move back home anymore. She had her hands full with her job and looking after her husband without cooking and cleaning for her son, too. She said he'd have to get work and stick with it, and he'd have to sleep on a friend's couch until he could afford to rent a room. She told me she'd left one of those pool parties early with a headache. Left her husband there and came home to find Wallace had broken the kitchen window and was trying to climb inside."

"How long was that before she died?" Brian asked.

"About a month, I'd say. It was mid-summer, or the party wouldn't have been going on. No one wanted their kids up at all hours during the school year. I was firmly in favor of that, being an educator myself. It's very important for children to get sufficient rest." She peered at Brian from under her hat brim, her eyes sharp and almost coal black in the shade. "Do you have any children, Sergeant?"

"No." Brian made notes on his pad. "How did Mr. Bowman and Wallace react to Hester's death?"

"Mr. Bowman closed himself up in the house and didn't come out for two weeks. He kept up the ban his wife had put on Wallace returning home. In fact, Wallace didn't even attend Hester's funeral. It was a very small gathering. I made a hot dish and took it to the house after the funeral, but I didn't stay long. Bowman was drinking heavily and crying. He said he'd never appreciated Hester until she wasn't there anymore. Soon afterward, he put the house up for sale. I heard he'd quit his job and moved away, but I never heard where."

"What happened to the house?" Brian asked as she paused for breath.

"It eventually sold. Took a while. The market was down." She looked pleased with herself for using that terminology and squared her shoulders. "He left all the furniture. That went into a dumpster. Then the family who bought the house remodeled everything before they moved in. What a mess the neighborhood went through. A huge dumpster was brought in, and that was filled and exchanged three times. They tore out walls and threw out all the appliances. Even the bathtub."

"Sounds like a gut job," Gabe said, interrupting the lengthy description of urban rehab.

Brian gave him a half-smile of thanks. He was getting frustrated with the woman's rambling and had been about to interrupt in a more direct manner.

Mrs. Dewett nodded. "That's right…a gut job. I watch all the HGTV shows, you know."

"I'm sure you do," Brian told her. "You're very knowledgeable. But did they change anything in the back yard, where Mrs. Bowman was found?"

"Well, yes, they did. I went to their housewarming when everything was done, and they said they bought at a low price because of the home's history." She leaned forward and lowered her voice. "The murder, of course," she hissed.

"Of course." Brian nodded and tried to look encouraging. A little prompting and redirection went a long way with this witness, but wading through extraneous details about remodeling sent the part of his mind that was still detached into visions of the various stages Treasure had gone through. The distinctive odor of sawdust seemed to creep back into his nostrils, along with the echo that had accompanied their feet as he and Kaylen walked through the cavernous space before all the walls went up. He shook off the memory and redirected himself that time, instead of Mrs. Dewett.

"They wanted to make sure the whole place looked different," their witness was explaining to Gabe. "They had a pool put into the back yard and a big concrete patio. I thought they should have left more grass. Concrete gets very hot in the summer for small children to play on, and they were expecting their first child. I told them." She nodded sagely.

Brian couldn't help himself. He was getting hot, too. The sun was no longer behind the palm tree. Gabe was the only one still sheltered from its rays. "I'm sure you did," he said, making no attempt to hide the irony in his tone.

Dewett glared at the interruption and closed her mouth, which formed a firm, disapproving line.

"Are you ready for that ice cream?" Brian asked, quickly. If he pissed her off, she'd want to go back to the rest home. Then he'd probably have to go through the whole time-wasting hassle again another day.

"I'm almost finished telling you about the new people who moved into the Bowman house, Sergeant."

She must be using her teacher-to-student voice, Brian thought with a sudden trace of amusement. He could see her in a classroom, looking down her long nose at a bunch of kids who didn't want to be listening to anything she said.

"If you wouldn't keep interrupting, we could both be done with this interview," Dewett told him. "I'd like to get out of this heat and eat that ice cream inside the café, where it'll be cooler." She pulled a lace-trimmed handkerchief from a pocket in her capris and wiped her brow. "I'm beginning to sweat."

"Sorry," Brian said, doing his best to look suitably apologetic.

Mrs. Dewett folded her hands together on her lap. "Well, let me see, where was I?"

"Talking about their vision for the back yard," Gabe said.

"Ah, yes." Dewett dabbed her upper lip with the handkerchief. "Let me see...well, at their housewarming party they told all of us they'd thought about canceling the sale after they found out about Hester's death, but the house was such a good price, they couldn't pass it up." She brushed a few remaining cookie crumbs from her pants. "That's really all I can tell you." She looked at her watch. "Time to wake Gertie. We have just enough time for that ice cream before we have to return to the rest home."

"Did Mr. Bowman have affairs with any of the women in the neighborhood?" Brian asked as Mrs. Dewett slid forward on the bench prior to standing.

She looked startled. "What makes you think he did?"

"Did you have an affair with him?"

Mrs. Dewett got up from the bench. She tried to move quickly, but she'd been sitting too long. She had trouble drawing herself upright. But even if her body wouldn't cooperate, her glower and her tone made up for it. "That's none of your business," she snapped.

"It's definitely my business." Brian got up, too. He had the advantage of being able to stand over her and made the most of it. She had to strain her neck to maintain her accusatory glare. "I aim to solve Hester Bowman's murder. That requires me to ask questions you might not like, but you need to answer."

Bowman cranked herself erect and jammed her hat down as the breeze almost lifted it off her head. "I already told you everything I know."

"I don't believe that for a moment, lady."

"Well, I never…"

"No more sidebars about remodeling and those new neighbors. I want to know about the Bowmans and their interactions with the neighborhood. I think you know plenty about that, but you've been playing around while getting afternoon snacks out of us. Don't try to outsmart me. Not gonna happen, Mrs. Dewett."

Her mouth had almost dropped open. Almost. Brian had thought she was a tough nut. Now he knew for sure.

"I came here to make it easier on you," he told her. "I can make it a whole lot harder by taking you down to the precinct and sitting you in one of those small rooms I know you've seen on those cop shows you watch on TV."

She refused to make eye contact.

"I'm asking you again, Mrs. Dewett, and for the last time before we go to one of those rooms. Did you have an affair with Bill Bowman?"

"Yes." When she looked up at him, her gaze was unwavering; unapologetic. "Short, wild and very much regretted. When they first moved in." She shook her head and the sunflower bobbed around on her hat. "I didn't realize

I was just one of his many conquests. Who would have thought a short, fat and balding public works supervisor would be so good in bed?" She sighed and mopped her face. "Are we done? I'm really hot, tired and humiliated."

Finally, Brian thought. They'd stopped meandering around and gotten to the point while the day turned into a humid furnace. "I wanted the truth, Mrs. Dewett. It's my job to get all the information I possibly can. Hester Bowman's murder needs to be solved, and I mean to do that. Stepping on people's feelings happens frequently during investigations."

"It's a horrible job, and you're the one to do it," she said. "You have no feelings yourself."

"Maybe I do, maybe I don't, but that's not up for discussion." He moved around until his shadow gave her some relief from the sun. "Now, before you leave, how many other women did he have affairs with in the neighborhood?"

"I wouldn't know."

"Come on, you've got to have some idea. You *knew* these people. You were the concerned neighbor who gave good advice."

"I did," she agreed. "I always took the opportunity to educate."

A nice way to talk about meddling, he thought. "Yes. So, give me some names."

"Well, there was Donna Richie and Mary Quintero." A new wrinkle appeared between her brows as she thought. "Joyce Lumberger, too, and her daughter, Polly. Those I know for sure, because we all talked." She tapped an index finger against her long, yellow front teeth. "Rumors flew about Gillie Maxman and Florence Harding, but they denied they'd ever been closer to him than the next chair at one of the parties." She grabbed her hat as it threatened to take off in the hot breeze and squinted up at Brian. "I think that's why he came in the Speedo. Fast off and fast on."

Brian got a disturbing visual.

"He would go inside with whoever was throwing the party while the husband was busy working the grill and making sure the hamburgers and hot dogs didn't burn," Dewett continued. "Or he'd use one of their bedrooms with another guest. Then when he'd got what he wanted, the affair, if you could call it that, was over. A lot of his so-called affairs were more like one-night stands, although he made a few exceptions. I was one of them. I lived alone, so it was easier for him. He was able to sneak over after Hester went to bed. He was drunker than a skunk most nights, but it never affected his performance."

"Who was the last woman you know he was seeing before Hester's death?"

Mrs. Dewett stood silently pondering the prospects. "Probably Grace Meadows," she said after a long pause while the breeze shifted and tipped her hat back from her face. She blinked in response to the glare and pulled a pair of sunglasses out of her pocket, setting them on her nose.

"She lived on the street behind the Bowmans," she told Brian. "Not Bill's usual route, but I think he'd gone through all the women on our street who were open to his overtures. He got in trouble when it came to Grace's husband. I heard them arguing one night, standing on either side of the block wall between their properties. They couldn't see each other, but they sure heard each other. So did I. I put on my back-porch light to let them know they were being loud, and they did lower their voices, but I still heard. I couldn't sleep until they quit, so I took a lemonade onto the back deck and sat to wait them out. They barked at each other for a few more minutes, then I heard Bowman's patio door close. Chuck Meadows must have stayed outside to calm down. A cool breeze was blowing for the first time in days, and it brought the smell of his cigarette smoke over to me."

"That was the only time you heard them arguing?"

Mrs. Dewett nodded. "The Meadows' house went up for sale the week after that, and the family moved away. Before Hester's death, if that's what you're going to ask next. You don't quit, do you?"

"Never. I'm your worst nightmare, Mrs. Dewett, if you've got something to hide. Better give me everything now, or I'll come visit you at the rest home."

"There's not much else." Her thin shoulders rose and fell in a small shrug. "I did hear rumors the Meadows family moved because Grace was pregnant. If that was true, the baby couldn't have been her husband's. He'd had a vasectomy the year before. He'd told the whole neighborhood he couldn't mow the grass because of his surgery. A lot of the men sympathized, and that grass got mowed all season. You'd have thought he'd lost his masculinity."

She snorted. The sunglasses slid down her nose and she looked over the top of them at Brian, like she thought he wasn't a very good representation of masculinity, either. He resisted the urge to glare right back, telling himself Mrs. Dewett was using another old trick from her days as an educator. Maybe it had worked when she was teaching school, but he'd be damned if he'd react to that tactic from a woman approaching eighty.

"That's all I know," she said.

Away from the shade provided by her hat brim, her eyes were no longer black. Instead, they were a disconcerting shade of pale brown with grey around the rims, like washed-out cold coffee. Brian felt a stir at the pit of his stomach that had nothing to do with the events of the morning. He had a sixth sense where suspects were concerned, and he felt it at that moment.

Something about Mrs. Dewett was disturbing, and it had nothing to do with her past as an educator. He heard Gabe moving around behind him. He'd have his clerk research her background as soon as they got back to the precinct. He wanted to know more about this retired teacher.

"Who told you the rumor about Grace Meadows?" he asked. He didn't want to miss a beat in their conversation. He felt she'd notice the pause.

"Joyce Lumberger," Mrs. Dewett said without hesitation. "I think she was steamed about Bill dumping her for Polly. She should be." Dewett gave a more dignified and much smaller snort, accompanied by a slight toss of her head. "Here she was, twenty-five years older than her daughter, who was twenty-two when she had the brief affair with Bowman while she was home from college for the summer. They met when she was working at the local ice cream parlor. Joyce and her husband left on vacation and Polly invited Bill over. Joyce came back and walked in on them. She was livid. Polly was sent back to school early. She had to agree to bunk in with her parents' friends, who lived close to campus. She had a curfew. Her parents told her either adhere to it or they wouldn't pay her tuition. She was sensible enough not to risk them following through with their threat." Mrs. Dewett nodded her approval.

"So what happened after graduation?" Brian asked, when Mrs. Dewett's gaze moved to a contemplation of the traffic flowing past on Biscayne Boulevard.

"Polly never came home again during the holidays; she stayed for summer school and had a part-time job she didn't want to lose. When she graduated, she moved to the Midwest. Michigan, if I remember correctly. Joyce managed to repair her marriage, and the couple moved to Texas."

"A lot of people seem to have moved away because of Bill Bowman," Brian said. "I can't believe no one said anything to the police about all this."

"We made a pact to keep quiet," Mrs. Dewett said. "But I know you're not going to stop bothering me until you've found out every last little detail about the neighborhood. I'm too old to go through that just to keep that secret. I never wished Hester dead, but someone must have. I can't imagine why. I told you she didn't have an exciting job, and she was nothing to look at...lank brown hair, thin as a rail, big hands and feet. She had one of those quiet, mousy personalities. How could she have made any man angry enough to kill her?"

"Didn't have to be a man. A woman could have done it. Hester doesn't sound like she would've put up much of a fight."

Mrs. Dewett shook her head emphatically. "Not a woman. I think it was either Bill or Wallace. They kept it in the family." She started to walk away. "I've got to wake up Gertie," she said over her shoulder. "Time for us to get back."

"Fine, but I may need to talk to you again," Brian said. "Don't leave town."

Mrs. Dewett stopped and pivoted to face him. "Fat chance of that," she said. "I've got terminal cancer. Just got the diagnosis. I wondered why I was getting short of breath when I walked. I've got six months if I'm lucky, so I've been told. Lucky? Ha!" She tossed her head again as she walked over to Gertie's bench. The snort came next, loud and clear. "Lucky would be to drop dead out here in the sunshine, not die in one of those beds at the rest home." She poked her friend less than gently.

Gertie awoke with a start. "Ouch," she said, blinking and moving away from Dewett's jabbing finger. "What's up?"

"Time to get back for our afternoon snack," Mrs. Dewett said.

"Ah, yes." Gertie peered at an oversized wrist watch. "I must have nodded off."

"You must," Dewett agreed, rolling her eyes at Brian. "We'll have to take a rain check on that ice cream, Sergeant."

Brian watched as Gertie struggled to her feet and the two women set off slowly together.

Gabe left his shady spot under the tree to join Brian. "I feel sorry for her," he said.

"Don't," Brian told him. "That woman's had a full life on her own terms until now, and that's what's pissing her off."

"She got really mad when you asked about those affairs. How did you guess she'd had one with Bowman's husband?"

"Shot in the dark," Brian said. "I figured if he'd had affairs with most of the other neighbors, he might have decided to include her because she was available."

"I'm going to send her flowers," Gabe said as they walked back to the Camaro.

"That's why you'd never make a good investigator," Brian told him. "You're too soft-hearted."

"You've got a heart buried somewhere in there, Boss; I'm sure of it."

"Buried. There's a figurative word."

Gabe shook his head, but didn't comment.

"Did you get the names of all those women she mentioned, who supposedly had affairs with Bill Bowman?" Brian asked. "I saw you scribbling on a pad."

"I did." Gabe produced the small notebook and showed Brian a neat list of names. "I'll follow up on them when we get back."

Brian's phone alerted him to a text. "Trehorn," he told Gabe. "We'd better get back to the precinct so he can ask me more questions about this morning's robbery. He's probably realized Buxford isn't gonna make any headway and wants to take over."

CHAPTER EIGHT

"WELL, it sounds like you've had a real fine day." Jim Paxton handed Brian a beer from the cooler beside him on his vintage motor yacht.

"That's one way to describe it." Brian popped the top and took a long drink. As usual, it was crisp, cold and very welcome. He settled back in the chaise across from Jim's and watched sunlight glinting on the water. *Fanciful Folly's* gentle rolling movements calmed his spirit almost as much as Jim's reassuring presence.

"I've been doing that preliminary research you asked for," Jim said. "Taking a trip to Baton Rouge is the next step if you want to keep going on this."

"I figured it would be." Brian nodded. "I did a search on Google Earth. The house on Webber Street is still there."

He couldn't bring himself to say anything else. Coldness had blanketed him at the mention of his childhood home. The same coldness that had stopped him from zooming in when he'd seen the row of dilapidated houses beside the railroad tracks. Dark memories threatened to seep out from his soul. When he'd looked at the roof of that house where he'd spent the majority of his childhood, he'd wondered again whether opening Pandora's box was necessary. It was, he assured himself silently as he sipped the beer. If he wanted to put the ghosts of his past to rest, and if he wanted to completely commit to his new life with Kaylen, he had to know the truth.

"You sure you want to do this, buddy?" Jim asked, echoing Brian's misgivings. "We can stop this investigation right now."

"Hell, if I didn't want answers to the questions about my past, I wouldn't have asked you to start pokin' around in the first place." Brian finished his beer and took the replacement Jim offered. "I can't move forward with Kaylen until I know my full family history. Too many gaps, especially in my early years. So many things don't add up; don't feel right. Why were Tim and I so different physically? Yeah, he could have inherited more from his father's side than our mother's, but we were *completely* different. I used to look at my mom and wonder what *my* father was like. But she'd never talk about him, and she had no photos or keepsakes. Nothing. If I persisted in asking for details, she'd start crying. I didn't want to make her upset, so I quit."

He took another can from the cooler, but Jim must have added more beer at the last minute. That one was warming rapidly and didn't taste good anymore. He put it down on top of a small table between the chairs. "There's too much risk for Kaylen.," he said. "I could turn out to be the son of a serial killer."

Jim didn't comment. No empty reassurances. He only nodded, like he fully understood Brian's dilemma. Brian never understood how his friend, who had come from a solid Midwestern background and a 30-year marriage devoted to one woman, could possibly *do* that. But somehow, Jim did. His reassuring presence was a god-send. Kaylen adored him, and they had both trusted Jim with their lives.

"Kaylen texted me. Angela's pregnant," Brian said, changing the subject. He'd had enough personal sharing for one day.

"That's real good news." Jim chuckled. He lifted his beer can. "A toast's in order."

"Yeah." Brian was still getting used to reactions that apparently other people thought were normal. He followed Jim's example and grabbed his lukewarm beer. "You make it."

"Okay." Jim raised his can a little higher. "Here's to Angela and Jonathan. May Angela have a worry-free pregnancy and a fast and safe delivery of a healthy newborn." He paused, looking at Brian. "I gather they don't know whether they're having a boy or girl yet, or didn't tell Kaylen?"

"No." Brian clinked cans. "I guess they want to keep that piece of news to themselves right now."

"That's their prerogative." Jim drained his beer and tossed the empty can into a pail behind the cooler. "I saw several broadcasts about those murders you got mixed up in this morning. You didn't come off too well, buddy. Why do you go out of your way to alienate the media?"

Brian felt his hackles rising and tried to tamp them back down. He reminded himself that Jim was a straight-shooter who had earned the right to ask questions and make comments.

"They don't act friendly enough toward me."

Jim shrugged. "That's nothing new."

"Especially that one reporter," Brian added. The thought of her set his teeth on edge.

"Which one?" Jim looked like he knew the answer, but wanted veri-fication.

"Cassandra Bunting…the one running around in heels and a skirt, looking like she was on her way to interview some local celebrity when she got reassigned to her first murder scene. She let that damned painter run free and loose with her microphone. Then the station aired the inter-view, so now I've got more bad publicity. More muck to wade through. It never ends."

"So because that woman was wearing a skirt and heels, she wasn't a real reporter?" Jim's eyebrows rose. "You'd better not let Kaylen hear you talking like that. She conducts business in three-inch heels and cock-tail dresses."

Brian shrugged. "Unless *I'm* with her. Then she wears flat shoes, like she thinks she's gotta look shorter than five-eleven."

Jim's brow furrowed. He took another beer from the cooler. "What is it with you, today?" He popped the top and beer frothed out. Jim tut-tutted and grabbed a towel hanging over the back of his chair. "I should have kept another six-pack in the refrigerator. It's warm isn't it?" He pointed to Brian's unfinished can on the table.

Brian waved away his friend's apologies. "It's okay, Jim. One was enough, anyway. The first one's always the best."

"You don't sound like yourself, this evening." Jim wiped down the can. "Well, your new self, anyway. You sound like the sarcastic Brian Swift who got into hot water on a regular basis and kept himself walled away from everyone."

Brian couldn't sit still any longer. He got up and walked over to the *Folly's* rail, where he welcomed the salty breeze chilling his face before turning back to Jim. "I'm frustrated," he told his friend. "I got left outside this investigation and pretty much hog-tied."

He folded his arms across his chest and leaned back against the rail. Jim didn't offer a comment.

"I should be leading that damned investigation," Brian complained. "I was the first officer on-scene. But Trehorn assigned two detectives from his supposedly new-and-improved Homicide squad. According to him I'm a witness, nothing more."

Jim crossed his ropy legs and nodded, looking strangely like an Eastern sage despite the Polo shirt and khaki shorts. "So, you let him get to you." He tut-tutted. "I thought you knew better than that by now. You reacted to him thumbing his nose at you by barking at a reporter. Ironically, the reporter you dubbed a professional. That left the other one, Miss Skirt and Heels, without her scoop, so she found the loudest and most obnoxious witness she could, and he wiped the parking lot with your reputation."

"Yeah, he did that all right." Brian wondered whether he'd have fared any better if he'd given Cassandra Bunting a few comments. Probably not. After sparring with Mireille Shagassi, he doubted he'd have had any civility left in him.

"Buddy, it's time for you to start constructively fighting back," Jim said. He got up and joined Brian at the rail. "You took enough of that bull-crap during the investigation over your brother's death. You were cleared of any charges." He looked like he wanted to give Brian one of his reassuring shoulder pats, but evidently thought better of it and jammed his hands into his pockets. "You've got to defend yourself and keep on doing it until all this nonsense stops."

"Easy for you to say." Brian watched a gull wheeling on air currents above the *Folly.*

Jim chose not to respond to that dig. "Call the reporter you sniped at and offer her an exclusive," he advised. "I know it's hard for you to talk about yourself, but you've got to change the public's perception of you."

Brian glanced toward his friend and saw concern plainly written in every line on Jim's craggy face. His advice was usually sound, and this occasion was no different. "It's an option, I guess," he allowed.

"Talk to her on your boat," Jim urged, pressing his advantage. "Make it a relaxed atmosphere where you'll look and act calm. And then try to imagine you're talking to someone like Kaylen, so you loosen up."

"Sitting on the *NTK,* which was bought with Tim's money? Oh, yeah, that'll make me look as innocent as a gilded lily, to use one of your favorite expressions."

"Buddy, you've got nothing to hide."

Brian started pacing. It always helped when he felt agitated. "IAB would love me to make myself available to a reporter and her probing questions," he said as he turned at the bow and returned to pass by Jim. "Might give them fodder for a new look into any links I had with Tim's businesses, even though they found no evidence I'd played any part in them the last time they investigated."

Jim went back to his seat and sipped his beer while Brian silently paced and thought. After a few minutes, the agitation eased and he went back to sit across from Jim again. He refused another possibly warm beer.

"Internal Affairs put me through hell," he told Jim. "I'm not going to stir up any more crap that'll start me down that path again. An' if I give an interview that isn't sanctioned by the department, I'll get flak from every-one, starting with Hal and workin' all the way down to the janitorial staff."

He noticed he'd reverted to the Louisiana drawl he'd worked so hard to escape, stopped and took a couple of deep breaths. Jim waited without comment.

"I need clearance before issuing statements, anyway," Brian said, thinking aloud. "Something I should have thought about before opening my mouth this morning."

Jim gave a decisive nod. "That you should."

"But when Mireille Shagassi shoved that microphone in my face and asked me where all the blood came from, I wanted to reassure Kaylen, if she was watching, that it wasn't mine." Brian ran a hand through his hair. "Christ, I fucked up. I've been keeping my nose clean all these months working cold cases, then for one moment, I reacted like Joe Citizen instead of a homicide detective. Fuck it…Hal'll never let me back into Homicide after this crap."

"Your remarks weren't that incendiary," Jim said. "Well, maybe when you told her she needed to get out of your face…"

"She asked me whether the coffee shop deaths had anything to do with Tim's murder and the cartel," Brian protested. "Then she suggested Kaylen's success was due to her playing fast and loose with two brothers as well as marrying an old billionaire with one foot in the grave. I about blew my stack."

"You *did* blow it." Jim shook the can in Brian's direction. "She pushed all your buttons, and you reacted in a knee jerk manner."

"I reacted as a jerk. There's a good summary."

"Oh, buddy. You think that's the be-all and end-all of things, don't you? I disagree. It's still fixable."

"Is it?" Brian shook his head. "I doubt any of this will ever blow over."

"Not by itself, it won't." Jim gave up on the beer and put his can on the table. "You're going to have to appear a whole lot less defensive," he advised. "Reporters love defensiveness. They jump right on it, and then they start using words they know from past experiences will get reactions, especially from you…they know you've got a short fuse."

"Damn right, I do. And not only when it comes to me, or Tim…"

"I'm not done." Jim sat on the side of the chaise, to face Brian more head-on. "Don't go getting protective on Kaylen's account. She can handle herself. She's proved that numerous times, and she'd be the first one to tell you to leave her be if she knew you were holding back because of her."

Brian's cell started ringing. He checked. "Kaylen. Her ears must be burning."

"Go talk to her," Jim said. He got up and stretched both arms above his head. "She'll calm you down better than I can. Once she's done that, we'll figure out a way for you to set things right with the local news teams, or at least with that one reporter." He stopped in mid-stretch, one arm overhead, the other hand on his hip, and winked. "You know…the professional. What's her name again?'"

Brian tried to ignore a stir of exasperation over Jim's lighthearted approach to a media threat. "Mireille Shagassi."

Jim nodded. "That's right. While you and Kaylen are chatting, I'll try to find out more about the other reporter. Bunting, right?"

"Yeah, Cassandra. Thanks, Jim."

"Of course."

Kaylen's call had gone to voicemail. Brian headed for the dock. He would rather call her back from the *NTK*.

"I'm not going anywhere until I get on a flight to Baton Rouge," Jim said, slowly following Brian. "You'll find me right here."

Brian's cell started ringing again.

"Kaylen needs your support," Jim added. "She's anxious about that new club opening."

Brian stepped onto the finger pier between the two boats. "Yeah, I know."

Jim leaned over the rail. "Don't go there unless she does," he recommended.

Brian waved his agreement.

He returned her calls as soon as he was on his own boat.

"I thought you were coming to Bannisters?" Her voice had a sharp little edge. "I got worried."

"I'm almost on my way; I came home to change clothes. I was talking to Jim." Brian unlocked the door to the salon and walked inside, closing it behind him.

"Are you still with him? If you are, say hi from me and tell him I'll stop by in the next couple of days. I'll bring one of his favorite hoagies from that sub shop close to Bannisters."

"You'll have to tell him yourself. I'm back on the *NTK*." The first thing Brian noticed was a red jacket of Kaylen's, lying on the floor. He picked it up and shook it before tossing it onto the back of the couch. "I've gotta get out of these work clothes."

"Ah, what thoughts that phrase always brings." She sighed.

"What? Being on the *NTK?"*

"No, of course not. You know exactly what I mean." Her voice had lowered. "You. Without clothes."

"Soon, princess, soon," he promised. "I'll get out of my clothes and give you my undivided attention."

"You'd better. It's been too long. Almost a week, in fact."

"I know. I count the days, too." He thought about her arms around him. Her long legs wrapped around his hips...

"Work," she broke in. "For both of us, it's always work. We're going to have to set some sort of schedule, because this spontaneity thing isn't doing it for either of us."

Brian craved coffee. He walked into the galley. "I agree," he told her as he dumped grounds into the basket.

He couldn't think of anything more profound. They had only gotten together twice in the past two weeks. He'd put in extra hours to tie up the Kowalski case while Kaylen had been equally busy keeping her club opening on track. He poured water and pushed the button to start the brewing cycle.

"So how are we going to fix this?" Kaylen asked.

"We agreed moving in together right now wouldn't solve anything," he said, turning away from the coffee maker. He leaned against the counter and ran a hand over his face. He'd needed a shave, too.

"*You* said it wouldn't, and I went along with that, like I've been doing for over a year. That goes for *everything* you've asked for." The edge was back in her voice.

Brian couldn't handle any more reproaches at that moment. "Look, hon, we're both tired, and this isn't a good time to be discussing long-term plans," he told her, trying hard to keep his tone neutral. "Let me get ready and come to the club. We can talk about anything you want after it closes."

"Oh, Brian." Her sigh sounded like it came from somewhere deep inside her. "You're beginning to drawl, and I know I'm sounding snippy. I won't stay at Bannisters until closing. We can chat over a late supper at the condo. Maybe we'll both still have the energy to make love. I'd like that a lot."

She was trying to compromise, and Brian appreciated the gesture. "I'd like that a lot, too," he said, and heard the warmth in his own voice. "I started fantasizing about being with you as soon as you started talking," he added.

A stir of desire made him want to be with her right at that moment. But the coffee dripped and gurgled, the *NTK* rocked gently at her moorings, and suddenly, Kaylen wasn't saying anything.

Brian decided he had better be the one to break the silence. "Supper sounds good. And how about I stay the night at your place and go straight to work from there?"

"That's an offer I'm definitely *not* going to refuse." She sounded a lot less tense.

Phew, Brian thought. "Love you, hon," he told her as he poured strong coffee into a mug.

"Love you, too. Even when you're grouchy."

So much for disguising his feelings. Kaylen knew him like no other.

As he left the galley, he caught sight of someone climbing onto the *Folly.* Someone wearing green high-heels and a black leather skirt.

"I've gotta go," he told Kaylen.

"What's up?" Her bantering tone had vanished.

"Jim may have unwelcome company. At least, unwelcome as far as I'm concerned. It's one of those damned reporters from this morning."

"Miss Social Media?"

"Yeah. How d'you know?"

"I looked her up after seeing that awful interview with some guy in overalls. I think she's trying to move from talking to vendors at street fairs into reporting hard news. I've seen some of her horrible attempts at investigative reporting. My advice to you is keep quiet and stay out of sight," Kaylen said. "Jim will send her packing. And he'll stop her from trying to interview you, too."

"I damned well hope he doesn't say anything to her." Brian felt a stir of unease. He'd kept a low profile at the marina. Some neighbors knew he was a detective, but had, as far as he knew, never said anything to reporters, not even when a fire had destroyed his first boat, the *Destiny.* But would this time be different?

"Please call me if you change your mind about coming to the club tonight," Kaylen said. Despite her upbeat tone, Brian heard the undercurrent of anxiety.

"I'll be there," he promised. "But maybe a little later than planned."

"I love you," Kaylen said again. She didn't say anything else, but as she hung up, Brian knew she wanted to tell him to be careful.

CHAPTER NINE

"LISTEN, little lady, you're barking up the wrong tree here," Jim said.

Brian had managed to maneuver himself into a secluded corner of the salon to hear what the reporter wanted from his neighbor.

"I did my research," Cassandra Bunting said. "I know you're his friend. You'll be able to give me a much better idea of what Detective Swift is really like."

"If you did your research, you'd know his rank is Detective Sergeant," Jim said.

"See, you already set me straight on his title. Just think how much more insight you could give me. I've only read the media reports. I tried to set up an interview with him, but the police department refused."

"That's a shocker."

"I heard he might have a boat here at the marina."

"Did you?"

Brian heard Jim rummaging around in the cooler and had to smile. Kaylen was right…Jim was doing a great job of acting remarkably disinterested in the reporter.

"I spoke with several other boat owners and the marina staff." Bunting's tone had become slightly more strident. "No one seemed to know his name or which slip his boat's moored at. That's unbelievable.

He was all over the news this morning. The shooting at the coffee shop. Several victims. You must have heard about it."

"I don't watch the news." Jim's voice was bland. "I fish and hang out here."

The sound of a pail filled with empty cans being shaken punctuated gull cries and slapping waves against the *NTK's* hull. Brian decided Jim was more than capable of handling Ms. Cassandra Bunting, Crack Investigative Reporter. Knowing he could count on a blow-by-blow later, he retreated to the head and took a shower.

Forty minutes later and wearing a tux, he walked back into the salon. He'd packed an overnight bag, and after a quick check to make sure Bunting was nowhere in sight, he locked up the *NTK*. Jim was MIA. It was already 9:30 PM., and either his friend had gone to dinner or called it a night, as no lights showed on the *Fanciful Folly*.

Brian used caution leaving the boat and walking through the parking lot. He'd moved his cars closer to the dock after getting jumped in the secluded back lot. That was almost two years ago, he told himself as he loaded his bag into the trunk. But he never felt completely at ease, and knew he probably never would. His training demanded he keep sharp at all times, and having the shit kicked out of him had heightened the sense of self-preservation and alertness.

He buckled his seatbelt and turned the key in the ignition, hearing the Camaro's powerful response. Next to it stood the non-descript sedan he used when the flash of the restored car might cause issues. He glanced around for Jim's Kia Sportage but didn't see it.

Driving to Bannisters, Brian tried to rid himself of the negative elements from his day. He wanted his evening with Kaylen to be filled with pleasure, but she already had an agenda, and spending more time together was without a doubt the first topic for discussion. He didn't know how he was going to respond to that demand. His work, her business...as important to both of them as their relationship.

He reneged on that last thought. Kaylen was always willing to put their relationship ahead of anything else, even her new club. She always made time for him, even if it was a shorter amount than either of them would have liked.

No more trysts in her office, though. Not since she'd found

surveillance equipment installed without her knowledge. So far, nothing had come of whatever had been recorded. But the knowledge that someone had recordings that not only included all aspects of Kaylen's business but of her spontaneously making love with her boyfriend on the office couch, always made him want to start sweating.

Too many of Kaylen's backers were conservative older friends of her deceased husband. Her reputation had been damaged by her relationship with Tim after the truth surfaced about his prior contacts with a drug cartel. Then she had further jeopardized those backers funding her next project by dating Brian. Not only was he Tim's brother, but he'd been accused of bribery.

But the commendation Brian had received, added to the revelations from Tim's journal seemed to have alleviated Kaylen's strained relationships with her backers. Arrests had been made in the community. A shake-up at Miami-Dade Police Department had occurred. And Bannisters was a success. Kaylen had more than demonstrated she could run a business, and run it well. She'd used that success to secure funding for Treasure. But if the sex tape surfaced, she had told Brian numerous times, much of her support would vanish, practically overnight.

Brian pushed away his misgivings as he entered Bannisters' parking lot. No more street parking for him. He had a reserved space close to the side entrance and the code to access the building. He noticed a couple of busboys smoking over next to the dumpsters and waved to them. They waved back. He knew every member of Kaylen's large staff. He felt comfortable in her club and looked forward to seeing Rob, Kaylen's manager, and Marvin, the head waiter.

He wasn't such a fan of Julio, the head bartender, or recently-hired maître d', Alphonse. Julio had attitude, and Alphonse was almost as obnoxious as head chef, Emrico. But Kaylen managed all their personalities successfully and kept them in line. Julio had once thought about jumping ship for more money and a promotion. He'd thought better of it after a conference with Kaylen. But he was never a trusted employee again. She kept him on because she said he was a gifted mixologist and a hard worker. Brian hoped an even more gifted mixologist might come along soon to change her mind.

As he punched in the code and opened the side door, his wandering thoughts settled briefly on Ziggy Stavros and the rest of the Stavros clan. Ziggy's marriage proposal to Kaylen might have been unsuccessful, but he had found enough backers to open a restaurant in South Beach. Seafood was his specialty.

The emphasis for Treasure seemed to be in direct competition. Kaylen's new head chef specialized in southern Italian dishes, which highlighted olive oil, tomatoes and seafood, although she had also given him instructions to vary the menu with a selection of meat dishes and fare that would appeal to the spicier tastes of the Miami community.

No more themed clubs, she told Brian. Maintaining the 40's vibe for Bannisters was enough of a challenge, and she hadn't found another era that appealed to her as much as the Big Band. Brian found the gaudiness of Treasure's interior overwhelming, but Kaylen swore she had a winner, and he certainly had no expertise in décor. He had given her full rein with upgrading the *NTK*'s salon and main cabin when he ordered the *Destiny's* replacement. She had picked tasteful neutral colors he liked a lot, but he still thought she had brought in too much furniture for the salon, in particular.

"Hi Brian." Rob Diaz, heading for his office, stopped in the hallway. "How's it going?"

"Fair. I'd be lying if I said I'd had a good day." Brian grimaced as pleasant thoughts of the *NTK* were replaced with the morning's events.

"I saw the news." Rob nodded. "I'm glad you're okay. That was a lot of blood."

"Yeah. Kaylen called right away. She thought it was mine."

"She's in her office," Rob said. "She told me she's leaving early tonight. That'd be a good plan for both of you."

"Any packages or other gifts for her today?"

"No." Rob's mouth turned down. "You were expecting something?"

"Maybe. Sam Wilson left a calling card on Tim's grave. White roses."

"That bastard." Rob sounded quietly furious.

"Yeah. I've got to tell Kaylen. Keep sharp, Rob. Call me immediately if you notice anything out of place."

"I will. You want me to alert any other staff?"

"No. Kaylen always wants to keep any of this low key, and I'll respect that for now."

Rob nodded. "I've got to get back to work. I'll leave my door cracked and keep an eye on things back here as well as out front."

"Thanks. I appreciate that." Brian walked over to Kaylen's door. It opened as he was about to knock.

"I thought I heard your voice." Her smile looked a little strained. "Come in."

She closed the door behind him and sank into his arms. When he kissed her, she returned the kiss with passion, but her body was tense.

"I'm fine, princess," he assured her.

"You're not, or you wouldn't be trying to distract me with that horrible nickname." She gave him a slight push. "Go sit down; I'll pour us some Chardonnay."

"I'd rather have a beer. I had a couple of cans with Jim earlier, and I don't like mixing drinks."

"Okay." She opened the mini fridge and took out a bottle. "Widmer Brothers? I'm trying new brands. I just subscribed to BeerAdvocate and DRAFT Magazine. I've learned a lot about wines over the last couple of years, but there are so many craft beers, it's pretty daunting. Especially since I'm not very fond of some of it." She wrinkled her nose. "Dark beer tastes and looks like motor oil."

"Anything's fine...even the motor oil stuff." Brian refused her direction to sit and walked over to take the bottle and opener from her. "It's okay to act worried, hon. I know you are, but I wasn't the target today." He opened the beer and took a sip. In response to her raised eyebrows, he nodded. "You know me...no expertise here, but it's pretty good."

"I'm still trying to convince myself you were never in any danger." She poured herself a large glass of Chardonnay with slightly shaky hands. "It was the blood. You know what that does to me...those flashbacks."

"Did you use the tactics your shrink gave you?"

"Yes, of course, but that image on TV brought back memories. I felt dizzy. It's the first time I've seen blood on you since you got shot."

"If you still have doubts I'm intact, I'll unbutton my shirt. You can see my scarred-up chest looks the same as always. Nothing new, I swear."

"Now I know you're worried, too. You never joke about your scars." She took a sip of the Chardonnay, almost spilled the wine and used both hands to put the glass down on the counter.

"I'm trying to lighten up." He tried grinning at her.

Kaylen wasn't having any of it. "Drink your beer," she told him. "Dark and powerful suits you a whole lot better than light banter. Any time you start joking, it ends up as sarcasm, and sometimes, I'm the butt of it."

"Don't think you're being singled out, hon. I don't play favorites. I'm an equal opportunity offender."

A definite crinkle had appeared between Kaylen's brows. "I still hate you, sometimes," she said.

"I know. I like that about you." He put down the bottle.

Time for a big distraction.

"Let's get out of here, go back to your condo and make love until dawn." He kissed her again, nuzzled her neck and cupped a breast.

Her eyes closed briefly as he fondled her, but the frown remained. She drew away from him. "You'll be tired and cranky when you go to work tomorrow. Not the best idea you've had."

"Oh, hon, it's not the worst, either, is it?" He found himself wanting to be with her for much more than distraction purposes.

"No, I guess it's not." She wrapped her arms around his neck. "We could both do with some togetherness after this morning." Her gaze met his. A trace of a smile appeared at the right side of her mouth. "I'd settle for making love until say, one in the morning. Is that good enough?"

"Now *that* sounds like a plan." Relief filled him. She was willing to put aside her own misgivings and meet him halfway.

He decided he'd put off telling her about the roses until after their lovemaking. She was far too edgy. He'd make sure he got her tired and relaxed before giving her any more unpleasant surprises.

He watched her take her purse from the bottom drawer of her desk and her jacket from the back of her chair, her movements graceful and sensuous. He still thought she was the most beautiful woman in Miami. He should be pinching himself to make sure he wasn't having some really long, highly distracting and pleasurable dream. He rushed her out of the club and into his car.

"I guess I'll take Uber home tomorrow," she said.

"I guess you will." He felt her hand on his thigh as they headed toward Coconut Grove.

CHAPTER TEN

HE TOLD her about the roses after they made love and she was lying in his arms, her hair spread across his chest. Her forehead rested against his cheek, her breath gentle on his neck.

Kaylen reacted to his watered-down account of finding the flowers by jerking up onto one elbow and leaning over him, her widened gaze locking with his. Brian tried giving her reassuring caresses, but Kaylen wasn't going to be easily calmed.

"Why didn't you tell me this before?" she asked. "And how did you find time to go to Tim's grave in the middle of a murder investigation?"

Despite frequent assurances that she trusted him completely, Brian thought she always harbored a sliver of suspicion that he might not truly be the flip side of his brother's deceitful character. Especially after he'd been forced to lie to her when they first met. Lie about everything, he thought. It was a wonder she had forgiven him, let alone learned to trust him at all.

Kaylen struggled away, sat up and pulled on the white silk robe he knew matched the nightgown he loved to take off her…the one with the spaghetti straps that slid down her arms. Brian felt a stir of desire and hoped Kaylen wouldn't notice as she drew her hair from beneath the robe, shook it into a stream of glistening chestnut down her back and stood up.

"Where are you going?" he asked, hoping against hope she wasn't walking out of her own condo as soon as she'd put on street clothes. "Come back to bed."

"I can't talk to you about this while we're naked in bed." She glared at him. "You're lucky I'm not kicking you out of here right now. I'm going to make coffee. I'll see you in the kitchen."

"Better make it decaf," he said to her departing back.

God, she was gorgeous. He watched her hips sway as she marched out of the room without a backward glance. He wondered whether she'd forced herself not to look at him. Glancing down at himself and seeing his partial erection, he thought he should be glad she hadn't.

Grabbing the sheet from the bottom of the bed, he pulled it up to his chest. His decision not to worry her with a phone call had backfired. He rolled to his side and groaned into a pillow that still held her perfume. He inhaled deeply and tried to understand why she was so upset. He hadn't lied, but he *had* withheld information until he had her relaxed, he admitted.

He rolled back and stared up at the ceiling while he listened to crashing glass and cups in the kitchen. He wondered whether she was planning to hit him with the carafe instead of brewing that coffee.

"I'm gonna take a shower," he called.

"Of course; anything to avoid a confrontation," she shot back.

"Okay, no shower yet." He got up and pulled on his boxers. After a moment of reflection, he also put on his pants before joining her. He stayed in the dining room, safely on the other side of the breakfast bar, while she dumped coffee into the basket and started the coffee maker.

"Hon," he attempted.

She stopped him with a glare. "Don't say it. Don't you dare try to tell me you're sorry and expect me to accept it. I'm really angry, Brian."

"I can see that, but why?" He perched on a bar stool and tried to look at ease.

She shook her head. "I thought you understood me better than this."

"I thought so, too. What's got you in a knot?"

"A knot? *Really?* You wait until you think I'm all sweet and satisfied and then you drop that *bombshell* on me? After I spent the entire day *worrying* about you?" Her hands slammed down onto the counter, elbows locked, and her eyes spat fire across the breakfast bar.

There was a lot of slamming going on, Brian thought. An unjustified amount in his opinion, although he decided commenting on that was asking for more trouble. Instead, he opted for his calmest tone and direct eye contact.

"I talked to you as soon as I could after the murders," he said, keeping all traces of harshness out of his voice. "You know my job can be dangerous. Usually not as hazardous as working a fresh homicide, but it's not like I purposely booked a murder appointment on my way to work so I could have some excitement."

"I know." Kaylen threw up her hands. "Good grief, I know." She ran her hands through her hair, snagged her fingers on tangles and winced. "I've been doing really well all these months, haven't I?" Her tone hovered between demanding and plaintive. "Do I ever kiss you goodbye and say 'Don't get killed today?'" Her voice started to quiver. She blinked rapidly. "Do I ever ask you to be careful?"

Brian watched her grab a napkin from the holder on the counter and dab the corners of her eyes. He'd really hoped she wouldn't break down. Seeing her cry always made him feel guilty, but it certainly wasn't his fault he'd walked into the aftermath of a slaughter. He got back to his feet.

"No," he said, walking into the kitchen. "And I really appreciate that about you. Very much, hon. You *know* that."

He slid his hands beneath her forearms, cradled her cold elbows. Warmed them with his palms. He had no choice but to look right at her. With her head raised, her gaze was level with his. Her eyes definitely swam with unshed tears, and she was biting her lip in an obvious attempt to control her emotions.

"But you can't expect me never to land at a fresh crime scene or walk into some risky situation." He gently squeezed her elbows. "I thought we had that straightened out."

Kaylen sniffed and stopped biting her bottom lip. Slightly reddened, it made her mouth very kissable, but Brian restrained himself. She needed reassurance from words right at that moment, not actions.

82

"We did." She cleared her throat. "We do." She pulled away from him, wiped her eyes and blew her nose. "I don't know what's wrong with me, Brian. I shouldn't be acting this way, picking a fight with you. Maybe I'm being unreasonably harsh because you waited too long to tell me about Sam's roses."

She pointed her finger at him; a gesture he knew meant she was recovering her poise. He decided to wait her out and see what she had to say before defending himself. He'd screwed up again. Being on a constant learning curve with Kaylen's feelings could be downright exhausting. He felt like telling her to shelve the lecture, because all he really wanted to do was go back to bed and sleep. He'd shower in the morning.

If she'd only let things be.

But she wouldn't. That pointing finger of hers always signaled a lengthy discourse. She was about to educate him yet again on how he needed to be more communicative and insightful. Both attributes he already knew he sorely lacked and couldn't change, even for her.

"In fact," Kaylen said, "that's probably *why* I'm so upset. You should have told me before we left the club. Now I'm thinking that when I saw Rob's worried expression, I should have known something was up. I suppose you had already told him...my employee...yet you didn't think it was important enough to tell me until after you'd gotten what you really wanted out of me, and that's sex."

Brian was completely astounded. "That's ridiculous. I would never use you like that."

Kaylen, arms now folded, tossed her head in response to his consternation.

"The truth is, I wanted to calm you down before I told you." He searched for the right words. "I thought if we made love, you'd really know I'm okay. That the events this morning, however bad the scene was, didn't...well, they did affect me personally, because I know those people at the coffee shop as friends, but I didn't get flashbacks or any other adverse effects, and I wasn't lying when I told you I wasn't injured. I didn't expect you to react to the news about the roses the way you did. My mistake. I told you I'm sorry. I don't know what else you want me to say."

She rubbed her temples, like her head really hurt. "Sometimes you make me so mad, I remember the days I really *did* hate you, and I understand why."

He had no answer for that. She *had* hated him at times in the early days they were together, and he also understood why. Those were the days when he didn't care about her feelings. Days when he was in denial of caring about her, anyway, because she was his brother's girlfriend, but he longed to make her his.

"I was planning to tell you first," he qualified. "But then I met Rob in the hallway. When I *did* see you, I knew you needed convincing I wasn't injured. You believed I was hiding something; some wound I'd secretly had sewn up."

He wanted to give her a reassuring smile but he didn't think she would be receptive to that, so he paused to take a deep breath, and he saw Kaylen do the same.

"Look," he said in the calmest, kindest tone he could muster. "I promise I'll unload on you immediately if anything else like this ever happens again." He watched her face carefully. Her frown had eased slightly, and he didn't see any more tears. "No delays. An immediate text if I can't call right then. You *know* my promises are good."

The frown dissipated. She nodded slowly. "They are. You're a man of your word, and that's a real blessing."

She placed a hand on his arm. Brian began to hope she was going to forgive him and they could salvage the evening.

"I know it's not always easy for you to open up the way you do with me," she said, her voice low and soft.

Suddenly, the stiffness left her posture and she crumpled, leaning against him. Her arms slid around his waist. Her cheek rested against his. Brian's heart rhythm increased to a fast trot. He loved it when she initiated contact, and especially that evening, after she had been so upset.

"It's *not* easy," he said. "There're so many things I'd rather not tell you. I could have just tossed those roses into the dumpster and said nothing, you know."

"I do."

The coffee maker beeped, announcing the end of the brewing cycle.

To Brian, it was like a punctuation mark in their discussion. They both looked at the full carafe.

"You want some, now I made twelve cups?" She gave him a tentative smile.

"I never refuse coffee. Cops have it running through their veins." He almost added a joke about bleeding regular roast, but stopped himself.

No sense in reminding her of anything to do with blood. The resulting flashbacks from the gunshot wound that had almost taken his life had plagued Kaylen for close to a year. Now the news coverage had triggered a reoccurrence. His left shoulder ached in response to that thought, like a reprimand for giving her a graphic reminder, however unintentional.

She poured two mugs, handing him his before adding cream to her own. "How many?" she asked.

He was startled. What was she talking about? Did she know he'd been shot once before? He didn't think so. His other scars masked the two tell-tale reminders on his chest of an altercation in an alley earlier in his career.

Then he realized she had reverted to thinking about Sam's calling card. "Roses?" he asked casually, before taking a sip of his coffee.

She nodded and looked at him over the rim of her own mug as she drank. Her hands were steady. He suddenly noticed she was no longer wearing her wedding set on her right ring finger, and wondered when she'd taken George Bannister Roberts' rings off. The solitaire diamond had dwarfed the one Ziggy Stavros had tried to place on her left hand a year ago, during a time when her relationship with Brian had hit a bad patch.

Brian wondered when she would start making noises for him to make a commitment. So far, she hadn't after he'd told her he loved her but wanted to take things slow. How much more 'slow' was she going to tolerate?

"Yes, of course, the roses." The crease reappeared between Kaylen's eyebrows. "Well?"

Brian reeled in his scattered thoughts. "A half-dozen. No card. Sam probably thought it wasn't needed, and I have to agree with him. Message received. He's back in Miami and probably watching one or both of us, either himself or by using others to do his dirty work. I hate to even say it, but I'm wondering whether he's mended his fences with the cartel and they're regrouping."

Kaylen put down her coffee. The frown stayed. "But nothing else ever happened after he sent those other roses with the note," she reasoned. "It's been over a year. Surely he would have done something... tried to mess with me about that awful tape. Now's a good time for him to hit me with financial damage. I'm almost over-extended because of Treasure."

"Yeah, I know." Brian nodded and drained his mug. "I've been kinda worried that things have been too quiet."

"Did you find out what that reporter wanted?" Kaylen asked. "The one who came to Jim's boat."

"Not really." He placed his empty mug in the sink. "I eavesdropped a couple of minutes, but he was handling things so well, I decided I'd talk to him later and took my shower. By the time I got back on deck, they were both gone. I didn't want to call Jim during his dinner. You know how he hates cold food."

Kaylen nodded. "I do." She picked up her mug again and glanced toward the kitchen clock.

"One-thirty," Brian said. "Much too late to call him now. Most nights he's in bed by ten. I'll talk to him first thing tomorrow."

"You're not staying here tonight?" She looked and sounded very disappointed.

He hurried to reassure her. "I am, but I've gotta leave early. I'll try not to disturb you."

"Disturb away; I want a goodbye kiss." She cradled her half-finished coffee in both hands. "In fact, I want a kiss right now. I hate arguing with you. It feels really wrong."

"Even when you're the one who's right?"

"Like tonight?"

"Yeah." He nodded. "Hon, I really screwed up."

"You did." She gave him a half-smile. "And in return for you admitting that, I'll try harder not to completely panic if I see you on TV with blood on you."

"I hope you never have to see that again, but okay, that sounds like a plan."

She cleared her throat and made a business of straightening napkins leaning out of the little holder on the breakfast bar with one hand while the other still held her neglected mug. "I feel awful for those people at the coffee shop. Did they all die?"

"No. The owner survived, but he's in the ICU. We're all hoping he pulls through and can give us more information on what happened. The only camera inside the shop didn't do a good job. Badly positioned. They must have entered from the rear. When I arrived, the back door was propped open, like one of the employees took out the trash or maybe went to get something from a vehicle. All we saw from the security footage was the backs of the perps, all wearing hoodies. It was like a shooting gallery."

He stopped. Kaylen's eyes had widened. He could have kicked himself. He'd shared too much information without thinking. Yet again.

She swallowed hard. "That's horrible. If you'd arrived even a few minutes earlier, you might have been killed, too."

"If I'd arrived a few minutes earlier, I would have been able to stop them."

"You can't guarantee that."

"I can't live my life thinking about my own safety first, or do my job on defense," he warned. "Situations like that, I make my best choice on how handle it and then usually, I go in. There's no standing around outside waiting for back-up if there's an active shooter on-site."

Kaylen rubbed her left temple with an index finger. "I'm getting a headache."

"A tension headache," he said, taking her mug away and placing it in the sink. "Enough coffee for both of us." He debated a moment, choosing his words carefully before turning to face her. "Look, hon, you've got to trust I'll be fine. I don't take unnecessary risks. Used to, but now we got together, those days are over."

"Thank goodness." She stifled a yawn. "Oh, I'm worn out, mentally and physically. It's still one of the hardest things about our relationship, me accepting you being in danger as part of your job."

"There are many hard things about our relationship." He turned off the coffee maker, threw the coffee grounds into the trash, tipped the contents of the carafe down the sink and rinsed everything out.

"My neck hurts." Kaylen rolled her head from side to side. "My shoulders, too. Either from stress or some of those moves you made on me."

"Then I'll have to make up some new moves." He stood behind her and gently rubbed her neck and shoulders. Her robe gaped open in response. She wasn't wearing anything beneath, and his hands moved down to cup her breasts. He loved the feel of her skin, soft as velvet. He untied her belt. Brushed the robe aside to slide one hand across her stomach and down into the thatch of dark hair between her legs while the other teased a nipple.

"One of those hard things about our relationship is now pressing against me," Kaylen said breathlessly as his fingers found their goal and caressed her. "You're insatiable."

"Only when I'm with you."

He carried her back to bed and they made love again, but very gently and slowly. The passion had been spent, but the need for closeness persisted.

"I'm going to take that shower," he said afterward. "It'll save me time in the morning. You should get some sleep." He sat on the side of the bed.

"I'm going to shower with you, first." She rose up behind him, pressed herself against him and kissed his left shoulder, her hair gliding across his skin and tickling him. The slightest contact with her stirred desire in his tired body.

"No, you're not," he decided. "Otherwise we won't be sleeping afterward, and I know neither of us has the energy for any more sex tonight." He coiled one chestnut curl around his finger, fought the urge to turn around, push her back onto the bed and initiate anything else. "I'm going into the other bathroom and using cold water."

Kaylen shivered. "That's punishment." She tapped him lightly on his chest with one hand before releasing him. "Fine, you use one shower, and I'll use the other. I need warm water to help me relax; I'm still wired. If your skin is icy when you get back in bed, don't you dare try to cuddle."

"Cuddling would only send me back for an even colder shower."

Despite his resolve only moments before, he reneged on his promise not to touch her again until morning. He drew her into his arms. "Sleep well, princess. I love you. I promise I won't leave tomorrow morning without kissing you, just like this." He kissed her lightly.

"I love you, too, you difficult man." She kissed him back, equally lightly.

He took a long, marginally tepid shower before sliding back under the covers. By then, Kaylen was asleep. He watched her for a while before closing his eyes and allowing himself the luxury of oblivion.

CHAPTER ELEVEN

GETTING up and going to work was a lot harder for Brian the following morning. He carried an uncertain feeling inside that refused to leave. He took the route to the coffee shop, where he did a slow drive-by to check for looky-loos or familiar faces instead of doing a walk-around. His ability to scan a crowd and remember many of the people gathered at a scene had been a real gift for police-work.

He spotted a vagrant pushing a shopping cart loaded with garbage bags on the side street and pulled around to park curbside. The guy cast a glance at him from under an old cap before averting his eyes and continuing to push the cart, but at a faster pace.

Brian got out and crossed the street. "Hey, hold up. I want to talk to you." He flashed his badge.

The shopping cart ground to a halt. "I ain't done nothin' wrong," the man grumbled, eyes still downcast, although he had definitely glanced at the badge.

"Never said you had." Brian stood in front of the cart, effectively blocking the man's escape-route. He saw one large black trash bag was filled with crushed cans. Another held plastic bottles. "You come around here pretty often?"

The man shrugged. "A fair amount."

"How about yesterday?"

Still no eye contact. The man shifted his grip on the cart. "Maybe."

"What did you see?"

"Enough. I made myself scarce."

Brian pushed aside his irritation. "What's it going to take to loosen your tongue?"

"Maybe a ten spot?"

Brian took out his billfold and looked inside. He only had a couple of $20 bills.

"Let's hear what you've got."

"I tell you, you leave and I get nothing in return."

"Not gonna happen." Brian took out of one the twenties and held it up. "You give me what I want, you get this."

The man paused, seemed to come to a decision and nodded. "Mind if we step away from the street? My house is around the corner."

"Your house?" Brian looked at his companion's outfit and the shopping cart.

"It's not much, but it's mine."

Brian tried to think where there was a homeless camp in that neighborhood. He couldn't think of one. He followed the vagrant as he pushed the squeaky and rusted shopping cart down the block, around the corner and up to a small bungalow with peeling white paint. An old Chevy, even more rusted than the shopping cart, sat under the cover of a carport.

"I live on a fixed income," the man said. "I supplement it by cashing in cans, plastic, whatever I can find around the neighborhood." He took out a key and opened a padlock on the gate blocking the driveway, pushed the cart through and motioned Brian to follow. He hooked the padlock back onto the chain but didn't fasten it. "Not planning to lock you in here with me." His dry cackle came and left quickly. "Come on into the kitchen."

Brian followed the cart's squeaky progress down the pitted and weed-filled driveway to the Chevy. His potential witness parked his cart next to a row of trash cans, each filled with different recycling objects. The man dipped his hands into a bucket of water, washed them energetically and wiped them off on a rag hanging over a makeshift clothesline strung between posts on the carport before extending his hand. "Travis Schneider," he said.

"Detective Sergeant Brian Swift, Miami-Dade Police Department." Brian shook hands. "Why the disguise?"

"People don't take any notice of what they think is some homeless bum with a shopping cart." Mr. Schneider walked toward the house. "Come inside out of the heat and have a glass of lemonade."

He led the way up two chipped and cracked concrete steps and through a screen door into a utility room containing a washer and a utility sink. Another clothesline, weighed down with wet wash, obscured the entrance into the kitchen. Brian followed his host's example and ducked beneath a neatly clothes-pinned row of black socks to follow him into the kitchen.

Schneider waved toward a booth with cracked orange vinyl seats and a well-worn Formica-topped table that looked like it must have come with the house, which appeared to date back to perhaps the early 1950's. He took a jug of lemonade out of the refrigerator and brought it with 2 glasses over to the table. He filled both glasses, slid one over in front of Brian and took the other with him as he sat on the opposite side of the table. He drank half his lemonade without pausing for breath.

"Ah, that hits the spot." Schneider smacked his lips and looked pointedly at the full glass in front of Brian. "The glass is clean, and I made the lemonade yesterday evening."

Brian reluctantly took a sip. The lemonade wasn't bad. He saw a couple of seeds in the bottom of the jug and wondered if his host had lemon trees in his back yard. Fixed-income living supplemented by scrounging from trash cans surely couldn't include supermarket citrus. "So, you were pushing your cart around the neighborhood yesterday?" he prompted.

"I was." Schneider nodded. "I heard shots coming from inside the coffee shop, left my cart and hid behind the dumpster. Antonio always makes sure to leave a smaller trash container filled with cans and bottles for me to pick up each morning. Usually Rigo puts it out, but lately that new kid has been doing it. I don't remember his name, but he usually rides his bike to work."

Brian's initial surge of hope sank deeper than the lemon seeds in the bottom his glass. "So you didn't see anything?"

"Not at first. I was too afraid of being spotted. I know what small arms fire sounds like." He patted his chest. "'Nam. Sixty-eight and sixty-nine. I picked up a silver star and a bunch of shrapnel." He waved his hand around. "Low cost VA loan made this possible. But I came back with a drug habit and never held down a solid job. Wife left me after ten years. Couldn't take it any longer. Good wife, too." He sighed. "But I learned to cook by watching her, and I'd been brought up in a house with a father who insisted on doing all the maintenance, so I've managed to fix this place up enough to keep a roof over my head. I smartened up and got counseling for the drug problem. I've been clean for ten years."

He was getting side-tracked. Brian guessed Travis Schneider rarely got to talk to anyone, let alone someone pretty much trapped inside his kitchen. He decided to gently steer the conversation back on topic while giving his host some leeway for chit-chat. He figured he'd get more for his $20 if he played his cards right. "I lucked out," Brian said. "You're a good witness."

Schneider drained his lemonade. "I'll do my best, Sergeant." He winked conspiratorially. "We both come from the same side, after all."

"That, we do." Brian gallantly drained his own glass but refused a refill.

"I heard six shots," Schneider said. "I counted them while I was running behind the dumpster. Then nothing, but I heard the side door slam and took a chance. I flattened myself against the dumpster, like I'd been taught in the army, and did recon. I saw that kid, the one with the bike, getting thrown out the back door. Looked like he had a chest wound. Bad one, but he was still moving. Tried to get up. Guess he was gonna make a run for it, but I could see he wasn't going anywhere. No strength left. Then two men came out, wearing black hoodies and sunglasses. Don't know how they'd managed to see anything inside the shop, but that made it hard to identify them."

"Any distinctive characteristics?"

"One was a good four or five inches taller than the other. Stockier build. The shorter one was in front. He was the one who threw the kid out the door, I would guess. This black van pulls up and they all get into it. I heard a door open on the side. That's how they must have gotten the kid into it, because he sure couldn't have climbed in by himself. Probably got picked up and thrown in there."

"You didn't call nine-one-one?"

"No phone. Can't afford one of those smart-things. Don't even have TV anymore. My old set went belly-up a couple of years ago. Sometimes I go sit in the senior center if I feel like I'm missing out on any of the day-time shows, although I usually find I haven't missed a damn thing."

"I suppose you don't have a landline, either."

"A what? Oh, you mean a house phone? No. Couldn't keep up with the bills. Got cut off a couple of years back. Still have power, water and sewage, but sometimes I run late on those, too." Schneider sighed heavily. "Now you know why I collect cans. I don't want my neighbors to recognize me, so I wear the rig when I'm out. I make sure no one sees me come home. Neighbors around here all work. I'm the last hold-out of the original owners. I'm waiting to get into a VA home. It's been a long wait. Lots of guys in worse shape than me want beds."

Brian felt a stir of sympathy he knew he wasn't going to shake after he left his witness. "Anything else you can tell me? Make of the van? License plate?"

Schneider took a moment to reflect, his wrinkled hands sliding up and down his empty glass. "I think it was a Chrysler. I've seen those around while I'm waiting to cross at the light and take my cans to the center. My eyesight's not good enough to read a license plate."

"Did you hear either of the men speak?"

"They were arguing, but low-volume, so no."

"Clothing? Apart from the hoodies? Jeans? Boots or shoes?"

Schneider shook his head. "Again, with my eyesight, details tend to escape me, although those sunglasses were real visible. The light kept catching them. I think the guys were wearing black pants and boots. I didn't see anything white, like tennis shoes."

Brian placed the $20 on the table and added another. "You've been a big help."

"Hope you keep my involvement on the Q.T." Schneider took one $20 bill and left the second one. "We agreed on the price before you came inside."

"And you gave me a lot more than I expected for my money." Brian would have given Schneider twice as much if he'd had more available cash. "Take it. You've earned it."

"Okay. You twisted my arm." Schneider put both bills into a well-worn wallet he drew out of his back pocket.

Brian hoped the old vet's failing eyesight would at least be good enough for a couple more details. "Did you see the kid's bike while you were there?" he asked. "And in what direction did the van take off?"

Schneider nodded. "I did. The bike was leaning against the usual tree, but it wasn't chained up, like the kid had been on the way in and gotten side-tracked. He never left that bike unlocked. It was his transportation, or he'd have to take the bus and transfer twice, so he told me one time. As for the van, it U-turned and headed into the subdivision, the way you and I came, but instead of turning right at the corner, it kept going straight. I couldn't take the chance the driver would spot me in his rearview mirror, so I waited until I could barely hear the engine. Then I made a break for it and came home. Left my cart right where it was. Went back for it last night, after everyone left. Nobody had disturbed it."

And no one had probably had the foresight to think it was out of place next to the dumpster, either, Brian thought, his exasperation back full-force. So much for Trehorn's new and improved homicide squad.

He shook hands with Schneider and left, his host padlocking the gate behind him. Brian glanced around at the neighboring homes before walking back to his car. Schneider was correct...all looked abandoned for the day, carports empty and shutters drawn. Silence was broken only by an occasional barking dog and the distant sounds of the main street only a couple of blocks away. He wondered where that van had been going. The area behind Hibiscus Lane was residential.

CHAPTER TWELVE

BRIAN DROVE down Hibiscus for two miles before he found what he thought he might be looking for…an industrial park with a large self-storage facility. He pulled into the lot, parked outside the office and walked into the reception area, where he found a young guy who looked like he was fresh out of high school and feeling the burden of working for a living. A badge on his overalls proclaimed his name was Oscar, associate of Premium Self-Storage. His attitude said otherwise. Leaning over the register with a look of complete boredom, he stared right past Brian and fixed his attention on the parking lot. His jaw worked slowly on a piece of gum, visible briefly as it rolled across his tongue to settle on the other side of his mouth.

Brian identified himself, but Oscar barely made eye-contact, much less straightened up and looked interested.

"Any new rentals since yesterday?" Brian leaned one forearm on the counter and invaded Oscar's space.

"Do I have to talk to you?" The gum rolled back across the kid's tongue.

"No; I can go straight to your boss." Brian leaned in closer. "You want me to do that?"

The gum stopped rolling around. "He's not here. I'm in charge right now, and our customers have rights. Privacy rights." Oscar's chest expanded. A touch of color appeared high on his thin cheeks.

He countered Brian's direct gaze with a look he must have practiced in front of a mirror, probably designed to intimidate the customers, Brian thought, exasperated. A waste of time and effort, plus the result made the kid look slightly cross-eyed and squinty. Brian felt like grabbing Oscar and slapping him around a little, but he controlled himself. He didn't need a complaint about police brutality to land on Hal's desk.

"Our investigations take precedence over a lot of things, including privacy rights," he told Oscar. "You're not spilling secrets by telling me if you rented storage to any new clients yesterday." Brian fell back on his anger-management techniques by starting a slow count of one to ten in his head in case the next thing out of Oscar's mouth was even more irritating.

"Well..."

Oscar considered his response a whole lot longer than Brian's ten-count. Brian started a reverse count from ten to one. After that, all bets were off except whether he'd grab Oscar's bobbing Adam's apple or his shirt.

"I suppose that's right," Oscar said, and he wasn't slouching anymore after he apparently noticed the set of Brian's jaw. "But management wouldn't like me revealing anything about our business. I'll have to wait until my manager gets back to make that call. It could be an hour or more."

Brian's hands left the counter and headed for Oscar's throat.

Luckily for Premium Storage's young associate, a door opened behind Oscar and a middle-aged African-American man in a navy-blue uniform came through it. His badge said 'Wayne, Shift Supervisor.' He walked up to the counter and cast a sideways glance at Oscar, who moved several steps away. "Is there a problem?"

"Not yet, but we're getting close." Brian showed his credentials again and asked Wayne the same question he'd posed Oscar.

"Two units," the manager said.

"Either of them rented by someone driving a black van, possibly a Chrysler?"

Wayne nodded. "Let me check the log, but I think it was around ten o'clock yesterday morning." He looked pointedly at Oscar, who colored-up and moved aside. Wayne gave a couple of clicks and stared at the screen. "Ten-ten, to be exact. Unit one-thirty-six. The largest one we have in the back row."

"I'm getting a warrant," Brian said. "If they come back while I'm working on that, I'll be in my Camaro, parked right out front."

Wayne nodded again. "Will do, Detective. I'll come out myself." He looked at Oscar. "I'll handle the desk. Why don't you go check those units that were supposed to be emptied yesterday? If there's anything left in them, let me know. Otherwise, you can clean and get them ready for rental."

Oscar looked mutinous but he left, slinking out the door at a speed just a hair faster than a death-march.

Brian kept an eye on the kid while he made the necessary calls. Trehorn was understandably livid about the undermining of his investigation. He initially wanted Brian to leave the storage facility, then changed his mind after Brian pointed out the Chrysler could return before other detectives arrived on-scene.

"Any evidence leaves that storage bay, it'll be on your head, not mine," Brian pointed out.

Trehorn blew air into the receiver, the result a mix between a whistle and a snort of disgust. "Fine. Stay there until Reynolds and Villanueva arrive," he barked.

Brian thought Trehorn probably had difficulty stopping himself before adding "you bastard" or worse. He waited while he listened to orders being issued to the two detectives in a raised voice.

"This is probably a false lead, Swift," Trehorn said. "But my department leaves no stone unturned or ignores any tip, however flimsy. If the van shows up, I don't want you to interfere. Follow discreetly if it tries to leave. Unit one-thirty-six, you said?"

"Yeah. That needs to be on the warrant."

"I do realize that, Swift. This isn't my first rodeo."

Brian didn't need sarcasm. He figured he'd done enough favors for the homicide detectives already that day. "Are you afraid I'll solve this case while your squad keeps busy interviewing the crowd from outside the coffee shop yesterday?" he asked.

"No way in hell. You couldn't solve your way out of a shitter. We're working on several promising leads, not that I need to justify my squad's actions to you or anyone else. "

"You need to justify yourself to the chief," Brian pointed out

"Of course. You do, too, so don't think you'll make any brownie points by running to Hal Shaw and telling him you think I made bad decisions. If Hal asks me anything, he'll get an explanation he can't argue with in any way, unless it's to do with you. Then he'll probably say I'm wasting time I could better spend elsewhere, because you are still, for whatever reason, in his good graces."

"My arrest and conviction record proves I do my job. You've seen it. I don't waste anyone's time, yours included." Brian barely managed to bite back the curse he knew Trehorn was waiting to pounce on.

He needed to put a lid on his anger. The lieutenant outranked him, and arguing with the guy could lead to a charge of insubordination. *Another one.* With a great deal of effort, Brian ignored his desire to tell Trehorn where to go and what to do with himself when he got there.

"A black van drove off from the coffee shop right after the murders and then took off through a residential area," he said, striving for a tone he would use toward any of his friends during a disagreement. It proved to be difficult but manageable. "Someone driving a black van rented a large storage unit an hour after the crime was committed," he continued when Trehorn merely grunted in response instead of interrupting. "I have a witness who told me the missing employee from the coffee shop was loaded into a black van, which he thought was a Chrysler with a sliding side door. In my book, that's more than enough reason to obtain a warrant and search the storage unit."

"I have to agree…this time." Trehorn sounded like he was speaking through gritted teeth. "We'll obtain the warrant. As soon as the Homicide Squad detectives arrive, you leave."

"Like hell I will."

Brian hung up. He thought about calling Hal, but opted instead to update Mills and give Gabe instructions to find out when the warrant was issued and by which judge. Feeling he couldn't do anything more, he settled back in his seat to await developments.

He didn't wait long. Less than five minutes later, his phone started ringing. Brian looked at the caller ID. Chief Shaw. *Of course.*

"Swift," he answered.

"Trehorn wants you busted down a rank or two." Hal's dry tone held a note of exasperation.

"I'm sure he does." Brian could well imagine what Hal had been told. But keeping to the facts would justify his actions. "Look, Chief, I stumbled onto a good lead in the coffee shop murders. I called Trehorn immediately. I'm on-site. He told me to leave. I refused. If my suspicions are correct, someone could turn up to move a body before those other two detectives Trehorn dispatched even get close to here."

"I told him that." Hal paused.

Brian waited him out. Hal never spoke spontaneously. His responses were always measured and definitive.

Hal sighed, long and hard. "You are the biggest damn thorn in my side, Swift," he said. "Stay there as senior officer. I'll square things with Trehorn and tell him to leave you alone when you're right and he knows it. I'm not jeopardizing a murder investigation because of some pissing match between you two. When you get through there, I want you in my office. I'll tell Alicia to interrupt me, whatever I'm doing."

Brian felt a stir of unease. *For what reason?*

Hal answered that question right away. "You've had two complaints filed against you," he said in a neutral tone. "One's from the reporter you tore into yesterday morning at the crime scene. The other's from some guy who was interviewed by another reporter. He says he has information that shows you were receiving kick-backs from your brother. I can't ignore his claim. We know Tim's businesses were legit at the time of his death, but this guy says he's talking about three years ago."

"Fuck," Brian said, wondering whether he was over-reaching by thinking the accuser might very well be that loud-mouthed painter.

"That pretty much sums it up." Hal's voice sounded even more measured than usual.

A dark sedan arrived at the lot, followed by a patrol car. No lights. No sirens. Doors opened.

"I've gotta go, Chief…back-up's here." Brian had seldom been more relieved to get an interruption.

"Call me whether you find anything in that unit or not," Hal said. "And don't get side-tracked on the way to my office."

"You've got it." Brian wasn't sure whether he hung up faster than Hal or they were in synch.

He left the Camaro to meet the detectives already walking briskly toward him. He knew one of them only slightly...Davion Reynolds, a young African-American who had survived a childhood in the Liberty Square public housing complex known colloquially as the Pork 'n' Beans. A very rough, extremely violent area well-known to all at MDPD. Somehow, Reynolds had managed to graduate from high school and leave that life behind.

The other detective, Villanueva, Brian knew even less. She had arrived in Homicide only days before he was placed on suspension. Then Tim disappeared...

Brian immediately put the brakes on yet another trip down memory lane and the resulting nightmare memories. He focused on what he'd heard about Villanueva. He couldn't remember her first name, but he did recall she had moved from Mobile. Jack Mills had spent more time with her before transferring to Cold Case. He said she was sharp and intuitive, both excellent qualities for what had the makings of yet another convoluted case.

Brian hoped they weren't carrying any pre-conceived notions about who was in charge on-site before Trehorn even arrived. Instead, hands were shaken and brief pleasantries exchanged before he gave them a quick report. Neither had any complaints about him taking the lead. The patrol officers rolled their car out of sight and monitored the perimeter. Brian, Reynolds and Villanueva fanned out as they walked between two rows of storage buildings. Wayne, the manager walked behind with bolt cutters.

Villanueva had secured the warrant. Dark-haired and petite, she carried herself on light feet that hinted at a background in the martial arts. Brian had heard Reynolds played in a soccer league when he wasn't working. He had no doubt either of them could apprehend a running suspect, but he missed Jack Mills, with his ability to evaluate any situation and adapt to surprises. There was no telling what they'd find once Wayne used those bolt cutters on the unit's heavy-duty padlock.

He motioned Villanueva and Reynolds to take up positions on either side of the door. Wayne cut the lock. Brian pulled it off and threw it to one side while motioning the manager to make himself scarce. Wayne was only too glad to do that, running for cover behind a utility cart.

Reynolds cautiously pushed up the door. Glock drawn, Brian carefully looked inside. Villanueva handed him a flashlight. The beam pierced the dimness of the interior. At first, the unit appeared empty, but a tarp at the back was definitely covering more than the concrete floor. A decided odor of decomposing flesh wafted toward the doorway.

Villanueva coughed and placed a forearm across her nose and mouth. "Sorry," she muttered.

Brian entered the unit, followed by the other detectives. They pulled on gloves and took a careful look under the tarp. Brian recognized Moises, his white t-shirt soaked with dried blood, his sightless eyes staring up at the ceiling. Flies buzzed. The odor intensified. They allowed the tarp to cover the body again.

"Call it in," he instructed Reynolds. Villanueva's olive complexion had paled. "You need to step outside?" he asked her.

"This isn't the first time I've been at a crime scene, Sergeant." She coughed and blinked rapidly. "But I'm pregnant and suffering from morning sickness, damn it." She tried to swallow, began retching, turned and bolted out of the storage unit.

Sounds of vomiting filled the air outside, not only from Villanueva but from Wayne, who had been unable to stay away. The day was just getting better and better, Brian thought as a hot breeze circulated around the storage unit, carrying the unmistakable odor of puke to join the decomp. His least favorite side of detective work. His and every other police officer. What he wouldn't give for a jar of Vicks at that moment. One swipe beneath his nose and the odor would be far less intense. But he'd stopped carrying it when he moved to Cold Case. Their bodies were far more skeletal in nature and any odors were minimal.

He knew one thing...he'd reek when he returned to the precinct, and he was supposed to go straight to Hal's office. Alicia Solis, Hal's assistant was in for a real treat. Brian wondered whether she'd puke, too. The chief's strict instructions not to take any detours on the way back from the crime scene precluded any side-trips to the *NTK* for a shower.

Since he'd already used the change of clothes he kept in the locker room and hadn't yet replaced them, there would be a distinct odor in and around the chief's office until the janitorial service turned up with heavy-duty deodorizers. He'd better call Jim while driving to the precinct and see if his friend would be willing to perform the services of a valet.

Trehorn arrived at the same time as the crime scene unit and the medical examiner, Dr. Farley Jones. The team began processing the scene with very little chit-chat. Brian waited on the fringes after briefing the newcomers.

"I've got to give you this one," Jones told Brian, standing outside the storage unit with a cup of black coffee when the medical examiner had finished up and walked back outside.

Wayne had thoughtfully brewed several pots of coffee for the crew, brought water and a clean towel for Villanueva and made himself generally useful. He had wanted to send Oscar with a hose to clean up the vomit, but Brian had refused until the investigators had processed the surrounding area.

Trehorn, following closely behind Jones, looked at the ground outside the storage unit. "Who the hell did this?" He pointed toward the two piles of puke.

"Me," Wayne said as he offered Trehorn a white Styrofoam cup filled with coffee. "I got more than I bargained for when I stayed around too long." He pointed toward Oscar, pushing a wheelbarrow slowly around the far side of the building. "He's bringing a shovel and a bag of sand. Soon as you give the word, Sergeant, he'll dump that and kill the odor." Wayne looked at Brian.

Trehorn gave a characteristic snort of distain, but refrained from commenting on Wayne's deference to Brian by walking back into the storage unit. Brian gave the word and Wayne waved at Oscar, who pushed the wheelbarrow forward at a pace that would probably bring him to the storage unit just before night-fall.

Villanueva still looked pale, but she was sipping water as she stood on the opposite side of the doorway, well away from the vomit. "Thanks," she told Wayne in an undertone.

"For what?" Wayne grinned. "I tossed my cookies. Twice." He left, but he cast a backward glance at Villanueva, who was taking a second look in his direction.

Brian moved over to stand beside her. "Hey, I thought you said you were pregnant," he whispered. "Flirting at a crime scene?"

"I am pregnant, but I'm not the one who is dead, and there's no father in the picture. My boyfriend couldn't handle me coming home with blood on my shoes." She shrugged. "I don't even know where he is now. I haven't told the department yet, either."

"Your tale to tell. Sorry to hear about your boyfriend, but these days, especially with your position, you could find him if you really wanted to." Brian looked over at Reynolds, busy talking to Trehorn. "What about your partner? Does he know?"

"Davion's cool," she said. "He offered to marry me if I needed to give the kid a father. We're tight. Not that tight, though. I'll be okay if I can keep from puking every five minutes. I'm going to come clean about this next week. There's no rule says I can't continue doing my job as long as I've got medical clearance and I can still perform all the duties." She grimaced. "Running down perps when I'm the size of a house may not meet those criteria. I'll have to take this one day at a time."

"Can you get back in there if you need to?" Brian jerked his head toward the unit.

"Sure. Whether I have to run out again remains in question." One corner of her mouth quirked. "You're different from what I heard."

"In a good or bad way?"

"Good." She sipped more water. "Better than good. I'm sorry you're not still working with us."

"If I was, you might change your mind. But don't believe half the stories you've heard about me."

"What about the other half?" She finished the water and threw the cup into a plastic trash bag hanging off one handle of the utility cart.

"Pretty accurate." Brian smiled at her.

Villanueva nodded, the quirk back at the corner of her mouth. "In that case, if you ever need any more help down in the basement, I'm your girl." The quirk turned into a full smile. "I doubt I'd have to run down perps on cold cases. It could be a good assignment for a girl who'll soon be the size of the Goodyear Blimp."

"That's true. You probably wouldn't have to run after anyone." Brian liked her no-nonsense attitude. She'd been dealt a lousy hand, but apparently, it wasn't in her nature to wallow in misery. "What's your background?" he asked. "Military?"

She nodded again, the gesture sharp and decisive. "Army. I wanted to be a sniper. I'm a really good shot. But I ended up as an MP." She paused. "Military Police," she clarified.

"Villanueva!" Trehorn's voice echoed around the storage unit. "Get in here and stop shooting the shit with Swift."

"Yes, sir." Villanueva extended her hand toward Brian. "We only had a short intro when I arrived on-site. I'm Deanna Villanueva."

Brian shook hands. "Brian Swift," he said. "Glad to make your acquaintance, Detective."

She nodded before walking briskly into the storage unit, her back and shoulders rigid. Brian wasn't sure whether her stiffened posture was the result of trying to prevent another wave of nausea induced by the odor or from having to deal with Trehorn. Perhaps it was purely reactionary; a hold-over from her years in the US Army.

"Don't you have a meeting with the chief, Swift?" Trehorn's voice boomed, enhanced by the suddenly-empty storage unit.

Moises' body was being rolled on a stretcher to a waiting ambulance. Brian looked at the body bag and thought of the young man who, only 24 hours ago, had thought he was riding his bike to another day at work, not to his death. Life could be so unpredictable and leave so suddenly, he thought. Then he wondered what had triggered such an unexpected moment of reflection. Possibly the visit to Tim's gravesite, or even Villanueva's predicament. He shook it all off, as he had many times before. Living in the moment was a lot less stressful than dwelling on the past or worrying about the future, even a future that included what promised to be a contentious meeting with Chief Hal Shaw.

"Yeah, I do," he told Trehorn. "You ready to get rid of me, or you need any more info?"

Trehorn strolled out of the unit. He looked unruffled by either the heat or the smell. "If I need anything else, I know how to contact you."

Brian noted Trehorn hadn't said he knew where to find him. Was the man anticipating him being out on suspension again?

Worrying.

Brian shook off the concern, reminding himself that casting doubt was Trehorn's specialty. "You bet."

He made sure he walked unhurriedly back to his Camaro and avoided glancing in his rearview mirror. He knew Trehorn was monitoring his every move.

CHAPTER THIRTEEN

KAYLEN STOPPED at nearby Bennett's Market on the way to the marina. She'd found pickings really sparse the last time she was in the *Need to Know's* galley. She grabbed a basket and scanned the list she'd made to save time. Cream for her coffee, Brian's favorite chocolate chip cookies with walnuts, a couple of bananas and a box of cereal. Milk, because he probably didn't have any left or the half-empty carton she'd used over a week ago would probably be out of date and sour.

Kaylen had stopped trying to get Brian to check the contents of the refrigerator or the boat's small pantry. His mind was razor-sharp for everything, it seemed, except groceries. She wondered whether that was a result of his upbringing, where poor nutrition had been the norm, or his constantly-packed schedule. Between his job, the boat and her, he never seemed to have much time left for anything like pushing a cart around a grocery store. But then, she reminded herself, neither did she. But what she deemed a priority was no more than an unnecessary inconvenience to Brian, who figured he could always stop by some fast food place when hunger got the best of him.

She walked into an aisle stocked with a wide variety of cookies and scanned the shelves. There they were, front and center—chocolate chip with walnuts. She placed a packet in her cart before another caught her eye. That one had chocolate chips with pecans. She wondered whether Brian would like those better.

He loved pecans. He'd told her about making a detour on the way to school in Baton Rouge so he could pass a yard with a pecan tree. If he was lucky, some of the ripe nuts would drop over the fence into the alleyway and he'd beat the squirrels to them. He'd stuff the pecans into his pockets and eat them for lunch. He borrowed a hammer from the janitor's cart to crack the hard shells, returning the tool before it was reported missing. He told Kaylen that Tim said he should stow the hammer somewhere on campus where they could both find it, but Brian refused. Tim was always the more talented and determined pilferer in the family, Brian had said with a wry smile.

Whatever information about his childhood Brian shared with her, and he shared very little, Kaylen thought, revealed a desperate time when he as well as Tim had to steal to survive. Purchasing cookies with pecans seemed like a frivolous attempt at giving Brian something he could never have had as a child. Kaylen almost put the packet back on the shelf, but she felt he always appreciated her gestures, even if he rarely commented on them. The cookies always got eaten quickly. Jim would probably like them, too.

"You'll never keep your figure if you eat all those," said a familiar voice.

Kaylen had hoped never to hear that voice again. She pivoted to face Sam Wilson as the packet of cookies hit the floor.

Sam bent over and picked them up. He shook the packet, which rattled like it was filled with pebbles. "Sounds like you'll be eating crumbs." He dropped it into her basket.

Kaylen didn't know if she could trust her face not to reveal her shock, let alone her voice, but she had to ask the obvious.

"What are you doing here?" she managed. Even to her, her voice sounded shrill.

"Shopping." Sam waved a half-filled basket at her.

Kaylen didn't look at the contents. "Get away from me," she said. Hand shaking, she fumbled around in her purse, felt the cold metal of the Sig Sauer but opted to pull out her phone instead.

"Oh, come on now, K.T." Sam shook his head, a rueful smile pulling his mouth up at the corners. "You're not going to call nine-one-one or Brian Swift, are you?"

"I certainly am." She started to press numbers.

Sam snatched the phone away.

"Give that back. Right now." She extended her hand, palm up. It was no longer shaking. Adrenaline had kicked in, for which she was extremely thankful. "Do you want me to start screaming?"

"No, of course not." He returned the phone to her. "Make an effort, honey. Be sociable. You and I haven't seen each other in a long time."

Kaylen kept the phone in her hand, but instead of screaming or running, which she would have done before being coached on confronting potential attackers by Brian, she opted to put on her bravest face and see what Sam wanted from her. She was armed and in a public place, she reminded herself.

"Not long enough," she told him, "and don't call me honey. You and I have nothing to say to each other after what you did."

"We used to be best friends. You valued my opinion more than anyone else's." Sam sounded wistful, wheedling. He thrust his face closer. "Now you're treating me like a stranger."

"A dangerous one." Kaylen shoved her phone back into her purse. She assured herself she could fire the Sig Sauer right through it if she didn't have time to get it out. She hoped that wouldn't make it misfire, but she was going to have to adapt to the situation. If she brought out the gun, store security cameras would see it.

Sam had to have been in on the plan to murder Brian, she told herself. A plan that had almost succeeded. An image flashed into her mind of him ignoring her desperate plea for help outside his home as Brian, shot and bleeding heavily from his left shoulder, lay slumped semi-conscious in the passenger's seat of the car. Instead, Sam had attempted to drag her from behind the wheel so his 'men' could finish what the thugs sent by the cartel had started. He had already had Tim disposed of like a piece of trash dumped in the Everglades. She knew he also wanted to remove the new man he considered his rival, and the biggest threat to Sam Wilson marrying George Bannisters Roberts' widow and getting his hands on her money...Tim's detective brother, Brian.

Anger surged. Her fingers slid down inside the purse and brushed the cold metal of the Sig again. But she knew Brian would never forgive her if she didn't deal with the situation in a more proactive manner than shooting the one man who might be able to name Tim's killers. Her fingers curled slowly into her palm, the acrylic nails biting painfully into her flesh.

Sam looked first at her face, then at her arm, with her hand still nestled inside the purse. "What are you doing?"

"Making sure you get what you deserve, although having you arrested won't bring me as much pleasure as shooting you dead right now."

Sam blinked. He backed up a couple of steps. "You're armed?"

"You bet I am." She leaned forward, feeling empowered by their height difference as she looked down at him. "I've always known how to use firearms. I told you that one time before. Remember? When I pointed Brian's Glock at you the day you refused to help us?"

Sam took another step back. "No need to threaten me. I'm completely unarmed and alone."

"Where's your posse?"

He shrugged. "No money left to hire bodyguards. K.T., I've got a lot of regrets. That day you brought Swift to my house, well, that's one day I acted really badly."

"Badly?" She closed the gap between them. "There's a gross understatement."

"K.T." He swallowed hard. "Honey…" His back hit the shelf behind him and he stopped, his breathing rapid and shallow.

"I told you…don't 'honey' me, and don't call me K.T. ever again, either."

"Okay, okay." He nodded slowly as though he was afraid to make any sudden moves, even positive ones.

Kaylen quickly pressed her advantage, worried that he'd see through her bravado and run before she got any useful information out of him. "Now, you want to talk, so talk," she prompted. "Tell me why you came back. You know you're a wanted man. Why take the risk?"

He straightened up, apparently deciding she wasn't going to shoot him immediately. "Miami's my home." He shrugged. "I missed it."

"You're going to get arrested. It's only a matter of time. Do the right thing...turn yourself in."

"And do time?" His bushy eyebrows rose at the thought. "I couldn't handle it. You of all people should know me better than that. I like comfort, good things, beautiful women. But I've missed you most of all." He leaned forward again. "I've been sending you little tokens, to let you know I'm back," he said, his voice low and syrupy. "Did you get them?"

"You know I did."

"Now, how would I know that, K.T., er...Kaylen?"

Kaylen's anger surged. "You had Bannisters bugged...you knew everything that went on in my business before you were found out. Now I have the place swept on a regular basis, you don't. Is that why you're here? Because you can't eavesdrop anymore, so you think confronting me will scare me into telling you whatever you want to know?"

"No...I just told you...I miss you. I love you. I want us to be together."

"Oh, come on, Sam. I'm not so naïve these days. Try telling the truth for once." She hoped she wasn't pushing too hard...he still had that tape to hold over her head. Was he hoping to blackmail her? He certainly wasn't stupid enough to hope she'd shield him from discovery and give him any form of affection, could he?

"I've got protection," she said. "I'm not scared of you."

"Ah...you're protected." Sam looked from one side of the empty aisle to the other. "Where are all these guardians of yours right now?"

He was definitely regaining his poise, Kaylen thought. She wondered why, and suddenly the disquieting thought that he might be the one who had come with reinforcements slithered into her mind. Kaylen found herself swallowing hard, and didn't like the feeling. "I don't need any of them to go grocery shopping," she said, trying to sound strong and in charge. "I told you, I'm armed, and I don't consider you a direct threat."

"Maybe not a physical threat, honey, but I followed you from your condo to this store without any trouble." He glanced around briefly. "Unless he's well-hidden or goofing off somewhere, I'd say you don't have a bodyguard with you. If I had brought reinforcements with me, instead of choosing to talk to you in a friendly manner, I'd have had you kidnapped by now."

Kaylen refused to give in to the chills flowing over her at the mention of kidnapping. "I've got a fully-loaded Sig Sauer trained right at your mid-section. No one is going to threaten me, least of all you."

Sam actually grinned. "I'm not sure I believe that, K.T."

Kaylen bristled. *The smug bastard.*

"I'm not going to prove I have it, if that's what you're trying to make me do," she told him. "There are cameras all over this store. I could get in real trouble for showing you the gun. But if you try to interfere with my shopping any further, I'll call Brian. He'll get here faster than you can run out the door, and he'll give you the beating you deserve before he hauls you off to jail."

"He's not going to be around to protect you much longer. He'll have too many legal problems he won't be able to talk his way out of."

Kaylen's anger paled in comparison to the absolute rage she felt at Sam threatening Brian. "I'll kill you, Sam. I swear I will, if you harm him in any way," she vowed. "I don't care if you're recording this conversation and you doctor the results. You're not going to ruin my life or my business, and you're definitely not going to take away the man I love, you piece of *shit.*"

Sam's mouth actually dropped open. Kaylen took her hand out of her purse to poke him in the chest with her finger. He winced.

"I never saw you for what you really are until Tim died," she continued, all the pent-up emotions and things she'd wanted to say to Sam coming to the surface. "I know George had been shoring up your business. You used your longtime friendship with my husband to manipulate him when he was dying. You're a leech of the worst kind." She pulled out her phone again. "And now, I'm calling the cops to come pick you up."

Sam had his back to the shelves behind him when she stopped speaking. Suddenly, the store sounded quiet. Even the piped-in music had stopped. Kaylen saw movement out the corner of her eye. Panicked that it could be from members of Sam's own security detail, she turned away from him to see two uniformed men advancing toward them, one a store employee, the second a security guard.

"I'll see you another time," Sam hissed.

With that, he threw his partially-filled basket toward the men, bottles and cans spilling out to roll all over the floor, before he hooked his arm around a display of Torani coffee syrups and swept those to the floor. Glass shattered, colored syrup erupted from the broken bottles to splash everything around them. Kaylen jumped back, colliding with the shelves behind her. Packets of cookies rained down.

By the time she recovered, Sam had already reached the end of the aisle. His white suit jacket flapped behind him as he walked rapidly out the front door. He was surprisingly speedy, but then, he'd lost a lot of weight since his days as a restaurant owner Kaylen reminded herself. The security guard broke into a run but slipped on the sticky, wet floor. Putting out a hand to steady himself, he latched onto the shelves and dislodged several packages of coffee.

The other man, wearing a tag that proclaimed he was the store manager, stopped before he came into contact with the mess. "Are you okay, Ma'am?" he asked Kaylen. "Your conversation with that gentleman was getting loud. Several customers complained they didn't feel safe. One said she thought she heard you threatening violence."

The security guard glared at the manager before stepping carefully through the spill. "Did that gentleman threaten you in any way?"

"He's an old business associate," Kaylen said, attempting to gloss over the incident. "We had a bad professional break-up, and this is the first time we've come face to face. I was about to call the police if he didn't leave me alone. Thank you for coming to my assistance." She put on her best game face and forced herself to smile first at the security guard, then the manager.

"Aren't you Ms. Roberts?" The security guard asked.

"That's me. Trying to do a little personal shopping." She held up the basket.

"I thought I recognized you. I work some shifts where you live. Are you sure you're okay?"

"Fine, yes." She nodded reassuringly at the guard before turning her attention to the manager. "So sorry about all this." She saw the man surveying all the broken and wrecked merchandise. "Please let me pay for the damage," she added. She would rather be remembered for that than for the altercation with Sam.

The manager looked relieved. "Why, thank you, that's more than generous. Would you like one of our associates to help you finish your shopping?"

"Oh, no thanks. I'd like to do that myself." She gave him her widest smile and hoped she looked completely unfazed by the entire incident. "I'm almost done, anyway. If you'd be so kind as to have a tally of the damage ready when I check out?"

"I'll get right on it." He waved a young man forward with a mop and bucket. "You'll need to close this aisle," he told his associate. "I'll personally take care of itemizing the damage," he assured Kaylen.

The security guard followed her from the chaos behind them. "Was that Sam Wilson?" he asked.

"Yes. You're very observant."

"I try to be. It's part of my job." The man's brow furrowed. "He looks different. Smaller. Thinner. And he's got a lot more hair."

"He does," Kaylen agreed. "I almost didn't recognize him myself." That was a lie. She'd always know Sam, regardless how much he tried to alter his appearance.

"He used to own a restaurant close to here," the guard said.

"The Hideaway." Kaylen nodded. "I'm sure he'll pop back up, unfortunately, but I don't think you or the manager have to worry about him coming in here again." She grimaced at the thought she might not be able to shop there again, either. Too much attention from shoppers and staff alike. "I'd like to finish up alone, if you don't mind."

"I'll watch the door and walk you to your car when you're ready to leave," he said.

Kaylen decided arguing against that would only draw more attention to her. "Thank you." She forced a smile.

She thought about calling Brian, but decided he'd already had enough drama for one day. She'd wait to break the news about Sam's return until they were alone on the *Need to Know*. That would give her time to process the confrontation herself and try to determine why she had learned so little. What a wash-out she would be as a private investigator, she thought.

Even mild-mannered Jim would have had Sam pinned against the shelves. Brian would have gone at least one step further and slammed Sam up against them. Both men would have gotten every detail of Tim's abduction and murder out of the man. She, on the other hand, had only danced around making stupid threats to shoot him, which he quickly realized she was not going to do. He had toyed with her and had the upper hand throughout most of their conversation, when she'd had the means to subdue him and have him taken into custody. Kaylen cringed. Brian was going to be furious, and she couldn't blame him.

She had a horrible feeling this meeting with Sam would soon be followed by others, and she was afraid she'd react just as stupidly. He'd tested the waters and found her as easy to lead and dominate as she had been when he was her mentor. She had easily reverted to being his student, the empty-headed socialite, she berated herself. Where had that woman gone who had once confronted him with Brian's Glock in her hand and been prepared to use it? Apparently, that version of herself had taken an extended vacation and might never return.

No, Kaylen thought, shaking off the mantle of victim. *Not gone. Momentarily lost.*

She made a solemn vow not to fall into that trap again. She'd control her emotions. Find and tap into her tougher self. The shock of seeing Sam for the first time since he'd fled Miami was over, and she would make herself react differently the next time he ambushed her.

She felt sure his ultimate goal was to destroy Brian and probably her, too, once the enjoyment of baiting her had soured. *But surely he couldn't believe she would ever allow him back into her life, could he?*

That would be crazy, she told herself. And *that,* Sam was not. Desperate? *Absolutely.* Conniving? *Definitely.* But deluded enough to believe she'd ride off into the sunset with him? *Impossible.*

She reminded herself that she wasn't the same person who had depended on Sam for support after George's death. She had leaned on him and on Sandy, her best friend in those dark days. Both of them had conspired behind her back. Lied to her. Betrayed her. Kaylen reined in her galloping thoughts, accelerating toward images and remembrances that would give her nightmare recollections. Sandy was dead, Kaylen told herself. End of that story. But now she knew for certain Sam was not.

She took one hand off her basket and held it in front of her. Only marginally shaky. She consulted her list, lying on top of the chocolate chip cookies with walnuts. An intact packet of chocolate chip with pecans was completely unreachable. Wet floor signs had been strategically placed on both sides of the sticky mess while the store associate toiled methodically to clean up and restore order. Kaylen headed for the dairy aisle.

Milk and creamer, she thought, pushing back against a barrage of disturbing thoughts whirling through her brain. Then the cereal and bananas, followed by a big tab at the check-out when she paid for all that Torani syrup, the cookies, and the coffee.

Damn Sam!

Kaylen concentrated on finishing her shopping, walking quickly and purposefully through the brightly-lit store. Other shoppers stared or avoided her by scurrying off to other aisles. But it wasn't until she lifted her legs into the car that she saw perhaps the real reason those shoppers had avoided her, and it wasn't because of the altercation with Sam.

She started laughing and crying at the same time. Grabbing a handful of tissues from her purse, Kaylen wiped her eyes and blew her nose. She looked at herself in the rearview mirror and shook her head at her reflection. She must have presented quite the spectacle. Her white pants were covered with syrup stains in every color and flavor Torani made.

CHAPTER FOURTEEN

When Brian arrived at the chief's office, Hal Shaw had a carafe and two cups on his desk. He took one whiff as Brian walked across the room and wrinkled his nose. "Decomp," he said. "You shouldn't have."

"Yeah, I know, but you told me to come straight here." Brian unbuttoned his jacket and sat in one of the brown leather chairs in front of Hal's desk. "Jim's bringing me a clean outfit. As soon as you're done with me, I'll go shower and change."

Hal's right eyebrow raised a fraction. "You don't keep extra clothes here? I know you've been working cold cases, but even rookies realize accidents happen in this line of work."

"I already used my spare outfit yesterday." Brian shrugged. "I didn't intend to find another body today."

"No, I guess you wouldn't." Hal rubbed his chin. "You unintentionally got involved yesterday in what is now a triple homicide. You unintentionally went back to the same crime scene today, followed up with a witness you just happened to find and based on a flimsy tip, went into a storage facility and discovered the body of the missing coffee shop employee."

"Yeah, I did." Brian began to wonder whether Hal believed he'd found Moises' body through good policing or other, less lawful channels.

"I've made discoveries on flimsier tips than I got from that witness today," he reminded the chief.

"You have." Hal took hold of the carafe. "Coffee?"

"Sure."

Brian tried to relax his shoulders, telling himself Hal wouldn't offer coffee if he was planning another dressing-down, but the attempt failed. Hal was noted for his sly interrogation methods, which included reassuring the subject before pouncing with both feet.

"Have you gotten an update from the hospital about Antonio Camardi's condition?" he asked, hoping to steer the topic of conversation away from himself, at least temporarily.

Hal poured two cups of black coffee, pushing one across the desk. "Upgraded to serious but stable."

"That's the best news I've heard in two days." Brian took the cup and drank. The coffee went down hot and satisfying.

Hal didn't pick up his own cup. Instead, he grabbed his pen and tapped it against the desk. "And now, I'll deliver the not-so-good news."

Obviously, the chief wasn't going to get sidetracked. Brian braced for impact and tried to remain as neutral as possible while they proceeded to review his less-than-optimal exchange with Mireille Shagassi before running through the painter's complaints. Brian listened to a watered-down version of the language he'd used on Shagassi before hearing familiar strains of his supposed-involvement with the uglier side of his brother's enterprises.

"So, what the hell is that damn painter's name, anyway?" Brian asked after Hal had finished.

"Beale Friendly," Hal said. "Yeah," he held up his hand. "I know it sounds like a fabrication, but he checked out, at least as far as having a driver's license, apartment lease, the usual. But we're going further into his background. He can throw out all the accusations he wants, but he has to have proof to back them up, and so far, all he's doing is acting the loud-mouth."

Brian's tension ratcheted down a half-notch. "Who's doing the checking?"

"IAB."

The ratcheting reversed. *Internal Affairs...again?* "Chief, you know how they feel about me."

"I know, I know." Hal leaned back in his chair. "But you got a fair shake from Gil Morrison after Tim's death, and he's agreed to take the lead this time, too."

"Okay." Brian nodded, but felt no real reassurance.

His memory of Morrison was still a little fuzzy. The IAB representative had come to the hospital while Brian was recuperating from surgery. Morrison's report had brought revelations about Tim's businesses that were enough to send Brian's already fevered mind into a tailspin. But that had been almost two years ago. Nothing illegal had been discovered on Brian's end, even if everything wasn't completely clear-cut and Brian himself wasn't deemed to be spotlessly clean in every nook and cranny of his life.

"Let everything play out," Hal advised. "Don't act defensive, and for God's sake don't get hostile with Morrison. I don't believe I need to counsel you to keep your distance from Beale Friendly, but I'm going to do it, anyway."

"As long as he keeps away from me, I won't go near him."

"Never meet with him unless you have a reliable witness. Never engage him in conversation either in person or by any other means. Don't allow him to get your words or actions into the public arena."

"I know, Hal...er, Chief."

Hal frowned at the inadvertent slip. "You don't. Not one hundred percent. Even now."

"I *do.*" Brian stopped. He couldn't get into a fight with the chief over his behavior. That would only prove he still didn't know how to handle himself in a stressful situation. He took a breath. "Chief, I think I should meet with Mireille Shagassi again. Give her a better interview. Make myself look less of a reactive jerk."

Hal took a sip of his coffee and ruminated. Brian followed suit, sitting back and sipping coffee while trying to convey complete control of his legendary hair-trigger temper. He couldn't even smell the decomp on himself anymore, which was a blessing. He hoped Hal had adjusted to the odor, too. Perhaps it would put him in a less judgmental mood.

"Okay," Hal said. "I'll authorize it. I'll have Alicia set it up."

"Fine. Anywhere Shagassi wants, although I would prefer keeping out of the TV station."

"I wouldn't want you anywhere near a TV studio, either. Especially not right now."

"I'm in full agreement with that." Brian risked cracking a half-smile.

Hal didn't return it, but he shook his head slowly. Brian hoped that was a sign of capitulation, at least for one day.

"Get out of here," Hal said. "I'm going to have to get a cleaning crew in here while I run home to shower and change clothes myself. I'm participating in a three o'clock update on this case, and I'm not taking any chances that I could smell anything close to the way you do right now."

"You've got it." Brian abandoned his cup and rapidly left Hal's office.

Jim had thankfully left everything he needed down in the basement office. Brian saw a garment bag leaning over the back of a swivel chair in front of Gabe's desk and a duffel on the seat. But Gabe stopped him at the doorway.

"No way, no how," he said, spraying an aerosol can in a wide arc. "I'm pushing everything out in the hallway. Once you've cleaned up, I'll order you some lunch and you can tell me what I need to do for you next."

"You're a real pal," Brian told him, back-pedaling.

Gabe rolled the chair out into the hallway, returned to Cold Case and closed the door. Brian heard more aerosol spraying and had to smile. As he took the bags to the locker room, he silently thanked Jim's neat-nick ways that protected everything from contamination until after the shower. Jim had even provided him with a couple of large garbage bags to keep the smell contained after he undressed.

By the time he'd eaten lunch, Brian felt almost normal again, a state he was certain wouldn't stick around long.

CHAPTER FIFTEEN

"THAT LITTLE REPORTER'S OUT for a scoop," Jim said the following morning as he handed Brian a plate of crispy bacon, scrambled eggs and hash browns. He waved his spatula toward the banquette in the *Need to Know's* salon. "Coffee's in a flask on the table."

"Thanks for cooking breakfast." Brian took his meal over to the table and sat. "What's the occasion?"

"Me giving you a report before you go to work. Easier to talk over a meal than deliver bad news on an empty stomach." Jim brought his own food to the table and set another plate stacked with toast beside the salt and pepper. "I take it Kaylen's sleeping in?"

Brian poured coffee into his mug. "Yeah, she worked last night. Rob was out sick. Caught something from one of his nieces or nephews."

Jim nodded as he scraped a thin layer of butter onto his toast. "Kids do that to you. Rob's got a big family."

Brian always wondered why Jim even bothered with the butter. He watched a generous dollop of marmalade land on the toast before it was cut into 4 equal portions.

"Kaylen's going to Treasure today." He tried to sound casual. "Want to ride with her? She'd like the company, and you could give her some input on the décor."

Jim chuckled. "You think it's over the top, don't you?" He popped a piece of toast into his mouth.

Brian watched Jim chew slowly and methodically, as he seemed to do everything else. He wondered, not for the first time in the last year, how his neighbor had become his best friend and strongest ally when their temperaments, backgrounds and ages were so different.

He knew that if he was actually hungry, his breakfast would have been eaten before Jim even made it to the table. Instead, it languished while he divided his time between watching Jim separate his eggs and bacon into equal portions and watching the *Fanciful Folly* bob at her moorings while a pair of gulls rocked back and forth on top of Jim's table. He knew Jim would be cleaning and polishing the marks off that table as soon as he saw them. Brian's own housekeeping remedy was to pay Carlos, his deck-hand, to take care of the *NTK's* upkeep once a week.

"I do think she's putting too much crap in there," he told Jim. "But I'm no interior decorator. The opening's in three weeks. She needs to stop ordering stuff. It's stressing her out, waiting for things to get delivered."

"I'll go." Jim pointed his knife toward Brian's untouched plate before buttering another piece of toast. "You're *both* getting too stressed over this opening. Eat up, and I'll fill you in on that reporter."

"I'm not really hungry Jim, and you telling me about that damn nosy woman isn't gonna give me an appetite."

"I added a little kick to the eggs. You'll like them. Eat those, at least. You know how I hate waste."

Brian broke a piece of bacon in half and popped it in his mouth to placate his friend. Jim hadn't needed to get up and fix more than his own bowl of oatmeal unless he had important news that couldn't wait until they did their customary chill-out with a couple of beers on deck after Brian got off work.

"Cassandra Bunting told me she's been working hard to get investigative reporting credits," Jim said, sitting back and cradling his coffee mug in both hands. "But until yesterday, she hasn't been able to convince the station to send her out on anything more than social news segments."

"That's nothing worth you cooking breakfast for."

"Don't get snappy with me, Mister. I'm laying the groundwork."

Brian rolled his eyes, but ate the rest of his bacon to keep from commenting further.

Jim tut-tutted under his breath and poured more coffee. Brian broke a piece of toast in half and buttered it. The mast creaked and the *NTK* butted up against the dock a couple of times before Jim continued. Brian finished the rest of the toast, which he ate dry and regretted it when crumbs lodged in his throat. He drank the orange juice.

"The reporter who was initially sent to cover the coffee shop murders got stuck behind a big wreck on the Palmetto," Jim said.

"Jim…" Brian set down his empty glass with more force than needed. "I've gotta work this morning."

Jim held up one hand. "I'm getting to the point. You need the backstory." He waved the hand. "And don't even think about sighing at me. You should have gotten more sleep last night."

"Okay, that's it." Brian pushed his chair back. "I'm leaving."

Jim folded his arms across his chest. "You want me to go with Kaylen today or not?"

"Fine." Brian pulled his chair back to the table. "But get on with it. I've got a morning meeting."

"Since Cassandra and her cameraman were close, she got diverted from the opening of a new bridal shop to covering that multiple homicide." Jim held up his hand again, forestalling any further interruptions. "She was still a mite shaken-up telling me what she'd seen when she got there, but then she got excited about the witness she'd found and forgot all about how disgusted she was seeing blood everywhere. She said some guy in painter's overalls gave her the best sound bites. She was really pleased and anxious to talk to you so she could get your side of things. She saw the interview you gave Mireille Shagassi and thought she could do better, being more empathetic." Jim chuckled softly. "Like that would sway you or make you into a good interview subject. We who know you better would definitely say Ms. Bunting was sadly mistaken."

"You've got that right." Brian poured more coffee. Not bad, he decided as he sipped. Jim must have added an extra spoonful of coffee grounds. Usually, his brew tasted pretty weak. *Coffee the Midwestern way,* he liked to call it. Brian called it dishwater.

"Cassandra said she's been researching both you and your brother in her spare time." Jim took a big sip of his coffee, wrinkled his nose and stirred in more cream. "She told me she's become quite the authority on the pair of you. She wanted me to intervene on her behalf and ask you to agree to letting her interview you on your boat."

"Did you tell her there's no way in hell I would meet with her under any circumstances?"

"I implied it." Jim smiled. "I still like my idea of you going a second round with Mireille after apologizing to her for flying off the handle. You could give her an update on whatever progress has been made. That'd repair some of the damage you inflicted on your reputation, maybe."

"Jim, you're going to have to butt out of this from here on out. I'm not giving any more interviews until the brass tells me what they want me to do, if anything. This is Homicide's case, not mine." Seeing the disappointment on Jim's face, Brian made more of an attempt to eat the eggs rather than push them around his plate. "However," he said between bites, "I did run your suggestion past Hal yesterday, and he's going to have his assistant set that up."

"Do you still want me to go to Baton Rouge?" Jim asked after a few beats of uncomfortable silence. "Or do you want to put that on a back burner while I'm chaperoning Kaylen around town?"

"I don't want to deal with any more unpleasant surprises right now, so hold off on that." Brian's left shoulder gave him a stab and he stretched his arms above his head. It was the first thing that morning that had given him any pleasure, however brief. He realized he hadn't run or gone to the gym all week. *Not a good move.*

"Look, I know something else is really troubling you, buddy," Jim said. "You don't usually snap at me and show your impatience like you're doing this morning. Why won't you tell me what's really going on?"

Brian stopped stretching. "Kaylen told me she saw Sam Wilson in Bennett's Market. Not only saw him, but had a damned *chat* with the bastard."

"I *knew* something was up." Jim slapped the table.

"I don't want to stop you investigating my past, but I can't keep tabs on Kaylen right now and do my job at the same time. I know she'll let you tag along when she goes to Treasure. That'll buy me some time until

I know more about that painter. Hal told me they have his name now. It's Beale Friendly."

"What kind of made-up name is that?" Jim's eyebrows shot up, right along with the tone of his voice.

"It's not, at least according to the info Hal had yesterday. I'll have Gabe do his own research. If there's anything hokey about the guy, I've got more faith in Gabe finding it than anyone else at the department."

"Let me do the background research on him," Jim urged. "That'll keep your name and your department out of everything."

"Uh-uh. I don't want you messin' around anywhere near him. He could be connected to Sam Wilson or the cartel."

Jim blew out softly. "You think that's why he's targeting you?"

"Yeah, I think there's a strong case for that. I'll give you more info as soon as I have it myself. But watch your back with that guy. Don't go trying to interview him yourself if the occasion arises." Brian hoped Jim would listen. "I'd feel okay about you pumping Cassandra Bunting to see if she knows anything more about him, since she's already talked to you and thinks you can sway me into giving her that exclusive," he added, tossing a carrot. "See what she thinks she has on Tim and me, too. Get chummier with her. I know you can do that."

Jim nodded, sharp and decisive. No rumination that time. "I can. Being chummy is one of my specialties. You can count on me, buddy."

A brief wash of relief flowed over Brian, but his instinct for danger was on high alert and the feeling passed almost as soon as it had appeared. He checked his watch. "Nine. We'd better clean up before we leave. I've gotta be at the precinct by ten." He piled the empty dishes on top of each other and carried them into the galley.

He still didn't know how much he wanted to involve Jim in Sam Wilson's reappearance. Despite Kaylen's firm assurances that with her firearm and Brian's months of training she felt confident she could handle any future contact with Sam, Brian still had doubts, especially if Wilson still had his cartel contacts. He *must,* Brian reasoned to himself as he dried the dishes Jim washed, for Sam to flagrantly follow Kaylen into a neighborhood market.

"Brian, whenever you start clamming up, it makes me nervous." Jim put the rest of the bacon into a plastic bag and stowed it in the refrigerator. "You're not acting or looking like yourself this morning."

"What are you talking about? I showered and combed my hair." Brian ran a hand over his face. "Crap. I forgot to shave. Why didn't you say something?"

"I wasn't sure if you'd decided to grow your beard back. But now you put your mugs away in the wrong place. That means you're more than a mite worried." He opened a cabinet, took two mugs from a shelf filled with glasses and transferred them to their usual place above the coffee maker.

"Telling me I've got stubble on my chin ten minutes before I need to leave for a meeting isn't helpful, Jim. Helpful would have been telling me the moment you saw me already dressed in a suit."

"Point taken." Jim leaned against the sink and watched Brian take off his jacket. "How's the coffee shop owner doing? Have you heard anything new?"

"No. I checked on him last night before we went to bed. Condition unchanged. He hasn't regained consciousness since the surgery, but at least his condition's been upgraded to stable." Brian pulled his tie over his head and unbuttoned his shirt. "It still doesn't look good, Jim. And he's the only witness left now that kid's been found dead."

"For which the homicide squad has you to thank." Jim took the dishtowel from his shoulder and hung it up to dry. "Nice piece of detective work, Sergeant Swift."

Brian shrugged off the compliment. "Nothing anyone else in the squad couldn't have done. Dumb luck I saw that guy pushing the shopping cart and stopped to interview him. Common sense led me along the route to that storage facility." He draped his shirt over a dining chair to keep it from creasing.

Jim shook his head. "Luck has nothing to do with it in my book. You followed up where others didn't."

Brian felt Jim's old skills had sharpened over the last year. He was in full investigative mode. "Yeah. You're right. I thought that myself. Trehorn's squad didn't do enough."

"Why doesn't Kaylen hire a bodyguard until Wilson's apprehended?" Jim asked. "If she won't agree to one full-time, I can pick up the slack.

That way I can work on Cassandra Bunting and keep researching your background."

"Kaylen wasn't at all receptive last night to me suggesting a bodyguard."

"But you think she's going to agree to me trailing around behind her, thinly disguised as a consultant on her decorating project with Treasure?" Jim took Brian's jacket from the arm of the couch and draped it over another dining chair. "Don't you think she'll smell a rat?"

"She might, but I'm hoping she'll think you're bored and wanting a diversion. Keep a low-profile as far as your surveillance is concerned, and don't tell her I asked you to do it under any circumstances, or she'll get mad with me."

"How gullible do you think I am?" asked Kaylen.

Brian's heart sank. She was standing right behind them, midway between the galley and one partially-open door to the cabin. Her hair hung over one eye, and she was wearing his terry-cloth bathrobe instead of her own, which was lace and much more transparent. She pushed the hair off her face and gave him a very direct stare. Brian knew by the tight set of her mouth that she'd been listening for more than the time it had taken to get out of bed and put on his bathrobe.

"Coffee?" Jim asked, brandishing the pot.

"Definitely." Kaylen walked over and perched on a barstool.

Jim nuked coffee while Brian got her cream out of the refrigerator and slid it across the breakfast bar.

"Thank you," she said to both of them as Jim placed the mug in front of her. "Now, why are you two trying to hatch a scheme without including me in your plans?"

"Insurance," Brian said.

"I already told you I don't need a bodyguard to manage Sam. I'll shoot him if he threatens me in any way."

"Easy to say when you're not faced with that situation." Brian had doubts she could actually do it. She had told him how much she'd hated going hunting with her father, and that was to put food on the table. Even though she now thought Sam was vermin, she hadn't put a hole in him when she'd had the opportunity.

"I'm sure you're speaking from experience." Kaylen tipped cream into her mug with a steady hand. "But after I stupidly let him escape, I made my decision. It's not going to happen again. I hesitated, not because I couldn't do it, but because I know how much you want to catch Tim's killers and we were so close, I might have killed him."

Jim passed her a spoon, and she briskly stirred her coffee without making eye contact.

"I do want to get the truth out of him, but not at the expense of your safety," Brian told her.

"I'll be fine," she assured him, her gaze as steady as her hand when she lifted the coffee mug to her lips.

"Hon, if you *do* shoot him during a confrontation, you're either going to kill him and end up in court, if not in prison, or you'll wound him and he'll sue you. For sure that'll damage your reputation. People love victims, not aggressors. Your backers could pull out, and you'd end up losing your business."

"I've thought about that." Kaylen carefully placed her mug on a coaster, as though she needed time to weigh her words. "You won't like hearing this, but I discussed my options with my attorney before I told you what had happened, and I talked to Angela and Jonathan, too. Jonathan said anything I need, it's mine, and that includes legal fees. I admit I was really shaken up after seeing Sam, which is why I called Angela before I talked to you. I needed to be calmer when I told you what had happened, so you wouldn't worry so much about me. You've got enough to deal with at work right now."

"And that's where I come in," Jim said. "I'm always here for both of you. You're like family to me. Kaylen, I couldn't live with myself if I knew I was hanging out on my boat while you were in danger. Let me spend my days with you until Wilson's apprehended. I promise you won't even know I'm there half the time."

She shook her head. "No way. I couldn't possibly ignore you if you were by my side all day. You'd get really bored, and it's a waste of your time." She reached across the breakfast bar and squeezed Jim's hand. "I'm rarely alone. I'm surrounded with staff at the club, there's the construction crew and decorators at Treasure. When I'm not working, most of the time I'm with Brian or home in my condo with security keeping an eye on me. The complex has very restricted access. I'm going to be fine."

"No, you are *not*." Brian ran a hand across the stubble on his chin, decided he had no time left to shave and grabbed his shirt. "Look, if Sam's back in Miami, the cartel has probably regrouped. He chose to confront you in a public place, where he figured you probably wouldn't call nine-one-one. He knows you better than anyone else, even me." He pulled on his shirt and quickly buttoned it before pushing it inside his pants.

Kaylen watched, her brow furrowed. "I've been asking myself why I didn't call the cops as soon as I saw him," she said. "I was startled, but I didn't freeze. I got out my phone, but I didn't use it. The only answer I can come up with is curiosity. I wanted to see how he was going to act toward me. Maybe find out what he was after."

"And did you learn anything? Get any insight? No, I don't think you did unless you've been holding back that information from me, too."

"I didn't, and I'm not withholding anything else, I promise." She toyed with her coffee mug, as though she needed a moment to regroup and perhaps avoid eye contact. "You're right, of course." She shrugged. "It was idiotic. The whole thing with Sam. I should have called you immediately. A nine-one-one operator would have needed too much explanation. You'd have cut right through that and sent a patrol car if you weren't close enough yourself." She placed both elbows on the bar and cradled her face in her hands. "He might have been caught right then."

"He might. At least we could have tried to apprehend him instead of him walking away and disappearing again."

"The thing is…" Kaylen hesitated, as though trying to find the right words of explanation. "…I knew he would never do anything to me himself…he's too cowardly. I think that's what gave me the courage to tell him to leave us alone. I actually threatened him." She half-smiled. "He made me really angry."

"Good for you," Jim said. "So he said nothing about the cartel?"

"No, he didn't." She grimaced. "I heard you saying Brian didn't sleep enough last night. I didn't, either. I couldn't stop wondering why he confronted me in that market, and I came to the conclusion his main goal was to remind me, while convincing himself, that he's still in charge of me." She toyed with the mug again, her eyes downcast. "And he managed to do that, didn't he? He called my bluff. I left the gun in my purse, and I let him get away."

Jim cleared his throat. Brian tightened his tie and shrugged back into his jacket. Kaylen dabbed her eyes with a napkin from the holder on the bar.

"So, he didn't tell you why he came back to Miami?" Jim asked.

Kaylen tossed her head. Her hair shimmered in the sunlight. Brian wanted to take her in his arms and tell her everything was going to be all right, but he had doubts. Nagging ones that had kept him awake half the night.

"He said he missed it here." She looked at Jim on the other side of the breakfast bar and gave a slight, derisive snort. "I don't know if I totally believe that, but it *is* home to him. *I* wouldn't come back somewhere I'd made a complete mess of my life, but I certainly can't speak for him. I realized toward the end of our friendship that I knew him so much less than I'd believed before Tim disappeared. So perhaps I'm completely wrong, and the only contacts he has left here *are* cartel members?" She turned to look at Brian.

He shrugged, feeling helpless and not liking it. "Your guess is as good as mine right now. Maybe the cartel offered him something he couldn't turn down, or they're holding something over his head."

"He could have run out of money, and they offered him more to come back," Jim said.

"Yeah." Brian nodded slowly as he thought about the possible reasons for Sam Wilson risking incarceration by returning where there was a warrant out for his arrest. "But not just money. Something else. Something bigger. He once wanted Kaylen's business."

"Which he knows isn't an option for him. The downfall of my business surely wouldn't be enough of a carrot, either," Kaylen said. "He wants to hurt me because I won't have him, either as a business partner *or* a suitor." She shivered and wrapped her arms around herself. "Ugh, the thought of that makes me ill."

"Trying to kill me didn't work out so well the last time, either," Brian said. "And they would have learned from that. So now they're back to ruining my career."

"I don't think they're going to let me off the hook, either, do you?" Kaylen asked. "How best could Sam hurt me? Taking away my belief in you and taking away my backers." She pressed the toes of one foot against the floor and pushed, moving the barstool back and forth as she deliberated. It squeaked.

"I'll have to fix that," Jim said. "I'll lube it."

"The Crossfields would never leave you high and dry," Brian said, thinking of the sex tape and how little that would affect Kaylen's relationship with her biggest backers, even if George Bannister Roberts' friends pulled out. "Wilson would know that."

Kaylen pulled the belt of the bathrobe tighter and shivered. "Surely… you can't think…"

"Jonathan runs a huge, lucrative import and export business."

"Yes." She nodded.

"Maybe Sam's goal would be to ruin you financially, but the cartel could have other plans. They can tell him anything he wants to hear and use him, and then you, to worm their way into Jonathan's business. Take a cut or run their drugs."

The color drained from Kaylen's face. "Angela and Jonathan could be in danger." She grabbed her purse and opened it, pulling out her phone. "I've got to warn them."

Brian stilled her with a hand on her arm. "Not so fast. No need to alarm them without good cause. What we're discussin,' it's all conjecture. We need way more evidence."

"And how do you suggest we do that?" Kaylen wasn't avoiding eye contact anymore. "I'll have to meet him again, won't I? And we'll have to get everything on tape."

"You've been watching too many cop shows on TV," Brian admonished. "But it may have to come to that." He looked down at his hand, still curled around her arm, and saw his watch. "Dammit, I've got to get out of here or I'll be late for my meeting. Look, both of you, don't get to talkin' about any of this today. I want you both to swear you'll stay together and do nothin' but take care of business at Treasure. I'll talk all of this over with Hal. Get more input before handing the information over to anyone else."

"You couldn't work the case yourself?" Jim sounded shocked. "Who better than you to take care of Kaylen and the Crossfields. Me, too, if it comes to that?"

"No one, Jim. All three of us know that. But remember, this is all fall-out from Tim's case. Jack Mills transferred to Cold Case; he didn't retire. Tim's murder is still an active homicide case, and any threats against Kaylen or her business or her backers could become part of that. And if I want to pursue Sam Wilson, I'll have to be real careful. Everyone in the precinct knows I'm too close to this case. My bias could taint any investigation, and when we do apprehend Sam, which I promise you we will, I don't want my personal involvement to jeopardize a conviction. Conspiracy to commit murder carries a really long sentence, and I want Wilson to serve every day of that time until he dies in prison."

Kaylen turned Brian's wrist to better see the time. "You're not the only one who has to leave. I've got a noon meeting at Treasure, and I need to shower and get dressed in something other than the cocktail dress I came here in last night."

"You can do that here," Brian told her. "No need to go back to your condo. You've got a couple of outfits hanging in my closet."

"Capris and tank tops." Kaylen stood up. "Too casual. I have to wear a business suit." She smiled. "I appreciate you hanging onto my clothes, though. Makes me feel more at home."

"How about I drive us to the meeting?" Jim said. "I can drop you at your condo, then pick you back up in say, an hour? I've got a couple of errands to run while you're getting ready."

"Is that your way of telling me I'm not going to be alone today?" She smiled, maybe to reassure both of them she wasn't going to be difficult about being chaperoned.

"Yes. Not so subtle, huh?" Jim took her mug to the sink. "Brian, you can go to work and not worry about her."

"I'm not gonna stop worryin' 'til Wilson's in custody. No more meetings with him under any circumstances, Kaylen. I want your promise on that."

"You have it." She held up her hand. "I swear. Enough foolishness on my part. I'm sorry; I didn't think about the consequences of my actions until it was too late."

"I should take your firearm away," Brian told her. "Then you wouldn't have a false sense of security. Even though we'd discussed what you should do if he confronted you, when that time came, you threw out my play-book and followed your own."

"I'm not going to do that again."

They locked gazes. She had taken a really bad misstep, and he wasn't going to tell her everything was okay. She mustn't throw his careful schooling out the window the next time she came face-to-face with Sam Wilson.

"Ahem," Jim interrupted. "I've got to pick up a couple of things from the *Folly*. Meet you in the parking lot in five minutes, Kaylen?"

"Sounds good." She slid off the barstool and placed both hands on Brian's chest. "I need to make sure I'm forgiven before Brian leaves."

Jim looked at both of them, colored up and left.

"I know how much you hate it when I don't follow your orders," she told Brian after Jim closed the salon door behind him. "Probably about as much as Hal does when you don't follow his."

If only she'd called him from the market, Brian thought. He might have apprehended Wilson, solved Tim's case and saved his own career already. But none of that had happened, and he had to set up another meeting with Hal to tell him how Kaylen had let Sam Wilson escape and see how they were going to handle baiting a trap for Wilson. They'd have to get him to meet her again, placing her in potential danger while they tried to find out what that piece of shit was up to now.

Kaylen's cheek nestled next to his. "I love you," she said. "I promise I won't take any more stupid chances, and I'll do my best not to shoot Sam if I see him again. Is that enough?"

"For now," he said.

CHAPTER SIXTEEN

JIM TOOK a leisurely tour of Treasure while Kaylen held another planning meeting with the architect, the contractor and her interior designer. A meeting she knew they all hoped was the last. She watched Jim periodically stop to look up, down and around while the architect reassured her enough changes had been made to accommodate any number of physically-challenged individuals in any area of the restaurant, bathrooms, and even the kitchen, since one wheelchair-bound chef had applied for a position and appeared to be more than qualified to meet Kaylen's criteria for a master baker and pastry chef.

Also addressed was the newly-hired head bartender's complaints about the narrow prep area that wouldn't comfortably accommodate him even without the two others hired to prepare less-exotic beverages. The bar area had been both widened and extended without losing table space or obstructing the all-important wait-staff flow.

Kaylen's own concern that the entrance was too narrow and dark to be welcoming had been rectified with brighter lights, a more neutral paint color and repositioning the scalloped draperies her patrons would pass beneath as they entered the foyer.

Poppy, the interior designer, had now made enough changes to her original designs, she assured Kaylen, to fully convey the vision of her client's concept without graduating from spectacular to gaudy and overly-pretentious.

Kaylen wasn't sure how she felt about that summary, but wasn't about to dispute it. She swore she almost heard a collective sigh of relief when she told all the team members that she felt she had achieved what she had set out to do, which was to open a club far different from Bannisters in appearance and theme.

The flamboyance and lushness of the new club's decor resembled a scene from *The Arabian Nights.* Everything sparkled, winked or glittered. Huge scallops of rainbow-hued fabrics hung from a breathtakingly-high domed gilt ceiling, whose weight was supported by soaring rococo columns and archways topped by gold leaf. White tables with gold chairs, glittering gold chargers holding turquoise dishes. Gold flatware in a baroque pattern, one of the compromises between Kaylen's wish for the ornate and the designer's desire to guide her client toward the lighter rococo period for the lynchpin of Kaylen's decor. Brian had told her she'd gone overboard with the design. Kaylen wondered what Jim would think of it.

"Well," he said when the meeting was over and he stood with Kaylen in the middle of her new venture. "I'd say if you were aiming for jaw-dropping, you achieved your goal and then some."

"Definitely what I'm aiming for." Kaylen felt a glow of satisfaction. "Brian thinks I should have gone with a theme that complemented the cuisine, which is exactly what I didn't want. No comparisons with Bannisters."

"Then you've succeeded. I heard you with those three over-burdened souls." Jim tut-tutted. "If I was the architect, I'd have quit long before now. The contractor, probably. The decorator, not so much. She acts like she's used to demanding clients."

"She is." Kaylen had to smile. "Poppy Fields has been in business for close to twenty years. She's transformed any number of spaces into hot tickets."

"Her name is *what?* Surely that's not her real name?" Jim's eyebrows had shot up.

"It really is." Kaylen had to laugh at his incredulity. "She told me her parents thought it was cute and catchy. She adored it from the moment she knew it was hers. Me, I couldn't even imagine going through school with that name. I used to get enough teasing about my corkscrew curls. I'd come home crying, and my dad would threaten to shear me like a sheep. That would shut me up. Even now I'm not so sure he wouldn't have done it."

"From what you've shared with me, your dad's a hard man." Jim picked up one of the gold forks from a place-setting on the table next to him and rolled it between his fingers. "What does he think of Brian?"

Kaylen watched Jim's steady gaze rise from the flatware to meet hers. She thought he was trying a little too hard to appear casual about prying. Jim's usual pattern...sidle up and chattily probe into your private life and thoughts. Like Chief Hal Shaw, she thought, remembering how he had blindsided her right out of the blue the first time he had her driving him to the precinct in her car. He'd asked her how she came to meet Brian, and she'd told him a lie while sweating profusely.

She moved around to the opposite side of the table and readjusted a slightly-askew napkin. "I haven't told him much."

That was the truth, so no need to start sweating.

Her father had called her husband, George, "The old man." Right before her wedding, which Preston Grant had refused to attend. He'd shown little sympathy when she'd broken down while informing him of George's death from cancer. She wasn't about to invite more abuse from her father during one of their infrequent phone calls by telling him she was now in a relationship with her murdered boyfriend's half-brother.

"Why ever not, honey?" Jim sounded shocked. "What are you going to tell your dad when Brian finally gets around to popping the question and you accept? I'm not doing double duty giving you away while being best man."

Kaylen thought Jim was being a bit presumptive, but she also struggled to explain why she was so reluctant to tell her father about Brian. She didn't want Jim to think she was hiding her relationship with Brian because she had inner doubts, but she wasn't ready to lay herself bare to yet more verbal abuse from rural Maine, either.

"I don't want to hear any more snide, hurtful comments from my father, Jim," she told him as she fiddled with the flower arrangement in the center of the table; a single mauve freesia with whisper-soft fern fronds.

Was it too little? Too much?

She glanced around the room, doubt filling her about so many aspects of her life.

"Why would you think his first response would be negative?" Jim followed her as she moved to readjust another place-setting two tables away. "He doesn't like the police?"

"My father doesn't like anyone," Kaylen said. "Although I think sometimes he might actually like Brian." She managed a half-smile at the thought of her father trying to get the best of Brian in an argument. "The actual reason I'm so reluctant is because I've heard more than enough negativity from my father over the years." She shuddered involuntarily. "He's such a difficult man. He barely talks, but then when he does, I frequently wish he hadn't. He doesn't know the meaning of tact or consider anyone's feelings before he gives his unbiased opinion. He always scolds me or belittles me, whatever I do. Nothing's ever good enough." She felt tears swimming into her eyes and quickly blinked them away.

"So, since you get no praise for being a successful businesswoman in your own right, you're withholding what should be joyful news to share with your father because you think he's going to make you feel bad about yourself and your relationship with Brian?"

"Exactly."

Kaylen's inner doubts surged to the surface. Suddenly, everything in the restaurant seemed wrong...the décor, the lighting, the very building and location. She should have been content with Bannisters' success, not try to get out from under George's influence and make her own path, she told herself. She wanted to sweep everything from the table onto the floor and start afresh.

"This club's perfect. You don't need to rearrange or touch anything." Jim's gentle voice pierced Kaylen's uncertainty.

She saw concern written plainly on his face, and with great effort, fought to shake off her doubts. She and her backers had sunk too much money into the restaurant for her to consider failure before the doors even opened.

"You need lunch, huh?" She plastered a smile onto her face.

"It certainly wouldn't hurt." Jim smiled back, but the smile didn't reach his eyes.

Kaylen's phone rang. She glanced at the screen, didn't recognize the caller ID and let it go to voicemail. As they passed a couple of painters touching up nicks and scratches made by the latest round of structural changes and walked out to Jim's Sportage, Kaylen's attention was drawn by the length of time it took for a ping to announce a message had been sent.

"You sure you don't want to find out who that was?" Jim asked as they settled into his SUV. "Might be something important."

"I suppose." Kaylen drew her phone out of her purse. "Where do you want to eat?"

Jim shrugged. "I dunno. What's good around here?" He carefully backed the Sportage from of its parking space, watching out for the jumble of assorted construction vehicles circling his SUV. "I never come to this part of town. Too upscale for my budget." He chuckled. "Is this meal going on my expense account, so Brian picks up the tab?"

"No, my treat today. You're driving us around, using your gas." She pointed to the right as the vehicle coasted to a stop at the parking lot's exit. "There's a bistro a couple of miles down the road. Their menu has a couple of Midwestern favorites, so I've been told by the concierge in my building. His wife works in this neighborhood and highly recommended it when I mentioned I was scouting locations for my new club. That may mean macaroni and cheese, meatloaf or," she shuddered at the thought, "tuna casserole."

"All good choices." Jim rubbed his hands together before pulling into traffic. "Brian must have told you I don't like spicy food. Where I grew up, meals were plain and filling. Nothing with hot peppers or stuff like that."

Kaylen gave him directions to the bistro before retrieving her message.

"Hello, K.T.," said Sam's voice. "I've got something you've just got to see and hear."

Kaylen saw herself, skirt hiked up around her waist, head thrown back and exposed breasts in Brian's face as they made love on the couch in her office. The audio was low but graphic.

Barely able to breathe, she closed the message. Another text had arrived. MORE TO FOLLOW, it said. Kaylen felt lightheaded. She managed to hit the power button for the window. Got it down. Hung her head out and tried to draw in air.

She heard Jim's voice far away, asking her if she was okay. His words were almost unintelligible through the ringing in her ears, the heavy beating in her chest and the rushing air whipping through her hair.

The Sportage bumped a curb and came to an abrupt stop. Jim got out. Moments later, Kaylen felt someone open the door. She almost fell out. Jim's gentle hands prevented her fall. He guided her back and lowered the seat while her head continued to swim.

A crowd gathered. Clamoring voices, some asking if they needed to call an ambulance. Jim soothed her; soothed them. Said she'd been to hot yoga and got overheated.

Kaylen protested she was okay, even while her voice trembled and betrayed her. Someone brought water and a damp towel from a karate studio a few doors away.

Kaylen wished she *had* passed out. Oblivion would have been a blessing. The sparring with Sam was over, and she might have caused that by threatening him in the supermarket. He had declared war on her. Not just on her, she thought. On them...the two of them.

Her reputation would be ruined, her business would be in shreds, and her backers, including her dearest friends, the Crossfields would lose all their investment. Hot tears cascaded down her cheeks. She didn't even want to think what could happen to Brian's future with Miami-Dade Police Department. That made the whirling in her head spin faster.

"I have to go home," she told Jim after she had allowed him to dab her with the towel. To prove she wasn't going to pass out, she swallowed a few sips of water, which threatened to choke her. She grabbed the towel, held it to her face and managed to spit the water into it without alarming him by coughing.

"She's probably pregnant," said a woman in the dwindling group still lingering.

That comment brought out a number of cell phones, which pointed

Kaylen's way and took photos that would no doubt end up on social media within minutes.

"I'm definitely *not* pregnant," Kaylen said. She sat up straighter.

Not that. No way. That's all she'd need.

Brian, too, she told herself. But they'd been so careful, and she hadn't forgotten to take any of her birth control pills, so she was pretty sure she was telling the truth.

"You've seen enough," Jim told the gawkers. "Leave her alone. She's *not* pregnant. I told you…she's overheated."

"I'm fine now," Kaylen said to no one in particular, hoping she'd included the entire group as she took a quick look at the curious faces. "He's right. I felt faint. It passed. Thank you to whoever brought the towel and the water. They were a great help."

Jim slowly brought the seat upright. He made sure the towel was dampened again and wrapped around the back of her neck and the bottle of water was in the cup holder beside her before he closed her door and got back behind the wheel.

"You're sure you're okay?" he asked after he maneuvered the Sportage back into traffic. "Was that woman right?"

"No, Jim; she wasn't. I'm not pregnant, at least as far as I know. The voicemail and texts were from Sam. They're too awful to share with you.."

"You can share anything with me," Jim said. "Anything, honey. You should know that."

"Not these. They're blackmail material. Really dreadful."

Jim's hands tightened on the steering wheel. His knuckles turned white.

Kaylen relented. He could be dreaming up even worse scenarios than the reality. "He has video taken during one of our most private moments," she said. "I've got to talk to Brian as soon as possible, but alone." She wiped her hot face with the end of the towel.

"I'll call," Jim said. "Make sure he's still at the precinct, then take you."

Jim had the Cold Case office number programmed into his car's system. Gabe answered the phone and said Brian was in a meeting with

Jack. He promised to interrupt them and tell Brian that Kaylen was on her way in to see him. Did she want to add to that message?

"No," Kaylen said. "Just tell him it's very, very urgent."

She tried to sip the water as she stared through the windshield, the road and the traffic ahead mere blurs while she tried to quiet the panic that threatened to engulf her.

CHAPTER SEVENTEEN

KAYLEN FELT the warmth of the afternoon sun on her left shoulder as she worked to regain her composure after Brian and Chief Shaw had both seen and listened to the messages Sam Wilson had left on her phone. Telling herself that only the two people in the room with her had seen the video did little to tamp down her anxiety. A desire to hyperventilate all over again made her open the bottle of water Alicia had placed on the desk for her and take a small sip.

Brian had gone to lean against a window-sill with his arms crossed. "Well, look at it this way," he said. "At least we don't have to wait any longer for that tape to surface."

"Can't you think of something more encouraging?" Kaylen ran one hand up and down the ribbed surface of the bottle. She wondered whether Chief Shaw was picturing them as he'd seen them in the video at that moment, and hoped his professionalism could see past that image.

"I wish you'd come to me as soon as you discovered there was a tape in the first place." Hal's glower radiated from one of them to the other.

"What good would that have done?" Brian unfolded his arms, placed both hands behind him on the window-sill and leaned forward, his steady gaze meeting Hal's. "Word of it would have gotten out somehow, and the entire precinct would know. You think I'd be able to do my job with that

142

piece of gossip circulating?" He nodded toward Kaylen. "And what about *her*? This surfaces weeks before her new club opens? You *know* this can't be a coincidence, Chief."

Kaylen didn't like being called *her*, but interrupting to point that out seemed ill-advised at that moment.

Hal leaned back in his chair. "Of course it isn't a coincidence. Wilson started planning this long before he returned to Miami. The man wants to retaliate. He lost his business, his house, and from what you've both told me, his dream of being with Kaylen. He's going to use whatever methods and connections he still has to put an end to your career, Brian, and your business, Kaylen. If he's completely successful, he'll even have you two pitted against each other instead of working as a team."

Hal grabbed his pen and started tapping it at high speed against the legal pad in front of him, the lined yellow page covered with concise notes in neat handwriting Kaylen wished she could read. But despite a knack for reading upside down and backwards, a trick that had given her numerous opportunities to gain insights or advantages during meetings with any number of people over the years, the small script coupled with the sheer depth of Hal Shaw's massive mahogany desk rendered the writing indecipherable.

"If you'd confided in me immediately, as you should have done as a member of this department..."

Hal paused to deliver a look toward Brian that Kaylen was very glad he hadn't directed at her.

"...maybe we could have figured out a better way of handling things." Hal put down the pen and folded his hands on top of the pad. He shook his head slightly. "I know why you thought you should keep this tape secret from everyone else, Swift, but from me? Who the hell do you think I was going to snitch to...the commissioner? The *mayor?*"

"No, of course not. I wasn't thinking straight. I'm sorry." Brian sat next to Kaylen and took her hand. "Look, can we move on? What do you want to me to do...resign?"

Kaylen knew her gasp was audible when both men glanced her way before returning to stare impassively at each other. The air filled with an undercurrent that made her want to jump out of her skin.

"If you think rumors would fly from talk about a sex tape, how do you think staff would react if you quit?" Hal's voice was low and icy. "They'd believe I forced you out over something that wasn't your fault. Are you trying to put the blame for your mistakes onto me?"

Kaylen felt Brian's grip tighten. She'd come to the meeting hoping Hal Shaw had a remedy that didn't involve Brian sacrificing his career over fifteen minutes of spontaneous sex with his girlfriend. That hope was leaving fast. She looked down at their clasped hands.

Miserably, she decided Chief Shaw's opinion of her had definitely tanked. She wondered whether Hal and his wife had ever thrown caution to the wind for a few moments of pleasure. Probably not, she thought, remembering Frances' kind but somewhat uptight ways whenever she participated in or hosted a work-related celebration.

Kaylen knew where Brian was concerned, she had no control. She loved him too much to think clearly, and this potential disaster was the result. George would have advised her to have more care. He had made sure she was protected, insulated. Since his death, she'd been flying solo and making a fine mess of it.

She wasn't going to cry, she told herself, biting her lip as tears flooded her eyes. It was an old trick, but it still worked. The tears stopped flowing as she tightened her jaw and the pain in her lower lip increased. Not for the first time in her life, Kaylen was glad she'd had plenty of practice keeping her feelings to herself during confrontations with her father.

Brian, always hyper-intuitive to even subtle changes in her reactions, shifted his attention to her. "Are you okay, hon?" he asked.

"No," said. "Of course I'm not okay. This is horrible."

"You had every right to expect privacy in Kaylen's office," Hal said, his voice gentler than it had been since their meeting started. "You're two consulting adults, for Christ's sake. My first reaction was to tell you to ride it out."

Kaylen saw genuine concern on Hal's face. She opened her purse, dug around inside and brought out a small packet of tissues. Reluctantly disengaging her hand from Brian's, she pulled out a tissue, dabbed the corners of her eyes and discreetly, she hoped, blew her nose, instead of trumpeting like Louis Armstrong, as Brian had once laughingly told her she usually did.

"It takes a lot to shock the average person," Hal continued in the mild tone he usually seemed to reserve for statements to the media. "Most celebrities, even local ones, aren't held to the high moral standard they once were." He focused his attention on Brian. "I don't recall any significant waves when Kaylen became involved with you right after your brother's death. In fact, you've both told me Kaylen's business profited from the notoriety, not that either of you would have wanted that, of course."

Kaylen wasn't sure whether she should protest or keep her mouth closed. The discussion seemed to be shifting into personal areas she would much rather remain off-limits.

"But what about the reporters and those interviews?" she blurted, scrambling to redirect the conversation. "I...I saw all the footage from the coffee shop." She glanced at Brian and saw the rigid set of his jaw. "I'm sure Brian did, too," she added quickly, while calling herself all kinds of a fool. He might still be seated next to her, but he had traveled miles away emotionally. She felt the chill and shivered.

"Yeah, I saw every piece of it. Thanks for reminding us of that, Kaylen." Brian got up and started pacing. "I lost my temper, which I'd been able to control for well over a year."

"Mireille Shagassi's a seasoned reporter," Hal said. "Although she's never interviewed you before, I'm sure she's been studying you for a while. After all, she's been covering the police beat for years."

"Yeah," Brian muttered, his voice low and angry. "She knew every goddamned button to push."

"Which is more problematic for the department than your other shortcomings," Hal said. "Not necessarily the accusations, which could be rebutted, but your lack of control with Shagassi has to be addressed. I'll issue a public statement that says you were under duress at the time, due to post-traumatic stress from your brother's murder."

Brian stopped pacing. He moved in close to Shaw's desk. "That makes me sound like a basket case who can't cope and needs to end my career," he protested.

"There's no other excuse for your behavior." Hal leaned back in his chair and folded his arms, his body language unmistakable. Brian was going to have to accept that explanation.

"Screw you, bastard," Brian said. "Trehorn's fuckin' incompetent, an' I'm not gonna sit back while both of you piss all over me."

Kaylen's dismay turned into shock. Hal Shaw had always been Brian's champion. But now he was hanging his detective out to dry, and Brian was responding as he always did when pushed into a corner... fighting back.

Hal's fist pounded the desk top. "That's *enough*."

Kaylen knew she'd jumped, and she was pretty sure Brian had, too.

Hal's gaze locked with Brian's. "What the hell were you thinking, shouting at a reporter?" He shook his head slowly. "There have to be repercussions for your behavior at that crime scene, and for your gross insubordination at this meeting."

Kaylen's mind whirled. Surely Hal wasn't going to put Brian on suspension again? After all the months he'd spent recovering from an injury that had almost ended his career? She looked again at the chief's face and saw no empathy. Her stomach flipped, nauseatingly. She staggered to her feet. Her ankles threatened to twist. She was still wearing the three-inch Luis Vuitton heels she'd worn for her meeting at Treasure.

"Are you ready for me to leave?" she managed, her voice as unsteady as her legs.

"Yes."

Hal and Brian had spoken almost in unison. Neither of them even glanced her way as she pulled the strap of her Gucci purse over her shoulder and side-stepped away from the chair. They were glaring at each other with open hostility.

Kaylen made an awkward and undignified rush for the door. It felt like she was crossing a 50-foot chasm instead of a thick Aubusson rug. Stepping into the outer office, she saw Alicia's fingers flying over her keyboard. Hal's assistant didn't even look up. No doubt, she'd heard the shouting, Kaylen thought. Whether Alicia had heard the words was another story, but not one that would be told around the precinct, Kaylen felt sure.

Unable to stop herself before she closed the door, she took a quick look at Brian to find him watching her.

"I'll call you later," he said. He gave her brief, very contained smile.

"Call Jim," he told her. "He can pick you up at the motor pool. Alicia will get you there."

"Okay." She nodded. "Thank you, Chief," she added before closing the door.

She longed to lean against the wall for a moment, but she had to get out of that building. Belatedly, she realized she was clutching her purse to her chest like a shield. When she dropped her arm to her side, the purse bumped heavily against her hip, like she had a brick inside. She had forgotten to check her gun before going into Chief Shaw's office, but no one had asked whether she was armed. The tension must have been rippling through the chief's inner sanctum even before their arrival.

After relaying Brian's instructions about the motor pool, Kaylen called Jim. Alicia gave them both directions to their rendezvous and escorted Kaylen to a nearby restroom, where she dabbed her face with a damp paper towel and tried to repair her makeup. She ran a pick through her hair, tugging unmercifully at snarls and tangles she'd gotten from riding in Jim's car with her head hanging out the window.

Thankfully finding the elevator empty, she stepped into it and leaned against its side, welcoming the faint vibration as it descended. When the doors swished open, no one took any notice of her. She tried to look casual and unhurried as she walked to the designated spot for her pick-up. Thankfully, Jim arrived shortly after she did.

"You must have been parked close by," Kaylen told him as she climbed into the passenger's seat.

"I went for coffee and then circled until I found a spot to wait." The Sportage continued idling at the curb. "What's wrong, honey? You look awful."

"And this is *after* I tried to tidy myself up. Jim, you didn't even tell me I looked terrible when you dropped me off." She heard non-committal noises from Jim as she placed her purse on the floor by her feet and fastened her seatbelt.

"How was the meeting?" he asked as he pulled away from the motor pool.

Stoic Midwesterner to the end, Kaylen thought. Jim would never bad-mouth a friend, even if it was in that friend's best interest.

"I'll give you all the sordid details after you take me to a bar," she said. "I've got to have a drink."

"That bad, huh?"

"Worse."

"All right; we'll find one."

"Not too close to here. I don't want to go anywhere cops frequent. We mustn't go where I could be recognized, either. I don't want to my unkempt appearance plastered all over social media."

"I know of a good place." Jim nodded. "It's on the way to the marina. Dark and secluded, and they've got booths."

Kaylen felt too tattered inside to even appear interested in where he was taking her or ask how he knew of a bar that would fit her criteria.

Jim cleared his throat. "I'm taking you somewhere that serves food, too. You need to eat. You haven't had anything except coffee today. That's probably what's ailing you."

"It's not," Kaylen said. "I don't care about food, Jim; I need a drink. I think the shit just hit the fan."

CHAPTER EIGHTEEN

"YOU DARED CALL ME A BASTARD?" Hal Shaw's fingers drummed his desk. "That was way over the top and completely unnecessary, Swift."

"I could've called you a lot worse. She wouldn't believe you'd put me on probation without good cause," Brian said. He couldn't stop pacing. The agitation within him hadn't left with Kaylen.

"Look, it's done. All of it." Hal rubbed his temples. "You're giving me a headache. For Christ's sake, sit down while we review the details again, otherwise you'll be telling me you've gone through all this crap for nothing."

"It's more fuckin' crap than you should have asked me to take." Brian threw himself into one of the chairs in front of Hal's desk. "I made a solemn promise to Kaylen after Tim's death. I vowed I'd never lie to her again, and I haven't. But to make this plan work, I can't tell her what's goin' down, or we may never put Tim's killers behind bars." He leaned forward and planted both elbows on Hal's desk. "I'm not gonna apologize for callin' you a bastard after the shit you've gotten me into with Kaylen," he told Hal, who remained impassive to the confrontational posture. "How will I ever make it up to her? She'll never trust me again. That's if she's even speakin' to me by the end of this."

Hal opened the bottom drawer of his desk and pulled out a bottle of scotch. "Look, I didn't twist your arm or threaten you." He poured two small glasses without asking Brian whether he wanted any and pushed one across the desk. "You agreed to this plan. You know it's the only way we're going to infiltrate that cartel and bring Tim's killers to justice. We'll net Wilson in the process unless the cartel takes care of him first. If there was another choice, I'd have green-lighted it."

"Yeah, yeah. I know all that. Doesn't make me like it."

Hal leaned back in his chair and took a sip of scotch, like he needed a moment. "For this plan to succeed," he said in a calm, measured voice, "everyone, including Kaylen and Jim, has to believe you're under investigation again and those bribery accusations have merit. I know you believe as strongly as I do that the cartel is ultimately behind Wilson's reappearance and threats. He's a coward, as Kaylen said. He wouldn't be this bold unless he believes he's got the support of his cartel buddies. Somehow, somewhere, we've got to connect that painter to the cartel, or at least to Wilson. Too much of a coincidence for him to suddenly rake those bribery accusations back up while Wilson's threatening Kaylen's well-being right before her new club opens."

"Damn it, you know I agree with you. But neither Kaylen nor Jim would say anything. I don't believe she'd betray me even if confronted by a cartel member threatening to cut her nose off. As for Jim, with his background in Naval Intelligence, we both know he'd never give me up."

"I'm sure you're right, but keeping them in the dark makes them a lot safer. What they don't know can't hurt them." Hal gently rocked his chair back and forth.

"But what if it does? What if one or both of them get taken by the cartel and tortured? What comfort will I get from knowing they won't be able to give any relevant information because they both believe I'm back under suspicion?" Brian tossed back the scotch. He didn't think it would help settle his agitation, but it was worth a try.

"You won't." Hal stopped rocking and leaned forward. "But you understand deep down this is the way things have to be. Regardless of whether Kaylen or Jim knows anything, they're still in danger. The Crossfields, too. Don't forget about them."

"I haven't. I've just pushed them onto a back burner while I'm trying to cope with the fall-out from this meeting an' I decide what I'm gonna tell Kaylen and Jim when I get back to the boat."

"You'll still have Mills and Gabe in your corner as well as me," Hal said. "I can't leave you out in the wind alone like the last time that happened. I'll hold a meeting with them. Mills needs to be your point-man here. No one's going to wonder why he's meeting with me while he's settling into his new position as temporary Cold Case supervisor. Gabe's a tech wiz and a squirrely bastard. He'll figure out ways to keep in contact with you, no matter what happens. And I doubt anyone will question why he's turning up at the marina after he took that sabbatical last year to join you up in Tampa." Hal managed a slight smile. "I think he dislikes Trehorn almost as much as you do."

"Using Gabe as a go-between would place him at risk. He told me last year he likes what he does and has no desire to get involved in field work. You're gonna be askin' him to do a lot more than his job description."

Hal twirled the amber liquid around his glass before tossing back his drink in three rapid gulps. Brian waited impatiently, knowing the chief was debating how to proceed with Gabe.

"Is he proficient at the firing range?" Hal put down his glass and leaned back in his chair again, the leather crackling.

"He doesn't even own a gun. Said he has no interest in learning how to use one."

Hal's eyebrows shot up. "Why the hell not? Alicia's a crack shot. She's got trophies."

"Not everyone at Miami-Dade is into guns, Chief." Brian managed to stop himself before he snapped a caustic comment about Alicia believing she was the Annie Oakley of Miami-Dade's administrative branch. "Gabe's a civilian who loves his job," he added instead. "Otherwise, working at a police department would be the last place you'd find him."

"Christ...a pacifist. The last thing we need for this particular operation." Hal ran his fingers up and down the empty scotch glass for a moment, evidently reflecting on the irony of Gabe choosing to work in a police department. "Convince him he's got to learn how to protect himself, even if it's only for this case."

"Chief..."

"No more discussion about this. He has to get over to the firing range. He's not going to be sitting on the sidelines anymore now he's gotten involved with you and your problems, so he may as well get comfortable with carrying."

"Okay…I'll talk to him if you ordering him to do it doesn't work… but these problems aren't exclusively mine." Brian felt the chief had distanced himself from Tim's case for far too long.

"Agreed." Hal nodded decisively. "Which is why those around you need to keep vigilant at all times. Something I really don't need to tell you, but I'm going to stress, anyway. I know you've got plenty of firepower at your disposal, and you're prepared to use it, but you're going to have to convince the rest of your posse to maintain the same level of awareness, otherwise we stand more than a chance of someone getting seriously hurt, or even killed." Hal's fingers left the glass to drum on the desk. "Check in with Alicia before you go," he said after a moment. "Tell her I said she's to make those arrangements for you to be interviewed by Shagassi again and that other reporter, too. The social pages girl who got those inflammatory sound-bites from the painter…what was her name?"

"Cassandra Bunting." Brian thought of the girl's ineptitude and pushiness. He wasn't relishing interviews with either reporter for many reasons, all legitimate, he felt, but he would rather go a couple of rounds with Shagassi than even a short one with Bunting.

Hal gathered up their empty glasses and placed them on top of the cabinet behind his desk. He stowed the almost-empty scotch bottle back in his bottom drawer. Brian wondered who had guzzled the rest of the liquor…Hal by himself, Hal and Alicia, or any number of other troubled police department personnel needing false courage. Hal brought out gum, which they both chewed to get rid of any lingering aromas of scotch while they ran over the facts Brian needed to stick to with Shagassi and the questions he needed to shoot at Bunting.

He assured Hal there would be no more hot-headed episodes and that he wouldn't divulge anything to Kaylen or Jim to ease their fears. The Crossfields were going to have to leave town. He and Hal both agreed the risk they would run by staying was too great. As Kaylen's primary backers, Jonathan's business and both his and Angela's personal safety and their effect on Kaylen's financial health made them prime targets for

Sam's vengeance, as well as any attempt by the cartel to infiltrate and gain a stake in either Jonathan's or Kaylen's business interests.

After leaving Hal and getting Alicia's assurance she'd work immediately on the two media interviews, Brian left the precinct. Aware his stomach was empty, he stopped at a diner. While he waited for his order of meatloaf, mashed potatoes and green beans to arrive, he wondered with a great deal of unease how Kaylen was doing. The expression on her face before the chief's door closed between them had spoken volumes…she was terrified for him. Now he needed to make sure she was terrified for herself. Jim and the Crossfields, too.

He thought back over the last two years and wished they were all back in the relative calm after Sam Wilson had fled the country along with Tim's killers. Then he retracted. That hadn't been a period of calm. It had been a period of total frustration and unrest, both for him and those around him.

No more, Brian vowed as he watched the waitress heading his way with a loaded plate. It was time for a little retribution.

Or a lot.

CHAPTER NINETEEN

"HAL THREATENED TO *FIRE* YOU?" Kaylen, still wearing a navy business suit and white blouse but shoeless, brushed her hair back from her face with an uncharacteristically awkward swipe and stared incredulously at Brian. One side of her suit jacket's collar stood up like a salute. "He placed you on *probation?* Why would he do that after all you went through? What sort of a supervisor *is* he?"

Brian shrugged. "He's a good supervisor. A fair one. He said it was the best thing to do for the department. More bribery accusations hanging over my head, piled onto the image issue from the melt-down during that interview with the reporter. He couldn't ignore any of it. And then I topped everything off by swearing at him. He could have fired me for insubordination, but he didn't. I was out of line."

"You seem to be having more issues with anger management now than you've had for the last year." Kaylen leaned forward and pointed her finger at him. "What's up with you, lately?"

"You swore at Hal and he threatened to fire you?" Jim was seated at the banquette in the *NTK's* salon. "That's not the first time by a long shot you two have had words. Why couldn't he tell you to take time off and cool down? Think things over and apologize? What's wrong with him? He's acting like a...a..."

"A dick," Kaylen said. "Let's tell it like it is."

"That's whatever you had to drink talking for you...both of you," Brian reprimanded. "Jim, I thought you had more sense. What were you thinking?" Brian didn't feel he needed to remind Jim he had gone with Kaylen to protect her.

"She was upset after getting out of that meeting," Jim said. "She told me she needed a drink, and after hearing what had happened, I joined her. You look like you need one yourself. Might help your disposition. Usually, you stand up and fight for yourself. Right now, you're lying down and letting a bunch of hogwash roll right over you."

"And then letting it back up and go right over you again," Kaylen interjected. "It's damn hot in here. Jim, did you turn on the heater or something?" She stood up, rocked slightly and braced her legs against the couch before trying to shrug out of her jacket.

Brian helped her with the second sleeve and tossed the jacket onto the arm of the couch before he helped Kaylen sit back down. "He didn't turn on any heater," he told her. "You've had at least one too many. Maybe more than that."

It had been a long time since he'd seen Kaylen over-indulge. She was always careful not to take chances with her reputation by doing anything like getting tanked-up in a public place. He couldn't believe she'd gotten so upset over the meeting with Hal that she'd resorted to alcohol. And Jim joining her? They had both lost their minds, he decided. And maybe it wasn't such a bad thing for him...he got a sense they both doubted the story he and Hal had concocted, but the alcohol was blunting their reactions.

He looked at Kaylen's flushed face and gave her what he hoped was an indulgent smile because those weren't in his wheelhouse. "You're soused."

"I am *not.*" She pouted, apparently at the thought of something so uncouth.

Brian wasn't about to argue with a drunk Kaylen. He turned his attention back to Jim. "The best Hal will do is review my case if and when I can prove my innocence," he said. "I'm going to have to do all the leg work. Internal Affairs doesn't want to waste any more time and energy, not to mention man-power and funds to investigate new accusations about old claims of bribery." He shook his head when Jim started to interrupt. "If I don't do the work, those claims are gonna stick around. The chief's tired of defending me and doing damage control. Trehorn's pissed at me for meddling in the coffee shop murders, and I've gotten on the wrong side of the press again."

"Most of that wasn't your fault," Jim protested. "But you could have been a mite more tactful with those two reporters."

Kaylen, who had taken a pick out of her purse and was trying to pull it through her hair, got up and joined Jim at the banquette.

Brian walked into the galley. He needed to start a pot of coffee and put some distance between himself and his friends while lying through his teeth.

"Hal said if I talk to any other reporters without clearing it with him first, it's my ass," he said, raising his voice over the sound of running water as he filled the carafe and poured its contents into the coffee maker. "I almost handed over my gun and badge for the second time. Probation was the best he could offer."

Kaylen was going to have his head for this.

He heard nothing but silence from the salon. "I can kiss any pay raises or the promotion I was in line for goodbye unless or until I can prove my innocence," he added.

There. It was done. The lies had all been told.

"So, you're really going to let Sam Wilson and the cartel roll right over you, not to mention that asshole Trehorn?" asked Jack Mills.

Brian saw Jack and Gabe both standing in the salon's doorway.

He didn't need anyone else giving him crap. He held up his hand. "Don't start with me, Jack. I've got enough shit coming at me in this room already. And Gabe, you should know better after the last time you ran up against a department head and had to take a sabbatical."

"I don't *want* to know better." Gabe nodded toward Kaylen and Jim as he headed for the galley. "Hi folks. You know me, I'm on Team Swift. Step aside Boss, I'll make the coffee. You all look like you need some." He pulled a canister of MDPD's coffee out of the gym bag he was carrying. "*Department* coffee," he said without cracking a smile. He left the bag on one of the bar stools before flipping on the light over the stove.

"I already put in the water." Brian left Gabe to it. "Why aren't you two at the office?" he asked.

"Cold Case isn't going anywhere this afternoon," Jack said. "Gabe and I both decided we needed a time-out. Hal didn't object. You could have heard a pin drop when we left that building."

"Don't jeopardize your pension," Brian told Mills. "You can't afford to get linked with me too closely right now. Being a coworker won't put a stink on you, but defending me by closing up shop for the day will raise a red flag." He looked at Gabe. "That goes for you, too."

"Have things like that ever worried me before?" Gabe opened cabinets until he found the mugs. "I can get a job anywhere, Boss." Mugs in hand, he turned around to face Brian. "I *prefer* to work with you."

Brian tried one more time to send Gabe away. "Look, if you insist on hanging around me, you're going to have to become proficient at the firing range and start carrying. Hal told me that, and he's right."

"You're being overly-dramatic." Gabe took cream out of the refrigerator. "I'm just a clerk."

"Who is now on his allegedly-corrupt supervisor's boat in the middle of a workday," Brian pointed out. "Nothing obvious about that, is there?"

"Nothing worth sweating over, unless you make a big deal out of it, Swift." Jack joined Kaylen and Jim at the banquette, looked askance at them and sniffed.

"Kaylen and I had a couple of drinks at lunch," Jim said, looking embarrassed. "We were upset about Brian getting railroaded again."

Mills gave a slight nod, then turned his attention back to Brian. "This is now officially the War Room. We're all here to clear your name and get that f'ing son-of-a-bitch Wilson into custody."

Kaylen's pick dropped onto the table.

"Pardon the language," Mills said.

Kaylen rolled her eyes. "Cops. Why do you all have to swear constantly? Is that something they teach you at the academy?" She grabbed the pick and tugged it through her tangles again.

Mills didn't have a chance to answer her possibly rhetorical question, if he even wanted to try, because Jim's fist hit the table with a lot more force than Kaylen's pick.

"Damn right it's the War Room," Jim said.

"You're all out of your minds," Brian told them. "And two of you have been drinking on top of that."

He couldn't believe the level of support he'd received since Tim's disappearance and death. He couldn't do anything right at that moment but be astonished and humbled.

"How do I even begin to thank you while trying to convince you to change your minds?" he asked.

"You're not about to change any of our minds, so cut out the ass-kissing and give us details." Jack stood back up, took off his jacket, unbuttoned the shirt cuffs and rolled his sleeves up to the elbows. "Gabe, did you bring that laptop for Brian as well as the coffee?"

"I did." Gabe pulled it out of the gym bag. "It slipped off the inventory list," he told Brian. "Oops."

"You could do time for this," Brian cautioned. "It has to go back right now, along with the pair of you."

Gabe waved away Brian's objections. "They'll never miss it until next year at the earliest, when they go around and start inventorying everything. We'll have Tim's case wrapped and you exonerated way before that, Boss. Then you'll be heading up Cold Case again."

Jack Mills nodded. "I felt like I was breathing fresh air for the first time in way too long when I walked out of that place today. There's a stench that's lingered since Hastings died and the Vice squad was investigated. Trehorn came in to finish the shake-up, but he's no peach, either." He cleared his throat. "Enough said. Now, go ahead and bring us up to speed. Exactly what pushed the chief over the edge? You swearing at him would never put you on probation. You're not going to convince me, so don't even try. It's gotta be something bigger."

"Oh, no." Kaylen wrapped her arms around herself as though suddenly chilled. "Brian, you're not going to give them every detail from our meeting with Chief Shaw, are you?" She looked at him. *"Please* tell me that's not happening."

"No, of course not." He wondered how she'd even think he'd do that, but she'd spent a lot of time with cops and had a fair idea of their methods. Brian knew he'd have to establish ground-rules and stick to them if he wanted to keep anything private. "But they *have* to know what Wilson's trying to do and how," he told her. "I'm planning to nail that bastard this time, while I more than scatter that goddamned cartel. I'm gonna make sure they pay for what they did. *Really* pay."

Kaylen abandoned her work with the pick. She locked gazes with Brian, her face pinched, her eyes weary. "I can't see you sending Tim's killers to prison. I know how badly you want revenge for him and for what they did to you." She paused and bit her lip.

Brian waited her out, as did the other three men.

"But I want to tell you right now," Kaylen squared her shoulders, "if you turn into a vigilante because you don't believe anyone but you can give these people what they deserve, I don't know how I'm going to react." She took her gaze from Brian to Jim and Jack Mills, opposite her on the banquette. "That goes for you two, as well." She studied her hands. "I almost lost you once, Brian. I can't do that again."

Brian was taken-aback. He heard Jim harrumph. Gabe suddenly decided to go back and clang mugs in the galley. Jack Mills jumped to his feet. "I'll help you with the coffee, Gabe," he said.

Jim hurriedly struggled out the banquette right behind Mills. "I'll get my own coffee," he said, moving so fast he almost ran into Jack, who wasn't exactly sauntering either.

Brian went to sit with Kaylen. He took her hand in his. It felt cold and slightly clammy. "Hon," he said gently when she kept her head lowered. "My first thought is always to protect you in any way I can. Next on the list is trying to keep myself intact. Revenge comes a distant third. But I'm not gonna sit back while these bastards ruin our lives and use blackmail tactics to stop us retaliating."

Kaylen nodded slowly and raised her head. "Your revenge, our self-preservation and both our reputations…all worth saving from my point of view."

"See, we're on the same page." He raised her hand to his lips.

"Look, I'll go along with your plan as long as it's to put Tim's murderers in prison," she said. "Sending Sam there for the rest of his miserable life would be the worst punishment anyone could give him. Going from owning a restaurant to eating prison food in a dining hall? Wearing a jumpsuit instead of one of his made-to-order white suits? Sleeping on a cot and maybe having a cell-mate who will scare the hell out of him so he's afraid to close his eyes? *That's* what I want to see."

She gave a half-smile before turning toward Gabe, bringing two mugs and a container of cream over to the table. She noticed her raised collar and fixed it back into place. "Thanks, Gabe. I don't need cream. I'd better drink it black," she told him. "I've got to get sober fast."

"Me, too," Jim said. "We both made bad decisions ordering that last round."

"How many damn drinks did you two have, for Christ's sake?" Brian asked, glad to change the direction of the conversation.

"We had two." Jim grimaced. "I had a beer the second round, but hers were both Boilermakers."

Jack Mills looked at Kaylen and shook his head. "I bet you'll be suffering tomorrow," he predicted. He pulled out his cell. "I'm ordering food. Sandwiches. We all need them."

Brian shook his head. "I ate at a diner." He looked at Kaylen. "A full meal. Nothing wrong with my appetite."

"We were *going* to eat," Kaylen said. "Instead, we drank our lunch."

"I'll pick 'em up," Gabe interrupted. "No delivery. We should avoid anyone seeing all of us together, even some kid delivering from a sandwich shop. In case we have snoopers."

"If anyone snoops, all they're going to see is the Cold Case squad eating with the supervisor's girlfriend and his neighbor," Jack said. "Let's try to keep it looking like that."

"I'll go get my deck of cards while we wait for the sandwiches," Jim said. "A round of something harmless like Hearts would throw anyone off the scent." He set his mug on the breakfast bar. "I'll nuke that when I get back."

"I would never play Hearts," Brian said.

"You don't gamble," Jim said. "No good even suggesting a hand of Poker."

"He'll play," Kaylen said. "Won't you Brian? For toothpicks? Jim can bring those over, too." She looked uncertain he'd agree.

Brian hated cards. His step-father had lost far too many hands, leaving the family with debts instead of paychecks when Brian and Tim were kids in Baton Rouge. But they had to look like there was more of a purpose to sitting around the salon in the middle of a workday than drinking coffee.

"Fine." He threw up his hands. "Have it your way, all of you. I've had one helluva day, and a hand of Poker and sandwiches with my friends sounds great. If we do a little sharing and plotting on the side, that'll be okay with me, too. But I want y'all to consider what you're getting yourselves into." He paused to smile at Kaylen. "Maybe not all of you. Hon, you've been my partner before. You know what torture that can be." He felt relief when she returned the smile.

"I think I can speak for the rest of us when I say we're well aware things could go south real quick," Jack said. "Gabe and I already discussed that while you were meeting with the chief. We're in this for the long haul. We both hope it won't end up being some dragged-out mess, but if it is…"

"Bring it on," Gabe said. He lifted his mug. "Cheers, everyone."

"Here's to the end of this nightmare, finally." Kaylen raised her own mug.

"What kind of sandwiches do you all want?" Jack Mills waved his phone. "I'll call Subway."

Brian's phone rang. He checked the caller I.D: *Hal.* "I have to take this," he told the group before walking out on deck and closing the salon door behind him.

"What the hell is going on?" Hal snapped. "Your coworkers walked out."

"I know. They both arrived here a few minutes ago."

"The precinct's like some three-ring circus right now. I can't have this. Tell them to get their asses back immediately."

"I already tried that. With Kaylen and Jim right there with them, I don't have any valid arguments. I tried warning Mills he could lose his pension. He swore he doesn't care."

"Damn cops with consciences. You couldn't ask for a better team, Swift."

"I know." Brian listened to gulls screeching overhead as a fresh breeze blew steadily against his face. "Chief," he said after the silence lengthened.

"I'm thinking."

"Sorry. Can't you think faster?"

"Who do you think you are?"

"The employee you just placed on probation."

"Where are you right now? You don't seem to be having any problems with eavesdroppers while you're smart-mouthing me."

"On deck. They're all in the salon with the door closed. They're ordering food."

"Tell Mills and Weston to come to my office immediately. I'll make sure Alicia marks their absence down as a remote meeting."

"What if they refuse?"

"You're their supervisor; act like one." Hal slammed down the phone.

"Ouch." Brian leaned against the rail and gazed up at billowing clouds scudding past on their way to shore as gulls wheeled on air currents and called out to each other. "Somehow, life used to be simpler," he told them.

"In what way?" Jack Mills and Gabe had left the salon. Gabe was jogging down the dock, presumably on his way to pick up their order.

"Jack, you and Gabe have to get back to the precinct right now. You've got a meeting with the chief."

"I already told you we'll go back when we're ready."

"I'm not *asking* you; I'm *telling* you."

"The hell you are. You got temporarily demoted."

"Go back to work, Jack. You and Gabe are to meet with the chief as soon as you get there."

"What the hell?" Mills looked at him, eyes narrowed. "Are you trying to tell me something without coming right out with it?"

"You've gotta take over temporarily as Cold Case's supervisor. It's the best way to help me. You can go to meetings with Hal and nothing will look suspicious. I'll arrange to get another detective transferred in to help you while I'm not there full-time. You'll like her a lot. She's sharp and opinionated." He managed a brief smile at the thought of Deanna Villanueva. "She might remind you of me."

"And Gabe? What if he refuses? He's more of a rebel than I am."

"He has to go back, too. And you've got to convince him to take weapons training."

Jack Mills grimaced. "You know he'll resist that."

"Tell him it's an order from the chief, and I'm backing him up.

Gabe's potentially in danger and completely unprepared. I can't lose anyone else, Jack."

Jack nodded, sharp and decisive. "I know. I'll talk to him. Try to convince him, although it'll be a hard sell."

"He'll get fired if he doesn't cooperate, and then all hell will break loose. I can't watch him as well as Kaylen, Jim *and* the Crossfields while I'm tryin' to bring in Sam Wilson and Tim's killers. And I'm gonna keep working the coffee shop murders, too. I don't give a rat's ass about Trehorn tellin' me to butt out. I've been pickin' up orders from that place for over a year. Those employees aren't just victims, they're friends. It's personal."

"I get that. All of it." Mills shoved his hands in his pockets and stared out at the water. "I'll get through to Gabe."

"Thanks, Jack. For not questioning my motives now and believin' in me when others didn't."

"Of course. Never doubted you for a minute before, and not now. We'll get them this time. You won't be working any cases alone, and that includes solving Tim's. That's my case, anyway, you schmuck. No trying to steal my thunder when they're all behind bars."

Brian waved his coworker off the *NTK* and informed Alicia that his two staff members were on their way back to meet with the chief.

He took a moment to breathe in clean, salty air while preparing himself to tell yet more lies to Kaylen and Jim. Several gulls had alighted on the rail in the stern, tails swinging as they resisted rolling and pitching movements that threatened to dislodge them. As Brian turned to go back into the salon, he startled them. All but one flapped away.

A shadow seemed to pass through him. He wondered if he'd soon be as alone as that one gull still clinging to the rail after those closest to him realized he'd lied to them yet again. At least he hadn't made Jim any promises, he thought. But would Kaylen forgive him?

Hal might have forced him into taking that risk, but Brian knew he'd have chosen the same path even if he had been offered a choice. Regardless of any potential damage to his relationship with Kaylen, he had to track down the men who had murdered his brother or he'd never have peace of mind again.

CHAPTER TWENTY

"IF YOU DON'T TAKE me, I'll go in my own car." Kaylen, hands on hips, faced Brian across the *NTK's* salon after everyone else had left. "Honestly, Brian, what are you thinking? I am not going to stay on the boat with Jim while you go over to the Crossfields and scare the pants off them."

Brian tried to keep the irritation out of his voice. "I'm not planning to do anything close to that. I'll tell Jonathan he has to take Angela on a spur-of-the-moment trip."

"Oh, that'll go down *so* well with him." Kaylen definitely wasn't trying to keep her feelings under wraps. "I know how you get." Her index finger wagged at him for emphasis. "And let me tell you, Brian, if you try dictating to Jonathan, he'll dig in his heels. You're not going to be able to order him around like you do me."

"I do *not* order you around." Brian felt his teeth clenching and tried taking a couple of deep breaths. "I reason with you. Even when you're trying to blow me off, like you were until a few minutes ago." He leaned back against the salon's closed door.

Kaylen stuck her nose in the air and refused to make eye contact.

"I did finally get through to you, though, didn't I?" Brian saw her flinch. "Whenever I can't be there, you need Jim with you. When you saw Sam, you couldn't even call for help, let alone use that damn gun you carry around in your purse."

Kaylen crossed her arms and tossed her head. Chestnut curls cascaded around her shoulders and caught a fiery glow from the sun. To Brian, the spectacular effect reflected her resentment at being told the unvarnished truth. But he realized he could have used more tact, and while talking sense into her, still left her with a shred of self-respect.

Despite the training he had given her, he reminded himself, she was still a civilian, and until she became involved in the fall-out from Tim's murder, she had been a young socialite who attended parties and charity events while being sheltered by two older men who doted on her.

"I resent you talking down to me, Brian." Kaylen's voice held a slight tremor.

Her mouth was turned down at the corners, and the little quirk that appeared on the right side when she was particularly angry, was definitely there. She turned her back to him and walked over to the couch, where she jammed her feet into her shoes.

She cleared her throat. "Since I think you're probably as upset as I am, I'm going to try to let your last remarks slide." She picked up her purse.

Brian took another deep breath and hoped that was the end of their disagreement, but when she pulled out her keys and dangled them on the end of one finger, that hope died.

"We'll take my car," she said. "You can drive."

Brian heard himself make a derisive noise before he could stop himself.

Kaylen paused only the space of a heartbeat before scooping up her jacket and swinging her purse-strap over her shoulder. She pivoted on her very high heels and walked toward him. Brian thought at first she hadn't heard his response, but the arch of her eyebrows told him different.

"I'm going to okay Jim acting as my bodyguard for now," she said, her voice tight and still slightly uneven around the edges. "But don't bother suggesting I leave town, too. I can't. I *have* to be at Treasure's grand opening. You *know* that."

She had heard, all right, Brian told himself. Snippy didn't even begin to describe her demeanor. He was going to have to figure out a way to compromise. He'd work on convincing her once he'd dealt with the Crossfields, who he hoped would be easier to convince they needed a security detail or an extended trip out of the country than his girlfriend.

But Kaylen wasn't done. Nowhere even close to it, he realized as she stopped in front of him.

"I've got too much to do over the next few weeks to go anywhere," she said, her gaze decidedly icy. "I'm sure Jonathan does, too."

Brian tried shrugging non-committedly. Kaylen had donned an invisible suit of armor and prepared for battle during the time it had taken her to gather up her stuff.

"His business is a lot bigger than mine, and it's still privately owned," she continued. "So when he and Angela want to take a vacation, his preparations take months. I'm not guessing when I say that; Angela told me. It won't matter how much you try to scare them. They're not going to pick up and leave, especially now Angela's pregnant."

Brian couldn't afford to waste any more time arguing unproductively. Highly annoyed, he couldn't resist a parting shot before capitulating. "We'll see about that."

Kaylen was no longer avoiding eye contact. She glared at him. "We will, indeed."

He picked up his own keys. "Come on, then. But we're taking the Camaro, not your Beemer." He held the salon door open and waved impatiently at her. "Step it up, Kaylen, before I change my mind and lock you in the cabin."

"I'd like to see you try." She stalked past him, her back rigid.

Brian used all his anger-management techniques as he followed her out the door and locked it behind them. He heard her foot tapping the entire time as he worked on the awkward lock he had never made a priority to replace.

He needed to take Jonathan Crossfield aside. Tell him it was in his best interest to comply. No emotion; no lengthy explanations. Jonathan was a no-nonsense kind of guy. Brian hoped he would recognize the urgency without pressing for a lot of information.

He helped Kaylen off the boat, but she was still giving him the stink eye when they reached the parking lot. He abandoned any thoughts of compromises. She needed to work with him, not pull a hissy-fit. He sped up and left her jogging along behind.

"Wait up," she called. "Did you somehow forget I'm wearing heels and a tight skirt? Usually, you notice everything."

"You insisted on coming." He stopped beside the Camaro and jerked open the passenger's door. "I'm not waiting around for you to change clothes."

"The mood you're in, I know you'd leave me behind if I tried."

Despite the tight skirt, Kaylen lowered herself into the car seat with more grace than Brian would have believed possible. He watched her long, shapely legs all the way into the vehicle. Her skirt slid up to mid-thigh in the process.

She fastened her seatbelt and began shimmying her skirt closer to her knees. Brian quietly closed the door. She knew he'd ogled her legs. He wasn't going to give her the satisfaction of knowing he was now having trouble controlling more than his temper.

He strode around to the driver's side. If she was spoiling to continue their fight, then she could vent all the way over to the Crossfields. Maybe by the time they arrived, she'd have gotten everything out of her system so he could concentrate on the task at hand.

But Kaylen said nothing until they had left the marina and Coconut Grove behind. She didn't even protest about Brian's speeding while they cleared multiple intersections right before amber lights turned red.

Brian appreciated the silence, even a loaded one. It gave him the chance to figure out how to convince Jonathan Crossfield and his pregnant wife to suddenly decamp with very few preparations.

The owner of a large company had to have a contingency plan for emergencies, Brian told himself while weaving around slower traffic. Even a private company had some sort of hierarchy, including a V.P., although that might be Angela. But there had to be a C.F.O., who hopefully wasn't a member of their immediate family. Otherwise, he reasoned, if Jonathan and Angela got into a wreck, who was going to take over until one of them was able to return to the helm?

"Brian, you should take Jim's advice and talk to Mireille Shagassi again," Kaylen said right out of the blue, not only breaking the uneasy silence but sounding annoyingly like Jim himself. "But on your own terms." She turned in the seat to look directly at Brian. "I disagree with you meeting her on the boat. It would make you more relaxed, but then she'd know where you live, and you don't need that. None of us do. I like being able to go to the marina without taking the risk I'll find a bunch of reporters camped out on the dock."

After Kaylen had been so quiet for the first part of the drive, he'd allowed himself to hope for the opportunity to organize his game plan before arriving at the Crossfields. But her nervous chatter wasn't going to allow for that. After taking a moment to swear silently, he told himself chatting about anything other than the Crossfields might do them both some good.

"Look, not running the risk of reporters harassing either of us is one of the things I really like about the boat, too," he told her. "Before the mess with Tim and those bribery accusations, I used to be able to come and go as I pleased, even when I lived in an apartment. Then I met you." He gave her a quick smile.

"Yes, and all that changed. You lost so much of your privacy." She cleared her throat again, like she was having trouble swallowing a lump that had lodged there. "I know how much that has concerned you," she said in a small voice. She held onto the dash as they swerved around a couple of lumbering older model sedans. "I☐I very much appreciate you putting up with things like that...all the things that make you uncomfortable...just to be with me." She paused, and her hand lightly touched his forearm. "I don't tell you that often enough. I'm sorry."

Brian tried hard not to flinch. He still didn't respond well to unexpected personal contact, even Kaylen's, but she was extending a shaky olive branch, and he needed to take it.

"You can't go back," she said, taking her hand of his arm. "Unless you've changed your mind about being with me because it takes too much out of you," she added quietly.

"Of course, I don't want out of our relationship," he said. He managed another smile he didn't feel because he sensed she needed it. "I could do without our arguments, and definitely without a spotlight on me wherever we go, but I'm adjusting. Maybe it's taking me longer to do that than you'd like, but it's not an easy process."

Unable to safely pass a mini-van with bumper stickers that announced it was driven by the proud mom of a middle-schooler who also evidently played soccer, he dropped in behind and slowed to the speed limit. "And the benefits of being with you so outweigh the negatives, hon, I can't even begin to tell you."

He glanced over at her. She was crying, tears running unchecked down her cheeks.

"Oh, Brian." She drew in a long, shuddering sob and opened her purse, presumably to fish out the small packet of tissues he knew she always carried inside.

"I'm not done," he told her.

His fingers tightened on the wheel as he fought to control his emotions. He wanted to avoid letting her know how little control he actually had left at that moment.

"It's the danger I could put you in that worries me." He sped up and passed the mini-van, catching sight of curious childish faces peering through the side window. "You and Jim. The guys at the department can fend for themselves." He thought of Deanna Villanueva. "And gals."

He slammed on the brakes as the light ahead turned red. They came to an abrupt stop. The mini-van coasted to a standstill behind them. He glanced in his rearview mirror and saw the middle-schooler's proud mom glaring at him for cutting her off. Yet another woman he'd pissed off that afternoon. He should start a head-count, he thought. Angela Crossfield would probably be number three.

He took another look at Kaylen and saw her gazing back at him. Tears sparkled on both her cheeks. Her eyes had narrowed, either as a result of the body-check from the seat belt or his hurried addendum. She knew Cold Case didn't have any female officers. He wondered if she objected to him using the term 'gals.'

But Brian didn't feel like segueing into some lengthy discussion about Trehorn's latest recruit when they needed to stay on topic, so he rushed to fill the gap.

"It's like ripples on a pond after a big rock gets thrown into it," he said, falling back onto an analogy that might be the easiest way for

Kaylen to understand how deeply his fears for her actually went. "The danger's spreading. Today it's the Crossfields. Tomorrow, it could be Rob, or even your new manager at Treasure."

He watched as several cars straggled through the intersection. A bus made a wide turn. Brian had to back the Camaro up to allow it to pass. The mini-van had to back up, too. The bus driver gave a quick wave of thanks before the big vehicle lumbered past. It was a long light. Brian's agitation grew. He should have taken another route, he thought, exasperated.

"You're exaggerating. You're trying to scare me into running off with the Crossfields," Kaylen said. "That's not going to happen. We all going to be fine...Jim, Rob and everyone else."

The light turned green and Brian didn't feel the need to try finding an answer for her last remark as he began watching for the turn-off to the Crossfields' small, private street.

"Sam has no interest in any of my employees," Kaylen prattled on. "And he doesn't know Jim from Adam."

"You don't know that," Brian said. "He could have access to a lot of information about all of us."

He checked his rearview mirror and saw the mini-van had turned off, leaving only a UPS delivery truck half a block behind. He quickly turned the Camaro onto the street where the Crossfields' compound was located, and a thick layer of green instantly enveloped both sides of the road. No tall trees, probably due to recent hurricanes, Brian thought, but thick vegetation that could be conducive to hiding a vehicle inside one of the deeply-recessed driveways leading to expansive gated estates.

"I don't think that's Sam's goal.," Kaylen said. "He wants to make his threat personal, so it really hurts me."

Brian felt her hand on his thigh that time. He placed his own over it and gave her hand a quick squeeze before drawing up to the gates of the Crossfield mansion, where it only took a moment to announce their arrival and gain entry.

"You're the one in immediate danger, Brian," Kaylen said as they passed between stands of palms. A few oaks towered over thick shrubbery. Vines climbed trunks. Thick, tropical foliage shut out the light and the view. The Crossfields had definitely replanted after any storm damage. The entire driveway was a potential harbor for a goddamned infiltrating army, Brian thought with dismay. He hadn't been to their home in a good six months, and his last trip had been in the dark.

Fortunately, as the house came into view, the dense foliage gave way to strategically-planted ornamental trees that did not threaten to obscure the view from any first-floor window or terrace. The bay stretched beyond, incredibly blue and touched by sunlight.

"The Crossfields are only involved because if they withdraw their support, my clubs will suffer." Kaylen reached down for her purse, on the floor at her feet. "I doubt Sam's scheming could close my business at this point, because I'm financially solvent now at Bannisters. It's the new business that will ultimately suffer from his meddling."

Brian parked in front of the multi-step front entrance. Kaylen waited while he walked around and opened her door.

"Have you been listening to anything I've just said?" she asked as he helped her out of the car, her skirt hiking up again.

Brian wanted to put his hands all over those tanned thighs of hers. He was annoyed with himself for getting so easily distracted.

"I've heard every word," he assured her. "But you're minimizing the impact. Hon, you'll go under if your backers withdraw their support. As far as my own safety's concerned, Sam has no confidence in the cartel's ability to take me out after what happened the last time they tried, so I figure they won't make another attempt to chase me with a car and shoot me. They'll be trickier. I'm beginning to think me arriving right after that coffee shop robbery had little to do with the robbery and everything to do with my goddamned predictable Wednesday morning pre-meeting coffee run."

"What are you talking about?"

"People needlessly losing their lives to put me where I can be hurt professionally, not physically. I received a commendation the last time the cartel tried to kill me. They don't want anything close to that happening again. What better way to hurt my career and make me downright disgusting to you than by destroying my image with a public disclosure that I *did* take bribes, and I used my brother's money to put myself on an even financial footing with you? Top that off by planting evidence so it looks like I killed Tim for his money and his girlfriend, and I go behind bars if I'm lucky. If not, I could get the chair."

"That's nonsense. My God!" Kaylen shuddered.

She ran up the marble front steps ahead of him, while Brian wondered how the hell she could do that in three-inch heels. With red soles.

CHAPTER TWENTY-ONE

"I STILL WISH you hadn't insisted on tagging along," Brian told Kaylen as they waited outside the Crossfields' front door.

Kaylen ignored him to fix her gaze on a huge planter filled with pink flowers, trailing vines and ferns. During the drive she had pulled her hair back and anchored it with a black ribbon, exposing her long, tanned neck. In her navy business suit and simple white blouse she looked even taller and more imposing than usual.

"I'm sure you do," she said. "Tough," she muttered under her breath. She tugged her purse strap further up her shoulder. "I should do the talking," she said. "You have no idea how to deliver bad news gently."

"The hell I don't." Brian felt the need to defend himself. "I've had to notify next of kin on more deaths than you've had manicures."

Kaylen gave him what he called her Medusa look. "You've always got to win any argument, regardless how pointless, don't you?"

Brian decided not to take the bait by attempting to answer her question. Kaylen was intent on jabbing at his self-control in every way. He'd thought she knew it wasn't his fault he was being accused of bribery yet again. If she trusted him as much as she said she did, then she shouldn't be getting on some high goddamned horse and demanding again that she should be the one to tell the Crossfields they were potentially in danger.

He wondered whether she was attempting to deflect her anxiety. If she was worried about the effects of his problems on her business and her own reputation, then why didn't she just come out and say so? Brian decided he still didn't understand the way Kaylen thought, and wondered if he ever would.

He pushed aside his preoccupation with Kaylen's thought processes and redirected his attention to handling the Crossfields. Maybe having her along to distract Angela while he talked to Jonathan wasn't such a disaster, Brian told himself as he reached around Kaylen to push the doorbell a third time.

"What's taking so long?" He stepped back to look at windows devoid of light or movement.

Kaylen shrugged. "Beats me. They knew it would only take a couple of minutes for us to get here from the gates."

Brian's preoccupation with anything or anyone other than the Crossfields vanished like a puff of smoke. "Get back in the car, Kaylen," he said. "Now."

Her mouth dropped open. "What is wrong with you? Didn't we wrangle long enough about this already?" Then she looked at his face again, and her own turned white. "You think? No...oh, God..."

He grabbed her arm and started to push her back down the steps even as he reached for his Glock.

Suddenly, the front door opened and the Crossfields' long-term live-in housekeeper stood on the threshold. A short, heavy-set middle-aged woman of Guatemalan descent, she had *Juliette* embroidered in blue on her heavily-starched white apron. Brian thought she resembled a nurse more than a domestic worker. She looked startled when she took in the little tableau in front of her, with Kaylen half hanging off the porch and Brian with his jacket thrown back and his left hand on the butt of his gun.

Kaylen used Brian's other arm to help pull herself upright. "Juliette," she said, her voice sweet and not at all reflective of how hard her heart must be hammering. "You took so long to answer the door, we thought you'd all gone out as soon as you heard we were coming." She smiled at the housekeeper, but her hand was still on Brian's arm, and it was shaking.

Brian kept his left hand right where it was. "Is everything okay?"

"Ms. Kaylen," Juliette said. "So nice to see you again. Everything is fine. Sorry it took so long for me to answer the door. Do come inside." She looked pointedly at Brian. "You, too, Sergeant."

Juliette's nephew had served time for running a chop shop. Juliette wasn't fond of the police as a whole, and having a detective on the front step with his hand on his gun probably wasn't garnering any goodwill. She waved him into the cavernous entrance hall behind Kaylen. Brian saw no immediate threat and lowered his left hand to his side.

He realized the housekeeper was looking puzzled as well as apprehensive while her gaze traveled from him to Kaylen and back again. He might not have trouble keeping his own emotions well-hidden, but he wasn't sure about Kaylen maintaining a poker face at that moment. He forced a smile. "Hi Juliette. How ya doin?'"

Juliette blinked rapidly. "Mr. and Mrs. Crossfield weren't expecting company. I'm afraid neither of them is dressed for socializing, and tomorrow is cleaning day in the sun-room. We are a little informal here."

Kaylen started to speak. "We know that…"

Brian guided her to one side with a firm hand around her elbow. "This isn't a social call. It's official police business."

Kaylen tried to pull her elbow away. Maybe he was clutching her a little too tightly, or maybe she was reading his vibes better than Juliette. He kept his attention on the housekeeper but loosened his grip on Kaylen.

Juliette's eyes widened. "Oh." She looked from Kaylen to Brian and back to Kaylen again, apparently seeking guidance from the person she knew best.

"You'd better tell Mr. Crossfield," Kaylen recommended. "When Sergeant Swift is on duty, he doesn't have a lot of patience for small-talk." She mouthed 'Ouch' to Brian and jerked her elbow away.

Juliette leaned forward. "Please wait here," she said in what sounded like a stage whisper. "I'll tell Mr. and Mrs. Crossfield." She scurried away on silent feet.

Rubber soles, Brian thought. Easy to creep around the mansion and hear anything she wanted to at any time. He closed the door behind them and moved Kaylen away from all the panes of leaded glass.

Her steps echoed on the marble floor as she walked toward an ornate table against the wall between twin marble staircases that joined together on a wide landing halfway up, then diverged again to end at opposite sides of the upper floor

Already spectacular, the staircase was further enhanced by an enormous chandelier suspended over the table with a long chain anchored in the vaulted ceiling. Brian made an effort to saunter unhurriedly behind Kaylen while he made a visual sweep of every visible space and piece of furniture within sight. He found nothing looked suspicious, and saw no shadows that didn't correspond with the effects of the lighting both from the chandelier, the generous leaded glass inserts and a copious number of windows set high on the exterior walls. Brian wondered how those windows were cleaned without bringing in scaffolding. Not his idea of a family home, but then, until Tim's inheritance took him from what some would call adequately-funded to a state of affluence, he'd never lived in anything larger than a one-bedroom apartment.

"What is *wrong* with you?" Kaylen hissed. "You grabbed my arm so hard you hurt me, and you almost made me fall down the front steps." She rubbed her elbow.

"Sorry. I'm feeling a little tense." *To put it mildly.*

Kaylen's eyebrows shot up. "A little? You haven't been yourself all afternoon."

"Neither have you. First you got drunk, then you insisted on coming along with me, and you've argued with me not only on the *NTK,* but all the way over here. No wonder we're both jittery and riled up."

"Of course I'm riled up." She sat on one of the spindly white and gilt chairs that flanked the hall table. "I'm worried, Brian. Worried about you, worried about your career, about Jim, Jonathan and Angela. About the future of my business." She shook her head slowly, side to side, her brow deeply furrowed. "You've gotten into so much trouble again, both at work and with the media. And now I have to wonder when Sam is going to release that sex tape to the public. When is all this ever going to end?" She laid her purse gently on top of the table. "I can't even go anywhere without a loaded gun in my purse." She looked up at him with that wry little quirk at the right corner of her mouth. "The gun I can't seem to get *out* of my purse, as you emphasized so clearly."

"Hon, I know, believe me." He sat on the other spindly chair. "Don't you think I'd like to have a normal life again?"

Kaylen grimaced. "When did you *ever* have a normal life? From what you've told me, you wouldn't know normal if it bit you."

She got up and walked over to stare at a portrait of Angela, seated in front of a fountain in what Brian knew was the small flagstone terrace between the formal living room and the sun-room where the Crossfields spent most of their alone-time.

He followed her and wrapped his arms around her. She leaned back against him for a moment, and Brian felt some of the tension slide from his shoulders. But then she pulled away, turned and poked her finger against his chest.

"You've been thinking way too much about everything, lately," she said. "Am I becoming too high maintenance, suddenly? Too much for you to handle while you're dealing with these new accusations and Sam Wilson's reappearance?" Tears came into her eyes. "Are you having regrets about *us?*"

Brian had to admit he was floored. "What the hell are you talking about? This has nothing to do with us personally." He gently cradled her elbows in his hands, mindful that he'd hurt her twice already since they arrived. He tried to make eye contact, but she was avoiding him again.

"It does. I know it does," she muttered, head down.

She squirmed away from his grasp. Opened her purse and pulled out that packet of tissues again. Dabbed her eyes while he fumed and wondered what to do about her. So much for worrying about the Crossfields refusing to leave. Kaylen's brain had left the building, and he needed it back ASAP.

"I know you're disappointed with me." Kaylen sniffed and dabbed her nose. "Even angry with me for letting Sam confront me and doing nothing to get him arrested."

"Hon..."

She waved away his protest. "I was stupid. I admit it. But I won't make the same mistake twice. I know he's going to contact me again, and I'll make sure he's caught the next time. He can't keep away from me. But what happens when you've got him in custody? How are you going to make him tell you who was hired to kill Tim and where they're hiding out?"

Brian threw caution to the wind. To hell with the acoustics of the cavernous entryway. "I'll do whatever's needed to get the names of Tim's killers. What happens to Sam Fuckin' Wilson while I do that, or if he's still alive when I'm done, doesn't concern me a whole lot."

"Brian, you're frightening me." Kaylen had lowered her voice, but it still echoed. She stepped closer despite her words. Her face looked pale and pinched. "You're talking about retribution... possibly murder to get what you want." She reached out a trembling hand. Touched the scars on the left side of his face. "Oh, Brian. Please don't get so caught up in exacting revenge on Tim's killers that you forget about the future...about what we have now; about what we could look forward to."

"I'm talking consequences. Justice for Tim. Putting a stop to any more threats." Brian moved away, and Kaylen's hand fell to her side.

He had nothing left to say to her at that moment. How long did it take for Juliette to go find her employers and tell them to forget about getting into formal-wear? If she didn't come back in less than a nanosecond, he swore he was going to find them himself.

To keep from striding off down the hallway Juliette had taken, Brian took measured steps around the entrance hall, remarking to himself, not for the first time, that it felt like a mausoleum.

Nothing homey about the Crossfields' family squat until you got to the sun-room at the back of the sprawling mansion. Maybe Angela and Jonathan felt that way themselves. They had said they spent most of their time away from all the formal rooms on the first floor.

Brian had never seen the second floor. He envisioned room after room of sterile furniture laid out by some famous designer whose name he had no doubt was familiar to Kaylen. Maybe there was a home theatre and even a master suite that also wasn't so sterile, but who knew? He felt the Crossfields were all about maintaining appearances, despite their friendliness and attempts to make him feel comfortable any time he and Kaylen were invited to visit.

Kaylen had called the sun-room their inner-sanctum. Reserved for them alone. She said the first time Angela took her there while she retrieved an old address book that held the number of a potential backer for Bannisters, Kaylen had remained in the doorway, feeling highly intrusive. She told Brian the furnishings were comfortable, even slightly worn in places. Unlike the rest of the house, it didn't seem vast and unlived-in. It was filled with Angela's carefully-tended potted plants and family photos ranging from the couple's wedding to nieces and nephews, favorite vacations and Jonathan's sport fishing. Angela's weaving loom and a basket overflowing with yarns stood in one corner.

Kaylen had said her friend loved to replicate patterns of some sort. Brian thought he remembered something about textiles from South America. Kaylen frequently chattered on about things he had never heard of, like they were common-place, which maybe they were in her world.

He still wondered how he and Kaylen remained a couple when their interests and professions were so different, but maybe that's why their relationship worked, he decided as he looked around what he thought was completely wasted space. His first boat, the *Destiny,* would probably have fit right into Angela and Jonathan's front hallway.

Having completed a circuit of the foyer and worn through his always-thin patience, he turned on his heel. *Time to invade whatever space the Crossfields were occupying.*

But Juliette was back, finally, almost running out of the hallway while smoothing her apron and pushing pins back into a knot of hair that appeared to have unraveled. "I'm sorry you were both kept waiting. Mr. and Mrs. Crossfield will see you now. This way."

She led them down a wide passageway adorned with large pieces of artwork between open doorways. Brian glanced into room after room dedicated to formal groupings, then a dining room that could easily seat thirty around the enormous table. A darkened home theatre. Brian took that off his list for the upstairs. Twenty bedrooms, he thought, or maybe ten with ten ensuite bathrooms so guests wouldn't have to share. So different from where he had grown up in Baton Rouge. Brian's mother and stepfather had thought themselves lucky to be able to rent a tiny house with 1 bedroom and indoor plumbing right next to the railroad tracks.

Finally, when they came to the end of the hallway. Juliette stopped. She opened a set of double doors and motioned Kaylen and Brian into a room bathed by dappled sunlight winking through palm fronds overhanging a terrace visible through three sets of closed floor-to-ceiling French doors. Despite the warmth of the day, the room felt cool and welcoming. As he followed Kaylen inside, Brian decided the Crossfields must spend the equivalent of his monthly salary on air conditioning just for that room. The upkeep on their mansion annually would probably cool the entire Homicide and Cold Case departments for at least that long.

"Thank you, Juliette." Jonathan Crossfield stood beside his wife, lying on a chaise with a cloth on her forehead and a small garbage can on the floor in front of her. "Iced tea for our guests, please."

Juliette nodded and squeezed past Brian, who was partially blocking the doorway. He watched her take off left, down an equally long hallway with open doors on both sides.

Jonathan beckoned them over. "Sorry for keeping you out in the front lobby for so long. Angela's not feeling well today."

"That's an understatement." Angela took the cloth off her forehead and handed it to Jonathan. "The doctor said if I don't stop throwing up, I'll have to be hospitalized."

"They're worried she's going to dehydrate," Jonathan said. He dropped the cloth into a small basin and wrung out another before placing it on Angela's forehead.

"Oh, Angela, I'm so sorry." Kaylen hastened across the room and sat on a couch opposite the chaise. "We wouldn't have come if it wasn't necessary. An emergency, really."

"What's wrong?" Jonathan's already-worried tone jumped up a notch.

Brian hastily closed the doors behind him. He didn't see Juliette, but he wouldn't want to bet against her being hidden somewhere close by, where she could eavesdrop before fetching that iced tea he didn't want. "It's nothing that can't be handled calmly. No frightening them." He shot a warning look at Kaylen.

She glared back. "You never sugar-coat things," she said. "Why should I?"

Brian hoped the Crossfields weren't going to give him as difficult a time as Kaylen had that afternoon. After abandoning all hope of taking Jonathan aside and talking man to man with him about protecting his family, Brian chose his words carefully. He told the shocked and initially incredulous pair what had transpired, and that not only Jonathan's business might be placed in jeopardy but their lives could be at stake.

During Brian's discourse, Jonathan took a seat at the end of the chaise and rested Angela's feet on his lap. He stroked her left foot absently as he looked at Brian with a mixture of disbelief and apprehension. Angela looked paler and even more distressed.

"You really think you're not over-reacting or reading this wrong?" Jonathan asked when Brian finally stopped detailing the possible consequences of them remaining in Miami. "After all, there were no real threats issued when Wilson confronted Kaylen, unless I missed something, and nothing ever directed at us."

"There's a distinct possibility the cartel's put itself back together and wants a piece not only of Kaylen's business but those of her primary backers, which puts you at the top of their list. If you don't comply, these people are ruthless. They *will* come after you. Kaylen's in danger, but so are you, and even more so, Angela. They'll have you right where they want you if they threaten her."

Jonathan's swift intake of breath was audible in the quiet room.

"What Sam said was that people close to me could get hurt," Kaylen said. "So it's not only *my* business he's after."

"She's right," Brian said. "He won't do it himself, but if you don't do what he says, there'll be repercussions, and it'll be from the cartel. He's their mouthpiece. He thinks he knows all of us, and what it'll take for us to comply, but he has no idea who he's fuckin' with where I'm concerned."

"Brian…language," Kaylen cautioned.

"It's okay," Jonathan said. "Nothing we haven't heard before."

"Look, I can take care of myself," Brian said. "I've convinced Kaylen to let Jim watch over her when I'm not around. But I can't protect everyone, and we're not going to get any help from the police department. Vague threats aren't enough."

"So you're telling me that until someone close to Kaylen gets hurt or worse, we can't ask for police protection?" Jonathan seemed to have moved past shock into anger. "That's bullshit."

Brian saw Kaylen's eyes widen.

"Brian's not the only one who knows how to swear," Jonathan told her with the ghost of a smile.

Brian liked Jonathan's attempt to lighten the situation. "I agree with you to a certain extent," he allowed. "Wilson didn't try anything physical when he approached Kaylen in the grocery store. He hasn't sent her any written warnings…"

"Except the roses," Kaylen interrupted.

"Which could be interpreted as gifts." Brian gave her a look he hoped would convey the need for her to keep quiet and let him do the talking.

"I can't leave." Angela slid the cloth down over her eyes. "I can't possibly travel in this condition."

Jonathan patted her foot. "Angela's not giving birth anywhere but in the hospital right here in Miami. Her obstetrician warned us today that she's having a high-risk pregnancy." His voice cracked. "I'm so sorry, baby," he told her. "I wanted this time to be as happy and stress-free for you as possible."

Kaylen slid closer to Brian. He felt her hand on his arm, placed his over it and felt it tremble in response. "What about hiring a security service for now?" he suggested.

"We've got a state-of-the-art system for the house already." Jonathan sounded indignant.

"I think he's talking about hiring bodyguards, honey." Angela took the cloth off her face and tossed it onto the edge of the garbage can.

"I'm not having some guy following me around and standing outside my office to listen in on all my private meetings and phone calls, Brian," Jonathan protested. "And I'm certainly not turning our home into a maximum-security prison because you think some vague threat of violence might have been made by Sam Wilson."

Brian realized Jonathan had taken a defensive posture. No suggestion made at that moment would sound even remotely reasonable. If he'd minimized the situation any more than he had, the Crossfields would have thought there was no credible threat at all. But he probably shouldn't have started off telling them to flee the country.

"Could you work from home for a while?" he tried.

Jonathan grimaced. "I'll have to, at least temporarily. I can't leave

Angela alone with Juliette, who doesn't even drive. I might have to rush her to the hospital."

"That's nonsense." Angela took her feet off his lap and sat up. "I'll be fine. I told the doctor I'll do whatever he says." She grabbed a full glass of water from the end table and greedily sucked on the straw. The glass emptied halfway before Angela started gagging. Jonathan held the garbage can up to her chin and she vomited.

He handed her a towel. "Dr. Singh said sip, remember?"

Angela wiped her mouth. "Ugh. I do remember. I should have listened to him, huh?" She managed a wry smile.

Kaylen cleared her throat. "Jonathan, why did you say temporarily?"

Jonathan slowly turned his attention from Angela to Kaylen. Angela mouthed 'thank you,' and sat back.

"Because I've got a trip coming up at the end of the month." Jonathan put down the garbage can and covered it with the towel Angela handed him. "I'll be in Europe for at least two weeks, maybe three. I moved the date back so I could have the new facility completed well ahead of Angie's due date."

Brian ran a hand through his hair. Although he knew Jonathan traveled frequently, he hadn't anticipated yet another complication.

"I'll be okay," Angela said. "Maybe Kaylen can stay with me. Then you could keep an eye on both of us, Brian, or talk Jim into doing it if you can't handle two women at once." She managed a brief smile.

"I think that's an excellent idea." Brian ignored the fact that Kaylen pulled her hand away from his. "Jonathan, would you at least agree to Jim keeping both Angela and Kaylen safe inside the home and maybe a private security detail outside while you're gone?"

"*Brian.* I've got my business to attend to," Kaylen protested. She turned to Angela. "Of course I'll stay here with you while Jonathan's on his trip, but I have to go to work. I'm already leaving Rob completely in charge at Bannisters. Treasure and its manager won't be ready for me to hand over the reins for months."

"Hon, let's tackle one goddamned issue at a time." Brian knew he hadn't tried to hide the irritation in his voice but decided, screw it. "You want me to solve everything and do it yesterday."

"I do not. I know your resources are well, limited right now." She bit her lip.

"Why is that?" Jonathan asked.

Great.

"Because he's got so many cases at work," Kaylen said. "And he's clearing them with such a limited staff. If Jim's busy looking after Angela now as well as me, then Brian's going to have to ask Chief Shaw for more help." She smiled at the Crossfields.

Brian silently thanked her for saving his ass. He didn't want them to know he'd supposedly gotten placed on probation. "I've asked Hal to get one of the Homicide staff transferred to Cold Case," he said, hoping to distract their attention.

"Oh? Who?" Kaylen looked surprised.

"You don't know her. She's fairly new, but she's got a lot of experience and wants the position." He tried to sound off-hand about it.

"A woman. That's a nice idea," Angela said. "Women have a way of getting information out of people that men sometimes can't."

"I agree." Brian nodded.

"So Jim could be here any time Kaylen is?" Jonathan sounded less stressed.

"Absolutely." Brian hoped Kaylen wasn't going to disagree.

"You won't make me learn to knit or weave, will you?" Kaylen asked Angela.

Angela managed a little laugh in response. A small amount of color had returned to her face. "No. I promise not to even ask." She looked at Jonathan. "And I promise not to over-compensate when I try to show you how I'm obeying Dr. Singh's orders. Now, how about some 7-Up and crackers? What happened to Juliette? She never brought in the iced tea."

Brian stood and unholstered his Glock. He saw Kaylen's hand go into her purse.

CHAPTER TWENTY-TWO

"You stay here with them," Brian told Kaylen as he headed for the door.

She nodded, the Sig Sauer in her hand.

"Surely you don't ..." Jonathan's voice trailed off.

"Where's the kitchen?" Brian asked.

Jonathan stood. "This is my house; I'll take you." He drew a Ruger out of the drawer in an end table.

"Since when have you had that?" Angela sounded surprised.

"A while. I didn't tell you." He looked at Brian. "I know how to use it. I used to hunt before I married Angie. I recently took a safety class, and I've got a license for it."

"Okay, okay. Keep your voice down. No sense in anybody outside this room knowing what you've got." Brian shook his head. He wished Jim had come with him instead of Kaylen, regardless of whether he'd taught her what to do if the occasion arose. She'd already failed the first important test with Sam Wilson.

"Sorry," Jonathan muttered. He tried to get in front of Brian.

"No damn way." Brian put up his hand. "You stay here. Give me directions."

Jonathan stopped, but he looked mutinous and pointed toward

Kaylen. "She's got a firearm. I'm not staying here. I'll let you take the lead, but I'll be right behind you. Take a left out the doorway and a right at the end of the corridor. The kitchen will be straight ahead."

Brian thought about telling Jonathan he didn't need any inexperienced back-up, but knew he'd be wasting breath as well as time. Another set of eyes might be a good thing. He motioned Jonathan into place and slowly opened the door to total silence except for distant twittering.

"What the hell is that noise?" Brian whispered.

"An indoor aviary," Jonathan answered, that time in an undertone. "Finches, mostly. We'll turn off before reaching it."

Brian chanced a look in the hallway and found it empty in both directions He wondered how far away the kitchen could be to hear no sound from it at all. He turned left and Jonathan slid in behind him. They passed several open doors on both sides. More cavernous rooms, all apparently empty when Brian gave them a cursory check. He continued, flattening himself against the wall where the hallways divided. He took a fast look, noting the kitchen also appeared empty. They advanced, fast and low. Nothing stirred. They cleared all sides of the massive central kitchen island first.

As they moved forward cautiously, Brian asked if Juliette would have left without telling them. "What if she'd run out of tea?"

"No way. She'd have come back to tell us." Jonathan touched one finger to the stove. "This is cold."

Brian glanced up at a huge pot rack suspended above the island. It was filled with more cooking utensils than he'd seen in Bannisters' commercial kitchen. He laid the back of his hand against an electric kettle. Took it by the handle and lifted it. "This is cold, too, but full." He pointed toward an empty pitcher and a tray of glasses. "Looks like she was about to make the tea. Is there any in the refrigerator?"

Jonathan turned around and opened a gigantic French door refrigerator. "No."

Brian jerked his head toward a door in the middle of a wall of cabinets and counter tops on the opposite side of the room. "What's in there?"

"The pantry, I think. I don't come out here much."

"Check the back door," Brian told him.

Jonathan tried the door, which opened onto a couple of steps down to a flagstone walkway. "She never leaves this unlocked," he said. "What the hell is going on?"

Brian carefully opened the thick, heavy pantry door. Inside, Juliette thrashed against ropes that held her hogtied and completely immobilized. Her apron was twisted and wrapped tightly around her mouth as a gag. She hadn't gone easily, Brian thought, looking at the amount of spilled and overturned dry goods surrounding her. A large canister with teabags scattered around it painted a picture. She must have gone into the pantry to get the tea and with the door closed, she was overpowered without any sound escaping to bring help.

"Call the cops, Jonathan," he said as he started to untie Juliette's gag. "We've left the land of vague threats."

Jonathan pulled out his phone.

A faint scream rent the air, chilling in its intensity. A shot followed.

Brian jumped up, grabbed Jonathan and threw him into the pantry, saw a knife rack on the nearby counter and threw that in with the two people on the floor.

"Cut her loose," he said. "And don't come out of there unless I tell you to." His last view before closing the door behind him was of Jonathan, phone between his ear and shoulder, using a knife to saw through Juliette's bonds.

Relieved to know Crossfield appeared to have a head for more than his business, Brian took off at a dead run, his heart hammering painfully in his chest.

CHAPTER TWENTY-THREE

"I'VE NEVER BEEN SO RELIEVED to see you in my life," Kaylen said. "They came in through there." She pointed the Sig toward wide open and very broken French doors. Splintered wood and jagged glass littered the floor. "I shot at them."

"She did. She was fearless," Angela corroborated, breathless but holding a knitting needle like a spear.

"How many? Which way did they go?" Brian's voice was a command.

As he strode toward the patio, Kaylen saw his eyes dart rapidly across her and do the same to Angela, huddled with her on the couch. No doubt assessing them for injuries, she thought. Totally focused and completely unemotional. She felt herself calming and lowered her gun before he told her to do so. She knew he was hyper-sensitive, and rightly so, about guns in his immediate vicinity.

But she would have liked him to at least ask if she and Angela were okay, she thought, slightly upset with him as well as the intruders who had terrified them only moments before.

"Kaylen?" His voice was sharper. "Snap out of it. How many?"

She jerked back to reality. "Two."

"Which way did they go?"

"I didn't see after they ran out." She got to her feet. She still felt a little shaky, but as soon as she'd seen Brian, she had felt her alarm subsiding.

"I think I may have hit one." She tiptoed behind him to the doorway. He took a moment to give her a warning look she had no trouble interpreting. "Don't you dare tell me to stay behind," she whispered. "Is that blood?" She pointed toward a trail of red spots starkly visible against the pale grey flagstones.

"Looks like it." Brian was scanning the vegetation surrounding the patio.

So *much* vegetation, Kaylen thought. One of the intruders could be lying in there injured or just as easily lying in wait for the first person who stepped out of the sun-room.

With that thought in her head, she watched Brian slide from the relative security of his position against the wall to a much less protected position behind a column supporting an overhang heavily covered with what Angela had told her was a species of Wisteria that provided beauty and shade to the patio without taking over the entire garden. But the rest of the garden completely obscured any view of the bay behind the house.

Privacy was a very bad decision, Kaylen thought, when you couldn't see where a pair of intruders had gone. Her heart sank as she watched Brian move to the next column, at the edge of the patio. Kaylen felt her chest tighten.

"Come back inside," she begged, trying to keep the fright out of her voice. She failed miserably and hated herself for not being able to sound strong and ready to cope with anything that came her way. "Angela's calling nine-one-one." She glanced back and read her friend's lips: *Where's Jon?*

Brian had moved to a column on the other side of the patio in that brief moment. Kaylen mimicked his movements and flattened herself against the column opposite him. "Where's Jonathan?" she hissed.

Goddammit, Kaylen. Will you shut up and get back inside?"

She saw as well as heard his exasperation. The withering glance he shot at her made her cringe.

"Brian..." She wasn't sure what else she wanted to say at that moment, but she wasn't going inside without learning why neither Jonathan nor Juliette had returned.

Brian evidently realized why she was being so uncooperative. "He's fine, hon," he told her. "He's untying Juliette. She's okay, too." He jerked his head in the direction of the house. "Please go watch over Angela and let me do my job."

Brian definitely didn't want her partnering him, Kaylen decided. But before retreating with her tail between her legs, she wanted one more piece of information for the Crossfields. "Do you think this was an attempted kidnapping?" she asked in her best stage-whisper.

Brian's sigh was audible. He leaned back against the column and shook his head, like he couldn't believe he had to deal with her. "Can't you ever let me tell you what to do, even when it's in your best interest?"

"Probably not." She watched him roll his eyes. "Well, was it a botched kidnapping?"

"Maybe." His attention was on the area beyond the patio again. She'd been dismissed.

"I hit someone, didn't I?" she asked. "There's too much blood for one of them to have scraped themselves on the doorframe or something."

"Yes, I think you did." His voice was low and measured, but filled with irritation. "Hon, Angela needs you; I don't. If you won't let me get after them, they'll escape, even if one of them is wounded. I'll be fine...I promise."

Kaylen still didn't want to leave him alone in that secluded garden, but she told herself Brian knew far more about ambushes than she did, and she was delaying the inevitable. He had to go after them, and he could pursue them in a far safer manner if she wasn't crashing along behind him because she was still wearing three-inch heeled Christian Louboutin dress shoes and a tight skirt.

He glided off the patio like the silent hunter he was. The enormous responsibility of his profession weighed heavily on her as she returned to the sun-room in the same manner she had left it. Her last view of Brian was a glimpse of one pale gray suit sleeve as he disappeared behind huge green leaves and thick ferns. No sound carried from his progress. Kaylen reminded herself that Brian was as noiseless and potentially deadly as those he was pursuing.

"Did you find anyone?" Angela asked. She had the phone in one hand and her knitting needle clutched in the other. "The dispatcher's staying on the line with me until the police arrive...the other police," she corrected herself. "I told them Brian's here."

"Thank you," Kaylen said. "I should have told you that. If they don't know he's on-scene already, he's in danger of getting shot, himself." She silently berated herself for still being a complete idiot where police procedures were concerned. She should *know* better.

She pulled a chair over beside the French doors, so she could keep watch in case anyone other than the love of her life came back. "Brian's gone to see if anyone's still on your property" she told Angela. "It looks like I may have hit one of them. There's a trail of what looks like blood drops going across the patio."

Angela's blue eyes widened. "He didn't want you with him? After you shot at them?"

"He wanted me to watch over you. He said Jonathan and Juliette are both fine, but he's untying her."

"Thank God." The tightness on Angela's face eased. "Tied up?" she asked. "Where?"

Kaylen barely heard her friend's response. She was still waging an internal battle with her own emotions. She wanted to sound reasonable and composed instead of disappointed and fragmented. She knew she was barely functioning, and it didn't sit well with her. Shades of her initial panic after Brian got shot. She *had* to pull herself together.

She reminded herself that she had proved her worth to Brian before. But when the occasion arose again, he didn't want her with him. Was it because he'd sensed she was on the brink of losing control, or he didn't trust her after how she had reacted to the incident with Sam? Maybe she deserved that, but hadn't she also redeemed herself by using her gun when there was imminent danger instead of only a mild threat of it? She certainly hadn't received any thanks for it, she told herself with a little surge of resentment..

"He doesn't want to have to look out for my safety as well as his," she said. *Reasonable. Arguable.* But not what Kaylen wanted from Brian. "I have to respect that, even if I don't like it," she said. "He's the cop." She looked down at the Sig. "I'm just a socialite who knows how to use a gun."

"I think you're a lot more than that," Angela said.

Kaylen heard footsteps running down the hallway outside the closed door. She jumped up and raised her gun, again.

"What's going on in here?" yelled a male voice outside the door. "Angie, are you okay? Kaylen? I hear your voices." Jonathan burst into the room.

Thank God he had spoken before coming through that door, Kaylen thought, her legs weak with relief. *She could so easily have shot him.* She lowered the Sig and saw how badly her hand was shaking.

"We're fine," Angela reassured Jonathan. "Where's Juliette?"

"Behind me, I hope." He went back out into the hallway and returned with one arm supporting the housekeeper. She had trouble walking, and he had to half-carry her to a couch, where he carefully seated her.

"I am okay, Mr. Jonathan," Juliette assured him. "My arms and legs are hurting from being tied up."

Angela rushed over to Juliette.

"Hogtied. I had to cut her loose." Jonathan looked around. "Where's Brian, for God's sake? And who was shooting?"

"Me; I was doing the shooting," Kaylen told him. "Brian's outside."

Jonathan started toward the patio, Ruger in hand.

"Don't," Kaylen said. "He doesn't want any of us out there. It looks like I hit one of the two intruders."

"There's blood on the patio," Angela said. "Kaylen saw it."

"Thank God you were here." Jonathan's voice quivered as he looked at his wife. "Those doors should have been locked," he said, his voice strengthening. "The kitchen door was unlocked, too. Juliette, did you let anyone inside?"

"No, Mr. Jonathan." Juliette adamantly shook her head. "I was coming out of the pantry with the tea when the back door opened and a masked man came into the kitchen. I was so scared. He ran right up to me. He must have hit me, and I fell." She tentatively touched a bruise on her cheek. "I didn't get knocked out, but falling took all the breath out of me. I couldn't cry out until he had dragged me into the pantry. He tore off my apron. I thought he was going to kill me." She paused and took a big, sobbing breath.

Angela patted Juliette's hand. "It's okay," she said. "You're safe now."

Juliette dabbed her eyes with a tissue Angela handed her before continuing. "No one could hear me scream, anyway. That door is so thick, and he had closed it behind us. When I opened my mouth, he stuffed the apron inside. I couldn't spit it out. I was afraid I was going to swallow it. I tried to fight him, but he must have found the rope the gardeners left outside the kitchen door a couple of days ago, and he tied me up. I didn't like the rope outside, so I put it into the pantry until the gardeners come back next week. I wish I hadn't done that." She took a sip of water from the bottle Jonathan brought her. "I tried to fight him, but he was so strong."

Angela put an arm around her housekeeper's shoulders. "You were so brave."

"I was so lucky." Juliette took another sip of water. "If he was going to kill me, he would have done it." She put down the bottle, rubbed one of her elbows and winced. "My arms and legs went to sleep, but now they're waking up, and they are so painful."

Angela took over rubbing Juliette's elbow. "Is that better?"

"Much. Thank you, Ms. Angela." Juliette nodded. "I am fine. I should make the tea."

"No one else is going out of this room until the police arrive," Jonathan said.

"I'm not going anywhere." Kaylen held up both hands, one still holding the Sig.

"Could you please both put those guns away?" Angela asked. "I don't think the police will want to see you with them."

"I'm not putting mine away until they ring the doorbell," Jonathan said.

"Me, neither." Kaylen sat back on the chair next to the French doors and beyond, the empty patio. "I wish Brian would come back."

And suddenly, as though her wish had been granted, there he was, breaking out of the undergrowth and striding across the patio. Relief surged through her. Kaylen jumped to her feet.

"Thank God, you're safe." She wanted to run out and hug him, but he didn't look receptive. He was all business, and she knew she had to be content that he'd come back safe and sound. *No clinging,* she told herself. He wouldn't like that.

"Did you find anything? Anyone?" Jonathan asked as Brian came inside.

"No sign of them, although they'd cut a path through the undergrowth that was easy to follow. I lost the blood trail outside your back gates, which were standing wide open. A bunch of tracks look like they're from an SUV. Someone disabled your security system and came right in." He turned his attention to Kaylen. "You definitely hit one of them. Look, what I need from you and Angela is a good description of your assailants."

"I can do that." Kaylen said.

"Me, too." Angela echoed.

"Good." Brian nodded his approval. "Juliette, did you get a look at whoever attacked you?"

"I did," she said.

No wasted words from any of them, Kaylen thought. She decided Brian's no-nonsense, commanding presence was getting the results he wanted. He might not be a touchy-feely man, but he certainly could put a stop to any signs of panic. Her own trembling had ceased as soon as he returned.

The doorbell rang. Loud knocking followed.

"Hold that thought," Brian said. "I'll get the door along with Jonathan."

Jonathan started forward.

"Put your gun away, first, will you?" Brian said. "We don't want anyone else getting shot around here."

"What about mine?" Kaylen asked. "I was the one doing the shooting."

"Put yours on the table over there." Brian pointed to the other side of the room. "Angela, you and Juliette stay on the couch. Kaylen, drag a chair over beside the couch, and stay on it. Don't any of you move until you're told to."

At long last, he gave Kaylen a reassuring smile before leaving the room with Jonathan.

CHAPTER TWENTY-FOUR

"THERE'S something you should see in the kitchen, Sergeant," a female uniformed officer told Brian in an undertone as he stood at the back of the sun-room and listened while the Crossfields, Juliette and Kaylen gave their statements to detectives from the Robbery Investigations bureau.

Brian surmised the Crossfields' address must have alerted the detectives' response. He realized his probational status couldn't have become general knowledge at the precinct, or being asked to participate in the investigation would probably have been nixed.

He nodded to Officer Mullins and followed her out to the kitchen. Scrawled across a large blackboard beside the pantry was a message: *WHERE'S THE MONEY?*

"What do you think that means?" Mullins asked, her dark eyes quizzical below arched eyebrows.

Brian tried to shrug non-committedly while his mind raced and he felt as though he'd been hit with a cold slap from a dead hand. "No idea."

"It could mean something to the Crossfields," Mullins said. "I noticed it when the pantry door was dusted for prints."

"Good catch," he told her. "I'll take care of it. You'd better see if you're needed outside."

"Yes, sir." She gave him a quick smile before walking briskly out the back door and down the steps to the path that led to a triple car garage and a number of uniformed officers searching the perimeter of the driveway.

When he was sure he was alone, Brian took a photo of the message with his cell then erased it with a paper towel. He wasn't sure whether Angela or Kaylen had been the intended kidnap victim, but he figured Juliette had been tied up as a distraction. The message on the blackboard had to be for him.

The cartel was definitely back, and they wanted the money Tim had accumulated from his connection with them. Maybe Tim had gone legit before his death, but the seed money for his enterprises may not have been laundered sufficiently. Also at play might be the contents of the attaché case now stashed in an out-of-state safe deposit box. Tim's intended get-away funds for his new life in Mexico. Just over a million dollars in $100 bills.

Brian had wondered when that money was going to become an issue. Now he knew. That time was now.

CHAPTER TWENTY-FIVE

"CAN'T you just give them the money and be done?" Kaylen asked as they sat in the stern of the *NTK* that evening. "I know you don't want to use it yourself, but you nixed donating it to charity in case the numbers on the bills came back to bite you. So it's hanging around doing nothing."

Brian had persuaded her she shouldn't go to Bannisters, not that she needed much convincing after seeing several news-vans parked along the street outside the Crossfields' home.

"I don't think it'll be that easy, hon," he told her. "These aren't reasonable people."

"I know, believe me. I was right there when they were being unreasonable." She stared out at the water and shuddered.

"Scare tactics seem to be the only thing they're using right now," he said, feeling he needed to give her some reassurance. "Although if you hadn't been armed, I don't know what would have happened to you and Angela."

"Better not think too much about possible outcomes, huh?" She gave him a half-smile. "You think Juliette got tied up as a distraction, don't you?"

He nodded. "They disabled the security system without any trouble whatsoever. State of the art didn't even slow them down. The Crossfields are much better off staying in a safe house, at least for tonight." He took her hand. "The only reason you're not there with Angela and Jonathan is because you finally agreed to hire a bodyguard."

"Who you sent home for the night." She slid her hand out of his, but then moved her chair so she could kick off her shoes and put her feet into his lap. "I know I shouldn't, but I like the thought of having you off work and around more to be with me."

"Oh, no." Brian tapped one of her ankles. "Don't you go thinking this is gonna be an everyday thing. I'm working a charter tomorrow, as a favor to friends of the Crossfields, so that bodyguard will be back. No taking any unnecessary chances. And don't tell me Rob can watch you at the club, either. He's needed to manage Bannisters. Besides, he's not trained as a bodyguard."

"You don't need to tell me. I agree. He's already doing more than his job description requires. If I asked him to take on guarding me, he'd probably quit. But those intruders had to be after Angela or Jonathan. They'd have had no idea we'd be there. We didn't even know it ourselves until we got into that argument, and I insisted on going with you."

Brian started rubbing her feet. He found it very therapeutic. "Maybe they had an inside track. I'll have to get everything swept for bugs again." He tried not to sigh, but found it difficult. "This is like a recurring nightmare," he muttered, mostly to himself.

But Kaylen heard, despite the creaking of the boats and the fresh breeze that had strengthened as they sat outside. "You've got that right." She sank down further in the chair. "Such a pity, when everything seemed to be going so well." She tilted her head back. "And it's such a lovely evening."

"It is," he agreed. "The stars are out, the moon's shining on the water, and we're together." He ran his hand up her leg. She had changed out of the business suit into a pair of capris and a tank top she'd left on the boat. Brian slid his fingers under the edge of her pants-leg to caress her knee before running his hand up her thigh to the junction of her legs.

"You're a lot different than my other bodyguard," she said, her voice taking on a playful quality.

"I'd better be." He pulled her onto his lap and kissed her while he caressed her back under the tank top, ran his hands over her breasts and unhooked her bra.

But as he started to lift the bra out of his way, she sat upright and looked directly at him.

"Brian, what good would it do a cartel to kidnap either of the Crossfields if what they really wanted was to hurt either you or me? Maybe both of us?"

Damn, damn, damn.

"Can't we forget about the cartel for tonight?"

He wanted to make love to her, not rehash reasons that had already been gone through ad nauseum on the way back to the boat. He tried to draw her back down so he could kiss her again while he cupped one breast and stroked her erect nipple.

"How can we forget everything that happened today?" She struggled off his lap.

The moment was gone.

"I don't have all the answers, hon," he said, making no attempt to hide his frustration. "In fact, I've probably got as many questions as you do. Maybe more." He ran a hand through his hair and found it matted with salt. Distractedly, he thought it was past time he got a haircut. He glanced at his watch. 9:30 PM. Still early. Maybe he needed to get dinner into her and a couple of glasses of wine. Then she'd be more relaxed and receptive.

"Are you hungry?" he asked. "We could eat something and get an early night."

"Okay." She sounded relieved. "I can whip up an omelet. You've got eggs and cheese in your refrigerator. I put them there after that shopping trip Sam interrupted."

"Sounds good. Coffee, too."

"Decaf, if you're planning to go to bed to sleep." She smiled, suddenly. "I know that's not what's on your mind. But I don't know whether you're going to get your way with me tonight. I'm still pretty shaken up. I got to use that gun, and let me tell you, I didn't enjoy pulling the trigger one bit."

"Maybe not, but you probably saved Angela and possibly yourself, too, when you did." He took her in his arms again, and that time, she didn't resist. "I love you for many reasons, Kaylen Roberts," he told her. "But I think what stands out most for me is your resilience. You're a fighter, and I have so much admiration for you, sometimes it hurts."

"I could say the same about you," she said, and then she initiated kissing him very, very deeply.

But they were interrupted again when his phone rang. They both sighed, almost in unison.

"I have to answer it," he said.

"I know. I suppose it's more bad news."

He looked at the screen. "Homicide calling. Better not be Trehorn. I'm not in the mood."

Kaylen patted his arm. "I'd better get started on that omelet." She went into the salon and closed the door behind her.

Brian was surprised to hear a female voice on the end of the line. At first, he thought Alicia Solis must be working late.

"Hi, Swift. How's your evening?" The voice was strong, well-modulated and cheerful. "It's Deanna Villaneuva," she said. "Sorry to call this late, but I was given the task of tracking down that reporter, Mireille Shagassi, and setting up another interview with you."

That was the last thing Brian wanted to hear. "Who told you to arrange that?" he asked, not even trying to disguise his annoyance. "Trehorn?"

"Whoa, cowboy. Don't shoot the messenger. It was Chief Shaw. He said his admin assistant's got a lot on her plate, so he delegated. I think he qualifies for ordering you around as well as the rest of us."

Still pissed, Brian grunted.

"Look, I should have started by telling you thanks for the recommendation," she said, ignoring his less-than-enthusiastic response. "My transfer's been approved. I came clean about the pregnancy so there are no misunderstandings, although I'll leave it up to you whether you want me to break the news to our coworkers or you want the honors yourself."

Brian felt his righteous indignation pop like some invisible force had put a pin through it. "That's good news, Villanueva." He felt a sense of relief at the thought of having her become part of his small unit while his life was back in turmoil. "Welcome to Cold Case."

"Thanks, Sergeant."

"Call me Swift. It sits better with me." He wasn't ready for her to call him Brian.

"Gotcha. What time you want me in the squad room tomorrow?"

"Eight-thirty. It's more of a closet office than a squad room." He'd figured he'd better get there at eight sharp to warn Mills and Gabe they were getting company. Despite his own satisfaction at having more help, especially from someone he'd liked immediately, he wondered how the rest of the team would feel admitting a new member into their tight-knit squad. Especially when she'd be the only one who didn't know about his supposed suspension being a ruse. They wouldn't be able to include her in some of their meetings, he thought. But she'd be boots on the ground while he couldn't be at the precinct, and very capable boots, at that.

"I talked to my doctor," she said. "He told me the puking should stop in a week or so, once I get past the first trimester. I sure hope he's right. I'm pretty tired of this."

"I bet." Brian didn't know what else to say to that. Now he had two pregnant women in his immediate circle, both puking their guts out on a regular basis. He wondered whether he had experienced a lapse of common sense when he'd suggested bringing Villaneuva on board. But that was before he knew about Angela Crossfield's severe nausea.

Hindsight, he thought sadly. *Hindsight, indeed.*

"So when and where's this do-over with Shagassi?" he asked.

"I've been given the job of coordinating everything, so I checked her availability," Villanueva said. "She's willing to meet tomorrow afternoon. She cleared her calendar. You get to say where and when; she'll turn up. She figured neutral ground, but private. Maybe someone's home. I suggested my apartment."

"You sure you wanna do that?"

"Yeah. It'll work out fine. I'll give you the address after the Cold Case meeting. What time? Shagassi asked me to text her this evening."

Brian ran through his plans for the following day. Nothing that couldn't be shifted around. "One," he said.

"See you tomorrow, Swift."

"Thanks, Villaneuva."

"No problem." She hung up.

Brian took a couple of minutes to breathe in the evening air before joining Kaylen for their impromptu meal. As he looked across the moonlit water beyond the stern, he had a lot of questions he couldn't answer.

When and where would the cartel demand the hand-off of Tim's money? How much was he willing to tell any of his friends and coworkers about the attaché case and how he'd kept it secret from the investigation into his brother's murder? How was he going to keep Kaylen out of everything, so she wouldn't meddle or put herself in danger? And would she still be able to stay on-track with Treasure's opening?

CHAPTER TWENTY-SIX

BRIAN ARRIVED at Deanna Villanueva's building at 12:45 PM the following afternoon. He had to stand outside and call her to be admitted into the front lobby. As soon as the elevator door opened and he stepped out onto the second floor, a door opened and Deanna popped her head out, signaling to him.

"Come on in." She stood aside.

Brian stepped into a short hallway. Deanna closed and locked the door behind him.

"The living room's straight ahead," she said.

Brian passed an alcove that held a small home office before walking into a living room that wasn't much larger. A galley-type kitchen stood on the other side of a miniscule breakfast bar. Beyond the living-room was Villanueva's bedroom, accommodating what looked like a double bed and a small nightstand. He wondered where the hell she planned to put that baby when it came.

"Pretty small, but it's home," she said from behind him. "You want a soda, water, ice tea? I'm off coffee because of the pregnancy, and the tea's decaf."

"Water's fine. Thanks." He looked at the possibilities for the interview. Either the breakfast bar or the loveseat would put them in very close quarters. He decided to wait for Mireille Shagassi to arrive and seat herself wherever she wanted to work. In the meantime, he took the water bottle Villanueva handed him and walked over to look through sliding glass doors that lead to the smallest patio he had ever seen.

"I liked your crew this morning," Villanueva said. "I hope they feel the same way about me."

Brian turned back to face her. He noted she was wearing a pair of faded jeans and a loose top that Kaylen had clued him in was a peasant blouse. She'd pointed one out in a store window in Coral Gables only a few days ago. When life had been fairly calm and normal for them, Brian thought with a trace of irony.

Villaneuva looked neat and comfortable with her hair pulled back into a pony tail and minimal makeup. Very different from Kaylen, who always looked like she had just returned from a fashion shoot. Brian liked both women's styles. They were comfortable in their own skin and knew what looked good on them.

"Mills said he was impressed with your credentials," he told her. "Gabe's easy going. As long as you treat him with the respect he deserves, he'll work any hours asked, any day of the week."

"You've been clearing cases that haven't been solved in years," she said. "I'm impressed, and very happy to be working with all of you, as I said this morning. I can learn a lot from you about teamwork and investigation techniques."

"As long as you don't use us as a stepping stone," he cautioned her. "I don't like that approach."

"I heard that, loud and clear from the guys in Homicide." She shrugged. "Doesn't worry me. I'm a straight-shooter, Swift. I expect the same courtesy in return, and my first impression is that's what I'll get in Cold Case."

"We're not as exciting as Homicide," Brian warned. "It's a lot of going over old material that's already been gone over many times before, looking for discrepancies in statements, getting use out of new forensic techniques whenever possible, and trying to jog memories that've been hidden away for years."

"You've been surprised yourself about how fascinating that is, haven't you?" She came over to stand beside him. "I wish I had a view of the water," she said. "Maybe by the time my lease is up, my finances will have recovered from the move. But then I'll have the added expenses of child-care." Her teeth worried her lower lip. "Not sure how all that's going to pan out, but I'm taking one day at a time." She took a sip of water.

"How's the nausea?" he asked, unsure whether she was going to start retching again.

"It's good today." She grinned up at him. "Don't worry, Swift. I won't need to rush off in the middle of this interview and leave you to be grilled by Shagassi without back-up."

The call-box alerted them to the reporter's arrival. Deanna answered the door and left Brian feeling awkward as he stood beside the breakfast bar. He heard murmuring before both women came down the hallway, Shagassi following Villanueva.

"Sergeant Swift." Mireille Shagassi was also dressed casually in a pair of pale green pants and a flowered blouse. A black attaché case hung over her left shoulder. She extended her right hand as she walked up to him. "Good of you to meet with me again."

"I probably should be the one saying that," he conceded, hoping that would be enough crow-eating to satisfy the reporter.

"I found your reputation for giving short and very direct responses wasn't ill-deserved," she said, but she gave a brief smile. "This is a more informal follow-up. I understand Detective Villanueva has some past experience with community relations."

Brian didn't know what to say to that remark. Villanueva hadn't included that little detail during her quick run-down of her job history while they were at the storage facility.

"A little," Villanueva said. "On active service. But that's ancient history. My position here today is to provide neutral ground for the meeting and maintain that position."

"Very well." Shagassi took the attaché case's strap off her shoulder as she surveyed the room. "Maybe we can sit on the loveseat, Sergeant? I can use the coffee table for my recorder, if you agree to its use, and I'll put my notepad on my lap. You do understand I need to take notes?" She unzipped the case and started to pull out a hand-held recorder.

Brian didn't want any of his words to be misconstrued, and putting everything on tape would make it impossible for him to try to recant anything. He took a moment to think about how to diplomatically refuse to be recorded.

"I believe Sergeant Swift would feel a lot more comfortable if you stayed with the handwritten notes," Villanueva said, stepping into the gap. "I believe that's what Chief Shaw wants."

"Understood." Reluctantly, it seemed, Shagassi returned the recorder to the case and took out her notepad and pen instead.

"I think you'd be more relaxed in my office chair," Villanueva said to Brian. "I'll share the loveseat with Ms. Shagassi. You're tall, and it's pretty low. Perhaps you can roll that in while I get her something to drink?"

"Good idea." As Brian went to get the chair, he heard Deanna asking Mireille what she preferred to drink, and then easing in a couple of comments about how insightful she thought the reporter's last few interviews had been.

Villanueva definitely had experience with community relations, he thought. She was going to be a good foil for his brash interrogation methods, and a real asset to Cold Case.

CHAPTER TWENTY-SEVEN

"So, you became entangled, so to speak, in the homicide investigation of the coffee shop murders against the department's better judgment?" Shagassi asked after they had gone over the current state of the investigation.

"You could put it that way." Brian took another sip of his water. He'd almost finished it, and they had only been talking for eight minutes according to the clock over the breakfast bar. He'd managed to sit with his back to the patio doors, which had an unobstructed view of a blank brick wall beyond the tiny patio. That allowed him to not only keep both women in sight but also the small entryway and front door.

"Had you ever seen that man in painter's overalls before?" Shagassi asked. She flipped back a couple of pages in her notes. "I understand his name is Beale Friendly." She permitted herself a brief smile. "He doesn't seem to be a gentleman living up to his name, does he? Not only was he belligerent toward you, but I heard through the grapevine that he was yelling at everyone in the precinct who came into contact with him later on, and I think he probably scared that other poor reporter half to death. The one he buttonholed at the crime scene."

Brian shrugged lightly. "I was too busy to notice what he was doing, and I don't listen to gossip at the precinct."

"No, I suppose you wouldn't." Mireille Shagassi paused, pen over pad. "Although you've been the brunt of a lot of it over the last few years, haven't you?"

Brian could have kicked himself. He'd walked right into that trap. Again, he warned himself Mireille Shagassi was a celebrated investigative journalist. She probably had a shelf filled with awards in her home, but he wasn't planning to hand her another one for a supposed exposé of his and Tim's corrupt dealings.

"I was cleared of all charges," he said, striving to maintain an even tone of voice. At all costs, he had to avoid any trace of the irritation he felt at her probing.

He'd had trouble controlling his emotions since the moment inside the coffee shop when Antonio had grabbed his jacket with a bloodstained hand and tried to speak. Brian knew he should have called Dr. Fleming and gone in for an appointment, but he'd been too preoccupied. The psychologist would not be amused. Neither would Hal.

"Whatever this guy Friendly is alleging is a false accusation," he continued, realizing he'd paused longer than he should have.

Both women were watching him intently, Shagassi with narrowed almond-shaped eyes, Villanueva with a slight crease between her brows.

"Unfortunately, police officers are frequently subjected to false claims," Brian said, trying to appeal to what he hoped was Shagassi's more linear way of thinking. "The public as a whole resents us until they need us, when they're more than glad to see us. Then they resent us again the next time they get pulled over for speeding."

Villanueva got up, went into the kitchen and brought more water for all of them. "Is anyone apart from me getting too warm?" she asked.

"I'm fine," Brian said. He looked at Shagassi. "You?"

"I'm actually a little cold," she said. "I should have brought my jacket in from the car. But don't worry about me, I'll be fine." She smiled up at Villanueva, who was about to lower the thermostat.

"My hormones must be to blame," Villanueva said. "Sorry for the interruption."

Shagassi shifted on the loveseat, uncrossed her legs at the ankles but kept her feet together, lined up evenly in her black, low-heeled shoes. "Well, Sergeant Swift, do you have any idea why this man should suddenly appear outside a coffee shop you were visiting right after a multiple homicide occurred, and then take the opportunity to accuse you of taking bribes right on camera?"

"No."

Brian wasn't wading into that quagmire. He had no idea whether Friendly had any connection to the coffee shop's staff, and he wasn't about to start searching for explanations to satisfy Shagassi. He wondered how the other reporter had managed to get so conveniently close to that disgruntled painter. Her unexpected arrival at the scene in the first place smacked of a lot more than some chance diversion from her original destination.

"Very strange, isn't it?" Mireille asked, her gaze unblinking, her face devoid of any emotion.

So much for the low-key approach, Brian thought. His belief that Shagassi couldn't keep that up for long was about to materialize. Despite any prior promises she'd made to get this meeting, her investigative chops were firing on all cylinders.

"It is," he agreed. "The detectives from the Homicide Bureau are in charge of the investigation. You'll need to go through proper channels to get a statement from whoever is assigned to that case. Maybe even Lieutenant Darrell Trehorn, himself, if he's available." *And agreeable, the snide bastard,* he wanted to add, but stopped himself.

She nodded. "I understand your reluctance to speak about a case in which you don't have, perhaps, an official interest. But you must have a *personal* interest, Sergeant Swift. I learned this wasn't your first visit to this particular coffee shop."

"No." He took a deep breath. For a moment, he couldn't maintain eye contact with her, which surprised him. "Those people have been friends. I've picked up coffee from Antonio, Aurelio and Rigo for the past year."

"For your Wednesday morning meetings," Shagassi said, quietly.

"Yes."

"I thought all officers were taught not to use the same routes and routines to avoid becoming predictable."

"We can't always do that. I needed somewhere reliable that could take an order and have it hot and ready when I dropped by to pick it up," he said. "There are limits to what we can do, Ms. Shagassi, to keep any number of potential assailants at bay while leading somewhat normal lives. If I was a target, I could have been approached at many other locations, including my home." He stopped himself from adding anything else. No sense in drawing attention to the marina, Kaylen or her clubs.

"I suppose that's true. But certainly, a small coffee shop is a preferable target to a large club owned by your girlfriend, who employs bouncers and has a well-known state-of-the-art security system."

"Ms. Shagassi, that's unfair and hostile," Villanueva said. "The agreement for this interview was to avoid personal attacks."

"This is all off the record," Shagassi said. "I only have my handwritten notes."

"We're depending on your memory and those notes to give Sergeant Swift a fair and unbiased interview now he's no longer under the duress of being at a fresh crime scene with numerous upset and in some cases hysterical witnesses," Villanueva said. She wasn't blinking. Her gaze was steady and Brian noted, clearly transmitting intimidation that he knew Shagassi must not be immune to, despite her training.

Mireille Shagassi sat completely still, both hands resting on her notepad. "Understood," she said.

"Good." Villanueva got up from the loveseat. "It's hot in here," she announced. "I'm breaking out the cookies after I turn down the thermostat and lend you a sweater, Mireille. I think we could all do with a five-minute break." She smiled at Brian. "I understand chocolate chip with walnuts is your favorite, Sergeant. I have those. Ms. Shagassi, I hope those are okay for you, too. No allergies to nuts or chocolate?"

"No." Mireille placed her notepad and pen on the little coffee table. "Why don't I help you by getting the cookies plated while you find me a sweater?"

She gave Brian a tight smile as she passed him. He took the opportunity to open one of the sliding glass doors enough to squeeze past a miniscule iron table and chair onto the balcony, He tested the railing before leaning against it to look down at the central courtyard. Behind him, he heard the two women chatting in the kitchen as though they were old friends.

He appreciated the time Villanueva had given him to regain his composure. He'd thought he was more than ready for that interview, but Shagassi had barely begun her questioning before he'd started to react. As soon as he left the building, he had to put in a call to Fleming.

CHAPTER TWENTY-EIGHT

"I'M SO glad you could come to stay," Angela told Kaylen as she led the way up to the second floor of a sprawling waterfront home located in an exclusive gated community in Coral Gables. "Jonathan thought this would be a perfect temporary home for us. Our friends will be out of the country for the next two months, and were so happy we could house-sit. They completely understand our need for secrecy. They didn't ask why we needed to relocate, but I mentioned we were having some renovations done before the baby comes."

"You've got an aptitude for thinking on your feet, Angela." Kaylen said "I wish I did. I tend to blurt things out and then wonder why I did that."

Kaylen wished Angela would move a little faster. She'd brought a large suitcase with as many of her toiletries crammed into it as she could get as well as several casual outfits. A garment bag filled with business suits and another with cocktail dresses still remained in her car.

"Is there a dumb waiter?" she asked when they finally reached the top and she was able to set down her burden.

"Unfortunately not. The staff have to tote everything up and down the stairs. That's going to be the one big drawback here." Angela grimaced. "There are no bedrooms downstairs. That case looks really heavy. I wish I could help you."

"Be glad you can't." Kaylen took a moment to pull her hair into a ponytail with a clip from her purse while she got her breath back. "Your friends must be very fit," she said as she rolled her suitcase behind Angela down a long hallway. "Please don't tell me we're going to rooms at the very end."

"We are. They're the best. They overlook the grounds and the water."

"I'd opt for a view of the parking lot or a utility shed to stay close to the stairs," Kaylen said.

But when they finally arrived at their goal, she quickly changed her mind.

Angela threw open a door and stood back. "Voila," she said, and gestured.

The view was absolutely stunning. "It's hard to find words," Kaylen said. Biscayne Bay glittered on the right side of one wall filled with floor-to-ceiling windows. Left and center, a canal sparkled. A private dock held one boat almost as large as the *Need to Know*.

"I knew you'd like it." Angela smiled in that self-satisfied way of hers that should irritate but somehow didn't, because Angela frequently really did know best.

Kaylen pulled her case into the room, where the wheels sank into a thickly-piled pale gray carpet covered with wreaths of delicately-hued flowers. She abandoned her luggage to pull back sliding glass doors and step out onto a wide balcony that accommodated a pair of upholstered loungers with a low table between them and a glass-topped table with two chairs waiting for an intimate breakfast or a romantic dinner.

"You want to see my room?" Angela grinned widely.

"Of course."

"Two doors down," Angela said. "I wanted you and Brian to have some privacy when he stays over."

"I appreciate the thought, but we need to be right next to each other. If something happened to you, I wouldn't hear anything." Kaylen followed Angela back through the expansive suite into the corridor. "And even though I absolutely love this, we need to be close to the staircase. We can't be trapped here at the end of the house.

Brian will never agree to this arrangement, and I have to agree with him."

Angela paused to open a door on the opposite side of the hallway and situated between their two prospective bedrooms. "Servants' access."

Kaylen saw spiraling stairs. "Okay, I feel slightly more optimistic."

"We'll be fine," Angela assured her. "No one outside of the friends who own this home, Jonathan, Brian and whoever else Brian trusts will know we're here. If someone follows you from either of your clubs, well, you'll have to be vigilant and lose them."

"I'm not a trained operative from the CIA or something, you know." Kaylen followed Angela to her friend's door.

"Maybe not, but you've had a lot more experience being on the lam than I do." Angela paused again, hand on the door handle. She looked up at Kaylen. "You told me you had to live off the grid for a while with Brian. I know he's given you a lot of training. You carry a firearm, and as I saw firsthand, you use it very effectively. I'm not at all worried. You shouldn't be, either."

"Brian says to always be vigilant. He never lets down his guard. Sometimes, not even when we're alone." She knew her tone sounded like a reprimand, but she wasn't sure whether she meant that for Angela or Brian.

Angela opened the door to her own suite. "Pretty similar to yours," she said. "I have the same view, too." She took Kaylen's hand and gently pulled her into the room. "This is going to work out. I'm sure of it. Jonathan was, too. So sure, he felt secure enough about everything to take off early for his trip. You can't believe how relieved I am. Now he'll be back well before the baby's due."

"I'm so glad he feels you're in good enough hands to do that." Kaylen felt a mixture of relief and trepidation. She knew Brian and Jim could watch over her own safety, but would they also be able to guarantee Angela's?

"I insisted I would be okay," Angela said. "I pushed him to go. One less person in Miami for Brian to worry about., and he'll be able to supervise the renovations after we decide what we want for the baby's room and the nanny's quarters."

Maybe this wasn't the first time the Crossfields had been forced to confront some form of a threat, Kaylen mused. They seemed to have recovered really quickly after their initial shock over the home invasion.

"How did you manage to convince him?" she asked. "He was so worried about you."

Angela waved away Jonathan's misgivings. "I told him I feel a lot better, and he knows me well enough to believe me. I promised I'll rest as much as possible and hang out here with you whenever you're not taking care of your business. Juliette's bringing my crafts over as soon as she gets back. She'll be with me when you're not here. She'll tell her family she's going on a trip with us, and we won't have reliable wi-fi or cell connections."

"Aren't you going to be incredibly bored, regardless of how many craft projects you have brought here?" Kaylen worried that Angela would sneak out shopping when she was confronted with many hours alone. "I'm so busy with Treasure and Bannisters right now, I barely have a minute to myself."

"I'll be fine." Angela waved away those misgivings with the same degree of nonchalance as she had expressed for Jonathan's. "You can help me with preliminary plans for the nursery whenever you have a few minutes. I'll send all the results to Jon so he can see what we're doing. He said he'd be useless for choosing baby furniture and paint colors, despite being ultimately responsible for the cause of it." She laughed. "My darling husband, who says he's never held a baby in his entire life. I can't say I remember the last time I did, either."

"You and me, both." Kaylen watched Angela head for a chaise overlooking the balcony and the water beyond. "Getting tired?"

"Yes, and a little nauseated, but I think it'll pass if I relax for a while."

"Can I get you anything? Mineral water? Crackers?"

Angela shook her head. "I'm fine, except maybe something to cover my feet?"

Kaylen saw a delicate gossamer-thin throw at the end of the bed. She brought it over and helped her friend tuck it around herself.

"Mmm." Angela leaned back and closed her eyes. "Sorry, but I'm so sleepy."

"I'll call Brian to let him know we've settled in and then I'm going to bring up the rest of my things and unpack," Kaylen said. "That should keep me busy for a while."

"What time is it?"

"Three."

"Can you wake me in two hours? If I eat on a regular basis, I feel better." Angela yawned. "Maybe you can have something with me before you go to the club."

"I'm not going anywhere tonight," Kaylen said. "Rob's in charge at Bannisters. This is a good time to test his skills. I'm confident he'll pass with flying colors."

"Me, too." Angela's voice was drifting off right along with the rest of her.

Kaylen's feet made no sound on the thick carpeting as she left the suite. She did leave both Angela's door and her own ajar. She took the phone onto the balcony and called Brian, but he didn't pick up.

She knew his meeting with Mireille Shagassi had been scheduled for one o'clock. She figured that must have wound up around 2:00 PM. Maybe he'd gone back to the boat for a while afterward, or even taken a late lunch and just didn't want to answer his phone right at that moment.

She thought about the meeting place. He'd said he was going over to Detective Villaneuva's apartment. Kaylen trampled all over a spark of unrest that flared up at the thought of him alone with either of those two women. Brian could spend time at *any* woman's apartment without anything happening that she wouldn't like, she told herself.

She left him a voicemail to let him know she was getting settled, mentioning nothing about Angela or their location. Brian had coached her extensively on what not to say. Although he believed their connections were secure, he wasn't taking any chances. She made two more trips out to the car to bring up the rest of her luggage and checked her phone for messages without finding any at all.

As she opened her suitcase on a rack she found in the walk-in closet and started to unpack, a nagging little voice in the back of her mind asked what Brian could be doing for two hours either with Mireille Shagassi or the Cold Case squad's newest addition. She'd heard something in Brian's voice when he mentioned Detective Deanna Villanueva that had surprised her…genuine like.

CHAPTER TWENTY-NINE

"DID you get a good grilling from that reporter?" Jim asked when Brian arrived back at the *NTK*.

"Damn right." Brian shrugged out of his jacket, pulled off his tie and unfastened the top two buttons of his shirt. "Like something out of the Spanish Inquisition. But she raised some good points that really got me thinking. Like, how could that damned guy, the painter whose name turns out to be Beale Friendly for Christ's sake, know I was going to be at the coffee shop that morning? I've never seen him there before, so he's not a Wednesday regular. Coincidentally, there's a shooting and he recognizes me?"

"Doesn't sound very feasible to me, either, buddy." Jim handed Brian a beer from the cooler.

Brian dropped his jacket and tie onto the back of the chair opposite Jim's, sat and popped the top on his can. "Okay, and how did he manage to snag an interview with that young reporter who was way out of her depth at a fresh crime scene?" Brian took a swig from his can and pointed his finger at Jim. "You tell me that."

"You want me go ask him or run a background check?" Jim leaned forward in his chair.

"No, I don't want you going anywhere near him. You'll put him on his guard. And I already asked Gabe to do the check. By tomorrow, I should know everything from where he was born right down to how many fillings the guy has in his teeth. Villanueva is gonna question the reporter, Cassandra Bunting. Everyone seems to think if I do it, I'll intimidate her and get nothing." He shook his head when Jim offered a can of peanuts from the table beside his chair.

"They know you well, my friend." Jim nodded sagely. "That interview took an eternity. But you look pretty good on it."

"I stopped by Fleming's office afterward. I've felt kinda jumpy since the murders."

"Good move." Jim drained his can and dropped it into a small trash can behind the cooler. "Who's Villanueva? You've got a new guy at Cold Case?"

"A new female detective. Deanna Villanueva." Brian filled Jim in on the details of her transfer.

His friend's forehead puckered when Brian told him Deanna was pregnant. "That's a hard road she's got ahead of her," Jim said.

"She'll cope." Brian shook his can and found it empty. "She's one strong woman."

"Did you call Kaylen after you left Villanueva's apartment?" Jim asked. "She was worried about your interview."

"I didn't. I'll do that on the way over to see her."

"And…"

"And nothing." Brian crushed his can and tossed it into the trash.

"You think the *NTK's* bugged?" Jim's eyebrows drew together.

"Probably not, but I want it swept daily. *Fanciful Folly,* too."

"This is worse than anything we got into last year," Jim said.

"Yeah." Brian didn't feel the need to elaborate.

"How'd the interview go, anyway? I feel like you're skirting the issue."

"I'm not. It went okay for the most part. Shagassi had trouble remaining completely neutral, but Villanueva stepped in and diffused the situation. I think she's gonna out work well."

"I look forward to meeting her." Jim's jaw jutted forward slightly. "Is she someone Kaylen should worry about?"

"What?" Brian looked at his friend in surprise. "Why in hell would you say that? Villanueva's a coworker. A good one. If she was a guy, would we even be having this conversation?"

"Well, no. There'd be no need." Jim got up. "You want a steak? I'm grilling."

"Too early." Brian glanced at his watch. "I'm gonna shower before I call Kaylen. I'll see if she wants me to pick up dinner."

"Tell her hi, and I'll see her in the morning. What time?"

"I have to leave at eight. Can you be there that early?"

"Please." Jim chuckled. "Usually I've been up a couple of hours at least by then. I'll get coffee on the way over, but I'll wait to cook breakfast until I get there. I'll make it for all of us…except you." He looked disapproving.

"Coffee's all I need in the morning," Brian said. "I've never eaten breakfast. And I doubt

Kaylen'll be up. She keeps clubbing hours and sleeps late even when she's had the night off."

"That she does." Jim stretched, leaned over and grabbed the trash can. "I'll take care of this on the way over to the *Folly.* See you in the morning."

"Thanks Jim."

"No problem. I'll invoice you." Jim left, his chuckle hanging around a moment longer than he did before being caught by the wind and taken out over the water.

Brian took his time going back inside. He appreciated the opportunity to decompress, much easier for him to do when he was out on the boat in the evening. After fifteen minutes, he decided he'd procrastinated long enough.

He got up, stretched and finished unbuttoning his shirt on the way into the salon, where he found Sam Wilson sitting on his couch and two unfamiliar guys, one pointing a Glock 17 from inside the galley, the other standing in front of the banquette with an AK47. Obviously, they weren't taking any chances with him.

"Hello, Swift," Sam said. "Come in and shut the door behind you. We need to talk."

CHAPTER THIRTY

KAYLEN CHECKED HER WATCH AGAIN. She wondered why Brian hadn't called. If he was running late, at least he could have texted.

She got up from her seat at the breakfast table and stood looking out the windows. Dusk had come and gone. Security lights illuminated the patio and the pool area beyond it. She saw her reflection in the glass and closed the blind. She and Angela were alone inside the house, but with two men stationed outside, one at the front entrance, the other patrolling the back patio, she knew she should feel a lot safer than she did. She'd refused when the man stationed inside the house had offered to stay past his shift. Now she regretted that decision.

She turned to face Angela, watching her from the middle of the kitchen. "I'm calling Brian," she said.

"I'm sure he's fine." Angela did not look at all like she believed her own platitude. "He must have been delayed. Maybe he had a flat and had to change a tire."

"He always calls or texts," Kaylen said. *"Always."*

Her call went to his voicemail. She left a brief message, asking him to call her ASAP. "Damned ASAP," she added. "I'm worried, Brian. Don't fool around. We need you over here."

"He's probably just hung up at work." Angela, her head now inside the refrigerator as she searched for something to eat, didn't look up.

Kaylen was glad. She knew her expression would have revealed her anxiety.

He should have left that interview hours ago, a nagging little voice in her head told her. If he'd been delayed, he'd have sent Jim over or asked the indoor bodyguard to stay late. Even if he'd stopped by the *NTK* to change clothes, he shouldn't have been more than an hour and a half late. He'd told her the interview was scheduled for an hour, and knowing Brian, he wouldn't have let it run over.

"I'm going to call Jim," she told Angela's back as her friend looked through take-out containers. "He usually knows when Brian's been home."

She watched as Angela brought out three Styrofoam clamshells, put them on the counter and popped them open to reveal congealed Chinese food.

Jim answered on the first ring. "I left him on the *NTK* easily forty minutes ago," he said. "He wasn't planning a long stay. Hang on, let me look and see if there are still lights on over there. I just finished making myself a steak."

"Thanks, Jim. I'm a bit concerned." *More than a bit,* she thought, her insides churning.

She listened while he took his phone with him, rustling sounds and footfalls accompanying him onto the deck.

"Lights are all on." Jim paused. "He's not alone."

"What do you mean? Who's there?"

"Hard to tell, but I saw a couple of heads. You want me to go check?"

A feeling of dread came over Kaylen. "No, Jim, don't do that," she said. "Call Jack Mills and have him check for us."

"You think something's going down?" Jim's voice had lowered.

"If it was nothing but a social call, he would have let me know. He would have asked you to come over and stay with us if he wasn't leaving shortly after you did. You know how fast he can get ready. And anyway, Brian wouldn't be hanging around chatting on the boat when he knows the inside security detail left promptly at five o'clock."

"Jesus, honey. Are you girls alone in that house?"

Jim's concern made Kaylen's churning increase. Her belly ached, and she felt her breathing quicken. "We are."

"I'll call you back as soon as I've talked to Jack. Keep all the blinds closed and your gun right with you." Jim hung up.

Kaylen paced and told Angela what Jim had said. Instead of the Chinese food, Angela brought out cheese and crackers. She opened a bottle of wine, pouring Kaylen a glass before taking out a mineral water for herself. Kaylen drank two glasses of wine while she waited, and told herself that jumping into her car and leaving Angela in the hands of the security detail wasn't a safe or sane option.

CHAPTER THIRTY-ONE

"I'D LIKE to keep this to ourselves," Sam told Brian out the side of his mouth as he lit a cigar. He shook out the match and looked around for an ashtray. "No need to involve anyone else in our little transaction." Seeing no ashtray, he dropped the match onto the coffee table.

Brian gritted his teeth but forced himself not to react as he saw the guy in the galley move forward, evidently waiting impatiently for any sign of resistance, however slight. Brian noted he was guarding his left arm.

"These were the two guys you sent to the Crossfields," he said. He wanted to call them idiots, but saw no sense in stirring up an already-volatile situation. A quick assessment had told him everyone was too spread out for an effective take-down at that moment.

"Kaylen's learned a lot from you since I last saw her," Sam said.

"She has."

Brian continued to mull over possible resolutions, finding the only workable one was a retreat. But since he'd followed Sam's order to close the door behind him, he'd lose any element of surprise when he not only had to turn and run, but stop to open the damn door.

Taking on the wounded guy with the Glock while the thug with the AK47 shot him wasn't a really workable solution, either. Even leaping on

Sam might not have the desired effect. His back would be exposed until he hauled Wilson's ass off the couch, and diving over the back of it to roll into his bedroom, then get up and slide both doors closed? *No way.*

For the hundredth time over the last few months, he sorely missed the *Destiny,* with its smaller footprint.

"There's no escape, unless you're planning to give my men target practice," Sam said.

My men?

Kaylen had said that's what Sam used to call his security team back at his compound two years ago. They might have fled the country with him. Brian asked himself if they could be the ones who had beaten Tim to death.

He took another good look at each of them. Maybe the one with the assault rifle might have gone a couple of rounds with his brother, but the other one? No fucking way. The guy was too short and puny to have gotten anywhere near 6'3" Tim the gym rat.

"Who killed my brother, Wilson?" Brian asked. No goddamned way was he going to miss out on identifying and then confronting one of Tim's attackers.

"We're not here to discuss your brother." Sam stopped slouching and sat upright. "I came for my money."

"*Your* money? My brother's businesses had nothing to do with you. He *earned* the money he left me in his will."

"Not *that* money. You're playing for time you don't have. We both know what money we're talking about."

"You might, but I sure don't." Brian took one small step back as he folded his arms across his chest.

"Arms up!" barked the guy with the Glock.

Sam jumped. "What's the matter with you?"

"He's gotta be packin.'" Glock guy pointed his weapon at Brian's midsection.

"Well, then, disarm him." Sam sounded exasperated.

"Go put your hands on the counter and spread-eagle your legs," Glock guy said.

Brian turned his back as he started to put out his right arm. He made a snap decision. Once disarmed, he'd be completely unable to defend himself except with his fists. While drawing his own firearm, he took a dive behind the recliner he had resisted being moved across the salon to give more space for the breakfast bar. He got off two shots before the AK47 came into play, and made them count. By the time he got back on his feet, Sam Wilson was the only intruder who wasn't lying on the floor.

Sam, his face even whiter than his double-breasted suit, stared open-mouthed at the man who had only moments before been his prisoner.

"Now, how about telling me who beat my brother to death," Brian said as he dialed 911.

CHAPTER THIRTY-TWO

PANDEMONIUM pretty much ensued over the next hour. Jack Mills arrived only moments after Brian had made his call, which ruined Brian's plans to get names out of Sam Wilson in whatever way he thought would bring the fastest results.

Jim came on the heels of Jack Mills, followed by two patrol cars, and finally several detectives from the Homicide squad itself, including Trehorn, dressed in a pair of cream shorts, tennis shoes and a red Izod shirt with a white cotton sweater draped over his shoulders, the cuffs tastefully folded inside each other to enable the sleeves to drape his chest.

Brian managed to call Kaylen. He told her he was fine, not to watch the news, and to wait for Jim to arrive before asking any more questions. Hal called and was assured that Brian hadn't instigated anything, and Sam Wilson hadn't suffered as much as a hair from his plugs being displaced. The two thugs who had accompanied Sam were dispatched in ambulances. One had sustained a gunshot to his chest, the other had taken one shot to his abdomen. He also had another gunshot wound, less recent and far less severe, to his left arm.

"My aim was a little off," Brian told the chief when he had a moment to bring Hal up to speed. "I had to fire while rolling on the floor."

"You were planning on killing them?" Hal asked.

"Maybe the big one. I thought he might have been one of the guys who murdered Tim. The other one was a punk who needed a defining moment."

"Christ, Swift."

Brian imagined Hal shaking his head.

"Stay away from reporters," Hal ordered.

"You betcha. I've already given one interview today. That was enough."

Brian wiped his face with a towel one of the paramedics had given him. His shirt, damp with perspiration, was stuck to his back, and he had bruised his left shoulder by colliding with one of the stools at the breakfast bar during his dive for cover. He admitted the recliner might have been positioned a little too close to the bar, but it had saved his life. His shoulder ached, but not alarmingly. He silently thanked Dr. West, his orthopedic surgeon, for inserting a plate and screws that could hold up to a challenge.

"How did that interview go?" Hal asked.

Brian brought his mind back to the conversation. "Good, I think. Shagassi seemed to get what she wanted, and I didn't say anything I can't live with."

"Villanueva?"

"Damn good."

"Maybe that transfer shouldn't have been approved. We might need her assets somewhere else, like public relations. Especially after a second incident hits the news where your name is front and center again."

"Chief, if you want me to do my job, then you're gonna have to be prepared for a few bumps."

"More than a few, Swift. When you sit down with Internal Affairs, play nice. Unless I get a different report from them, it sounds like these shootings were justified and we can all move on to Wilson's interrogation. I know *I'd* like a crack at the bastard."

"Yeah, you already know I do, but I doubt I'll be given the opportunity."

"Damn right. You're too close." Hal cleared his throat. "Good job,

Swift." His voice had lowered. He sounded a little less authoritative as he added, "I'm very glad to hear you're still in one piece."

Brian felt vindicated. "No more than I am, Chief."

"I'll ask for everything to be expedited so you get over to Kaylen and Angela Crossfield, although it sounds like they may not need any more protection."

"I'm not so sure about that," Brian hastened to correct his supervisor. "At least, not until they've looked at mug shots and positively ID'd the two I sent to the hospital as the ones who broke into the Crossfields' home. Tim's case was so convoluted, I'm not convinced yet that everything's been wrapped up so neatly."

"Me, neither. Particularly because of that guy who's trying to pin bribery accusations on you again."

Brian heard Hal's pen tapping rhythmically in the background, a sure sign the chief was leery, too. "Exactly," he said.

As he stood on the *NTK's* deck, he watched a small army of police personnel swarming in and out of the interior and on and off the dock as they gathered evidence. The night sky over the marina was still pulsating with emergency vehicle lights. Crime scene tape cordoned off slip 95.

"One crisis at a time, Swift," Hal reminded him. "First you wait around while this crime-scene gets wrapped up, then we'll see how and if we can tie Friendly's accusations and the massacre over at the coffee shop to what happened tonight on your boat."

Brian needed to think of something else. Maybe something more positive. "Anything new on Antonio, the coffee shop's owner?" he asked the chief.

"Yes. Upgraded from critical to serious this afternoon. I asked for clarification. He's conscious but his vital signs are unstable. No interviews. If he continues to improve, he'll be moved from the ICU in a couple of days. Then, and only then, will they let one detective ask him a few questions on a very limited basis."

"That's really good news." Brian felt the tension in his shoulders ease slightly. "I want to go check on him, but I know staff probably won't want to let me in, and his family might prefer I stay away."

"Let's play that by ear." Hal sounded empathetic. "If his condition continues to improve, we need to get in there and find out what he remembers. Anything he knows that'll lead us to the perps. You may be the best one to do it. He grabbed onto you. Doesn't sound like he was laying blame at your door."

"Not at that moment. In that situation, any familiar face would be welcome."

Brian thought of Kaylen, and how comforting it had been to see her at the hospital after he'd thought he was going to die. She'd thought he was going to die, too, and she'd told him not to do that because she needed him. Need was a two-way street with them, he mused, not at all comforted by any of the random thoughts that kept popping, unsolicited, into his mind to distract him from the scene inside his boat.

The *second* boat he'd owned and docked at the Coconut Grove Marina only to become a crime scene. Justified or otherwise, another incident at his boat slip that had brought emergency vehicles was going to be an issue for some, if not all the marina's occupants. And they would most certainly complain to the management company, who would then relay their complaints to the owners.

"Give your preliminary report to the officers on-scene and get over to Kaylen and Angela," Hal said, interrupting Brian's disturbing sidebar thoughts. "I heard Trehorn turned up with members of his squad, for whatever reason. No one died on your boat tonight. I'm sending them all home. You'll have to give a report to the Internal Affairs rep., which I'm going to insist happens tomorrow." His voice definitely sounded gruff. "You've had enough trauma over the last twenty-four hours. You'll get a call to set up the time."

"Thanks, Chief." Brian heard the unsteadiness in his voice…a sure sign his own composure was beginning to crumble. Those wandering thoughts were another symptom. "I want an attorney present at that meeting," he added.

"I was going to say you're getting one from the union. Swift, you always have to interrupt, like the rest of us are one step behind your reasoning skills."

Hal sounded like he was about to move from gruff to irritated. Brian quickly thanked him, assured Hal he was going to comply with anything and everything and got off the phone.

He gave a bare-bones report to the officer in charge at the scene, gave him spare keys to the boat and left. He had no idea whether Kaylen, Angela or Jim had eaten, so he picked up a couple of large pizzas and an outsized salad, so Kaylen wouldn't gripe at him for more unhealthy eating. He monitored his surroundings all the way to a sprawling estate at the mouth of a canal. He found it a little too isolated and secluded, but he liked the lack of vegetation close to the house. A desire for uninterrupted views of the water had their uses, he decided as he parked outside the front door.

Unexpectedly, Kaylen didn't take the time to gripe about his tardiness, lack of communication or anything else. She almost knocked the pizzas out of his hands in her eagerness to hug him. Jim laughed and took the food. Angela followed Jim and the food into the kitchen and declared her appetite was back.

Kaylen took Brian upstairs, where she pulled him onto the bed and wrapped herself around him, long legs and arms enveloping him in an embrace that made him know how afraid she had been.

"We saw the first news report," she said, her head on his shoulder. "When I saw the marina sign, I knew you had to be involved. Shots fired, they said. Then Jim called." Her voice trembled. "He said you were okay, but I wasn't sure I believed him. My heart felt like it dropped to my feet."

"I don't think Jim would ever lie to you, even if the news wasn't good."

"I never want to find out if that's true." Her voice was muffled and filled with pain.

"I'm sure you don't. But see, he wasn't lying this time." Brian shook her gently. "I'm fine, and Wilson's in custody. Best outcome." He managed to wrestle one arm from her grip to slide it around her.

"So, who got shot?" The amount of tension in her back was shocking.

Brian went on to give her as many details as he felt she could handle while he tried to tame the rigidity in her muscles.

"My God," she said when he'd finished a very abbreviated account. "I nearly lost you again."

"No way." He tried to kiss her, but she pulled away.

"You always think you're invincible," she said, her voice as accusing as her words. "That belief gets you into so many dangerous situations and absolutely terrifies me." She pushed her hair out of her eyes and wiped away tears. "I thought when you took the Cold Case position, you'd be much safer. Any bad guys you were chasing would be running slow and using old firearms because they were twenty years older than when the murders occurred. Yet here you are, confronting armed men on your boat. When is this ever going to end?"

Brian groaned and made no attempt to hide it. "You and I have had this discussion before," he told her, his other arm thrown over his eyes so he couldn't see her fright, and she couldn't see his frustration. "It's my job."

He stopped trying to hold her. There seemed no sense in trying to disguise his feelings. She'd have to stop complaining, if their relationship was going to continue.

"I *told* you I wasn't going to quit." He faced her troubled expression unwaveringly. "I love you, Kaylen," he said firmly. He wanted her to know there wasn't room for debate. "But I also love what I do for a living."

"A *living?* This isn't living, it's insanity." She scooted to the edge of the bed and placed both feet on the floor. "I can't discuss the long-term implications of loving a detective when I'm still so shocked and relieved to see you're not only alive but intact." She stood up, took her brush from the big bag of toiletries she had left on the dresser and ran it through her hair. "Let's shelve this until tomorrow," she said. "Those pizzas are getting cold, and I'm really hungry."

Brian stayed where he was and assessed his own current needs. The bed felt really comfortable, but he wasn't only tired, he was hungry. And definitely in no mood for extended discussions. "Fine, then kiss me and let's go have dinner with Angela and Jim," he said.

"I really hate you still, sometimes," Kaylen said. She looked and sounded perturbed, but she came back to the bed, leaned over and kissed him, long and hard. Brian felt some of the fatigue and tension leave him, but Kaylen didn't linger. She put down the brush and pulled him to his feet.

"Let's eat," she said. "And don't expect sex tonight. I want to fall asleep in your arms, but only with you cuddling me. I still feel really upset over everything right now."

Kaylen was definitely at odds with herself and with him, too, Brian thought as he followed her downstairs. She wasn't responding the way he'd thought she would, and figuring out how to calm her down and give her peace never came easily to him.

He checked his messages after they had eaten. Angela was resting in bed, and Jim said he wanted to clean up the kitchen by himself before going back to his boat. Kaylen had given up surfing channels and was busy looking through an extensive collection of movies in the entertainment room.

Brian found a text from Villanueva. 'Heard you kicked some ass today. Good going boss.'

Two more messages followed, one from Jack Mills, the other from Gabe Weston, both congratulating him on apprehending Wilson and promising coffee and donuts when he arrived in the morning.

His team understood what he did and why. Feeling less stressed after the affirming texts, Brian joined Kaylen, who had selected a period drama that didn't involve any police work, however remotely.

That night, for the first time since they had become a couple, they did not make love.

CHAPTER THIRTY-THREE

BRIAN AWOKE at 6:00 AM with Kaylen's back turned toward him. He slid out of bed and padded noiselessly into the bathroom with his phone. A quick text to Jim gave him the thumbs-up to take an early run while his friend filled in until the security detail arrived at 8:00 AM.

'ETA 30,' Jim responded.

Brian dressed in his running clothes and noted Kaylen hadn't moved when he collected his shoes and left the bedroom. He took one last look at her as he closed the door. He wondered whether she had slept as badly, although he hadn't sensed much movement from her side of the bed.

After knocking lightly, he carefully cracked Angela's door open to find her awake and reading. She waved at him. He waved back and whispered: "Jim's coming." She nodded and gave him a thumbs-up.

He made his way down to the kitchen, where he reluctantly used the Keurig prominently displayed with its handy rack of potential brews. He hated coffee from anything but his home drip system or the precinct. Both provided a brew strong enough to jolt him wide awake every morning, regardless of whether he'd slept eight hours or eight minutes.

Coffee before running probably wasn't his best option, but he needed the caffeine. He sensed trouble gathering like storm clouds on the horizon of his already-complicated relationship with Kaylen. She was showing strong signs that she wouldn't be able to make the transition that would be required of her if and when he returned to the role of a homicide detective. He wanted to be back in that role, the one he loved... maybe more than he loved her, he acknowledged with an uncomfortable gnawing in the pit of his stomach.

They had both known there would be rough patches and a lot of compromises, but he was beginning to feel that the fear factor was going to bring an ultimatum from her very soon. She had said...emphatically... that she couldn't face the thought of losing him to the finality of death. She'd already lost his brother.

Brian drained his cup. If they stayed together, she was going to have to face him dying at some point in the future. Why the hell would his age factor so heavily in her decision? He wondered whether because he faced death so frequently, he'd lost the ability to understand why others clung to the belief that they would never have to face losing a loved one.

He glanced at his watch. He still had about 5 minutes to kill, and he had no intention of wasting it pondering situations over which he had no control. He went through his stretching routine.

Jim's arrival was only two minutes later than the thirty he'd estimated. They exchanged a quick greeting and he expressed relief the night had been uneventful. Jim snorted his disgust at the Keurig, said he'd buy them a decent coffee maker once he finished his shift, and settled in to read his newspaper with a cup of French Roast, which he swore wasn't strong enough and barely more than lukewarm.

On that note, Brian left for a run around the estate before taking off up a service road. His strides lengthened, his breathing evened out, and the tension in his left shoulder finally left, taking a sharp ache with it. He returned to shower and dress in a suit for his meeting with Internal Affairs. Kaylen remained buried under the covers. She was used to his morning routine.

Before leaving, he made a point of pulling the sheet down from her face, kissing her cheek and whispering goodbye into her ear. She responded by flipping onto her back, grabbing his neck and returning his light kiss with one of her own.

"You be careful, today," she said, her face inches from his. "I want you back here this evening. No shoot-outs, okay?"

"I'll try my best." He crossed his heart.

"You'd better."

"See you later. You want me to bring pizza again?"

Kaylen rubbed her nose and squinted up at him. "Don't you dare. I'll have Rob send over tonight's special from Bannisters." She yawned and looked at the bedside clock. "Even if we have to reheat it, that has to be a far better choice than plastic cheese and pepperoni from who-knows-where. Call me when you know what time you'll be here, and I'll have the food sent over. I bet I can convince Jim to stay for dinner, so it won't be a hen party. Jonathan leaving on his trip earlier than he originally planned took away your opportunity for male bonding."

She gave a little giggle, much appreciated by Brian after his attempt to make love to her the night before had been rejected.

"Make sure you get the name of whoever's coming, and they're to bring I.D unless you know that employee well by sight," he cautioned, when she started gathering up the sheet and comforter in preparation for disappearing back under them. "Have Rob confirm that info when you talk to him, and make sure he doesn't tell the employee who the order's for…no one else needs to know where you and Angela are staying. Have the security guard bring in the order. Don't open the door yourself."

"Will do." She saluted. "Yes, sir."

She sounded insolent, but looked adorable with one nightdress strap sliding down her bronzed arm and her hair tousled. Brian wished he had awakened her earlier.

"Are you going to Treasure today?" he asked as he picked up his keys and billfold from the bedside table.

Kaylen nodded, curls flopping over her eyes. She brushed them aside and watched him holster his firearm and clip his badge onto his belt. "Yes. Planning to take Angela and Jim along with me, before you ask. I have a meeting with the decorator to finalize the last set of changes. I think we're done after today. I already okayed everything she emailed, but I want to see what it all looks like in the club setting before I sign off, in case the colors change with the lighting." She propped herself up on one elbow. "I wanted to ask you so much more yesterday, but I couldn't handle any more stressful news. You really shot two intruders?"

"I did." He sat on the edge of the bed to be closer to her while they talked. "Sam brought them. He wasn't harmed. I'm hoping to find out today what he knows about Tim's murder."

"They're going to let you do his interview?" Kaylen looked shocked.

"No way in hell that's gonna happen. Hal said he'd like to be the one, but that won't happen, either. We'll both probably be watching from the other side of the one-way glass, if Hal does want to hear any of Wilson's lies."

"I know you're disappointed, but I'm not. We both know you shouldn't be in any position to get your hands on him today." She took his left hand in hers and raised it to her lips.

"That's the truth." He kissed her lightly before disengaging his hand and standing back up.

"Mug books are being brought here this morning, as well as a photo array," he told her. "You and Angela need to look at everything to see if you recognize anyone, either from the home invasion or elsewhere. They could have come to Bannisters or Treasure, Jonathan's business or been the intruders at the Crossfield's home. Take your time over the process. Don't rush through. It can be confusing, maybe even overwhelming, to look at all those people staring right back at you."

Kaylen nodded. "It's not the first time I've done it. I had to go to the precinct when Tim was missing, after I got attacked in my condo. But I'll coach Angela before they get here. Do you know what time they'll come? My meeting's at noon. I was planning to take the three of us to lunch afterward."

"I don't know. You can call; find out." He jotted a name and number onto a pad sitting next to the house phone. "Make sure you do this today as well as go to that meeting, okay? Don't make yourself unavailable."

"I will." She reached out to stop him from leaving. "I'm not going to be difficult." She looked up at him, her expression open, unguarded. "I know how important this is to everyone."

"Thanks, hon." He kissed her again, lightly. "I've gotta go, or I'll be the one labeled difficult."

"You've got a meeting, too, or you know when Sam's being interrogated?"

"I've gotta answer some questions. Routine. Standard for an officer-involved shooting."

"Stay cool," she said.

He nodded before reluctantly leaving her alone and closing the door behind him. He hoped whoever he was going to give his report to wouldn't be Gil Morrison, the same guy he'd faced when he was still in hospital. He'd spiked a fever for days after that encounter. He decided not to stop for more coffee on the way to work and arrive over-caffeinated and jittery. Instead, he grabbed a bottle of water from the refrigerator and said goodbye to Jim, still pouring through the morning's news, before getting in his Camaro and leaving the lives of his three friends in what he hoped were the capable hands of the outdoor security detail.

CHAPTER THIRTY-FOUR

BRIAN ENDED his verbal report and looked across the table to see if IAB rep., Adam Borkowski, showed any reaction. Borkowski remained a human representation of The Great Sphynx of Giza. Short, bald and with black-framed glasses, at least he didn't resemble Gil Morrison.

Unlike the Sphynx, Borkowski also had a nose...a long, thin one with a bulbous tip. Brian's opinion of Internal Affairs had hit an even lower point than usual after his previous encounter with Morrison. This time, with an attorney at his side, he didn't feel quite the road-kill snack for a vulture.

Borkowski cleared his throat. "Anything to add, Sergeant Swift?"

"No," Brian said.

"Any further questions for my client before we leave?" the attorney asked.

Brian noted his attorney wore a suit Tim would have liked. His attaché case, soft black leather, looked new, like he'd picked it up on the way to the meeting. Brian thought the guy must have a very good gig representing cops. He'd introduced himself as Vincente Amelio. Brian was willing to bet he went by Vinnie to his pals.

"Not at this time," Borkowski said, his voice reminiscent of toe-scuffed gravel and delivered with spun-out syllables that sounded like they were being drawn out of his mouth on a clothesline. "But of course, IAB reserves the right to a second interview should the need arise." He looked at Brian over the top of his wire-rimmed glasses. "I would advise you not to speak with the media at this time, Sergeant Swift."

Brian barely stopped himself from shrugging. That might be construed as too casual for a solemn occasion. "Fine with me," he said, giving a curt nod instead. He pushed his chair back. "Am I free to go? I've got a meeting to attend with my cold case staff."

The IAB rep took off his glasses, pulled a tissue from a box on one corner of the table and polished one lens slowly and methodically while Brian half-stood, his hands on the arms of his chair. "I believe you are not only still on probation, Sergeant. Not only that, but you are now also on administrative leave until your officer-involved shooting is reviewed."

Brian sank back into the chair. He might skate by on the shooting, which after review should come back with a verdict of self-defense, but he had a feeling he was about to get yet another of the standard department lectures reserved for any officer in the midst of an investigation for perceived misconduct. Obviously, Borkowski hadn't been briefed that Brian had been used as bait for a trap that looked like it might have succeeded.

Borkowski started polishing the other lens. "You are on administrative leave. *Paid* administrative leave. You are, in fact, being paid to go home after this encounter is over. You will not be meeting with the Cold Case staff until you are returned to active duty, which will not happen until you have been cleared in the bribery investigation."

Brian pushed back his chair and stood. "I'm not staying around for any more of this crap."

"I beg to differ." Borkowski's clothes-line speech patterns had become even slower and more drawn-out. "You should have informed your client more thoroughly, Mr. Amelio," he said to Brian's attorney, whose neck had become noticeably redder around the upper edge of his shirt collar. "*I* make the rules. *You* will obey them, Sergeant Swift, or you will be placed back on suspension *without* pay."

Brian wanted to tell Borkowski what he thought of him and his rules, but Amelio jumped into the volatile atmosphere.

"Sergeant Swift, it would be best if you let me speak for you," Amelio said, his voice calm and well-modulated.

"Okay. You two talk about it as long as you want," Brian told them, fighting to keep the tone of his own voice civil but curt. "But while you're dragging all this out to earn your paychecks, I want to be fully reinstated, so my life isn't put on hold indefinitely. I was under suspicion for far too long two years ago. I went through hell before I was exonerated. Now my life's finally back on track, these unfounded accusations thrown out by some supposedly random bystander at a crime scene are threatening my career again. Have you even considered wondering why he was there, Borkowski, and how he managed to get air-time with some social events reporter who got diverted to the scene?"

"This meeting is no place for an angry response, Sergeant." Borkowski mounted his glasses back on his nose and restacked already stacked folders. "Of course, we have been reviewing even the minutest detail of these latest accusations."

He pulled a bulky old briefcase up from the floor, dropped it onto the desk and opened it to reveal an interior filled with dog-eared manila folders that had grubby white and colored papers sticking out of them. Borkowski made a gap in the middle and jammed Brian's folder into the jumble. He closed the briefcase with difficulty.

"Wouldn't *you* be perturbed?" Brian realized he shouldn't have had coffee on top of a restless night. His patience was wearing wafer-thin. "You're telling me to put my professional life on hold in the middle of what should be a joint investigation between Cold Case and Homicide."

"I'm sure Lieutenant Trehorn and his detectives can coordinate with your small staff as necessary, Sergeant, if you have trained your subordinates correctly." Borkowski slid the loaded briefcase to the edge of the desk.

Brian bit back the curse he wanted to deliver as a parting gift for the IAB rep. But if he didn't attempt to sound more reasonable than he felt, he could see himself spending a lot more time in the *NTK*'s stern with a cooler full of beer and a bunch of seagulls for company.

"Look," he told Borkowski. "I should be able to do my job while you two hash out whatever you feel you need to. When you get done, you can let me know the result, and I'll comply with whatever decision's been made, even if I don't like it. Until then, I should be allowed to coordinate these potentially overlapping cases with Homicide from my office, at least. No field work. Fair enough?"

"Sounds like a plan to me," Amelio said. "Borkowski? Any objections?"

The door opened and Gil Morrison walked in. Borkowski's expression shifted from gloating to shocked.

"I'll take over from here," Morrison told his subordinate.

Borkowski looked like he wanted to argue with Morrison as well, but evidently thought better of it by nodding curtly and making for the door.

"I'll take the Sergeant's file," Morrison said. "You will find all mention of this investigation has been wiped from the system already. This case is not to be discussed in any form with anyone except me, do you understand?"

"Yes." Borkowski's eyes widened. "I do."

"I'll debrief you after I conclude this meeting. Go get a cup of coffee, and I'll text you when I'm ready."

Borkowski nodded again, like he had no words left. He gave Brian's file to Morrison and walked out.

Morrison sat across from Brian and Amelio. "I've sent for coffee," he said. "I just finished meeting with Chief Shaw. Neither of us feel this investigation, if you could call it that, has any further merit. We now know a lot more about Beale Friendly and his reasons for submitting false accusations against you, Sergeant. Thanks in part to your Cold Case staff, particularly your clerk, Gabe Weston, it has come to our attention that despite his attempts to conceal his motives, Mr. Friendly has several reasons to retaliate for what he appears to feel are wrongs you did to him and a family member."

A discreet knock on the door brought a uniformed officer with a tray of coffee. She glanced at the three men in the room before withdrawing quickly. Brian figured she was either petrified at being in the same room with an IAB supervisor or she sensed the tension.

"Have you at any time recognized Mr. Friendly, Sergeant?" Morrison asked, stirring two packets of sugar into his coffee.

"No, but I don't remember everyone I've come into contact with."

Brian pulled his coffee cup toward him and wrapped his hands around the cup.

"Do you remember testifying in court after a wounded robber, shot by a security guard during an attempted bank heist, was murdered by a member of his own gang?"

Brian nodded. "Yeah, I remember that case. Pretty damn cutthroat. The guy was shot in case he decided to turn on the rest of the gang if he lived long enough to get taken to the hospital and patched up. I don't remember the name of the one who shot him, but I'm sure it wasn't Beale Friendly."

"That's correct. Mr. Friendly went by another name in those days... McCall. Had a little brother by the name of Winston." Morrison looked hard at Brian. "Now you remember something."

"I remember Winston McCall trying to beat my head in when I interrupted him holding up a convenience store. I kicked the shit out of him after I got my senses back. He about decked me with the clerk's baseball bat after he'd taken out the clerk with it. He would have killed me if the clerk hadn't come to and managed to grab the guy from behind. I'll never forget the courage that clerk had. He would have died if the gun McCall brought into the store hadn't jammed. A short little dude from Calcutta. Told me that was his first job in the U.S. Said he thought Calcutta was rough until he started working graveyards at the convenience store."

"And you walked in the door to buy a cup of coffee and disturbed a robbery in progress." Morrison grinned. "I'd have paid money to see that fight, but I digress...Winston was Beale's little brother. Beale's mother had married twice. Her second husband adopted both kids, but Beale didn't like the guy and once he turned eighteen, he changed his name back to Friendly while he was living in Arkansas for a while. Records in that particular courthouse were burned in a fire. I suspect our Mr. Friendly may have had something to do with setting the fire, but anyway, that's why there was trouble linking him with Winston McCall. Beale did not pull the trigger, and swore he tried to talk the shooter out of offing their partner. He did five years in the state pen after your testimony. He got out early for good behavior and because of prison overcrowding. He was supposedly rehabilitated and has been working at a water treatment plant for the past six months. No complaints from his supervisor or his parole officer. He's recently been working weekends for a paint contractor to pick up extra money. He told his parole officer he's saving up to buy a car."

"Okay, so now I see why he'd have painter's overalls, but if he's working at the treatment plant weekdays, why did he suddenly turn up at the coffee shop in his overalls and start yelling accusations?"

Morrison shrugged. "We haven't figured that out. But he hasn't been at the treatment plant all week. He's violated his parole, and there's a warrant out for his arrest."

"What about Winston?" Amelio asked.

"Paroled, too. Last job listed was working as a gardener for someone named Samuel Wilson. What a coincidence, huh? He hasn't been heard of or turned up on anyone's radar for the last two years."

Morrison took mug shots from a folder and pushed them across the desk. Brian looked down to see Beale Friendly, wearing painter's overalls and talking with Cassandra Bunting at the coffee shop crime scene in the photo on the right, and a much younger man, bearded and with shoulder-length hair in the mug shot on the left.

"Not much of a resemblance left, is there?" Morrison pulled out another photo and pushed it to the far left. "That's Winston. We don't have a recent shot of him. This was taken shortly before he got paroled."

Brian looked at a younger, leaner version of Beale Friendly but with smaller eyes and a longer chin. Thin lips and big ears that matched those of his older brother.

"Chief Shaw filled me in on your part in the recent operation, Sergeant. If it wasn't for the investigation into the shooting yesterday on your boat, you could return to active duty. Your expertise is needed to assist the Homicide bureau with their investigation into the coffee shop murders. They still can't figure out another link between Friendly and the coffee shop apart from you, and as you already pointed out to more than one person, Friendly turning up right after that multiple homicide and being available to shout accusations about you to news crews can't be a coincidence. Every star in the heavens would have had to align for him to be in the wrong place at the right time."

A huge weight fell from Brian's shoulders.

"Let me confirm the details and possible timeline for your reinstatement with Lieutenant Morrison," Amelio told Brian. "You and I can meet again this afternoon or tomorrow."

"You still need to make an appointment with the department psychologist because of the shooting," Morrison said. "You know the drill, already."

"I do, but I prefer to go to my own independent psychologist," Brian said. "Chief Shaw is aware of my preference."

"Very well." Morrison nodded and picked up his coffee.

Brian ignored the direction to go home and took the stairs to Cold Case, arriving in time to find his three coworkers exchanging information he found highly intriguing.

It seemed that Gertrude Pensky, Mrs. Dewett's walking companion from the assisted living facility had been found deceased on a park bench. Despite an initial diagnosis of heart failure, both Mrs. Pensky's primary care physician and subsequently the ME had not been convinced Mrs. Pensky had died of natural causes. An autopsy had been performed, and revealed she had ingested strychnine along with the large strawberry milkshake she had been enjoying while she rested in the shade.

CHAPTER THIRTY-FIVE

"GABE, let's start with a background check of Mrs. Dewett," Brian said. He'd eaten a bear-claw and a donut covered with a mixture of cinnamon sugar and toasted walnuts as well as two large cups of strong coffee. As a result, his mood had improved dramatically, and so had his thought processes.

"You think she's involved?" Jack Mills leaned back in his chair and scratched his forehead. "Arsenic and Old Lace at the nursing home?"

"An Agatha Christie-like murder?" Villanueva asked. "You think these two were poisoning other residents and then Dewett turned on Pensky?"

"Agatha Christie didn't write that one. It was a play by Joseph Kesselring." Jack Mills swirled coffee around in his cup.

"You're a play-buff?" Villanueva turned toward him.

"I majored in theatre arts before I decided criminal justice was a better option if I wanted to eat on a regular basis." He turned his cup toward her. "Now I donate to the arts."

"WPBT? Is that the local PBS station?"

"Yep."

"Can we get back to the case?" Brian asked, his elevated mood beginning to develop nicks.

"Sorry, Boss." Villanueva grinned at him. "What makes you think there's something sinister at whatever that retirement place is called?"

"He's got a gift," Jack Mills said.

"No, I don't," Brian said. "But when I was interviewing our Mrs. Dewett, something seemed off about her."

Villanueva started to open her mouth.

"His twitches are legendary," Mills said.

"I do not twitch," Brian said. "What the hell talk is that, Jack?"

"Whatever that sixth sense of yours is regarding possible perps, I've seen it in action, and I believe in it."

"Creepy," Villanueva said. "Not you, Boss," she reassured Brian. "This old gal you're talking about."

"Look, I know it's treading on Trehorn's toes again, but I want you and Villanueva to interview some of the staff at the retirement home, Jack. See if you can get to talk with Dewett, too. I doubt you'll get access to any of the other residents. Homicide will be interviewing them. But we've got history with Dewett. You can do a follow-up for our own investigation. Avoid making her suspicious. She likes orange soda and chocolate chip cookies. Take her some. Keep on topic but see if anything stands out to you...mannerisms, reactions...you know the drill. You'll have to call ahead and let them know you're coming, otherwise she might be out at some appointment and you'll waste your time. Lunch is probably some drawn-out affair that takes two hours, so take that into consideration. I don't want either of you hanging around that place longer than you have to."

"Thanks," Mills said. "My father died in a home like that."

"I'll look after you," Villanueva said with a broad grin. "You know, make sure they don't seat you in the dining room and give you a meal."

"Oh, shut up." Jack had to return her smile.

Brian heard something like a snicker out of Gabe before the clerk left to make himself busy at his desk.

"I'll hang out here and do some phone work," Brian decided. "Try to get in touch with neighbors at Dewett's last address once Gabe gets me more info."

Jack Mills hung back as Villanueva left, half-closing the combined conference and interrogation room door behind her. "Are you okay, Brian?" he asked in a low voice.

"Yeah, but I won't say the last few days have been easy, Jack." Brian ran a hand over his face. At least he hadn't forgotten to shave that morning. "It looks like IAB is going to accept my version of the shootings on my boat yesterday. It sounds like the other charges are going to be dismissed, too. Can you believe the accusations were coming from some guy I helped put away, because he's pissed at me? His name's Beale Friendly, for Christ's sake."

"Seriously?" Mills looked like he wanted to laugh, but he managed to stop himself.

"Yeah. Seriously." Brian placed his elbows on the table and rubbed his dry eyes with the palms of both hands.

"Look, we're *all* in your corner this time," Jack said. "Everything'll work out, and Mr. Friendly will be in the hot seat instead of you. And Wilson's in custody, too. He's a cream puff. He'll never hold up under interrogation."

"I dunno." Brian leaned back in his chair, extended his legs and stretched. After hours spent seated behind tables, it felt really good. "He's a great liar. He fooled Kaylen for years. I know she was a lot more naïve before Tim died, but she's told me she never had any doubts about Sam until she opened Bannisters. Then she saw another side of him. Jealousy, possessiveness…you name it."

"People do strange things when they're in deep financial trouble and a woman they're close to comes into a lot of money," Jack said. "When Kaylen's husband died, Wilson wanted to step in and have Kaylen *and* the money. That dream flew out the window when she became involved with you."

"Most of the money went to the four children from Kaylen's husband's first marriage, anyway," Brian said. "Wilson knew that. I guess he wanted whatever was left. He was desperate. Had to be to try burning down his own restaurant."

"And everything else he did," Jack said. "Don't forget he tried to have you killed."

"Not forgetting anything," Brian said.

"He'll do time," Mills predicted. "How much, is the question. They'll try to get him to share info about the cartel, and hopefully something useful in Tim's case."

"Plea-bargaining." A sour taste came into Brian's mouth.

"If that's what it takes. You'd better be prepared for that."

"Yeah, I guess." Brian felt conflicted. He knew deals went down every day to get cases solved, but wondered how far the justice system would be prepared to go to get information out of Sam Wilson. Immunity better be off the table or he might have to take matters into his own hands. Wilson would sink like a rock if he was thrown overboard somewhere out in the open water.

"Ready?" Villanueva's head poked around the door. She jiggled keys. "Who's driving?"

"Me, this time," Jack said. "You haven't been in Miami long, have you?"

"Long enough," she said. "I can find that retirement home if that's what's worrying you. Besides, we've got access to GPS. This isn't the early twentieth-century, you know."

"I'm more worried about the way you might drive in traffic," Jack said as he crossed the room and took the keys from her. "I heard you're ex-military. You can drive back. We'll take the long way, through subdivisions with low speed limits."

Brian could hear them arguing all the way out of Cold Case. He decided those two were going to make excellent partners.

CHAPTER THIRTY-SIX

KAYLEN HAD swum laps in the Olympic-sized pool and breakfasted on a big bowl of oatmeal loaded with cut up dates and blueberries, pecans and applesauce as she sat at a one of the dining sets on the outsized patio. She downed a small glass of orange juice and a big cup of coffee while Angela nibbled on dry toast and slowly drank a half-glass of milk through a straw. Beyond the patio, at the periphery of her vision, a member of the outdoor security patrol warily monitored the area, and no doubt remained displeased his charges had insisted on leaving the house.

"Are you nauseated again?" Kaylen asked Angela. "Yesterday evening, you ate pizza."

"A little." Angela gave a weak smile. "I'll feel better after I shower. I woke up early and read until I fell asleep again, then Jonathan called to check on me. I'm a bit of a wet noodle this morning."

"Do you feel up to going to the club with Jim and me? Brian doesn't want us to split up." Kaylen felt a little uneasy herself at the thought of Angela remaining alone in the enormous house." Jim'll be back at eleven-thirty. My meeting's at noon, then I was going to treat us all to lunch. I gave Brian our itinerary this morning before he left."

"You two argued last night, didn't you?" Angela abandoned the toast and dusted off her fingers.

"You heard us? I'm sorry, I thought the walls here were thicker."

"I only heard the more heated portions." Angela paused to rim her plate with one finger, her eyes downcast, like she was trying to figure out how to be diplomatic. "Look, I don't like to interfere, Kaylen, but you shouldn't be so hard on Brian. He's such a good guy, and he's got a really tough job, trying to balance his work with looking after us. You, in particular."

"I know." Kaylen suddenly felt as drained as the empty coffee cup beside her bowl. Brian shooting two people had pushed her stress level well into the red zone. "That's kind of what we were arguing about," she admitted. "Angela, I have such doubts that I can handle loving a man whose life is potentially in danger every minute of the day. I really thought, stupidly it turns out, that if he investigated cold cases instead of fresh homicides, he'd stay out of trouble." She leaned her elbows on the table and rubbed her throbbing temples. "But yesterday, he could have been shot again...killed." She grabbed a napkin to dab at the tears welling up in her eyes. "When he told me what happened on the boat yesterday, I could barely breathe. I swear, I thought I was going to pass out." Her nose started running. She dabbed that, too. "And he acted like it was nothing. *Just another day at the office,* he told me. So flippant. He wasn't hurt, he said, like I should brush off my horror the same way he brushed off shooting two intruders."

Angela pushed aside her unwanted breakfast, reached across the table and took Kaylen's hand in both hers. "I'm so sorry," she said. "I would have been horrified, too."

Kaylen tried to smile her thanks for the support, but was completely unsuccessful. "I've looked at him when he's asleep, Angela, and he's so peaceful. Not a care in the world," she told her friend. "Or at least I do it when I *think* he's asleep, because he often opens his eyes and stares at me, like he wasn't sleeping at all."

She hesitated, knowing Brian wouldn't want her to tell anyone about all his scars. She decided to compromise, because she needed to share her fears with someone, and she felt Angela had proved she could be trusted.

"There are two scars on his chest," Kaylen said. "Small. Raised. Circular." She placed one index finger on the right side of her chest to indicate the location of the scars. "I think he must have been shot some-time in the past. I've never asked him whether I'm right. I can't seem to do that, like knowing for sure will only make my anxiety worse."

"Maybe not." Angela's voice radiated understanding. "Keeping secrets never helps. And what if they're *not* old bullet wounds? Would you feel any better?"

"Probably not," Kaylen confessed.

She had originally thought those scars were cigarette burns inflicted by Brian's step-father, but the more she had gotten to know Brian, the better she understood he would never had remained still long enough for Ed Madison to grind the tip of a burning cigarette into his flesh. Although Brian had told her he'd been beaten with a belt and had hot soup thrown on him, she knew he had been running when the soup landed on his back. She didn't even want to think what Ed had threatened to get Brian to submit to being beating with a belt. Probably giving the punishment to Tim instead, she thought with an inner shudder.

"Ask him," Angela urged. "You need to know, so you can move past the wondering." She got up and took her plate and glass into the kitchen, shaking the toast into the garbage can on the way to the sink.

"Angela, you should have worked on that toast a little longer," Kaylen admonished as she followed in Angela's wake. "Do you want me to cook you something? I can't dish up anything fancy, but I could make pancakes or eggs."

"No, but thanks for the offer." Angela turned and leaned back against the counter. "I don't usually eat until I've been up a couple of hours. My doctor told me to stop drinking coffee, which was my go-to. I'm not so sure I'm going to be able to handle drinking milk instead." She pointed to the half-full glass beside the sink and stuck out her tongue. "Ugh. I've never been a big fan of milk in any form, so switching to something like almond or cashew won't help."

"What about tea? Mineral water?"

Angela wrinkled her nose. "Worse, maybe. Acid reflux is hell, let me tell you, and I'd have to drink decaffeinated tea, which I'm not fond of, either."

"Can you at least have an antacid for the reflux?"

"Probably, but getting something solid into my stomach in the morning does help. I keep making myself eat some sort of breakfast, because the past few days I'm beginning to feel better by lunchtime." She stopped leaning on the counter. "I'm going to get ready to come with you and Jim. If I can't make it, then the security detail's here to protect me. I'll make it easy for them and stay in my suite. I can watch TV this morning and nap this afternoon until you two get back."

"Juliette's still coming back in a few days, right?" Kaylen asked. The last thing they needed, she thought, was for Angela's live-in housekeeper to decide not to return from a week with her family in Nogales, where she had gone to recover from her scare in the pantry.

Angela nodded. "That's what she said the last time we talked on the phone. If she changes her mind, we'll have to cross that bridge. Until then, I'm going to act like Scarlett O'Hara and not think about it."

"Brian wanted to bring pizza again this evening. I told him I'll have Rob send over food from Bannisters, instead. I have this week's menu on my laptop. You can order from that or off the menu. Your choice. They'll make anything you want. Hopefully, you'll feel up to eating by the time we call in the order." She placed her breakfast dishes on the counter and disposed of several empty Keurig pods, clustered on the coffee bar.

"I thought Jonathan was having an affair one time, about a year after we married," Angela said.

Kaylen was cleaning the coffee bar. She stopped mid-wipe to turn and stare.

Angela leaned back against the breakfast bar that time, her hands folded across her stomach. "I didn't ask him about it until we had a huge fight a year later. He was astounded I could believe he'd do that to me. He'd never been unfaithful. He was working late and going in to the office on weekends because he felt overwhelmed after inheriting his father's business so suddenly. His dad died of a heart attack at fifty-three."

"Oh, my God." Kaylen didn't know what else to say.

"Jonathan was already working at the company when his father died, but he was still learning the ropes," Angela said. "Suddenly, he had the entire weight of that huge business on his shoulders. He felt such a burden to succeed for the sake of the workers, the board members and his mother, as well as me." Her eyes reflected anguish still vividly remembered. "I *so* wish I'd kept my doubts to myself or spoken up a lot earlier. I could have made that time period a lot less stressful for both of us. He told me he'd felt me distancing myself but thought it was because he was spending too much time consoling his mother. He thought I felt neglected, but instead of asking me if that was what was wrong, he held his thoughts inside, too." She gave a little laugh, barren of mirth.

"Brian confides so little in me, you'd be shocked," Kaylen said. "He has walls thicker and higher than Alcatraz."

"You'll have to give him more time, then." Angela pushed away from the breakfast bar. "But tell him how ready you are for him to share anything and everything he feels he can. Then the walls will start to come down. Men aren't good at opening up. It makes them feel too vulnerable. They always want to be the tough guys who protect us, no matter what the cost to them, mentally and physically."

"That's the truth."

Angela glanced at her watch. "Well, I'd better shower and get dressed if I don't want to be in my robe when Jim arrives. It's ten-fifteen, already."

"I need to shower and do something with my hair." Kaylen reached up to touch the matted curls. "This is a corkscrewed mess after the pool."

"Your hair's always beautiful," Angela said. "I inherited fine, wispy blonde hair from my mother's side of the family. I hope this baby gets Jonathan's thick locks." She laughed, and it didn't sound forced that time.

Kaylen followed her up the service stairs and hoped Jim wouldn't arrive as promptly as usual. She had her mind on a long shower with two shampoos and a lot of conditioner. She'd washed the chlorine off under the outdoor shower, but it had been a fast rinse-off.

While she stood under the hot water, her mind dwelled on what Angela had said. Did she really want to try asking Brian about those two small scars on his chest when the ones on his back were so large? To him, they might seem insignificant, but if she told him she noticed them, he might think if she noticed those, she might really obsess about the others.

She decided to emulate Angela, at least for the time being, and think like Scarlett O'Hara. It was much easier in some ways to put things off until tomorrow, especially potentially difficult heart-to-heart talks. But it was also the coward's way, and Kaylen told herself she had never been a coward before, except maybe where her own father was concerned.

CHAPTER THIRTY-SEVEN

THE OFFICE PHONE rang soon after Mills and Villanueva left. Gabe was still intently researching Winifred Dewett's background.

"I'll get it," Brian called from the miniscule office that now held Jack's name-plate on the door, despite Jack's objections to what he called a temporary situation.

Alicia Solis wasn't surprised to hear him answer the phone. "The chief told me to try Cold Case first," she said. "He figured you'd still be in the building."

She gave him the good news that Sam Wilson's interview was in progress, and he had clearance to observe. He scratched a note to Gabe and took the stairs two at a time up to the viewing room. He found Trehorn already inside. They watched Wilson rub sweat off his face and stammer that he wanted his attorney present.

Trehorn flipped off the sound. "Looks like we're not going to get much out of him."

"Not unless he's offered enough to turn on his handlers," Brian agreed. "Much as I'd like to see him doing twenty years, though, I need to know who murdered my brother. If he's not given a deal, I can pretty much kiss that info goodbye."

"The primary goal for any deal made with him is to get intel on the drug cartel." Trehorn took a drink from a can of soda.

"Murder has to take precedence," Brian said. "They beat Tim to death and dumped his body in a creek."

"Normally, I'd agree with you, but not when racketeering, drug trafficking and money laundering are the primary offenses connected to Wilson." Trehorn slowly shook his head. "I'm truly sorry, Swift, but a lot of agencies are interested in him, and they're going to make sure they get a piece before Homicide gets to interview him."

"My brother's murder'll take a backseat?" Brian felt his anger ignite. "Who the hell decided that?"

"Keep your voice down," Trehorn warned in a low tone.

"He can't hear me." Brian gestured toward the switch Trehorn had flipped off.

"Well *I* can, and so can anyone else out in the corridor." Trehorn tossed his can into a recycling bin beside the door. "If you get any louder, Wilson could hear you as well."

Brian was done with political correctness and respecting his superior. "Why the fuck do you always have to be so goddamned obnoxious, Trehorn?"

"I should be asking you the same thing."

That surprised Brian. "Why?"

"You've had it in for me since I arrived here."

"What?"

"Nothing wrong with your ears," Trehorn said. "You're pissed because you couldn't step into Hal's shoes when he left Homicide. You don't want me in a position you think should have been yours."

"No way in hell was I gonna get promoted to lieutenant," Brian said. "I was out on disability when you got here. I wasn't even sure I could return to active duty in *any* capacity. Homicide needed a new supervisor ASAP. I understood that."

"I walked into a dysfunctional department," Trehorn said.

"Hal...the chief didn't leave it that way."

"No, but the accusations swirling around you did the job. The entire department was divided and tense. You should have resigned and joined your buddy Jim Paxton as a private investigator. It'd fit your lawlessness like a glove."

"The hell it would." Brian glowered at Trehorn, who glowered right back.

The door opened. "What the hell is going on in here?" Hal walked in. "I arranged for the two of you to be here because you both have an interest in the outcome of this interrogation. Now I find you shouting at each other? I could hear you out in the hallway." He walked over to the window and looked through the glass. "Wilson'll have to sing louder than a flock of canaries to get any deals. His attorney's on the way up."

The door to the interrogation room opened shortly afterward. A silver-haired man with an attaché case walked in. Brian recognized well-known defense attorney, Bernard "Barney" Poulson. Hal flipped on the audio and Brian stepped forward to one side of the chief as Trehorn stepped forward on the other.

"Good morning," the attorney greeted Sam.

"Good to see you." Sam looked and sounded relieved. "I haven't said anything, Barney."

"Better to keep it that way." Poulson sat beside Sam and placed his attaché case on the table, but didn't open it.

"I want a deal," Sam said. "You've got to get me out of here. Out on bail. I can't stay in jail. It's not safe for me...I need protection."

To Brian, Sam Wilson sounded affronted as well as scared, like he didn't deserve to spend time behind bars. Nothing astonishing about that, Brian thought with a flash of anger. Pleading ignorance seemed to be the way Wilson thought he should go.

"One thing at a time," Poulson said as Gil Morrison walked in and sat opposite Wilson and his attorney, who unsnapped and opened his attaché case, taking out several papers.

Brian wanted to ask Hal what the hell the IAB supervisor was doing interrogating Sam Wilson, but the audio was on, and Hal glanced his way with a clear warning to keep quiet. Brian swallowed his protest and watched as Morrison placed his forearms on the table and leaned forward with the intense stare that seemed to be an integral part of his personality.

"Good morning, gentlemen," he said. "Are we here to make a deal? The charges are lengthy, and your client's going to be doing time for the rest of his life if we don't come to an agreement today."

"I'm innocent!" Sam protested. "I haven't done anything, and you've got no right to keep me here. Show him the motion to dismiss, Barney." He waved one hand toward Poulson, who did not turn his attention from Morrison or pick up any of the papers he'd pulled from the attaché case.

"You were trespassing in a police officer's home, accompanied by two armed men, Mr. Wilson," Morrison said, his voice calm and detached.

"I was kidnapped; forced to go to the boat," Sam said.

"Mr. Wilson, we agreed I would speak for you," Poulson said. His voice was as calm and detached as Morrison's when he placed a restraining hand on Sam's arm and shot a warning glance toward his client. "Please allow me to do that." He turned to Morrison. "Mr. Wilson was in fear for his life."

"From whom?" Morrison asked.

Sam opened his mouth. Brian saw Poulson's grip tighten on Sam's arm. Sam closed his mouth.

"Mr. Wilson was, unfortunately, forced to surrender his good name and his business to unscrupulous interests," Poulson said.

What a way to put it, Brian thought. The only truth to that statement was the unscrupulous part.

"And who was doing the forcing?" Morrison asked.

Sam actually squirmed. Whether it was over the restraining hand on his arm, the thought of his crimes or the word "force," Brian wasn't sure.

"What sort of a deal are we discussing here?" Poulson countered.

"Until we are given something of interest to us, there is no deal," Morrison said. "Coffee, gentlemen?"

"I'd like some," Sam said, eagerly. "The stuff I was given this morning was like dishwater."

"You'll need to get used to that unless you answer my questions truthfully," Morrison said.

He got up and went to the door, opening it and speaking with someone outside while Sam tried to mouth something to Poulson, who shook his head emphatically.

Hal turned to Brian. "Did you catch that?"

"I think he said something like 'give him everything,'" Brian said.

CHAPTER THIRTY-EIGHT

At 3:00 P.M. that afternoon, Kaylen, Angela and Jim drove back from a long, leisurely and celebratory lunch in South Beach, after Kaylen finally signed off on all the outstanding alternations to Treasure and declared the supper club ready for its grand opening. Kaylen and Angela chattered excitedly in the back of the Sportage, at Jim's request. He wanted to sit up front alone so he could listen to his favorite afternoon radio talk show, but it was interrupted by a news bulletin. Jim turned up the volume.

"Samuel Wilson, a long-time Coral Cables and Coconut Grove restaurant owner," the announcer intoned, "was killed in a drive-by shooting after being transported to a hotel following a lengthy interview at Miami-Dade Police Department. Mr. Wilson had been accused of racketeering and money laundering among other charges. According to sources at Miami-Dade Police Department, Mr. Wilson and his attorney were seeking a plea deal."

CHAPTER THIRTY-NINE

"THEY SILENCED HIM," Brian said.

Hopelessness had never totally engulfed him until that moment. Sam Wilson's death meant Tim's murder might never be solved. Brian stared at the scenery outside Hal Shaw's window without registering anything but blurred movement.

"They did." The chief left his desk to join Brian at the window. "He must have known a lot more about the cartel business and everything else than we got from him today."

Brian made an effort to focus his attention on his supervisor. "If I'd been allowed to interrogate him, I'd have gotten the truth, even if I had to beat it out of him."

"Which is why you couldn't be directly involved." Hal leaned on the window sill and looked down at traffic passing on the street below. "We were all too close to the investigation. That's why Morrison was chosen for the initial interrogation. Complete impartiality, but a broad knowledge of the history behind the allegations."

"They were a lot more than allegations, Chief. Wilson was too involved with the cartel not to know who murdered Tim."

"The D.A.'s office got involved after you left the viewing room. Morrison and the deputy D.A. both felt sure we could break through after

Wilson had the night to think things over. He was already showing signs he was ready to give up names and details, but his attorney wanted a better deal, and we'd had him sweating in that room for hours with only water to drink. No food." Hal shook his head. "There'll be a comprehensive investigation into how that van got through our security measures outside the hotel. We took him in a back door. No one outside law enforcement and the hotel management had any idea he was coming. The D.A.'s office agreed with Wilson and his attorney that he shouldn't go back to the jail. Too much of a risk."

"Another van." Brian turned and leaned back against the window frame. "Was it black? Stolen plates or no plates? It could have been the same one used to transport Moises Delgado's body to the dump site at the storage facility."

"If only your witness in the neighborhood around the coffee shop had better eyesight and could have gotten even a partial plate. That would have been a bigger help than his description of the perps."

"I agree, but at least he gave us a pretty good description of the van, as well. That dented right front fender's not as good as a plate, but it'll help narrow the field. Did anyone get a good look at the van involved in Wilson's shooting?"

Hal nodded. "Yeah, better than nothing, but color, possible make and that dented fender wasn't much info for a BOLO in this town. The black van today didn't have plates. Maybe that one didn't, either."

"No one had the sense to give chase after Wilson was shot?"

"Brian, you can't second-guess all of us," Hal said. "It was supposed to be a routine transfer, low key to avoid drawing a crowd or tipping off any media waiting around for a scoop."

"You think there was a leak at the precinct?"

"Maybe." Hal signed. "Like I said…there'll have to be a comprehensive investigation. I suppose the occupants of the van could have been hanging around all day, waiting for Wilson to leave, but he got taken out through the motor pool, and we had a decoy operating, too."

"Okay," Brian said, admitting defeat for that day. "I get it. Enough beating a figurative dead horse. What did Wilson give up already?"

Hal looked relieved by Brian's unexpected capitulation. "Not enough, obviously. Wilson said he could name names, dates and financial transactions, but he wanted immunity, relocation, and even compensation. His attorney wasn't the biggest problem. He tried to convince Wilson to settle for a couple of years in minimum security, followed by witness relocation. It was the best we could offer, given his probable involvement in your brother's death."

Brian felt a small measure of vindication for Tim. His brother's case had been mentioned, which Trehorn had been sure wouldn't happen. "But he didn't give up any names at all today?"

"No. His attorney flatly said until they had an iron-clad deal, Wilson wasn't saying anything else. That's when Morrison decided to have Wilson think things over at the hotel while the D.A.'s office and the Feds hashed out what they were willing to give if he and his attorney came back with more demands but definite signs that he was going to give up significant information."

"Fuck," Brian said.

"I agree, on so many levels." Hal went to his desk and opened the bottom drawer, taking out his scotch bottle and two glasses. "Heads are going to roll for this. The commissioner already called me."

Brian had no sympathy for whoever was going to feel the commissioner's wrath, up to and including Hal Shaw. Seeing Tim's killers brought to justice was a goal rapidly retreating into the distance. He had a suspicion he'd have to live with that outcome for the rest of his life.

"We haven't given up, Brian." Hal pushed a glass of scotch across the desk and pointed to it. "Drink up. You look like you need it." He tossed his serving back in one gulp and sat down. "The D.A.'s office is interviewing Wilson's attorney, who's rightfully concerned for his own safety. He swears Wilson wouldn't even give *him* the full story, but said the cartel doesn't know that. He thinks his career in Miami may be over, and he and his family may need long-term protection. He swears he had no idea what he was stepping into when he took the case. He was retained due to his reputation for extracting clients out of tight places, but he said Wilson's position was past tight."

"What a prick Wilson was." Brian eyed the scotch, but decided against it. He would rather take a few minutes to decompress on the *NTK* before changing clothes and driving over to deliver all the latest set of news to Kaylen, Angela and Jim. "I bet no one will be crying over *his* grave."

"Probably a safe bet, Swift." Hal's chair creaked as he rocked back and forth. "Get out of here. Nothing more you can do here until you return to active duty. Go be with Kaylen and your friends. The officer-involved shooting looks cut and dried self-defense, regardless of whether that one perp makes it out of ICU to a regular bed or a slab at the morgue. I already got Morrison's assurance they'll expedite the proceedings. You won't get anything else done here today, and until we have more of a handle on what, if anything, those two thugs who were with Wilson on your boat have to share, you're right...we've got close to zip."

"Did you get an update on their statuses?"

"One'll be ready to talk tomorrow...the shorter one with the two gunshot wounds." He gave Brian a tight smile. "According to ballistics, Kaylen was responsible for the wound to his arm."

"We thought she must have hit him." Brian returned Hal's smile. "She finally got the gun out of her purse and fired it."

"Pretty accurately, too, as long as she wasn't aiming for his big toe." Hall actually chuckled.

Brian wondered how many scotches Hal had consumed before their meeting. After the day the chief must have had, he could have been excused for upending the bottle.

"The other one," Hal continued, pouring more scotch into his shot glass, "the bigger one you thought might be involved in Tim's murder, is the one in the ICU. An extensive gut repair. His condition is poor. He's in the same ICU as Antonio Camardi."

"Any updates on Antonio?"

Hal nodded. "Much improved. He'll be interviewed tomorrow by Buxford."

"A piece of good news, finally." Brian felt like he could finally breathe a little deeper. "As far as the one I gut-shot," he shrugged, "I couldn't take the time to aim better, or I'd have had my head blown off."

"I'm still surprised that didn't happen." Hal started rocking his chair again.

"Hal...Chief...Wilson was looking for something he said I had... Tim's money."

"Cartel money," Hal said.

"Yeah, no…I don't know. We'll never know. I told him Tim's businesses were legit, but he'd have known that, already."

"Well, they didn't beat your brother to death for nothing." Hal stood back up and looked across the desk at Brian with a guarded expression. "Is there something you're not telling me? That you haven't told me since all this began?"

"Nothing that should affect this case," Brian said.

"That's not a firm no, Swift."

"It's the best I can do, Chief, while I'm not sure what's going on myself. I don't know whether whoever's left from the drug cartel thinks Tim took money from them as well as kept tabs on all their business, or whether Sam Wilson thought there was more to Tim's murder and drew his own conclusions."

"Conclusions that Tim had ripped off the cartel." Hal folded his arms across his chest.

"That idea crossed my mind, too," Brian acknowledged, trying to tread lightly while feeling out any information Hal had about the money Brian had recovered from a locker in the boxing gym close to his brother's apartment building after Tim's death.

"After Kaylen's husband died, someone was still shoring up Wilson's business," Hal said, watching Brian carefully. "There are two possibilities…the cartel or your brother."

Brian shoved his hands in his pockets and returned Hal's gaze. "I can't see Tim providing Sam Wilson with money for that. He wasn't much for throwing it down a dry well."

"Good analogy."

"Will it do any good to re-interview the guys Wilson had guarding his compound?"

Hal shrugged. "Probably not. I don't think he would have invited them in for little chats and updates on his financial status, do you?"

"Well, no, of course not, but if they were going in and out of the house, maybe they overheard something they probably didn't think was important at the time. What about his staff? He had to have had people cooking and cleaning at the house, and then there was the restaurant…

someone who worked there may have heard something or seen somebody they can identify in a mug shot."

"We've been looking at everybody. Combing through everything, Brian. You should know that without feeling you have to make suggestions. But what I need to know is that you're not withholding evidence. That you don't have knowledge you're not sharing because you're trying to run your own investigation on the side, using Jim for assistance, or even your Cold Case staff. You've got some very dedicated allies in your camp."

"I swear I'm not," Brian said. That was completely true. He had no idea who had taken out Sam Wilson.

Hal sat down heavily behind his desk. "This has been one long damn day," he complained. He pointed to Brian's untouched scotch. "Are you going to drink that or not?"

"Not." Brian watched Hal pick up the glass. "I'd better get back to Kaylen and Angela," he told the chief. "I doubt they're any safer with Wilson dead than they were when he was alive, but I guess time will tell."

"Wilson could have been behind the attempted abduction, burglary or whatever else was planned for that home invasion," Hal said, taking a sip from the scotch.

"Or it could have been planned by someone else, completely independent of Wilson or the cartel," Brian said. "Maybe kidnapping and holding one of the Crossfields for ransom was completely unconnected from anything to do with Kaylen, Tim or me."

"Maybe, but it seems wherever you and Kaylen go, there's trouble." Hal downed the scotch and eyed the bottle for a long moment before placing it back in the drawer.

Brian left, closing the door quietly behind him. He nodded to Alicia, who gave him a brief smile before returning to whatever she was working on at the computer. He decided not to check in with his team again. Instead, he went down to the garage, got in the Camaro and drove over to the marina. He needed space, quiet, and time to think before relieving Jim and giving Kaylen an unvarnished account of what had been happening over the previous few days. He wondered just how angry and disillusioned she was going to be when he got through. He began to regret not drinking Hal's scotch.

He stayed inside the *NTK* long enough to retrieve a beer from the refrigerator, noted the salon still looked like a crime scene and settled onto a chaise in the stern. He sent a couple of texts, one to notify Gabe he'd left for the day, the other to let Kaylen know he'd be there before the security detail changed shifts at 6:00 PM, when he'd give them an update on everything he knew so far. Then he opened the beer, took a long drink and watched gulls wheeling in the sky while he tried to make sense of the last 24 hours. It wasn't going to be easy.

CHAPTER FORTY

WHEN BRIAN RETURNED to the salon, he noticed an envelope taped outside the door. He dropped it onto the breakfast bar before going into the galley to start a half-pot of coffee. He pushed the button for the brewing cycle, pulled a knife from one of the drawers and slit open the envelope, which had the marina management company's logo in the left upper corner and his name neatly typed across the center.

Reading the one-page missive, he found he was being given a 'generous' 10-day notice to vacate his slip. He was notified that numerous other boat owners had signed a petition to have the *NTK* removed due to the shooting the previous day. According to the letter, no one felt safe after yet another incident where a heavy police presence was required at slip 95.

Brian was reminded how diligently the management company had worked with him under very trying circumstances when his first boat was destroyed by fire. They had calmed the fears of other boat owners and accommodated his needs for moorage when he took possession of his new and much larger motor yacht, even enabling him to remain at the same slip. It was brought to his attention that *Fanciful Folly* at slip 96 had been so badly damaged from the fire, she had required an extended stay in dry dock.

As though he needed the reminder, his attention was also directed to the *Naughty Nautical*, which had been moved by her owners to another marina, resulting in management having to bear the burden of finding an appropriate replacement, while losing fees during the extended period that slip 94 had remained empty, which Brian calculated to be less than a week.

He wanted to ball up the paper and trash it. *Naughty Nautical's* owners had been more than compensated for their inconvenience. Their shabby old boat, which had sustained water damage, had been upgraded with new paint and seats. The owners hadn't left the marina because of any negligence on Brian's part. They wanted a fresh start after he solved the 25-year-old cold case murder of their son. As for the boat at slip 96, Jim owned *Fanciful Folly* and would never have complained to anyone but Brian about the inconvenience of staying at a hotel while his boat was repaired.

The letter ended with the marina management wishing Detective Sergeant Swift well in the future.

"Yeah, I bet you do." Brian laid the open letter on the counter. His life at the Coconut Grove Marina was over. He'd have to find another home for the *Need To Know*. Somehow, he felt like a lot more than his moorage was about to change.

He poured himself a mug of strong, black coffee, unplugged the pot and skirted around bloodstains behind the recliner to get to his cabin, where he took off his suit and hung it in the small closet that had become even smaller now it held several of Kaylen's outfits. He noted she had added two cocktail dresses, one maroon with a low back that almost skimmed the curve of her buttocks. The other was a pale blue with rhinestones around the low-cut bodice and a slit that went from hemline to mid-thigh. He had told her those were his favorites. He wondered whether she was planning to wear one of them to Treasure's opening.

He paused to inhale the faint perfume that lingered on both garments before showering and dressing in jeans and a navy t-shirt. Walking back into the salon, he thought about calling in a crime scene clean-up crew, but decided to see if he could skip that step and send the *NTK* to have her salon completely refurbished. Since he was going to have to move her, anyway, why not make sure everything was brand new? God forbid at some point in the future Kaylen should find some bullet hole or blood drop that had been missed.

He'd rent a motel room while the work was completed, he told himself. That way, he'd have time to look for another home for his boat without sharing quarters with anyone else, including Kaylen or Jim.

But even if the salon got a new look, he thought that might not change his unsettled mood. He wasn't getting the same pleasure out of the *Need To Know* that he'd gotten from the *Destiny*. He'd bought a larger boat to accommodate his new life. He'd also stopped taking charters after he was reinstated. His original plan to spend his free time sailing around the Keys and out to the Bahamas had gone out the window with Tim's death and Kaylen's arrival in his life. Not only hers, he reminded himself, but Jim's, closely followed by all the coworkers, friends and acquaintances who had become part of the new and very different world he now inhabited.

He told himself that after Kaylen felt less stressed over the new club, he'd talk her into going on a trip with him. They could both do with the break. If she wasn't so preoccupied with the club opening, he would have used the time he'd have on administrative leave to take her away for a few days. Get away from the weird, confusing labyrinth the Friendly/Mc-Call brothers were inhabiting. At least this time he was on full pay, he told himself as grabbed his jacket from the back of a barstool and started to push his billfold into his back pocket. The jacket's sleeve caught on the barstool. Brian jerked it free, but the barstool fell over.

"Fine. Stay there, you piece of shit," he muttered, his frustration over the entire day focusing on the barstool. He kicked it. "You're going to the dump, anyway, once this baby goes to dry dock."

Focusing back on his billfold, he realized the reason it got caught on the way into his pocket was because he'd left a couple of small lock-picking tools in there. Gabe had called him at ten o'clock the night before the coffee shop robbery, saying his mother had dropped her keys somewhere outside and couldn't get into her house. Mrs. Weston had stared open-mouthed when he had her front door open in a matter of seconds, even without a porch light.

He pushed his billfold into the other pocket, opened the door and walked right into a blow to the face. The last thing he remembered was falling backwards and feeling a sharp pain in the back of his head as it hit the overturned barstool.

CHAPTER FORTY-ONE

"It's not like Brian to be late," Jim said, jiggling the keys in his pocket as he stood looking out a pair of sliding glass doors at the mansion's extensive grounds. "I'm not leaving until he gets here."

"We'll be fine," Angela said.

She had obeyed her obstetrician's orders to rest by camping out on the couch with pillows elevating her head and feet, despite complaining she was bored and needed her crafts. Kaylen stopped nervously flipping through the latest issue of Vogue and saw a movie was playing to itself on TV.

"The security detail's right outside. Go home, Jim. Enjoy your evening." Angela yawned and turned down the TV's volume.

"Having security outside isn't enough, Angela," Kaylen warned, throwing the magazine aside. "Brian said when he can't be here himself, the only person he trusts to watch over us is Jim."

She checked her watch. Jim had reason to talk about Brian being late. It was 6:45 PM.

"Let me check my phone again. Maybe he texted again, changing his arrival time." She leaned over and picked up her cell from the end table. "No, he hasn't." She looked at Jim's worried face and her heart rhythm did an ugly little skip-a-beat. "Do you think he's still tied up at work?

His meeting with Internal Affairs should have been over hours ago. Could they have asked him to help with the investigation into Sam's shooting if he's on administrative leave?"

"I doubt it, honey." Jim sat on the arm of the couch closest to Angela's feet..

Angela sat up and turned off the TV. "No one's paying any attention to it," she said to no one in particular. A crease had appeared between her eyebrows.

Kaylen tried calling Brian and got his voicemail. She left a quick message and sent another text telling him they were all getting worried. "I called him twice earlier today, but he didn't pick up or respond to the messages I left," she said, getting up. "Now he's close to an hour overdue." She turned toward Jim. "I think it's time to call someone else… maybe Jack Mills. He'd probably know if Brian left work already, and he lives close enough that he could run over to the boat and check whether Brian's still on board. Brian told me Jack always leaves work at five-thirty."

Jim nodded and took out his phone. "I'll make that call." He quickly left the room.

Kaylen heard him speaking before the door closed behind him.

"Don't even go there," Angela warned. "You're over-reacting, Kaylen, and you're making Jim anxious, now, too. Brian could have left his phone behind on the boat or lost it somewhere." She took a wrap from around her shoulders. "It could even have fallen into the water while he was getting onto the dock." She pointed toward the window. "That would be an easy thing to do; it looks like the water's a little rough tonight."

Kaylen looked outside again. Beyond an extensive terrace and the oversized pool, a swell rocked two jet skis tied up to the private dock.

"If he'd lost his phone, he'd find some way to contact me," she assured Angela. "He'd never leave his phone behind or forget to charge it. He's always on top of things like that. He has to be."

"Even Brian's human," Angela said with a little smile. "We've all misplaced our phones at some point."

"No." Kaylen shook her head emphatically. "He wouldn't. Being late and not letting us know why isn't what Brian does. Something's wrong."

She wrung her hands, because they were already twining around each other as though they needed the contact. "I said some things earlier that I regret now, but no matter how angry or disappointed with me he is, he would never desert us."

"No," Angela said. "I'm sure he wouldn't." She pulled the wrap back around her shoulders, apparently feeling a sudden chill. "I may not know him as well as you and Jim do, but I'm certain he's reliable."

Jim came back into the room. "Jack's on his way over to the *NTK*. He's having a patrol car meet him there."

"Brian won't like the patrol car," Kaylen protested. "The marina management won't like it, either."

"No lights," Jim said. "But they have to contact management to get the gate opened."

Kaylen sat in one of the deep, oversized chairs flanking the fireplace and sank into its depths. "He'll be really angry with me if he walks in right now."

"Better angry than missing," Jim said.

"That's how *you'd* look at it. Brian would probably think differently." Kaylen saw the remote sitting next to her chair and ignited the fireplace. Cheerful flames licked fake logs. "It's cold in here," she said when Jim, who was wearing a short-sleeved shirt, raised his eyebrows..

She'd expected Jack Mills to go alone, not turn up with reinforcements that were probably completely unnecessary. What if Brian had stopped off to pick up a surprise take-out order and flowers, as he sometimes did the nights she wasn't working? she thought, suddenly.

"He probably had a flat on the way over," Angela said, attempting to be the optimist in the room. "Or maybe he was grilling a suspect. You said he's working a cold case that may be connected somehow to a recent death."

"Angela, Brian doesn't talk about grilling suspects. You've been watching too many old movies since you were told to rest." Kaylen saw her friend pout at her reprimand. "He told me he'd handed that nursing home case over to Jack and the new team member, Villa-something."

"Villanueva," Jim said.

"Yes, that's right."

Kaylen tried to sound off-handed about the new team member. She didn't like or share Brian's enthusiasm for Deanna Villanueva. The new team-member sounded all too competent and friendly.

"I'm trying my best not to get too concerned, Angela," she said, rushing to fill what she realized was turning into an awkward silence. "I'm sorry if I offended you with that lecture about you watching too many movies. I know you've got to do something apart from sleep while you're stuck on the couch."

Kaylen felt the need to cross her legs. One foot jiggled spontaneously as soon as she did. She started to uncross them, but thought Jim and Angela would both notice her agitation and perhaps wonder whether all of it wasn't connected to Brian being...what? Overdue? Missing? Or how was it termed...in the wind? Kaylen cringed. She'd probably been watching too many old cop shows, too.

But what if he's with Deanna Villanueva? asked a niggling little voice at the back of Kaylen's mind. Maybe Villanueva had gone over to the boat for some reason or another. If she had, then Jack Mills was going to catch them together, and then what a mess that could turn out to be.

Kaylen berated herself for turning her back on Brian when he'd tried to make love to her the night before. If he *was* with the newest member of the Cold Case team, then it was probably because she had pushed him into the woman's arms.

She had done an internet search on Detective Deanna Villanueva and found a news photo of an attractive, compact woman with a charming smile holding a plaque from the city of Atlanta. Detective Villanueva had done something very civic. Kaylen thought it would be easy for Brian to like Deanna Villanueva, and it would be equally easy for her not to like either him or Villaneuva for that.

"You have nothing to apologize for," Angela said, breaking into Kaylen's decidedly unkind thoughts. "I'm worrying, too. I'm hiding out in someone else's house with armed guards patrolling outside and wondering whether I'm going to turn into target practice for a hit man."

"I'm responsible for that," Kaylen said.

She massaged her throbbing temples while she tried to get an image out of her head of Brian in bed with Deanna Villanueva. She had been so rude to him, she knew she would have to take the blame if the image turned into fact.

She thought back to the first night she had initiated getting into bed with Brian. He'd been so badly beaten, he could barely move, yet she'd felt safe and protected lying beside him on the narrow bunk in the *Destiny's* little cabin. So much had happened since then. Some good, and some really, really bad in the broadest of terms. But through it all, she reminded herself bitterly, they had always pulled together as a team.

Last night she had broken them apart, and she didn't know if they would ever be the same again... or even if she wanted them to be. One thing she did know...she didn't want Brian to be with anyone else, which she acknowledged was not only irrational but ridiculous and horribly self-centered.

She had never left that shallow persona of the popular socialite completely behind, and it had nothing to do with the Crossfields' influence or any of her other friends, for that matter. Brian didn't fit in that world of hers, and he never would. Not only because perhaps he couldn't, but because he chose not to do so. Sometimes perversely, she thought, remembering, with a flicker of anger, his dismissal of her dismay over Sam revealing that sex tape.

Princess. That's what he really thought of her. He'd never call Villanueva anything so derogatory.

Kaylen abruptly slammed the door on her spiteful thoughts. As she silently rebuked herself for taking an ugly little detour into Shallow-Land, she was forced to admit she was nursing a giant case of jealousy.

The revelation hit her like a blast of artic air. It might be unbecoming, it was probably completely unwarranted, but it was definitely what she was feeling. She hadn't experienced that shocking reaction since she was in high school, when she'd been passed over as a prom date by a sometime boyfriend who went with one of the cheerleaders instead, leaving Kaylen dateless and sullen. In those days, she'd been a tall, gangly teenager with unfashionable corkscrew curls. Those Mainers should see her now, she thought. But they wouldn't...no reason to go back to Maine when she could argue over the phone long-distance with her father.

"You are not responsible for any of this," Angela said, breaking into Kaylen's disturbing mental monologue. "You had no idea Sam Wilson was going to turn up on Brian's boat and bring cartel members with him."

Kaylen brought herself up from the chair's depths, where she'd sunk despondently, and moved to a wingback chair close to Angela. "I don't think they were from a cartel. I recognized one of them from the photo array they showed us after the home invasion. He was a member of the private security team Sam used at his compound. He called them his 'men.'"

"Oooh." Angela shivered. "That's so creepy, I've got chills." She energetically rubbed her forearms.

"That guy looked at me while he was pulling Sam away so I didn't run him over the night Brian got shot," Kaylen explained. "As I turned the wheel and accelerated, the headlights shone right on his face." It was her turn to shiver. "I never forgot the contempt and anger. The memories came flooding back as soon as I saw him again. Part of my PTSD, I guess, but this time, I'm almost glad to have it."

They all sat in silence after Kaylen finished speaking. She clasped her hands together and willed away the images that plagued her..

Jim cleared his throat. "Angela, why don't you turn that movie back on? We can't sit stewing as we wait for Jack to call or Brian to show up. And Kaylen definitely doesn't need to be thinking about bad things happening to Brian." He stood up. "I'm going to get a beer and fix you a mixed drink, Kaylen. You want something, Angela? Another spritzer?"

"Please." Angela held out her half-empty glass. "This is warm."

"I don't even know what movie was playing," Kaylen said, cranking her mind away from the flashback before she smelled the blood, which was always the worst part. "I hope it wasn't a thriller." She tried to laugh, but the sound burst from her throat like breaking glass.

"It wasn't." Angela said. "*While You Were Sleeping* has no violence in it at all."

"So it's one of those chick-flicks you girls are so fond of." Jim took Angela's glass to the wet-bar. "Do you think this house's owner subscribes to something like *Popular Mechanics,* so I can get some reading done? I already got through with the newspapers, and *Forbes* isn't on my wish-list."

"Sorry, Jim. I don't think Marshall ever has a need to fix anything around here. I think *While You Were Sleeping* is more of a rom-com than a dedicated chick-flick. It's got a lot of comedic elements. You might get a chuckle out of it." Angela snuggled down under a fluffy blanket she pulled from the back of the couch, dug around under a cushion and came up with the remote. "It happens at Christmas. We can all look at the snow we never see here."

"Great," Kaylen said. "I can be reminded of my early years in Maine, where we measured snow in feet every winter." She pulled a pillow from behind her back and hugged it in an attempt to ease the gnawing in her gut. "Like that's going to soothe me in any way. Jim, I don't care what drink you bring me, but whatever it is, make it a double."

CHAPTER FORTY-TWO

BRIAN AWOKE with his head on his chest. He tried not to move; a decision made easier by the thought of how much worse his headache would probably feel if he did. He found he was tied to a chair. The concrete floor within sight had been painted gray with patches of red and yellow where the paint had been scratched. Stark lighting probably meant fluorescent fixtures. He cautiously looked from one side to the other. The effort netted him more pain, lightheadedness and nausea. No doubt about it...he had a concussion.

Ice-cold water hit him full in the face. The abrupt shock jerked his head up. He fought dizziness and gasped for air as a second wave of water struck him. He inhaled enough to choke. Coughing and spluttering turned to gagging. His stomach emptied its contents all over his thighs.

"Pig," said a deep voice. "In more ways than one."

That elicited a sharp, barking laugh from another man.

More water hit Brian.

"Stop," he managed between coughing and gagging. He retched again, mucus streaming from his nose to join the other bodily fluids running off his chin.

"You puked. It stinks."

Brian heard what sounded like a plastic bucket hit the floor hard enough to crack it.

"Fuck," said the voice.

Something dragged across the floor. Almost slithered. What did the guy have...a fucking python? Brian struggled to focus on his surroundings. His vision swam. Nausea surged.

More water hit him. That time, a strong, sustained jet. No snake. A goddamned hose. But at least it was directed at his chest. The stream lowered, soaking his body, legs and finally his feet. Water gurgled down a floor drain some distance away.

"Unless you're planning on drowning me, that's enough," he yelled, before whoever was using the hose decided to send it back up to his face.

"Keep your mouth shut unless I ask you a question," said the deep voice. "That's enough, Clem," he added.

The hose shut off.

Brian tried to ignore pulsating pain as he raised his head and squinted at two figures, one taller and thinner than the other. The shorter one had a stocky build. Brian wondered which of the two had punched him in the face.

"I still think we should have followed orders and put him in the cage," Clem said, his voice reedy and higher-pitched. "He could get loose. We got warned, remember?"

"He's handcuffed and tied up. How d'ya think he's gonna get us?" asked the one with the deep voice, who was slowly taking shape. Dark hair, glistening under the fluorescent lighting, like it must be greased. The smaller one had a barrel chest with slim hips and muscled thighs. A boxer's build, Brian thought. He didn't need to waste any more brain power deciding who had K.O.'d him.

He blinked in an effort to clear his vision further. He needed to remember features, not blurred images, when he escaped. His lungs were still on fire from coughing. Breathing wasn't easy, and he felt sure he'd inhaled enough water to give him a serious case of pneumonia.

"I told you this was a bad idea, Win," the smaller one said as he moved front and center. "We should have put the wires on first."

Win turned to his partner. "We're supposed to give him a chance to be reasonable before we do anything else. Remember *that?*" He turned his attention back to Brian. "You hear that, Swift? We're gonna give you a chance to come clean; maybe walk away from this."

Neither had a discernable accent, Brian thought, trying to fix his attention on observation versus reaction. But his brain had fastened on the word "wires," added it to the experience of water soaking through his clothes and pooling around the chair, then informed him that he had to get free and out of there before his captors fried him and probably themselves, too.

He wondered if they had a connection to Sam Wilson. If they did, then must have taken him prisoner in an attempt to finish Sam's hunt for Tim's money.

"I hear you," he croaked, moving his head slowly while casting surreptitious glances at his surroundings. "I'm dizzy. What the hell did you hit me with?"

"My fist," Clem said. "Right in your face. Decked you with one punch."

"You must be hell in the ring," Brian said.

"A goddamned wrecking ball," Clem said.

"Shut up," Win warned. "Swift's the one needs to do the talking."

"Or what? You're gonna punch me in the face again?" Brian saw no reason to shut up and wait for more abuse. "It feels like I've already got a concussion. You could knock me senseless again."

"Your head hurts because you hit it on a barstool," Win said. "If you'd cleaned up the inside of your boat, you wouldn't have a concussion. I didn't hit you *that* hard."

Brian decided they couldn't have been involved with Sam Wilson or a drug cartel. If they were telling him his boat was a mess, they knew nothing about the shooting, and probably had no idea Wilson was dead.

His scattered thoughts tried to reorganize themselves. These guys were named Win and Clem. Win had to be Winston McCall. Brian looked up again, and that time, his vision wasn't quite as blurred, although his head still ached when he moved his eyes. He thought of the mug shot and tried to age-progress the photo in his mind. Yes, the tall, thin man standing some distance away could be Winston McCall, but his partner didn't look anything like him or the latest photo of Beale Friendly.

"How did you get me here?" Brian asked, risking another question. "You couldn't have carried me through the marina."

"Of course not." Clem chuckled. "We rowed over to your boat in a dinghy. Easy to load you into that. Then we used an outboard motor to get you out of there. No rowing with three of us aboard."

Win moved closer. "Enough sharing from us. We're the ones asking the questions from here on out. Where's the money your brother stashed with you? It's not on the boat. We searched the whole place."

"My brother didn't stash anything with me."

Brian's blurred vision caused him to miss seeing Clem's fist. He took a vicious punch to his jaw.

"He can do this all night," Win said. "He'll break every bone in your face, then we'll get started on the rest of you. I'm hell on breaking fingers one joint at a time, and he's a real master at giving electric shocks in places that'll really damage your ability to father kids."

Win's low chuckle sent the hairs on Brian's arms up into a parade-ground-worthy salute. He decided it was going to be a really long night. He had no idea where he was, and neither did anyone else, unless his phone had remained somewhere with his captors. If they'd tossed it into the water, he'd have to tell them where Tim's stash was located and hope they'd have to use him to get into the safe deposit box. He didn't really care about giving them Tim's money, but he'd become a real fan of staying alive over the last couple of years, and he wasn't ready to give that up.

CHAPTER FORTY-THREE

BRIAN DECIDED he had to be in a warehouse or another storage facility...
one that held some sort of a cage he couldn't see, probably designed to
keep valuable items secure.

He thought back to the unit where Moises' body had been discovered.
No cage in that one, but the manager had said that was their largest
option, not their only one. Being taken there was a long-shot, but as his
vision cleared even more, he noticed a rolling service door behind his
captors.

His partially-numb legs were cramping from being held immobilized.
Win and Clem stepped back and drew close together. When he heard
them arguing in low voices, their attention away from him, Brian
checked out the handcuffs they'd used, hoping the lock was within reach.

He couldn't figure out how long he'd been gone. Either there were no
windows, or it was so dark outside, they were hidden in the shadows. He
took stock of his physical condition. He'd taken a couple of punches to
the face by a middle-weight boxer. He doubted they had drugged him, for
which he was thankful. When he did manage to free himself, which
Brian promised himself would happen, he wondered how much his legs
would hinder him. The painful cramping was increasing at a rate compa-
rable to the progression of a numbness that had now spread to his butt.

His fingers found the lock. "You're making a big mistake kidnapping me," he called as he shifted into a position that would give him access to his tools.

"No one's gonna find you," Win answered. "You can either give us what we want and maybe get turned loose, I can beat it out of you, or if you continue to act stubborn, Clem can see how you like the shock treatment. He likes to use the wires, don't you, Clem?"

"I do, indeed." Another high-pitched, barking laugh.

Like a hyena must sound, Brian thought. He'd never get a chance to hear one in person if he didn't pry his tools out of his back pocket. It wasn't easy, with wet denim making the metal slippery. If he dropped one of the tools, he reminded himself, he'd not only alert Clem and Winston, but he'd be unable to pick the lock at all.

"We'll drag you out of the water before he attaches the wires," Win said. "Then we can hit you with the hose if you still don't talk after he turns on the current."

The hose. This had to be a small warehouse, Brian decided. No storage units he'd ever seen had a water supply inside any of them.

"Oh, good," he said, striving for snide yet casual. "I'll be clean, at least." He told himself he had to keep them talking, so they didn't start working him over or focus on his movements.

His body was beginning to shake. *Damn, it was cold.*

"I told you he wouldn't give it up easy," Clem said. "Let's get the wires on."

"We stick to the plan. I'll beat him for a while. That should get him talking."

Win sounded less sure the plan would work, but whoever was in charge had given strict orders, and Win wasn't about to choose another path. Their leader had to be prone to even more violence than his posse, Brian thought.

He felt the coldness from the concrete floor join the wetness seeping through his clothes and clinging to his skin. Soon, his teeth would be chattering. He was in for a decidedly painful incarceration unless he freed himself fast, and if he didn't make opening those handcuffs a priority, his fingers would be too numb to do the deed. Thankfully, he still had shoes on his feet, although he couldn't count on them staying there much longer, especially when Clem got busy hooking him up for a power transfer.

Whoever had sent them to do the dirty work must have felt certain they could get the information, which meant he was going to be beaten to a pulp and then electrocuted, probably whether he gave up the location of the safe deposit box quickly or tried to wait for a rescue that might never come. His wrists were partially numb, but he still felt his Rolex was missing. Kaylen had told him there was a tracking device in it when she'd given him his gift last Christmas. She told him to relax, because she wasn't going to use it to find out where he was at all times, and they'd laughed. She told him the device was actually there to enable the watch to be found if it was lost or stolen. Brian could only hope that the next time one of his captors came closer, he'd be able to see one of them wearing his watch, and that Kaylen would remember to tell Jim or Jack, or whoever was hopefully looking for him, that there *was* a way to find him.

Otherwise, he reckoned he'd be going out of that warehouse in a body bag even if he did give up the location of Tim's money. Finally, Brian managed to slide the tools out of his pocket. He had to stretch his hands and wrists into a very uncomfortable position to insert the tools into the lock. As he worked to free himself, he wondered whether Kaylen would bring two bunches of red roses every week if he was interred with his brother at Woodlawn Park Cemetery.

CHAPTER FORTY-FOUR

"HE'S NOT ON THE BOAT." Jack Mills' voice came loud and clear through the speaker on Jim's phone.

"Any signs of a struggle?" Jim asked.

"The salon's still a complete wreck, but so's the galley. Everything moved around, stuff all over the floor, including the contents of the refrigerator. Bedroom's trashed, so's the head. Someone's been searching the place. I found an open letter from the marina management, giving Brian ten days to vacate. It was dated today, so I've got to assume Brian was in here. I can see he'd be upset about the letter, but I can't see him emptying his refrigerator all over the floor and throwing everything out of cupboards and drawers."

"I *knew* something happened to him." Kaylen's worry had turned into full-blown panic. "Didn't any of the owners on the nearby boats see or hear anything unusual?"

"The slip to the left of the *NTK's* empty. The manager said those people pulled out after the shooting and said if they don't get their slip-fees back, they're suing."

Kaylen grabbed Jim's phone out of his hand. "Who cares about that? Did the manager see anything? Was the marina completely deserted, for God's sake?"

Jim gently but firmly took back his phone. "Honey, they're doing their best."

"That's not enough. The *Need to Know* isn't the only boat in the marina. Ask someone else, Jack." She barely stopped herself from reminding him he was supposed to be a detective.

"Kaylen, you have to settle down," Jack said. "Detective Villanueva and two patrol-officers are canvassing the entire marina. If anyone saw anything, they'll find out what."

Kaylen tried calming herself while she listened to what was now a one-way conversation because Jim had muted the speaker. She tried using Brian's method for calming himself…measured pacing with long, even step-lengths. She directed her steps to end at the gigantic kitchen island, which Jim had made his command post, well away from Angela in the TV room. Kaylen felt torn between remaining with Angela or keeping on top of any developments in the kitchen. She couldn't do both.

Feeling left out of Jim's one-sided conversation, she chose Angela. But her friend, brandishing the TV remote, told Kaylen to go back to the kitchen. *While You Were Sleeping* had moved to the last couple of scenes. Angela said she was perfectly capable of replacing it with another movie they had chosen together that afternoon and shooed Kaylen away after extracting a promise from her to bring any updates as soon as she had them.

"I can't take much more of this," Kaylen told Jim when he put down the phone. "The PTSD had almost gone until now. My heart's drumming away like I'm walking up a hill. I'm pretty sure I'm having a panic attack."

"Your reaction's normal," Jim said. "My heart's not exactly beating like I'm about to take a nap." He took two glasses from the cabinet above the bar area, added ice, a jigger of scotch and a splash of soda.

"Brian's always in trouble," Kaylen said, taking her drink. "I've tried to ignore that because I love him and he's so capable. But I'm a basket case."

"You were stronger than most when those thugs broke in at the Crossfields,'" Jim reminded her. "Whether they came for you or Angela, what you did sent them packing."

"I shot a man, Jim." She looked across the island as he settled onto a barstool. "I hate guns and violence, yet I'm wrapped up in it on a daily basis. I want to go back to what I was before…well, mostly what I was…" She took a gulp of her drink. "I like partying with my friends and running my business. I don't want to be known for shooting someone."

"Can't you be both a socialite and a businesswoman who's able take care of herself in any situation?" Jim placed his drink on a coaster. "You own two clubs. Brian's been worried about what could happen at Bannisters. Now you're going to have two locations that could get held up."

"I've got Security checking everyone who comes into the club. My policy is no weapons, no drugs, and no meetings of any kind except for social occasions. I want my clientele to feel safe and secure when they come to enjoy themselves. Parties of all kinds are encouraged." Kaylen took a sip of her scotch while she tried to get control of herself. Her panic wanted to take full flight and leave her completely irrational. "Brian always over-reacts and sees the blackest outcome to everything," she told Jim. She decided the scotch was loosening her tongue a little too much. "If I listened to him, I'd never leave my condo," she added, striving for a note of humor that sounded more of a whine than a joke.

"Oh, honey." Jim finished his scotch, got up and took his empty coffee cup over to the Keurig. He stood looking at it, cup in hand. "I hate these things."

"Here, I'll do it." Kaylen selected a light roast and made Jim's coffee. She felt better keeping busy instead of nursing an alcoholic drink. She glanced up at the clock: 7:30 P.M.

"I'll start dinner," she said. "Better than getting drunk again and making a complete fool of myself. And Angela has to eat. Doctor's orders. What have we got?"

Jim placed both the scotch glasses in the sink. "Ground turkey. Pork chops. A roast in the freezer."

She fought to keep her mind off Brian's situation while she did a mental run-through of her very limited repertoire of recipes that didn't need a lot of ingredients. "No chili or tacos; they'll give Angela heartburn. I can make burgers or pork chops. The roast can stay where it is. I'm not tackling that this evening."

"Let's have the burgers." Jim left his coffee and went to the refrigerator. "We've got lettuce if there aren't any buns. We can have wraps. I'll take care of the rest if you get those burgers cooked."

"We should check on Angela, again." Kaylen looked out the windows and watched one of the security detail wave reassuringly at her. She fought a sudden desire to start crying.

"I'll go." Jim left the room.

Kaylen went into the cavernous walk-in pantry and brought out the rest of the ingredients to make the burgers while her mind kept asking her where Brian was and conjuring up all manner of disturbing scenarios that mostly involved torture with branding irons, clubs or whips. Kaylen resolved not to watch any more TV shows or movies with violence for the next year at least.

Jim came back. "She's asleep. I left the movie playing so we can make as much noise as we like out here."

"I'm not hungry, but if I don't do something constructive, I'll start running through the house screaming at the top of my lungs," Kaylen said. "That would wake Angela up, movie or no movie." She opened the ground turkey and plopped the meat into a bowl, chopped onion and then decided against adding it in case that would upset Angela's stomach, too. She decided to use poultry seasoning, garlic salt and a dash of pepper, keeping the meat slightly bland.

"You are the most atypical socialite I've ever seen," Jim remarked as he took lettuce and tomato out of the refrigerator.

"I grew up on a farm in rural Maine, Jim." Kaylen finished patting the burgers into shape and warmed up the grill at one end of the island. "It wasn't until I met Sam that I got manners. He really groomed me for a new life. Then he introduced me to George, and I wanted to be able to mingle with the people he knew without being an embarrassment. George said Sam had done a fine job of mentoring. If he'd seen me when I first arrived, he'd have said Sam was a miracle-worker."

She took the empty bowl over to the sink to cover for a sudden lack of composure. Sam was gone. The last link to her early life in Miami. She cleared her throat while she ran water.

"George was a wonderful man," she said, "but he never saw me with all those rough edges that would almost certainly have made me completely unpalatable."

She owed Sam so much. More than she could ever repay, she told herself, even though he had betrayed her in the end.

"I could never picture you as anything different from what you are now." Jim smiled over his shoulder as he washed lettuce in a sink next to the bar area and put it into a spinner.

"Oh, I was different, all right." Kaylen checked the burgers and adjusted the gas grill slightly to prevent cooking the outside of the meat too quickly. "A skinny, naive nineteen-year-old with long, frizzy hair when I arrived at Sam's restaurant and asked for a job. The complete opposite of what I am today."

"How did you manage to snag a job, if you had no experience?" Jim asked.

"I'd waited tables that summer up in Maine. Only a small lunch crowd, but I didn't tell Sam that when he interviewed me."

Jim chuckled as he brought condiments out of the refrigerator and set them on the counter. "You always had spunk, huh?"

"I was highly-motivated to get that job, Jim. I'd been milking cows at the crack of dawn and doing the same thing in the afternoon. I was also expected to put all meals on the table at home. Believe me, my dad ate a lot of burgers, but they weren't made from turkey. I also made chili and meatloaf a lot."

Jim poured them both a cup of coffee and placed one next to Kaylen on the counter.

"He liked his mashed potatoes with gravy," Kaylen said as she flipped the burgers. "He reluctantly agreed to eat a sandwich at lunch the days I worked at the diner after I told him I could buy anything I needed with the money I earned instead of asking him. It took him a while to realize I actually required what he thought were unnecessary staples like shampoo or," she made air-quotes with the spatula in one hand, "'new' clothes from the local thrift store. He ate Bologna and cheese, mostly." She shuddered at the thought of that slimy, tasteless and misnamed deli meat. "I watch the meals being prepared in the kitchen at Bannisters and even after all this time, I still marvel sometimes at the masterpieces chefs make out of a piece of meat and a bunch of vegetables."

"So you left home and came to Miami, and Sam gave you a finishing school education before introducing you to George?" Jim cut a tomato.

Thin slices. He arranged them artfully on a plate, scraped Kaylen's unused onion slices onto it, then added the lettuce.

"When you say it like that, it sounds like that's exactly what he did."

Kaylen leaned one hip against the counter and watched Jim slice a couple of dill pickles into thin strips while she thought back to those first days she'd spent in Miami.

"Oh, my God," she said, a horrible realization dawning on her. "Why didn't I see that before? Sam was grooming me on purpose...for his friend. To make George like him even more or feel indebted to him when he asked for money to shore up his business. Sam played us both. Me for being vulnerable and open to flattery. George for being lonely and in need of consolation."

Why *hadn't* she ever thought of that before? She'd been led into that role like the teenage bumpkin from Maine that she had been at that time. Kaylen's heart felt like it was having trouble maintaining beats.

She'd been so completely gullible, and unfortunately, so had George, who was newly-divorced and about as susceptible to flattery as the young woman to whom he was introduced. In a manner of speaking, Sam Wilson may have brain-washed George into liking her as much as she had been groomed to like Sam's charming and very rich older friend.

Kaylen had to sit down. Her knees were trembling like they weren't going to hold her up much longer. She used the counter for support while she made her way to one of the chrome barstools, which she now noted to have seats that were disturbingly close to the color of blood.

She decided she had been lied to by just about every man she had come into contact with in Miami, including Brian. The only men who had never lied to her were Jim, hopefully, she thought, reserving a little doubt even for him, and her father. If Preston Grant was the package truth came in, she wasn't sure whether she preferred some degree of deceitfulness to the unvarnished version. Jim flipped the sizzling burgers again while she sat lost in thought on the opposite side of the grill.

"Are you all right?" he asked.

Kaylen tried to shake the swirling thoughts out of her brain. "No," she told him, "I'm definitely *not* all right. Far from it. Not many people know where I came from, Jim. I never talk about the farm in Maine, but not necessarily because I'm hiding anything. My dad is never going to come here, or he would have when I got married. He told me he tore up the invitation to join me for what he called basically the ceremonial throwing away of my youth on an old man. So I doubt he'd talk to a reporter who knocked at his door and wanted an exclusive." She smiled ruefully. "He'd give that person a piece of his mind, too, and my dad never minces words."

"He sounds like a real pill." Jim started loading the cooked burgers onto a serving dish. "I would have loved to be a dad and do all those things with my kids that make a family. I'd have been so proud to walk my daughter down the aisle, and I'd have respected her choice of husband."

"You'd have made a great dad." Kaylen blinked back tears again.

"We'll never know for sure." Jim covered the burgers with foil and popped them into the oven to keep warm. He pushed a couple of buttons without really looking at them. "It's easy to say what you'd be like when you've never had the experience. Maybe I'd have resembled your dad after a couple of blizzards. You said there were animals. They'd have to be fed regardless of how bad the weather was up there."

"Cows. They had to be milked twice a day. Chickens needed feeding, and I had to take their eggs away from them." She grimaced at that memory. Some things never lost their edge. "We had a couple of real peckers amongst our hens. Great layers, but they weren't into allowing anyone to take the fruits of their labor. Can't say I blame them, but we had to eat."

Jim went into the pantry and came out squeezing a bag of buns. "They're fresh," he said. "You want one?"

Kaylen shook her head. "No thanks. I've had so many calories lately, I've gained five pounds. Not enough exercise. Brian told me not to swim anymore, and he nixed the gym, too. See, I'm a prisoner." She made herself get up from the stool. "I'll set out the plates and glasses. I shouldn't be talking about Brian with resentment, especially when we're not sure where he is, and he's not here to defend himself. Which he does very successfully, I might add." She bit her bottom lip. Jim must think she was part heartless-bitch and was giving that side of herself an overdue airing.

"It's okay, honey. You don't need to explain yourself to me. I know you're mad with him for getting into hot water again, and terrified that he's gotten into more trouble than he can handle." Jim placed buns on the top of the still-warm grill.

Kaylen took three plates and glasses out of the cabinets, hesitated, then added another set before placing them on the table in the breakfast nook. "I wish Jack would call and give us another update. Do you think he'd get mad if I call him and ask him for one?"

Jim tapped the top of each bun lightly, found them to his liking and scooted them from the grill onto another serving dish. "He knows how worried you are, honey. He'll call as soon as he knows something. We should let him do his job." He took a bottle of Sauterne from the wine fridge and uncorked it. Without asking Kaylen, he poured two glasses and brought one over to her. "Drink up."

"I'm not using liquor as a crutch," she said.

"More satisfying than anti-anxiety medication." Jim lifted his glass. "Here's to Brian coming back safe and sound real fast."

"Cheers to that." Kaylen clinked glasses. She smelled burning. "Oh, no…the burgers. Did you set that oven on warm or something else?"

Jim's knowledge of what he called the new-fangled stoves had caused him to push the wrong button out of a large array of choices. But their burgers were thankfully only lightly charred. He stopped Kaylen throwing them out and starting over with pork chops. Using one of a large variety of knives from a caddy, he shaved away thin slices from the generous servings. "There. Good as new."

"I hope they taste okay." Kaylen eyed them doubtfully. "We may need to use a lot of ketchup."

"What are you two burning in here?" Angela asked as she drifted into the kitchen with a blanket trailing behind her. "I'm actually hungry, so let's eat." She placed an arm around Kaylen's waist and squeezed. "You have to keep your strength up. Brian would want that."

Kaylen burst into tears.

CHAPTER FORTY-FIVE

BRIAN SWORE silently as he tried his best to make his numbed fingers work the tools and open the lock. It was taking far too long, and his arms were tiring from being held in the same contorted position. A discussion had started over whether to get food before they tortured their hostage or wait until Clem had worked up an appetite by punching Brian to a pulp. It didn't sound like either of them expected him to give them any useful information. They were there because they'd been told what to do, and they were going to follow orders.

Finally, he got a break.

"I'm going for pizza," Winston announced. "I don't care what Beale says when he gets here. He's probably eating dinner right now. I'm hungry, and there's a pizza place only a few blocks away."

"Beale's not gonna like this," Clem warned.

"Let's get this over with," Win said. "We both know Swift's not gonna talk. Hook him up while I'm gone and fry him. You want pepperoni and mushroom? Two large?"

"Why don't you get yourself one of those and get me a Canadian bacon and extra cheese?" Clem pulled out what Brian thought was his billfold and produced a couple of bills. "Forty enough?"

"Probably. But you want sodas?"

Clem pulled out another bill. "This should do it."

Brian knew he had sixty bucks in cash. That had to be his billfold. Winston grabbed the cash. Something gold glinted on his wrist. Brian hoped it was his Rolex.

One side of the cuffs swung open. Brian grabbed it with a sense of relief greater than any he remembered feeling in his life. He pushed the lock picks back into his pocket and flexed his fingers, hoping to restore circulation. He still had one big problem, and that was Clem. He'd have to somehow get the guy to come within grabbing distance while his partner was out buying pizza. Thank God for hunger. His stomach growled on that note.

"Hungry, Swift?" Clem chuckled, hyena-like. "I'd love to wait until Win gets back and give you a slice of my Canadian bacon with extra cheese before throwing the switch, but that would be an unnecessary waste of pizza, and the smell of burning flesh would ruin our meal. I'm going to hook you up and do the deed while Win's gone, like he said."

"Won't Beale be upset if you don't get something out of me?" Brian asked.

"You know, Win's afraid of Beale, but I'm not. He's not my brother. I signed on for this one job. Then I'm out. They wanted my particular specialties, and paid me well up front for them." He went over to a corner and dragged out a small cart filled with what must be the tools of his trade, pushing it to within a couple of feet of Brian. "This group's too messy and primitive for my liking. Take Win for instance. He wanted to beat you. What's the sense in that? I could see if you were going to talk with a few jolts."

He took a couple of wires from the trolley and waved them. "All I'm going to do is clip a couple of these onto you, douse you with the hose again and throw the switch. You'll feel yourself cooking inside, but it won't last long."

Brian waited. Clem came up close and squatted. "I'll start by pushing your pants legs inside your socks, so we get good grounding."

Brian seized him.

It wasn't pretty, because his hands and arms were still partially numb, but once he dragged Clem across his thighs and got him in a better choke-hold, it worked. After thrashing around and kicking, Clem went limp.

Brian dropped him onto the floor and heard a satisfying crack as Clem's head hit the concrete. He managed to stand, his legs still attached to the chair's front legs. He had to act fast, or he'd be caught by Winston or even Beale Friendly, who would surely turn up at some point to make sure his orders were being carried out.

Brian used wires and cables from Clem's delightful little handy torture cart to tie up his prisoner. He found a utility knife in a bag on the cart and sawed through the ropes tying him to the chair. Freedom had never felt so good. He dragged his prisoner into the cage. Clem was still breathing, but a large blue area had formed on the right side of his face where he'd hit the floor. Brian still thought he needed gagging.

He found a rag hanging off a dolly parked near the roll-up door, ripped some off and shoved that into Clem's mouth, then tied the rest into a gag in case Clem came around and spat out the wad of material. He almost used the handcuffs, but decided he might need them for someone else. A half-dozen boxes inside the cage provided enough cover for Clem's body. Brian figured Winston wouldn't notice they'd been moved.

Suddenly, he heard the door start rolling upward. He had no time to do anything else but put himself back onto the chair and drop his head.

"Are you two getting anything out of Swift, or are you too busy with your dinner break?" Cassandra Bunting asked indignantly as she clip-clopped across the concrete floor in the same green high-heeled shoes she'd worn to the crime scene.

"We had to stop and eat," Winston protested. The door rolled down into place.

"Beale's going to be really, really disappointed in you," Cassandra announced. "You didn't even bring enough food for all of us. I suppose you used money from Swift's wallet. Didn't he have enough to cover a couple more pizzas and two big bottles of soda?"

CHAPTER FORTY-SIX

KAYLEN'S PHONE rang while she, Angela and Jim were finishing their make-shift dinner.

"I know you're worried sick," Chief Hal Shaw said. "I didn't want you to think we've given up looking, but there's no sign of Brian, anywhere. I'm calling to see if you can give me any more information. Have you checked your text, voicemail and email messages lately?"

"Yes, every five minutes or less," Kaylen said. "The last text I got from him said he was going to be here before the security detail changed at six. It's almost nine o'clock. Something terrible's happened to him. I know it." The tight band around her chest tightened even more. Kaylen's heart was doing its irregular two-step again.

"That letter Jack Mills found on the boat. Do you think Brian could be despondent?"

"Despondent? What sort of word is that? Do you mean he'd take his own life over losing his boat slip? No, of course not. But I know he was really frustrated and angry about being placed on probation. About the bribery charges and then the shooting. And I...well, I could have been more supportive." Embarrassed to be discussing her private life with Hal, and very aware that Jim and Angela were sitting silently looking at her, she got up from the table and left the room to walk down the long hallway toward the front entrance. "We quarreled last night, if that's what you're asking, but we made up this morning, and he didn't seem overly stressed about the meeting with Internal Affairs. He told me to be careful."

"Did that seem unusual to you, him asking you to be careful?"

"No. He always tells me that, and he means it, especially lately, with all that's been going on at home and work." Kaylen pushed hair out of her eyes and wished she had pulled it back into a ponytail.

"We had problems locating his phone," Hal said. "It finally turned up in a small dinghy that was adrift in Biscayne Bay."

"What?" Kaylen had to lean against the wall for support.

"Jack Mills said that dinghy doesn't belong to Brian," Chief Shaw broke in. "Brian's is still on his boat."

"How…how did you find the phone?"

"GPS coordinates."

Behind the swirling thoughts, something important was trying to break through Kaylen's panicked mind. "Chief Shaw," she said.

"Yes, I'm here. Listen, we're sending out a team to assist the Coast Guard."

"He's got a tracking device in his Rolex," Kaylen said. "I gave it to him last Christmas. The salesman told me about it. It's so the watch can be tracked if it's lost or stolen."

"Have you got the paperwork, or does he?"

"I do. I kept it, because I know Brian doesn't have a lot of space for storage on the boat."

"I'm sending Jack Mills to get you." Chief Shaw hung up.

CHAPTER FORTY-SEVEN

"IS HE EVEN CONSCIOUS?" Cassandra Bunting asked, clip-clopping closer to Brian. "Are you sure Clem didn't kill him while you were gone? Look, his equipment's over here."

"I'm pretty sure," Winston said.

"Well, where is he, anyway?" Cassandra sounded really ticked off. "Beale's not going to like this. You know how he is."

"Clem probably went out to take a leak. We've been here hours, and Swift still won't talk. I'm eating."

Brian smelled pizza. He could almost visualize the pepperoni and mushroom.

"You have *not* been here hours, Win. I thought you said you were going to beat the location of the money out of him. He doesn't look like you roughed him up much."

"He fell backwards and hit his head when we went to the boat to pick him up," Win mumbled, presumably with his mouth filled with pizza. "It took some time for him to come around and start making sense."

"Great," Cassandra said, her voice dripping sarcasm.

Cassandra's musky perfume overpowered the smells of pepperoni, cheese and tomato sauce as she moved closer. Brian started feeling nauseated again.

"He looks dead to me," Cassandra said.

The slap she gave Brian would have awakened him if he *was* dead. He'd had enough abuse for one night. He didn't have enough energy left after subduing Clem to jump up athletically, but he saw her confusion and fear as he rose from the chair and grabbed her, swinging her around and putting her in a similar choke-hold to the one he'd used on Clem, but allowing her to breathe.

"I'll break her neck," he threatened as Winston dropped his pizza slice onto the open pizza box resting on a metal utility table, stood up and took a couple of uncertain steps forward.

"Do what he says," Cassandra croaked. Her voice reverberated against Brian's arm.

"In the cage," Brian told Winston. He tightened his hold on Cassandra, who obligingly managed a terrified whimper. "Now!"

Winston shuffled in quick-time over to the cage and stepped inside. "Don't hurt her," he begged. "She's Beale's girlfriend. She hasn't done anything."

"She slapped the shit out of me. That's assaulting a police officer," Brian pointed out. "Take off my damn watch, Win, leave it outside, then get onto your stomach at the back of the cage."

Cassandra Bunting made a noise like a lone goose would make when searching for its flock as he half-dragged, half-pushed her over to the cage.

"We can discuss your charges later," he told her before he threw her in on top of Win, slammed the door, attached the padlock hanging open on the hasp and closed it with a sigh of relief.

His legs and feet, prickling and throbbing, were coming back to life with a vengeance. He badly wanted to stomp his feet to hasten the process, but Beale Friendly could be on his way over to the warehouse right at that moment, and he wasn't going to alert the part-time painter by doing a tap dance.

"He'll get you," Winston muttered from beneath Cassandra.

Cassandra scrambled off him and came over to grab the bars, her face framed between them. "You'll never get away with this," she snarled. But she didn't sound so sure of herself, locked in a cage with Brian on the other side of it.

"You'd better hope I do," Brian said. He picked up his watch and put in back on his wrist as he walked over to the where her purse lay beside the unopened pizza boxes. He opened the purse, finding her phone inside along with a small automatic tucked in with an enormous bag of makeup, her wallet and keys.

His own billfold was resting under the open pizza box. He shoved it into his back pocket, took the purse with him and cautiously rolled the door up high enough to crawl out of the warehouse. He sat in Cassandra's Nissan Sentra and used her phone to give Hal a fast update. Hal told him to watch himself in case Friendly beat the reinforcements that would home in on the location pinging from Cassandra's phone. Brian told Hal what he thought about the entire operation Hal had convinced him to participate in and enjoyed swearing loudly and at length while doing so.

Beale Friendly arrived moments before those reinforcements. He turned out to be the most uncooperative of the abductors. He swore and took swings until Brian, hungry, wet and cold, landed an uppercut to Friendly's jaw that put an end to the entire episode. By the time Jack Mills and Deanna Villanueva arrived along with two patrol cars, Friendly was wearing the handcuffs and sitting in the back of the Sentra.

"I'd better call Kaylen," Brian told Hal when he checked in to assure the chief he was safe.

"You'd better," Hal agreed. "After she got through being relieved, she started sounding angrier the more I tried to explain to her what exactly had happened."

"Yeah, I was kinda worried that might happen," Brian said. "I'll tell you right now, I refuse to be used as bait ever again. You almost got me killed, and I still don't know who murdered my brother. Certainly not these people. They were after money they thought he'd left with me."

"I thought you'd taken your own life there for about thirty minutes," Hal said. "Then I realized you would never check out before finding Tim's killers. I made sure I told Kaylen that."

"I'm sure that made her feel so much better."

"Yeah, well, no plan is ever foolproof," Hal said.

"You've got that right," Brian agreed as he watched Friendly and his little gang being led away. Cassandra Bunting glared at him. He nodded to her. She had quite a wrist, he thought, moving his jaw around.

He wanted to put off talking to Kaylen until he'd had a chance to get in on Bunting's interview, but told himself if he did, she would be even angrier. He wondered if she'd be relieved enough to hear his voice that she'd bring him dry clothes.

If she was still too angry after he called, then he hoped Jim wouldn't be as upset about being left out of the loop. He called Kaylen. She picked up on the third ring. "Hello, hon," he said.

She hung up on him.

CHAPTER FORTY-EIGHT

"LOOK, IT WASN'T THE CARTEL," Brian explained, trying to remain patient and supportive of Kaylen's outrage.

"So, you and Hal and whoever else you both included, which wasn't me, or Jim for that matter, concocted a plan to use you as bait to attract Tim's killers. Is that right?" Kaylen's dark eyes flashed fire. "But what you attracted instead was that painter and the reporter and two guys sent to take you prisoner and torture you until you told them where you had hidden Tim's money, after which they planned to kill you."

Brian nodded.

"So, even though that plan failed, you're still expecting the cartel's hit men to come after you?"

"Maybe, yes."

Kaylen crossed her arms and shook her head at him. "I can't believe this. You kept all of it from me? You lied, again? And not about anything small. You could have been killed, Brian, and you held my hand in that meeting with Hal and gave me the biggest line of bullshit."

"I had to. But after this bungled attempt, Hal agreed I had to come clean to you."

"You had no right to keep us in the dark. All of us. Jim, Angela, Jonathan. Who else was left out of this plan?"

"Everything was on a need to know basis."

"Yes, and without even considering the impact on anyone else's life, you made that decision."

"I had to."

"Don't tell me Hal ordered you to, because you never follow orders."

"I did this time. Hon, we decided this was the only way to flush out Tim's killers. But what we weren't factoring in was Beale Friendly and his little gang. I have to get over to the precinct and see what comes out in their interrogations."

"Nothing. I bet they ask for their lawyers and you don't learn anything." Her voice was as sharp as broken glass.

"Maybe the D.A. will cut them a deal, so we do." Brian didn't want to even consider he'd spent a couple of hours tied to a chair, being doused with water and threatened with electrocution for nothing.

Kaylen uncrossed her arms.

Brian thought she was going to shrug or even, if he was lucky, tell him she was still really upset while she hugged him and told him how glad she was to see him safe. But she didn't.

Instead, she left him in the *NTK's* galley, grabbed her purse and keys from the recliner, and walked out onto the deck.

"Where are you going?" Brian wondered what the hell she was doing. "We're not finished."

Kaylen stopped, turned, and gave him a look so cold, Brian almost flinched.

"Yes, we are," she said. "Completely finished. We're through."

"Hon, I know you're really angry, and I deserve it, but you don't mean that."

"I do mean it." Her icy gaze held no tears. "Don't follow me and try to convince me you love me, Brian. You've never loved me enough to consider my feelings above your own overwhelming desire for revenge. This relationship was always on shaky ground, and now it isn't even on that."

Brian watched her walk away. He followed her onto the deck. Without even a backward glance, she stepped down onto the finger pier, walked across the dock and entered the parking lot. She disappeared from sight between darkened vehicles. He heard her car door open and close. The BMW left quietly and unhurriedly, the purr of its engine diminishing until it was lost within the gentle lapping of waves against the *NTK's* hull.

Kaylen was past angry with him, Brian realized. She had just shut him out of her life.

CHAPTER FORTY-NINE

Kaylen was right about Beale Friendly and his cohorts invoking the right to seek counsel, but after deals were made, in what remained of the night, they talked. As Brian watched from the observation room with a frequently-replenished cup of coffee in hand, he learned a lot, and began to fill in details that might have remained subject to interpretation for a considerable amount of time.

The younger Friendly had indeed started out as a part-time gardener and handyman at Sam Wilson's compound. But his background as an armed robber evidently became an unexpectedly desirable attribute, advancing his career from mowing lawns to joining the ranks of Sam's protection squad. Kaylen had correctly identified his mug shot as the man she had seen helping Sam the night Brian was shot.

Beale Friendly proved to be less forthcoming than his little brother, but he grudgingly admitted to hearing from Sam Wilson that Tim had absconded with a lot of drug cartel money, and maybe a lot of Sam's too. Sam had spread that rumor around thickly to cover for his lack of available funds to pay for his lavish lifestyle, the upkeep of his restaurant, and most importantly for Winston McCall, his staff's wages.

At 6:00 AM, Jack Mills came into the room with two cups of fresh coffee and a couple of bear claws.

"I stopped off on the way in," he said, handing Brian one of the cups and a pastry. "I heard you never went home. Gabe's already in. He said ever since he went with you to interview Mrs. Dewett, something about her has bothered him. When he found out Gertrude Pensky, her walking companion had died, he looked into Mrs. Dewett's background. It was a long search, but he thinks death has followed her around a little too much."

Brian's attention, split between Jack and the monologue still going on in the other room, took a jump in Gabe's direction. "In what way?" He took a sip from his coffee. Hot and strong. Like a jolt of adrenaline to his tired body.

"Gabe said Dewett was married three times," Jack said, walking over to the window and checking out a scowling Beale Friendly arguing silently with his attorney since Brian had turned off the volume in the viewing room. "Outlived them all. Her parents and two siblings, too."

"Gabe's got a point. That's a lot of funerals."

Jack pointed his half-chewed bear claw in Brian's direction. "There were a couple more. She also had two fiancés who were nice enough to make her the prime beneficiary of their wills before they died."

Brian looked at Jack over the rim of his cup, and saw Jack watching him intently. "You're the acting Cold Case supervisor right now," he reminded his coworker.

"*Acting* is the word," Jack said. "I remember you issuing an order yesterday that covered Gabe as well as me. For someone on probation, it sounded pretty definitive. Gabe signed up at the range."

"I'm not in the office," Brian said. "And I've been told in no uncertain terms that I can't be until IA gets through with their investigation. Damn, I wish one of these guys, or even Cassandra Bunting, would give up information about the guys who murdered Tim."

"If a cartel was involved, do you really think any of these guys would tell the truth even if a sweet deal was offered?" Jack looked at Beale Friendly again. "Would *you?* I know I wouldn't. Not if I valued my life." Jack finished his coffee and tossed the empty cup on top of an overflowing garbage can beside the door.

Brian looked toward the heavy-set man sitting back with his arms folded across his chest. His court-appointed attorney was acting as the mouth-piece at that moment. "They all do what Friendly tells them, but even all these hours later, none of them will go higher up the food chain than saying Sam Wilson was involved in a lot more than his restaurant business." He rubbed one hand over his chin and felt the stubble. He wondered if he smelled as bad as he probably looked. "They admitted to being the ones responsible for the robbery at the coffee shop. Antonio Camardi was finally well enough to identify Winston McCall and Clem Green, but not Beale Friendly."

"I wonder whether he was inside or outside," Jack mused. "Maybe he was wearing those overalls to hide blood spatter."

"If he was, then I doubt he'd still have them hanging around in the paint truck." Brian unsuccessfully fought a yawn. "Trehorn's gonna have his work cut out for him unraveling this mess."

"Be glad it's his mess and not yours," Jack said. "What about Cassandra Bunting. What's her angle?"

"She's Beale's girlfriend."

"No kidding? That little cream-puff reporter?"

"She's no cream-puff, Jack. She showed a very different, aggressive side to her personality when she arrived at the warehouse last night. After she finished yelling at Winston McCall, she slapped the hell out of me."

"Well, well." Jack walked closer to the glass and peered intently at Friendly. "Who would have believed that, watching the footage of their interaction outside the coffee shop?"

"No one, probably. I wouldn't be surprised if she used the interviews she conducted for her social news segments to case homes of local celebrities. She could've obtained detailed itineraries under the ruse of fitting her time with them into their busy schedules, so she could feed all that info to that big sack of shit in there."

Brian finished his coffee and balanced the cup on top of Jack's in the full trash can. Even stooping to make sure the cup didn't land on the floor made his head pound.

" Damn," he told Jack. "I've got a massive headache, not just from lack of sleep and spending hours listening to all of them trying to talk their way out of probable long prison sentences, but from hitting my head on my own barstool, for God's sake. You got anything for pain in your pocket?"

"No, but I can get you some." Jack stopped peering through the glass. "I'm going down to see what else Gabe has dug up on Dewett."

"Make sure he goes home early," Brian said.

Jack nodded. "No overtime on cold cases, huh?"

"Not unless they're definitely linked to a recent homicide." Brian nodded, despite the hammering going on in his head. "Great work, both of you."

"I'll make sure to tell Gabe that. He may faint, but it'll be worth it to see the look on his face."

"Jack..."

"It's okay, Boss. We know you care, even if you rarely show it." Jack saluted and left.

Brian flipped the sound back on and listened to another half-hour of rambling testimony before deciding he'd heard the highlights and could get a report of anything else that might be of interest. He was fading fast, and Jack hadn't returned with the promised pain-reliever.

Brian decided to use the elevator instead of running down the stairs to the basement. Right before the door closed, Darrell Trehorn slid in through the gap.

"I heard a rumor," Trehorn said. "A little bird told me your clerk's been here half the night researching some old bat who used to take afternoon walks with Gertrude Pensky. Apart from some chronic back pain and a sleeping disorder, Mrs. Pensky was a reasonably healthy woman in her late eighties. Those walks she took with her friend and roommate, Mrs. Dewett, had managed the back issue and helped with the sleep disorder. Her physician said she took very little medication and wasn't anywhere close to dying. Yet she'd ingested enough strychnine to kill a horse. Both the staff at the nursing home and those at the café where she bought the milkshake swear none of them had access to the stuff. Both places had contracts with exterminators to take care of any rodent concerns."

"Mrs. Dewett may be a serial killer," Brian said.

The elevator dinged its arrival at Homicide. The door opened and Trehorn stepped out. "Your clerk'll probably get called to testify at

Dewett's trial. You took him with you to interview a person of interest in one of your Cold Cases. How do you even begin to explain that?"

Brian wasn't sure if he was supposed to respond to that question, but since he was on his way down to find out what else Gabe had dug up on Winifred Dewett, he confined himself to unnecessarily pushing the button for the basement again.

Trehorn blocked the door open with his hand. "We need to talk about possible links between Sam Wilson and those coffee shop murders," he said. "I heard Beale Friendly's younger brother used to work for Wilson."

He took his hand away and the door started to slide shut.

"Christ, Swift," he said, right before it closed. "Are you going to get mixed up in *all* my open cases?"

Brian swore he heard Trehorn laughing right before the elevator started back down to the basement.

CHAPTER FIFTY

KAYLEN HAD trouble maintaining eye contact with Jim. "I can't continue seeing you," she said. "I've got to break ties with Brian in every way."

The lump in her throat was painful. She swallowed with difficulty. Unwanted tears sprang into her eyes. So much for being strong and trying to look like this conversation wasn't affecting her, she chided herself silently.

"I'm so sorry," she said.

Jim wasn't making things any easier by staring at her with a great deal of concern on his kind face.

"I'll miss you horribly," she blurted.

She opened her purse and dug around inside, coming up with one crumpled tissue. She had already used several on the way over to the *Fanciful Folly* that morning, and she was far from running out of tears.

"You're not out of danger, honey." Jim's quiet, steady voice broke through Kaylen's misery. "Please don't make a such a huge mistake, cutting us both out of your life. Brian loves you, and you know I do, too."

"I *do* know." She dabbed her cheeks. The tissue became wet as well as crumpled as tears continued to well up. "Don't worry about me, Jim," she said. "I've made arrangements for a private security company to take over from you. Chief Shaw called me this morning and recommended them."

She stopped speaking and swallowed painfully. Hal had called to give her far more than a referral for security services. His voice had been filled with concern. He'd told her that although it was her business what she did with her life, he had to intervene on Brian's behalf. Brian had been following orders. He'd made an impossible choice.

Too hurt to listen to the chief's reasoning about Brian's motives for his lies, she'd nonetheless decided to contact the security company Hal had endorsed. He knew the owner, a former cop. There were no back-channels to the department, he had assured her. Whoever she drew for protection answered only to his employer. Kaylen had called as soon as she said goodbye to Hal for what she expected to be the last time.

"Your replacement's meeting me at Treasure," she told Jim. "It's all arranged." She glanced at her watch. Tears continued to blur her vision, but she was able to make out the time. "In thirty minutes. It's the final meeting with the staff before we open." She tried a watery smile. "Can I give you a hug? It's the last one."

"Of course, you can hug me, honey. Any time you want to." Jim spread his arms wide.

The lines on his face seemed to have deepened while they spoke. Even the sun had gone behind a bank of clouds rolling toward the marina. Kaylen leaned against Jim's chest and drew comforting warmth from him as his arms enfolded her. When she pulled away, she saw a wet spot on his shoulder where she'd rested her face.

She forced herself to look straight ahead as she climbed onto the finger pier and walked briskly toward the dock. She'd known Brian wouldn't be on the *NTK,* but its looming presence across from *Fanciful Folly* was an all too visible reminder of its owner.

She'd have to move, she told herself as she sped across the dock and jogged uncomfortably toward her car in her three-inch heels. Her lease was up in a couple of months. She had been planning to purchase the condo. Now, she wanted to be as far from the marina as she could get, keeping in mind she would have to find something convenient for commuting to and from two business locations instead of one.

A half-empty box of tissues sat on the passenger's seat of her BMW.

Kaylen blew her nose hard, pulled down the visor and dabbed carefully at streaks running down both cheeks. She pulled out her makeup bag and hastily repaired the damage. She was *not* going to regret her decision to sever all ties with Jim as well as Brian, she told herself, while her rebellious heart ached in protest.

Kaylen jammed her makeup bag back into her purse and put on her sunglasses. "Snap out of it," she told her reflection before flipping up the visor. She reminded herself that keeping busy was her best course, and that she'd have more than plenty of work to occupy her over the first few painful weeks.

She decided she had enough time to pick up a cup of coffee on the way over to the club and recover her poise before meeting her new bodyguard. His photo and resume had been sent to her phone. She glanced again at his impassive expression before pulling out of the parking space. No hint of a smile. Steely eyes. A complete contrast to Jim's reassuring, kindly presence.

What did she expect? she asked herself as she left the marina for the last time. No more romantic involvement with men for a while, she told herself. Since she would be staying with Angela at that mausoleum of a house until Jonathan returned from his business trip, she'd minimize the chances of bumping into either Brian or Jim for a while, anyway.

She glanced at Mizelle's as she passed. She wouldn't be able to go there, anymore, if she was staying away from the marina. She'd become a regular at so many of the little restaurants, bars and shops in Coconut Grove since meeting and falling in love with Brian. Kaylen's misery at the mounting toll of losses became crystal clear as she glanced in her rearview mirror in time to see the sign for the Coconut Grove Marina disappear from view.

Who had said that it was better to have loved and lost than never to have loved at all?

Kaylen had no idea, but firmly believed that person was a complete idiot.

CHAPTER FIFTY-ONE

"I THINK Mrs. Dewett really *is* a serial killer," Gabe said.

"And what brings you to that conclusion?" Brian sat on the chair opposite Gabe's desk and put his feet up on a stack of file boxes. Gabe's little office was filled with boxes, his desk littered with empty take-out containers and coffee cups.

Jack Mills brought a garbage can from his office and swept all the debris from the desk into it.

"Thanks." Gabe gave him a quick smile. "My can's full."

"So I see." Jack looked disapprovingly at the overflowing container. "How much paper did you use last night?"

"A lot. I printed way too much, probably, but I couldn't keep track with all the tabs open when I needed to recheck info and follow up on requests I'd made to other departments."

"Other people were up in the middle of the night?" Jack frowned, his brows at an acute angle. "You didn't wake anyone up, did you?"

"No...well...maybe a couple of them." Gabe looked embarrassed. "But I got results." He moved his chair so he could see Brian around the edge of the computer screen. "Boss, everywhere she's lived over the past twenty years, someone close to her has died."

"She's old. People around her age die all the time," Jack protested.

"Not *all* the time," Gabe said. "She's gone through three husbands, two sisters, and a brother-in-law, as well as the two fiancés. All of them left her the bulk of their estates, and now Mrs. Pensky's dead. So are two of the roommates she's had in the five rest homes she's lived in over the past four years. Where there were no roommate deaths, Mrs. Dewett was asked to leave shortly after her arrival because she was disruptive at night. Roommates complained she was going through their things after lights-out."

Brian had been mounting a head-count of possible Dewett victims. "That's eleven fuckin' people counting Gertie Pensky." He jerked his feet off the boxes and sat up straight. "Who *is* she, the Green River Killer's mother?"

"She's been moving around a lot," Gabe said. "That's why it took me all night to follow her. I was having trouble back-tracking, so I decided to start at the beginning, instead. I found her birth certificate, then the marriage and death certificates. There were newspaper articles, obituaries, you name it." He stopped to rub his eyes.

"Jack, you need to help Gabe by putting everything in chronological order," Brian said. "Gabe, have you left enough of a paper trail for Jack to do that?"

"Sure." Gabe pointed to several neatly stacked manila folders on one side of his desk.

"Jack, you need to take charge of this case and let Gabe go home for a while. No protesting." Brian held up his hand when Gabe opened his mouth. "This case is yours...both of you. I'm stepping out of this, as interesting as it sounds. I've left a report on the interview I conducted with Dewett that day we met her in the park. Gabe, you can add anything you observed to that, but not until you've slept, showered and gotten yourself into a change of clothes."

"Boss, you never stop for any of that when you're working a case," Gabe protested.

"This one's gonna overlap Homicide's investigation," Brian said. "I don't want you tired and missing anything of even the slightest possible importance. Jack can get the report pulled together from those files. I don't want Trehorn handed anything that can't back up suppositions with facts. You know what we need for that, Jack...the rest of the whatever Gabe doesn't already have. Medical reports, ME reports..."

"I got those," Gabe protested.

"On everyone? Going back years? What about the period between Dewett's birth and her first marriage?"

Gabe's eyes widened. "Boss, you think she started when she was a teenager?"

"Maybe even before that," Jack broke in. "She could've had a violent history as a child. These monsters don't suddenly start killing out of the blue in adulthood." He looked at Brian. "Unless a traumatic event triggers something dormant."

Brian nodded. "Yeah." He got up. "I've gotta keep movin' or I'll fall asleep myself. I'll see if upstairs needs anything else from me before I go do what I just told you to do, Gabe, and that's go climb into my bed."

He yawned and stretched, both of which felt really good. Something that didn't hurt emotionally or physically was a real luxury.

"Great work, Gabe," he told his clerk.

Gabe smiled and immediately started tidying up his desk, as though he was embarrassed by Brian's praise. Gabe always expected that giving 150% was normal for everyone, Brian thought. He should get a raise. Brian added putting in the necessary paperwork to his to-do list, then remembered he couldn't make any changes until he was back on active duty. He added his ceramic mug to a pile in the sink.

"I'll take care of those." Jack Mills took off his jacket and rolled up his sleeves. "Gabe needs a few minutes to get those files into order for me, anyway."

"You've got plenty to keep you busy without either of us underfoot today," Brian said. "You can use Villanueva, too, when she gets in from her medical appointment. If you've got questions, you can reach me anytime. I'm a light sleeper."

"I wouldn't doubt that." Jack started running water and squeezed dish soap onto a sponge.

Brian made his way upstairs to check on his own abduction case. After hearing everyone had been booked, he went into Hal's office, where he heard the bad news. The press had gotten wind of possible arrests in the coffee shop murders as well as in the attempted abduction case involving socialites Kaylen Roberts and Angela Crossfield. Mireille Shagassi was already requesting an exclusive with Brian. Hal said he'd refused until the department was ready to make any official statement, but he'd told Shagassi he'd make sure she got news of that upcoming statement before any other news-services were notified.

Brian texted the update to Jack and Gabe, unwilling to get into a discussion about what would come next. He was too frustrated with police work and too demoralized to face making any attempt to resolve his issues with Kaylen. Maybe, he admitted to himself, he was too tired and hungry to do anything but take care of those immediate needs with a burger and fries, followed by a long nap.

He took a little-used and considerably longer route back to the marina. On the way, he cruised through a fast food drive-through that wasn't on any of his regular routes. The *NTK* now had new locks and a refined security system, including cameras, thanks to Jim volunteering to supervise the work.

Brian had never felt the need for any supplemental security measures before, but times were changing, even for him, he decided grudgingly. Maybe for good. He might never come face to face with Tim's killers. Maybe they were out of the country. Dead, even. Cartels didn't tolerate failure, and as far as successfully hiding Tim's remains and keeping his detective brother away from cartel business were concerned, those killers had failed miserably.

The first thing Brian wanted when he arrived back at the *NTK* was a shower. His clothes had dried, but were sticking to him. He found someone had cleaned up the place. Probably Jim, he thought. The blood-stains were still front and center on the salon floor, but he skirted around them to peel off all his clothes in the cabin. He stood under hot water for much longer than usual. By the time he got around to his food, it was completely cold. He ran the fries through a cycle in the toaster oven Kaylen had insisted on bringing aboard for her bagels, which she liked crisp and piping hot. He nuked the cheeseburger. Squirting ketchup onto a paper plate, he stood at the breakfast bar and reviewed the camera footage while he ate.

His viewing included the *NTK*'s deck, the dock and Jim's *Fanciful Folly*. It also showed him Kaylen having what seemed to be an intense conversation with Jim on his boat. Brian watched her hug Jim before wiping her eyes and briskly walking away. Jim watched her with concern written plainly on his face, visible even from the distance between the two boats.

Brian threw half his burger and fries into the trash. They tasted like ketchup-covered cardboard. He knew Hal had recommended a security outfit, and hoped Kaylen had accepted. Hal had warned him there were no back-channels available to determine whether she had hired that company or someone else who might have less interest in making her safety paramount.

He stopped reviewing the footage and went into his cabin, shutting the sliding doors behind him. He left his phone on, but closed the blinds and got under the covers dressed only in a pair of boxers. He felt cold and alone. He got out of bed again, pulled on sweats and sank back into bed, only to fall into an uneasy sleep where he tried fighting off intruders with limbs that felt like they had turned to lead while cold water from fire hoses doused him again and again.

CHAPTER FIFTY-TWO

TREASURE OPENED two weeks after Kaylen had shot a man entering Angela's home. Kaylen was assured by the Robbery Bureau detectives assigned to the case that Beale Friendly had masterminded the attack, and she had no further need for extraordinary security measures.

Kaylen wasn't completely convinced that robbery had been the ultimate goal when those two men burst into the sun-room, but knew her doubts might be without merit, and she no longer had Brian to use as a sounding-board. In fact, she no longer had Brian in any capacity, and her body and mind still ached with the loss.

As she cut the ribbon outside Treasure for its official opening, with a select number of guests eager to see inside her new endeavor, and a small contingency of local press present, she felt an unwelcome and totally unexpected dip in her mood. She'd been so eager for that moment, but when it arrived, it felt like an anti-climax.

An hour later, a much larger crowd streamed through the gigantic set of wooden doors. Their exclamations of delight and awe at the over-the-top décor and sheer size of the club fell short for Kaylen. Her enthusiasm remained muted, as though everything filtered through a veil. She smiled on the outside and fought depression on the inside.

She'd never felt lonelier. Brian should have been at her side. Jim had originally planned to leave for Baton Rouge the day after Treasure's opening, so he could attend. Jack Mills, Gabe Weston and a number of detectives from the Homicide squad had accepted invitations weeks before. All of them had cancelled at the last minute except Brian.

She'd hoped to see a card or flowers from him, wishing her luck, but she told herself that was an unreasonable hope, since she had told him she never wanted to see or hear from him again. She asked herself for the thousandth time since that day…had she acted unreasonably?

No, she told herself. She had *not* been unreasonable. That stipulation he'd agreed to when they decided to go forward with their relationship wasn't one that could be broken whenever it was convenient for him. She couldn't continue to love a man when every day she'd have to wonder whether he was being completely honest with her.

As her socialite friends and business partners swarmed around to congratulate her, Kaylen missed everyone who had come into her life since she'd fallen in love with Brian. Even while George's influential business associates told her what a success her new business was already, inside, she wept.

While she greeted, chatted and thanked everyone in front of her, she felt the presence of a stranger at her back. Her new bodyguard, impersonal and unobtrusive to everyone but her, stood only a few steps away. He blended into the background, as he was designed to do, but Kaylen was aware of him and hated every minute of his presence.

One of the last guests to arrive she hadn't even expected to see, despite sending him an invitation.

"Hello, Kaylen." Ziggy Stavros smiled his thousand-watt smile and extended his right hand. "Congratulations on what I see is another successful venture."

Kaylen automatically took his hand. It felt strong, warm and held hers in a grip that was friendly, but not overly-intrusive. He brought her hand to his lips and brushed the back with a light kiss.

"Thank you." She forced a smile.

"For what?" His brow furrowed. "I have done nothing."

"You came, instead of sending good wishes. That means a lot." She felt that damned lump rise in her throat again. A waiter passed by, a tray loaded with champagne flutes balanced in front of him.

Ziggy stopped the man and took two glasses, handing one to Kaylen and raising the other in a toast. "My restaurant can survive without me for a few hours." He smiled. *"Salud, ya-mas."* He clinked his glass with hers. "All the very best for the future. You must drink, Kaylen, for the wishes to come true."

"I know *salud*, but not the other words. Are they Greek?" She took a very small sip of the champagne, wary of drinking at Treasure's opening, even though she knew she didn't need to worry about Tim drugging her drink and making her ill, as he had at the celebration for Bannisters.

"Loosely translated it means 'to your health,'" Ziggy said.

Kaylen clinked glasses again. "To yours, too," she said. "I really appreciate you taking the time to come to my opening. I've heard your restaurant's very successful. You and I could become rivals in the future."

"You only serve dinner. I serve lunch, too," he said, cupping her elbow and guiding her away from a boisterous group being led to a large table in the middle of the club.

Kaylen felt more than saw her bodyguard step closer. She shook her head slightly, to let him know Ziggy's contact wasn't a threat. How she wished for Jim, who at least knew many of her acquaintances by sight.

"I have plans to expand my menu to include lunch sometime in the future, so watch out." She managed a weak smile.

Ziggy inclined his head. "I will welcome your friendly rivalry when it occurs. And I would not have missed this event for all the tea in China."

Kaylen felt her smile widen as she relaxed for the first time that evening. Ziggy's formal speech patterns remained charming and familiar. Friendly. Caring.

"Can I request the pleasure of a dance with you?" he asked.

"That would be nice."

She stopped another waiter with a tray of empty glasses and gave him her almost-full flute. She wasn't going to take any more risks, she decided, pushing aside flashes of Tim, of being ill, and then the obliteration of all other memories at Bannisters' opening. Almost two years ago, she'd been drugged and taken away to what was now a completely remolded future.

Perhaps not completely remolded, she thought as Ziggy drew her arm through his.

"Let's take this slow," she said.

"Of course." He smiled again, but with less incandescence. It was a reassuring sight. "Let us start with your first dance this evening."

"Okay," she said.

Life had to go on. She had made that promise to George Bannister Roberts as he lay on his deathbed, and she vowed to keep it. Unlike some people she knew, who couldn't keep their promises, she thought as Ziggy drew her into his arms and they began to dance. She refused to remember dancing with Brian for the first time at Bannisters, when he had finally agreed to allow their relationship to become public.

Ziggy was young, handsome and available, both emotionally and physically. But she meant what she'd said about taking things slow. Her heart couldn't take any more disappointments, she told herself as they whirled across the floor beneath the twinkling lights and Ziggy smiled at her. No more disappointments…ever.

CHAPTER FIFTY-THREE

"How about taking a trip with me?" Brian asked Jim as they sat on chairs facing the *NTK's* stern.

It had been two weeks since Brian had returned to Cold Case as its supervisor, but he still felt unsettled and out of place. He'd had sessions with his shrink and a conference with Hal. Treasure had opened a month ago. Very successfully, according to all the news reports. He'd had no contact with Kaylen, nor did he expect to.

"I'm taking the three weeks' vacation I'm owed," he told Jim. "I need a break."

Jim nodded. "You do." He took a long pull from his beer. "Is Carlos available to crew?"

"Yeah. I checked with him already." Brian put down his own barely-touched drink, which didn't even taste good. "I know it's gonna be a long trip, and I totally understand if you don't want to leave port right now, but I'd like you to come with us."

"Right now's as good as any other. I've got no real plans other than to find out if you still want me to go down to Baton Rouge."

Brian rubbed a hand over his face. "Not right now. I don't need any more shake-ups."

"Understandable." Jim put down his bottle. "Did you try talking to her?"

"No. She made it clear we were done. I've gotta respect that." Brian gazed out at the horizon and felt the need to see what was beyond it.

"Give her a little time. She'll come around."

"I don't think so. Ziggy's back."

"That bastard didn't waste a minute, did he?"

"No, but he's familiar, and maybe that's what Kaylen needs right now. No more surprises."

"I suppose." Jim nodded slowly. "Can't say as I like it, and I bet you don't think much of it, either." He stretched his legs out in front of him, crossed them at the ankles and wiggled his toes in his flip flops. "You want to take an extended trip, I'm in. I wouldn't mind a change of scenery myself, right now." He cleared his throat. "I've got a confession to make. I started communicating with Nola Chesney after we came back from Tampa."

Brian had picked up his beer bottle. He almost dropped it. *"Nola Chesney?"*

Jim nodded. "Yep, *that* Nola Chesney."

"The widow."

"Yes. She called me after her husband's death. Asked me if I would go up to Tampa and help her with the funeral arrangements. Said no one else came to mind."

"And things developed from there, huh?" Brian had to smile. "She seemed like a nice woman. Kaylen liked her."

"She is. Very nice." Jim's own smile looked a little sheepish. "Better than all those other women I've dated since moving to Florida."

"Jim, I'm glad for you. Will it screw things up with her if you go with me?"

"No." He looked even more sheepish. "I told her you and Kaylen were having problems and I needed to cancel my weekend trip up there so I could be here. You need support right now, buddy, more than I need a weekend with Nola."

"Is this getting serious?"

"Not yet. Maybe. I don't know." Jim finished his beer and took another from the cooler. "I've been living alone for more than ten years,

Brian. I like being on the boat, like you do on yours. There isn't room on the *Folly* for more than me. Nola likes it up in Tampa, too. I don't think either of us is committed enough yet to even broach the subject of one of us needing to relocate."

"I'm better off alone," Brian said. "I'm done with trying to please someone else and all the rest of that crap."

"I disagree, but I'll leave that thought for now. You need time and space. This trip'll be good for both of us. When do we leave, and where are we going?"

"Bahamas to start?"

"Sounds good."

"What about Monday morning?"

"Two days to prepare? That'll be enough. We'll lay in supplies; get our affairs in order. Do you think Jack Mills would be willing to keep an eye on the *Folly?*"

Brian couldn't help smiling. "I'm sure he'd be happy to do that, Jim, if he can sit on deck and act like he's the owner."

"As long as he takes his trash with him and doesn't leave any marks."

"You'll have to square that with Jack. I'm not getting in the middle of your arrangements."

"Fair enough." Jim nodded slowly. "I can see how that might be a problem for you, seeing as you don't even notice the rings your beer cans leave on the table."

"Oh, Jim. Don't start with me."

Brian didn't feel like saying anything else. He needed those three weeks. He wanted to be at the top of his game, and right then, he knew he was not.

"I've been promoted," he told Jim. "As soon as we get back to port, I'll return to Miami-Dade as a lieutenant, and the new Homicide supervisor. Trehorn accepted a position with the FBI."

"Well, I'll be a doggoned monkey's uncle," Jim said. "Congratulations are in order." He lifted his bottle in a toast.

"Thanks." Brian lifted his own bottle and clinked it against Jim's.

"You should send Kaylen a text or an email or something," Jim said.

"No, I should not," Brian looked hard at Jim. "And you're not gonna, either."

Jim became engrossed with finishing his beer.

"I mean it," Brian said.

Jim settled lower in his chair and tipped his cap over his eyes. "This beer's made me sleepy," he said with a slight smile. "Think I'll take a little nap."

"Yeah, and I'll get going on our steaks." Brian took the empties into the salon. He glanced back at Jim. No movement, but Jim hadn't promised not to give Kaylen the news.

Brian thought she might offer her congratulations, but then again, she might not. She'd made it abundantly clear he was out of her life for good.

The ache in his chest told him Kaylen could definitely become the biggest regret of his life.

THE END

ALSO BY HEATHER AMES

Brian Swift & Kaylen Roberts mystery/suspense series

Indelible (Book 1)

A Swift Brand of Justice (Book 2)

Swift Retribution (Book 3)

Suspense

Night Shadows

Romantic Suspense

All That Glitters

Contemporary Romance

The Sweetest Song

Upcoming

Ghost Shop series (mystery/suspense with a paranormal twist – Book 1) 2020

Book 4 in the Brian Swift & Kaylen Roberts mystery/suspense series

ABOUT THE AUTHOR

Heather Ames knew she was a writer from the time she won first prize in a high school novel contest. An unconventional upbringing gave her opportunities to travel extensively, leading to nomadic ways and an insatiable desire to see the world. She has made her home in 5 countries and 7 states, learning a couple of languages along the way. She is currently pitching her tents in Portland, Oregon, and after a long career in healthcare, made her dream of writing full-time come true.

Heather is a current board member of the Harriet Vane Chapter of Sisters in Crime and member of Toastmasters International.